REBECCA JOSE

FREE DOWNLOAD!

THIS BOOK CONTAINS GRAPHIC
SCENES CONTAINING VIOLENCE,
FOUL LANGUAGE, AND SEXUAL
CONTENT AND MAY NOT BE
SUITABLE FOR CHILDREN.

PARENTAL DISCRETION
IS ADVISED.

TRIGGER WARNINGS

PLEASE BE ADVISED OF THE TRIGGER WARNINGS IN THIS BOOK AS LISTED, NOT IN ANY PARTICULAR ORDER…

1. PARENTAL DEATH

2. DEPRESSION

3. SUICIDE

4. SEXUAL ABUSE AND RAPE

5. MURDER

6. PSYCHOLOGICAL TORTURE

OTHER BOOKS BY REBECCA JOSE

This book is dedicated to all my fellow Indie Authors who supported me throughout my journey and are still with me as I trudge along the world of Self-Publishing.

Special thanks go out to my TikTok fans, friends, family, and all my fellow Booktokers for all the love and support you have given.

Extra-Special thank you to:
Will Gray
JC Fuller
RR Carter
Otto Schafer

You were some of the first fellow Booktoker Indies that took me under your wings, gave me great advice, and let me ride the journey with you. I hope you all find everything your hearts desire!

CHAPTER 1

Shadows loom on the edge of my vision, twisting and writhing around the sides of the decorative mirror frame. I ignore them as much as I am able. The reflection staring back at me widens its dark brown eyes as the darkness emanating from it invades my periphery.

They are coming for me.

I blink rapidly, and the image in the mirror does the same. She was once comfortingly familiar to me, but now, she is a frightening stranger. A shudder runs through me when my eyes meet the eyes in the mirror. Those eyes are no longer mine. The entire face has changed, but it was the eyes that went first. When did those eyes change?

My dark brown, almost black, eyes lack the luster of before. Dark circles rim the delicate skin underneath them. My once slightly dark skin is sickly and pale, contrasting sharply against the mop of deep auburn curls that frame my face and flow over my shoulders.

I trace the lines of my prominent nose pocked with blackheads from neglecting my skin regime. I continue across my high cheekbones, the skin underneath sunken in from too much weight loss. My gaze travels lower to my full cupid-bow lips that have not seen a smile in many days. Finally, my gaze follows the worry lines that have recently formed around my mouth and in between my brows.

I remember when it all started, the first time I looked into a mirror and did not recognize my own reflection. It was the day my mother died. I believe a part of me died with her, and that is why I began to change.

The shadows close in, and I can't breathe. So close. Too close. I'm suffocating. One tiny tendril touches my cheek, and the coldness of its shadowy caress makes me suck in a breath. The iciness flows into me, freezing the air in my lungs and squeezing my heart with icy tendrils. My entire body shakes as my teeth begin to chatter.

If one tiny tendril feels like this, what will happen to me when they surround me like I know they will do? How will I survive the bitter cold of this darkness?

I will not survive. I have seen to that myself. No one is coming to save me. No one is going to stop my life from flowing out of me, dripping in red rivulets down my hands from the slashes on my wrists and pooling onto the floor.

The scarlet-red color descending down my arm catches my eye, causing me to focus again on my reflection. My eyes widen in fascination and fear at the sight of my life's blood pouring out of me.

I really did it.

They had tried to make me stop and bend me to their will. The dark tendrils had wrapped around my wrists and tried to handle me like a puppet on a string, but I had resisted. I had found the strength somewhere deep inside me.

Just like my mother had said I would.

However, she had said I would find the strength to survive, not kill myself, to get rid of a mass of destructive shadows that had forced me to mutilate my friends.

I shrug; semantics…potato, potatoe…

Before the shadows can try to pull the knife away from me again, I slash at my arm once more. The knife cuts through the tender flesh of my opposite forearm as if it were cutting through butter just before the tendril of shadow forces me to drop the knife to the floor.

Too late.

More blood flows, bubbling from the fresh, deep gash traveling down the length of my forearm.

I have never seen so much blood.

The trembling of my body intensifies as the cold envelopes me, and the blood and darkness surround my vision.

I close my eyes, blocking out the sight of the shadows and the blood. Maybe it will all end quicker if I don't see what is happening. Maybe I will wake up and suddenly realize this was a long, drawn-out dream.

But I doubt it. It had all been real, and I am ending this nightmare by dying.

Another wave of freezing cold washes through me as another tendril of darkness wraps around my neck, cutting off my air and stealing my concentration. I lose my focus, and the shadows take over again.

They have me in their grasp and will not let me go.

They will try to stop me from dying.

But it is too late.

I am already sinking into the black oblivion of death. I can feel it pulling me down, beckoning me to give in. As I succumb to the darkness of death consuming me, my thoughts diminish to the old cliché of reflecting on my life. It does not "flash before my eyes" in an instant as some say it does when it is time to die. It is more like a slow burn, a torturous stopping of time in a moment when I just want it to end and be done with it.

It is as if I have all the time in the world to play my story in my mind, from beginning to end. I do not want to relive those moments, but I have no control over my body or my thoughts currently. They stole my concentration, and now they have me. The shadows control everything.

They may be too late to stop me from dying, but they are not done torturing me yet.

Fine. Bring it on. They took everything from me, so I have nothing left to lose.

Bring on the memories…

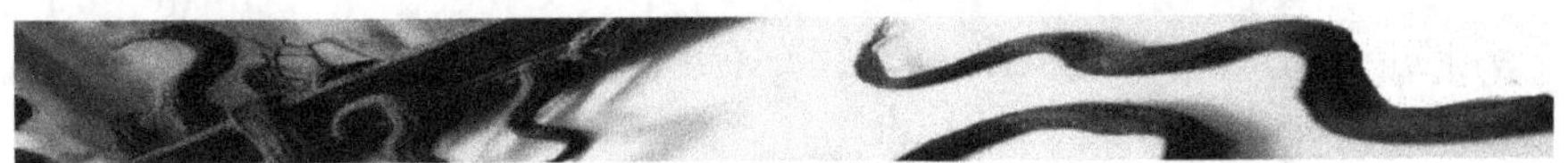

"Sophia, put on your coat. You will catch a death of a cold," my mom says as we head towards the door.

"Mom, you know I never wear a coat until the temperatures drop below freezing," I say as I sling my purse over my shoulder, car keys in hand. "Besides, I am wearing my thick sweater and boots."

"Well, at least take your coat with you," Mom replies. "The temperature just might drop if we stay out too late."

"We are only going for some last-minute Christmas shopping," I say with an exasperated sigh.

"Did you remember your Tio Vicente in Phoenix?" Mom asks. "You know he would be heartbroken if you didn't send him something. He still celebrates Christmas."

Tio Vicente was Mom's brother. *Tio* was Spanish for Uncle. My English-speaking father called him Vinny because he could not pronounce Vicente correctly. Therefore, I called him *Uncle Vinny.*

I glance over my shoulder as I take my coat from one of the many pegs on the wall beside the door.

"Yes, mom. I remembered Uncle Vinny," I answer.

"Well, even though I do not celebrate Christmas, I still have the ladies from the Kingdom Hall coming over for our Bible study, so I have to get snacks and such." I know my mother, and that look on her face says we will be longer than expected.

I sigh, turning back toward the front door as I say, "I only have one more gift to buy, Mom. Can you make it quick? I need to get back to close up and do tonight's paperwork for the restaurant. My manager needs to leave early."

I can practically hear my mother's curious frown as she asks, "If you already have gifts for Vicente, your staff at the restaurant, and your friend Tamara, who else could you be missing?"

 I brace myself for her reaction and answer, "It's dad I need to buy for."

Silence falls.

Holding my breath, I stop short of opening the front door to turn and look at her.

Katalina Dominguez-Boralis stands a few feet away, staring at me with her almost-black irises. Her raven-black hair lays straight down her back and over her shoulders, her short bangs hiding her forehead and touching the tops of her brows. Her short, broad nose flairs as her full lips purse into a disappointed look. She sighs as she steps closer to me, raising a brown-skinned hand to my face.

"Oh, mi hija. What could you possibly buy for someone who has been dead for years?" Her thick, Latino-accented voice is laced with sadness and remorse, causing tears to prick at the backs of my eyes and blurring my vision.

Her reaction surprised me. She usually responds with anger when I speak of my father. She hates it when I ask questions or recall a fond memory.

But this…

This is new territory. I have never seen her respond to the mention of Eric Boralis with anything but contempt. They had been going through a divorce, even though my mother did not believe in divorce. He did, though.

Then, he died in a freak accident on the job, but Katalina still held a grudge even after his death.

I blink several times to fight back the tears that threaten to spill over as my mother strokes my cheek fondly. I swallow past the lump in my throat and attempt to answer her question without letting my emotions show in my tone.

"I just want to get some flowers for his grave. I have gotten him flowers all three years he has been gone, mama," I answer, using the name I used to call her when I was a child; when my dad was still alive, my parents were still together, and life was still full of happiness.

Katalina's eyes soften as she stares into mine, so much like hers that people often confuse us for twin sisters instead of mother and daughter.

"Yo entendé," she responds, switching to her native tongue as her emotions rise. "Eres mi vida, mi corazón, et tu padre sintió lo mismo cuando estaba vivo. We loved you with all our hearts."

I repeat her words in English inside my mind. *I understand. You are my life, my heart. Your father felt the same when he was alive.*

"I know, mama," I say aloud. "I loved him, too. But I also feel the same for you. I don't know what I would do if anything ever happened to you."

Mama's smile was kind yet sad as she responded, "You would live, child. Just like you did when your father died. I was wrong to say that you would never make it without me. Many things I have done these past few years have been wrong."

I blink, and the tears fall. They slide down my cheek as she continues.

"You are stronger than you know, hija. You always were. It was I who was weak. I just didn't want you to move out and leave me."

Mom pauses and shrugs. Her tone turns humorous as she continues, "Besides, your Uncle Vinny would never let you be alone. You could go to Phoenix and live with him."

I scoff as I wipe the tears from my cheeks. "Yeah, right. Who would take care of the restaurant? Besides, Mia hates me. She thinks I am too white to own a restaurant specializing in Mexican cuisine."

Mia is my cousin, Uncle Vinny's daughter. She had been

unpleasant to me when we were little and now was a total bitch. It did not help matters any that she owned her own company and was insanely successful.

Mom waves a hand dismissively. "She is a brat, that one. Uncle Vinny has his hands full with her, but he would never abandon you. He would probably move here to help you. That's how much he loves you."

Mom's hand drops from my face, and she clutches her purse strap as she picks it up from the table under the pegs beside my front door.

I frown as I drape my coat over my arm and turn back toward the door, following my mother's movements.

"Why are we even talking about this, anyway? I am still here, Mom. I just live in a separate house. I would never leave you, and it isn't like you will leave me, either. You are not on your deathbed or anything. So, why all the talk about me being alone?"

My mother's tone is eerily serious as she says, "You never know what may happen."

A chill chases its way down my spine as trepidation fills me. How did this day turn so dark? I woke up planning a bright, cheerful holiday shopping day to spend time with my mother this morning.

This is how I like to spend the day before Christmas Eve since she doesn't celebrate Christmas. She knows this. So why is she so dark and foreboding all of a sudden just because I want to buy flowers for my dead father?

What happened to this day?

Suddenly, I am jerked from the memory as the shadows surrounding the mirror inch ever closer, snapping my attention back to them. Looking back on this memory now, as the strands of darkness envelop me in their freezing embrace, I slowly begin to realize something my brain refused to believe at the time.

Katalina knew. My mom knew that she was going to die that day, and she was trying to prepare me.

Well, I was not prepared.

She was right when she said I would not make it without her. Even though she had apologized and said she was wrong, she was right.

She was right about Uncle Vinny, too. He had moved here to help with the restaurant. It would have closed down had he not taken over. I neglected everything in my life when Mom died and the shadows appeared.

I lost everything. No, I let go of everything.

Uncle Vinny runs the restaurant now, and Mia manages the funds. She pays the restaurant bills, my personal bills and medical care, and buys my groceries with the profits. Any extra is put into a savings fund for me to use when I am ready to live again.

And I am too entrenched with the shadows to care.

The fact that I am about to die at my own hand should attest to that.

I shake myself from my thoughts and focus on the mirror again. It won't be long now. My vision is fading, the world spinning, and the mirror's reflection is fuzzier than ever.

The shadows tighten around me, the tendrils around my neck and wrists holding me in place.

Too late. They are too late.

I repeat this mantra to myself over and over, even as icy tendrils wrap themselves around the gashes in my flesh, trying to stop my life force from leaving my body.

It is cold, colder than winter, colder than snow, colder than ice.

Colder than death.

My reflection moves in the mirror even though I am standing still, and I startle. My eyes widen as the reflection changes, and suddenly, my mother is staring back at me with those almost black eyes.

Disappointment shines in their onyx depths. Her lips never move, even as her voice plays in my head.

"Hija, you have forsaken me."

"No, Ma. I could never…," I begin, but she cuts me off.

"You have killed yourself. Why would you do such a thing?"

"But it isn't what you think," I whisper roughly. "I had no choice."

The smile that spreads on Katalina's lips is one I have never seen on my mother's face. She speaks to me inside my mind, her lips never moving from that cruel grin.

The tone is uncaring, cold, and calculating, and the sound is as foreign to me as the look on her face. *"You are right. You have no choices. I make the choices now."*

A shudder runs through me as I suck in a breath, maybe my last one. This is not my mother. She was never this cruel. This is just another trick of the cruel shadows that have been following me since she died.

The ones controlling me now.

"I'm dying," I tell the reflection. "Now, you will never be able to come out again. You will never control me again."

The laugh echoing through the dark, empty room is menacing, and the voice in my mind is even more so.

"I never controlled you. You did all that on your own. But you did give me power, and now I can control you. Do you really think I will let you die?"

But I am dying. How can they stop nature from taking over? I have lost too much blood. There is nothing they can do.

Or, so I thought.

A rare moment of clarity consumes me, and the cold releases me from its grasp. In those moments of understanding, sensation returns to my body, and I am thrown into the presence of reality.

Voices shout urgently, asking me my name and if I know where I am. Lights blind me as the overhead light is turned on in my bedroom.

I see the officers in my bedroom doorway. I had not spoken to anyone in days, not since the shadows had forced me to do despicable things during a group meeting. But I knew they would be here to pick me up eventually.

My voice was scratchy as I look at the officers and say, "Why don't you save yourselves some paperwork and just let me die."

"Just stay calm, Ma'am," One of the officers says. "We are just going to get you some help."

Both officers move further into the room, and then multiple hands pull me away from the mirror.

"Get the paramedics here, stat!" The officer cries to the other officer as he begins to wrap my bedsheets around my arms.

No, no, no.

Please, do not save me. Let me die! The shadows are dangerous. I must die so they will die.

I try to scream out, try to get away. I thrash and pull, trying to pull my arms free from their grasp. They are holding too tightly. I cannot move, and the hold is stopping the blood from flowing.

No! This cannot be happening!

How can this be happening?

No one knew I was here, and no one knew what I had been planning. I thought I had more time before the police came to pick me up because the shadows caused me to…

No.

I would not think of that now.

I need to focus on getting away, on killing the shadows that rage inside me.

I scream and thrash some more, managing to pull the arm with the deep gash free. Blood bubbles from the gash again, and I cry out in victory.

"Get the tranquilizer out," The officer holding my arms says.

I hear sirens in the distance, and my soul cries in defeat. I struggle again against the officer who is holding me, but then I feel something prick my upper arm. A burning sensation runs through my veins, and it only takes a few seconds for something to take over, something more potent than the control of the shadows.

My world spins as the tranquilizer the other officer injected me with kicks in, and I succumb to a different kind of darkness than death.

This had all been for nothing.

The shadows will never let me go now. They are relentless.

My vision goes black, and I succumb to the darkness of dreamless sleep.

CHAPTER 2

"Focus on the light," the man in the white lab coat says as he holds a penlight in front of my eyes.

He waves it back and forth, watching intently as my eyes follow the light.

"When am I gonna get to go home?" I ask in a whining tone.

"When we are sure that you won't try to off yourself again," The doctor says sarcastically.

"Nice bedside manner," I shoot back, but there is a hint of a smile on my face.

Besides Jeremy, the one friend I have made here, my doctor is the only person who has made me smile for a long time. I have been here in the psych ward of a private hospital for six weeks now. I was in the psych ward at our local public hospital in Daisville, Kentucky, for two weeks before I came here.

I needed privacy for an extended stay. I work with the public, and I did not want my deranged psychotic breakdown to hurt my business if anyone found out I was on the 'crazy floor' of the hospital.

I am sure Uncle Vinny has done a great job caring for the restaurant and covering for me. At least, I hope he has. I still do not have clearance to call anyone or have any visits, so I am unsure what he told anyone about my whereabouts.

On the brighter side of things, my head is clearer than it has been in months. Since…well…since my mother died.

I can say that now without seeing the shadows creeping around in my periphery. I can remember her fondly now without the memory of her death torturing my brain. In fact, I have not seen the shadows for a while now since Doctor Harper found the medication that works to treat my schizophreniform.

That is what they say I have. It is a temporary mental disorder closely related to schizophrenia, brought on by tremendous and sudden trauma. The condition caused a psychotic episode, causing me to have hallucinations. The shadows had been nothing but a hallucination, and their possession of me was all in my head.

"Seriously, Sophia. I don't think you are ready to go home just yet. There is still another issue you must address." Doctor Harper says, piercing me with his icy blue stare.

I stare into that intense gaze, my heart pumping as it always does when he is around. I know, I know. I probably have erotic transference syndrome on top of everything else that plagues me, but he is so fucking hot.

His dark hair is cut short and combed back from his face, but sometimes his bangs fall almost to his brow line. It makes me want to run my fingers through it when that happens. His strong jawline is usually covered with a five-o'clock shadow that has me yearning to run my hand across his masculine features and feel the roughness of it along my palm.

His dark-lashed sapphire eyes are like something from a dream, and my heart flutters when those blue orbs look my way. All of this on top of that straight, strong nose and dimpled chin, and I am putty in his hands.

My favorite feature is those lips. I am utterly infatuated with those full, kissable lips. I love the smile he gives me when we are teasing each other. Whenever he speaks, I watch them as they move, imagining what they would feel like pressed against my own cupid-bow lips.

"Sophia, are you listening to me?"

The sound of my name coming from those lips snaps me out of my reverie, and I blink several times to clear my thoughts.

"I'm sorry, what did you say? I must have zoned out for a moment," I respond.

He rolls those gloriously gorgeous blue eyes at me. "I said you need to address the other issue in group, or at least talk about it with your therapist, Marcel, in your solo sessions."

Sighing heavily, I drop my gaze to the floor. "I can't talk about it yet."

The euphoria of enjoying the sexiness that is Doctor Harper Andrews fades as my mood goes into that dark place my mind hides in when it does not want to face reality.

I had hurt those people. Badly. My friend…well, ex-friend now… even lost an eye. The hallucination that I was under the influence of the shadows at the time was a lie made up by my subconscious mind.

There were no shadows.

It was me…all me…only me. I had hurt those people and destroyed my friend's eye.

The temporary insanity plea my attorney got for me kept me out of prison and landed me here, but the guilt that consumes me will hold me prisoner forever.

"I would never want to hurt anyone, at least not consciously. I have no idea why I would want to subconsciously," I mumble incoherently. "So, I don't know why I hurt those people."

Apparently, Harper speaks fluent "mumble" because he answers as if he heard me.

"I know you would never want to hurt anyone consciously," He says in that sexy tone that has my toes curling in my hospital-assigned, slip-proof socks that are supposed to be slippers. "You hold too much guilt over that. You were going through something you could not control."

"You need to speak to Marcel. She is a good therapist and very skilled in hypnosis. She can help you let go before the guilt consumes you and holds you in your depression."

"Can't I just go on taking my medicine and pretend it never happened?" I ask humorously.

Harper does not laugh.

My friend with the missing eye would probably not find it funny, either.

Harper runs a hand through his hair, pushing his bangs away from his face as he blows out a breath. "Fine. I can't force you to talk about it, nor can she. But someday, you must face yourself in the mirror again. You're not going to get out of here before that happens."

I know he is right. I have not looked in a mirror since I have been here. God knows what I look like. I brush my hair every day, wash my face, and brush my teeth. I do what is necessary and what I can do without seeing myself. I have not styled my hair or put on makeup in so long that I do not even know if I still remember how.

Not that I can put on makeup. They do not let us have makeup here. Or hair accessories. Still, sometimes I would like to know if I look presentable. I am just afraid to look.

The mirrors are where the shadows live.

Still staring at the floor with my head hung low, I answer, "I know. I just don't know how I can face myself with all this guilt on my shoulders."

"How about I give you some reading material that can help you do some exercises on your own, maybe work up the courage to talk about it aloud?"

Harper's tone is so full of hope that it makes me raise my gaze to meet his eyes, and I see that they are as full of hope as his voice was. I offer a small smile and say the only thing I can to that look.

"Alright, Doc. Bring me what you want me to read, and I'll read it. I'm not promising anything, though."

Harper's beaming smile pulls me from my dark mood as he answers, "Perfect. I will bring it tomorrow."

"Fine," I say. "I guess I'll be reading all day tomorrow."

Harper chuckles and says, "On the bright side, your vitals look good. Your blood pressure is a bit high today, though. Not high enough to worry about yet, but I'll keep an eye on it."

I feel my skin heating with embarrassment. I know why my blood pressure is high. Harper's sexy ass, and I do mean sexy ass, would shoot any woman's blood pressure up. I would probably have a stroke if I ever saw it naked.

Hell, I would probably die from pleasure if I got to see any of him naked. His muscular frame induces a yearning to squeeze his biceps, steal a feel of his pecs, and run wandering hands all over his solid abs. I bet he has washboard abs.

"Sophia, you are zoning out again," Harper says, his tone humorous. "Was there something else you wanted to talk to me about?"

Yes, I would like to talk about how close your body is to mine right now and how much higher my blood pressure would go if only you would close the distance and…

"SOPHIA," Harper exclaims loudly, but his mouth is curved in a knowing smile.

I blink several times and focus on that heartbreakingly handsome face. "Yes, doc?"

Harper chuckles and shakes his head in mock annoyance. "You can go back to your room now."

"Umm, okay. I guess I'll see you tomorrow, then," I say as I jump down from the examination table and return to reality.

Unfortunately.

It's too bad I cannot live in my fantasy land.

Harper turns, gives my shoulder a solid pat, and turns around. He waves dismissively before tapping keys on the computer attached to the stand-up workstation. He hums a little tune as he types.

Apparently, I am dismissed.

Sighing, I shuffle to the door, momentarily glancing over my shoulder to bid Harper goodbye. I think better of it when I notice the concentrated set of his shoulders as he types furiously while staring at the computer screen.

I turn back to the door, open it, and stroll into the hallway. The nurses' station is a few paces to the right, surrounded by a bullet-proof glass wall that keeps irritated, crazy patients from attacking the nurses when they refuse to hand out extra pudding and gelatin.

To the left are locked double doors leading into the station. They are always locked, and a scan card is needed to open them. An intercom system to talk to the nurses is attached to the glass wall next to the glass doors.

Past the closed-off nurses' station is a community area where the patients of this secluded ward can watch television, play chess or one of the various board games, or simply sit and socialize with one another. Not that there is much socializing other than the occasional fight over what to watch on the television or argument over who cheated who at one of the games. The rec room also doubles as the group meeting room where we hold our group psychiatric sessions.

Past the rec room is another hallway with various doors on either side. These are the patient rooms. We each have our own bedroom with a bathroom and a lovely metal door that can lock on the outside when we need to be put in isolation.

There is a single window in each room to let in the sunlight, but the glass is bulletproof and unbreakable by anything we have in our rooms. They do not open on the inside, and bars are over them as added protection. A key to the bars and window is placed in a metal cage outside. Firefighters can access the key to open the window and bars in case of a fire.

We even have our own cafeteria, located through the double doors at the end of the hall where our bedrooms are. The kitchen where they cook our meals is closed off from the dining room by a set of metal double doors. You can glimpse the kitchen through the window where we set our dirty trays and dishes after meals.

It is nothing more than a prison for people who are not in their right minds or who have no right mind. I was not in my right mind when I got here, but I feel as if I am now. However, I cannot leave until they release me.

And Harper won't release me until I talk about that day.

Ugh.

I shuffle toward the hallway where the bedrooms are and stop at the second door on the right. This one is my room. The other rooms belong to the other patients.

The patients on this floor are dangerous to themselves and others, like me. We are all stuck here until the therapists and doctors deem us worthy of being part of the public society outside these walls once more.

Or until we die.

Whichever comes first.

So, I am stuck here, as I should be after my insane attempt at suicide. I am thankful that the police came for me when they did. I had left those people all beaten and bloody on the community hall floor, so it was a matter of time before they came for me anyway. I am thankful that I did not kill any of them, or else I would be facing murder charges instead of wanton endangerment and assault.

I am thankful to be alive. I am thankful that I was able to afford a good attorney who got my attempted murder charges dropped down. I am thankful I have a good therapist and a wonderful doctor, and I can afford a private facility.

Even though I am not here of my own accord, I am thankful for the opportunity to heal.

After I lost my mom, I could not deal with my grief constructively and began seeing the shadows. I thought I was going crazy. As it turns out, I was.

I thought support group meetings would help me deal with the grief and help me not feel so alone. Maybe it would even help keep away the shadows.

And for a while, it did.

I had enjoyed meeting once a week with others who had lost their mothers, and my best friend, Tamara, had gone with me for moral support.

I am sure she regrets it now. At least she only lost one of her eyes.

Guilt flares inside my gut, so I shut out the memory of that fateful day and force my mind to think about a good memory like Doc Marcel taught me to do. My mother's smiling face fills my mind as the memory takes over.

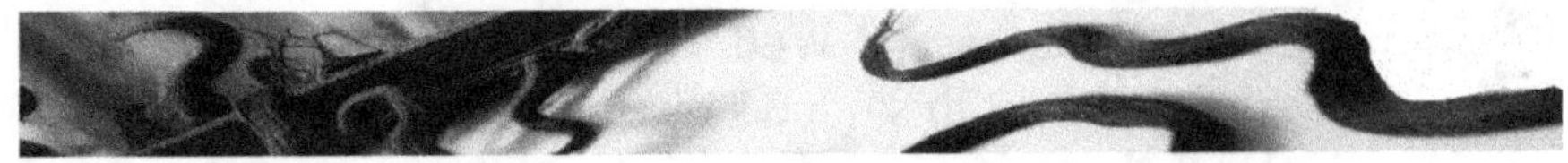

We piled in the car to go shopping, and Katalina was fussing at me for not wearing my coat as she always did.

I ignored her like I always did as I climbed into the driver's seat. When we were settled and buckled into our seats, I pulled out of our driveway and headed toward the shopping center in the next town.

It was a cold December day. The sky was gray with cloud cover, and the roads were wet from a morning rain that could have been snow had the temperature been five degrees colder. The temperature was supposed to drop later that night, making traveling difficult due to the freezing water on the road.

"We go in and get out. No loitering," I said sternly, darting a quick glance at my mother.

She smiled and said, "Yes, I know, dear. You do not want to drive in the dark, especially on wet roads with the possibility of black ice, plus you have to close the restaurant tonight."

"Exactly," I said, then chuckled. "Aren't you supposed to be the mom?"

Mom laughed. "I am the mom, but you are grown, so the roles are now reversed. It is my turn to be a pain in your ass."

My laughter joined my mother's in the close confines of the car as we traveled down the road. Traffic was sparse, making our commute shorter than usual.

That was fine with me. I hated the traffic of the city.

I was surprised, however, since the next day was Christmas Eve. I figured there would be tons of people out doing last-minute shopping. I supposed they feared the rain would turn to snow or ice as the temperatures dropped.

I was not afraid of ice or snow.

We pulled into the large mall's parking lot with its various stores and massive food court. I found a spot near the entrance to the store we liked to shop in, and we both piled out of my SUV.

"Do you think we can grab dinner at the food court while we are out?" Mom asked, pointing toward the sign for her favorite restaurant.

I shrugged nonchalantly, answering, "Sure, if we hurry in the store."

Mom quickened her pace. "Well, what are you waiting for then? Let's get in there and get this done so we can eat."

I laughed as I shook my head.

I jerk myself back to the present. That is as far as I want to go into this memory for now. I could go on if I wanted to. I had done it once before in my session with Miss Marcel, but I was not in a state to relive her death right now.

The door to my room stands open, as do most of the other doors. The one to the right of mine is closed. Why is Jeremy's door closed? The doors are supposed to stay open as long as we follow the rules and play nicely with the other patients.

Come to think of it, I had not seen Jeremy all day, which is unusual considering I spend every day with him. He would have been waiting for me outside Doctor Harper's exam room. Did he get released? Is he in isolation? I need to find out.

I turn away from my open door and knock on Jeremy's door. There is no answer. I try the knob, but the door is locked. I do not bother to unlock the door. That could get me into serious trouble.

Instead, I return to the nurse's station. A nurse is always on duty behind the glass wall surrounding the station. Surely, whoever is working the station today would know something.

I knock on the glass and push the button for the intercom.

"Why is Jeremy locked in his room?" I ask when the red-headed nurse glances up from whatever she is doing on her computer.

"He was released today," she answers into the intercom in a bored tone. "He isn't even in there."

I frown in confusion. "But he had another episode only a week ago. Why would they release him so soon?"

Jeremy faked the episode because he did not want to return to the world yet, especially without me. But no one else knows that, so I keep my mouth shut.

Nurse Amy narrows her emerald eyes at me as she forcefully pushes the button as if it is such an inconvenience and says in a snarky tone, "Not that it is any of your business, but he was released to Doctor Harper's care, and that is all you need to know."

"I was just worried about my friend. You don't have to be so snappy about it," I say indignantly, releasing the button.

Nurse Amy rolls her eyes and focuses back on her computer. Huffing, I turn back to my room and stomp off. When I enter my room, I slam the door shut behind me.

That will probably earn me isolation or some other punishment. It is against the rules to have our door shut during the day. However, if they send Doctor Harper to lure me out of my room, I can ask him about Jeremy.

I sit in the chair beside my window, staring out at the hospital's garden courtyard as I wait for someone to notice that my door is shut. At least my view is nice. Sometimes, we are allowed to go into the courtyard under strict supervision when the weather endures. But I get to look at it all the time.

I contemplate Jeremy being gone.

I had grown fond of Jeremy over the past six weeks, not in a romantic way, but in a brotherly way. I never had any siblings. I was an only child.

If I had a brother, I would want one like Jeremy.

He is sweet and sensitive, fun to be around, and fucked up like me. He had been the sole survivor of a house fire that had killed his parents. He turned to drugs to solve his depression, which only made the depression worse and turned Jeremy into an addict. He suffered from hallucinations just as I did, but I was not sure what Jeremy saw because he never talked about it. He had struggled with his addiction and depression for months.

There were three other patients on this floor. The lady in the last room on the opposite side of the hall suffered from several afflictions. The young man in the room across from mine suffered from extreme bipolar disorder and was on his sixth suicide attempt. And, lastly, the older lady who thought she was a dog half the time was in the room on the other side of Jeremy's. I wasn't sure what the name of the affliction she suffered from was.

Dogmania? I snicker at my own joke.

However, none of these people had taken an interest in me, nor had I been interested in getting to know them. Jeremy went out of his way to make us all feel welcome, but with his room right next to mine and us having so much in common, he spent most of his time with me.

The door to my room opening startles me from my thoughts. As I had predicted, an angry Doctor Harper stands in my doorway. I rise from my bed where I had been sitting and turn to face him.

"Sophia, why are you acting out so soon after leaving my office? You know you are not supposed to shut your door, much less slam it."

The deep, angry tone sends shivers down my spine, half from fear and half from…

I clear my throat nervously. His voice is sexy, but it is downright seductive when he is angry. There goes my blood pressure again.

"I slammed my door because I was angry," I answered, trying to keep my voice from wavering. "Amy shouldn't be such a bitch."

"Sophia," Harper says my name sternly as if reprimanding a child. "What is your problem?"

I cross my arms. "I was just asking about Jeremy, and she snapped at me. You know how fond of him I am."

Harper's visage softens, and his tone is kinder as he replies, "Oh, yes. Jeremy. What did Amy say?"

"Amy said he was released to your care, and that is all I needed to know," I said. "She said it in a snarky tone. It pissed me off."

Harper only nods. "I see. I did release him to my care this morning. I forgot to mention that to you during our session."

I don't respond and glare expectantly at him. Finally, after several moments of silence, I throw my arms out in a wide shrug.

"Well, are you going to tell me where he is?"

Harper takes a breath and says, "You know I am not allowed to divulge private information about one patient to another."

Yes, I did know that. However, I was hoping that Harper would tell me anyway. That was stupid of me.

"Can you at least tell me he is safe?" I asked defeatedly.

Harper just stares at me for a moment before answering, and I cannot read the look on his face.

"He is safe, better than safe."

I slump into my chair as I nod. "Ok, then. What is my consequence going to be for slamming my door?"

The corners of Harper's luscious mouth lift into a smile as he answers humorously, "I think I know the perfect thing."

I narrow my eyes suspiciously. "What?"

Harper's smile is delightedly malicious. "You will clean my private office tonight."

I groan and slump further, but Harper turns and leaves my room before I can complain, leaving the door open. I have heard horror stories about that particular "job". They say he is meticulously particular about the cleanliness of his office.

However, I have not heard anyone talk about his private office. If he is so meticulous over his regular office, how much more so will he be over his private one? I have personally never been in his private office. Very few people have.

His personal, private office is in this ward too, on the other side of a set of locked double doors. It is a dead-end hallway with only Doctor Harper's office, a bathroom, a janitor's closet, and a storage room.

And I will be in there with Doctor Harper tonight.

Alone.

For hours.

Well fuck.

CHAPTER 3

My heart threatens to beat out of my chest, and my breath comes in short bursts. I need to calm down before I hyperventilate. My blood burns through my veins as visions of Harper's mouth all over my body invade my mind.

Stop it! I tell myself. *He does not see you that way, so stop it!*

I take a deep breath to center my racing emotions as I approach Doctor Harper's office. The locked double doors that lead to his private office are at the end of the hall. I am supposed to meet Harper in five minutes in the medical office, which now stands open before me.

I take another deep breath and step in. Harper looks up from the computer and smiles.

"Are you ready to begin?" Harper asks.

"As ready as I'll ever be," I answer, trying to sound casual.

In reality, my body is a bundle of nervous energy and sexual tension. My heart is racing, my breathing uneven, and my groin is hot, wet, and throbbing.

Harper stands and moves toward the open door. I step aside so he can move past me and take the lead as he heads out the door. His hand brushes mine as he passes, and I suck in a breath as I jerk my hand closer to my body. The heat from his fleeting touch burns through me as I follow him to the double doors.

He pulls the keycard that unlocks the double doors out of his pocket. He touches it to an electronic pad on the wall beside the door. The pad beeps, the red light on the pad turns green, and the double doors open with a "whoosh".

Harper tucks the keycard back into his pocket, turns, and motions for me to follow. I follow, the doors swishing shut behind me and closing me in with him. My eyes roam up and down his muscled body as he walks in front of me, and I enjoy the view of his firm, slightly rounded ass. It looks sexy, even in scrubs.

I swallow hard as my sexually charged nerves quiver with longing.

The familiar fantasy of Harper slowly undressing me plays through my mind, and I fall into my own head. My breath hitches in my throat at the thought of running my hands over that ass as he fucks me…

"Sophia, snap out of it," Harper says.

Heat rises up my neck and cheeks as I realize that Harper has turned toward me, and I am now blatantly staring at his…

Gulp…

Bulge.

I had almost run into him as well. I stop suddenly, snapping my gaze up to his face quickly. "I…umm…I must have zoned out again."

Harper narrows his eyes worriedly. "You do that quite a lot. Maybe we should run more tests, see if something is wrong with your brain."

Oh, there is something wrong, all right, but it is south of my brain.

"No, I don't think that's necessary. I just have to learn to pay better attention," I say with a nervous laugh.

Harper's worried gaze turns suspiciously humorous. "If you say so," he responds. "I probably wouldn't have found anything anyway."

I cross my arms over my chest and glare at him. "Ha ha, very funny."

He chuckles and gestures with his hand. "Come on. This way."

He turns and walks toward a door on the right side of the small hallway and inserts a key in the lock. He glances toward me before attempting to unlock or open the door.

His gaze turns serious, along with his tone. He straightens his stance, saying, "This is my private office. Therefore, everything you see here is just that. PRIVATE. Only my most trusted patients get to come in here, so I am trusting you. You cannot tell anyone what is in here."

"What do you have in there, Doc?" I ask, my brows rising curiously, even as trepidation fills my tone. I back up a step.

Harper eases a bit and lets out a short laugh as he answers, "It isn't anything dangerous. I didn't mean to scare you. I just value my privacy, is all."

"You didn't scare me," I lie.

Harper gives me a disbelieving look. "Just promise me you will keep what you see here to yourself."

I nod as I say, "I promise. I can keep a secret."

"If I didn't think you could keep a secret, then you would not have been invited here," Harper says with a wink.

I place my hands on my hips as Harper finally turns to unlock and open the door. "Invited? I wasn't invited. I was ordered to come here as a consequence of slamming my door."

Harper chuckles as he opens the door, then turns to me before entering the room. "Yes, but this consequence is like an invitation. Not every patient will see this office. Only those I deem worthy."

I scoff as I follow him inside. "Sounds more like a private club than an office."

"In a matter of speaking, it is a private club," Harper says, gesturing around the room.

I focus on my surroundings and gasp.

At first glance, it is like any ordinary psychiatrist's office. A rich mahogany desk and an ordinary plush cloth desk chair take up the center of the room. Two plush leather office chairs sit in front of the desk.

In the far corner sits a comfortable-looking, gray tufted chaise lounge with a small doctor's chair next to it. The chaise is situated so the person sitting there can see the large window that takes up the entire back wall.

The window overlooks the garden courtyard, which makes sense since his office is on the same side as my room. This view is from another angle, however. Harper's view is lovelier.

He can see the beautiful fountain bubbling up in the center of the courtyard, with all the eye-catching flowers surrounding it and the elegant sitting bench beside it. In contrast, I cannot see any of it around the many bushes, flowers, and the giant oak tree that grows on the side where my room is.

The two side walls of the office are taken up with floor-to-ceiling bookshelves that stretch from one corner to the other on both walls. However, only a few shelves hold books, with expensive-looking bronze bookends holding them upright.

Normal-looking office, right?

Wrong.

The first thing I notice is the lighting. It is dark outside, so there is little light even though the curtains are open. It is dark and eerie, yet I feel a strong sense of peace and safety. The main electric lights are off.

Very strange.

Several taper candles are lit and placed into a candelabra sitting on the desk. It turns my attention to the desk, which directs my focus on the second very-not-normal thing in this room. A large human skull on the desk, acting as the centerpiece instead of a nameplate, casts shadows from the candlelight all along the desk's surface. It is far too big to be a normal-sized human. Maybe a giant's skull?

Alright, so that might not be too strange. This is a medical facility, so there are plenty of fake anatomy pieces throughout the place. Did it have to be so big, though? And what is up with the candelabra?

The next strange thing is the model that hangs from the ceiling and dangles above the desk. Many people hang galaxy models in their offices showing all the planets, moons, and the sun. But do any of them have extra moons around the Earth?

I don't think so…

But Harper's does.

There are three of them. One full moon is in the center, and two crescent moons are on either side of the full moon. To make it more bizarre, a large, six-pointed star enclosed in a circle hangs above the full moon in the center.

Weird.

My eyes drift to the shelves on the side walls. The shadows are thick here in the sides of the room, and I shudder as I stare into that darkness. The memories of shadows still haunt me, but I take a calming breath as I step further into the room to steady myself.

Thankfully, Harper hits the switch on the wall beside the door, and the electric light fixture on the ceiling lights light up the entire room, downplaying the shadowy candlelight.

Thank God. I would have probably had a meltdown over the shadows in the room.

Harper moves to snuff out the candles as I curiously return my attention to the shelves. The shelves do not contain many books. They contain something else, far from typical in any professional office. The colors are breathtaking and intense, catching the now bright lights and dancing them around the room. My eyes roam over the shelves, trying to take them all in.

They are rocks, but these are no ordinary rocks. Some are solid, some translucent, and they range from various shades of different colors. They vary in shape, size, and texture. Some are rough, like any rock, and some are smooth, like marble or polished glass.

And the rocks are not the only strange things on the shelves.

There are jars of liquid in various colors, small containers of what looks like herbs and spices from a kitchen, miscellaneous items like feathers, incense, and shells, and the most extensive collection of candles I have ever seen, each sitting in antique-looking candle holders or candelabras like the ones on the desk.

Finally, I notice the books. They are not ordinary books. I read some of the titles and gasp, covering my mouth with my hand to stifle the squeak of surprised fright that bubbles up from my chest.

Ancient Egyptian Gods and Goddesses, The History of Witchcraft, Spells and Incantations for Everyday Life, and *The Witch's Guide to Modern Living* are some of the titles.

What the hell is Harper Andrews into? He is a psychiatric doctor, for God's sake! Shouldn't he be into…oh, I don't know…golfing with his doctor buddies and things like that?

"What the heck is this place?" I ask in a hushed tone. "Because it is not an office."

"You don't like it?" Harper asks in a sarcastically mock hurt pitch.

I shoot him an annoyed glare, tapping my foot as I cross my arms over my chest. "I don't even know what all this stuff is. How the fuck am I supposed to form an opinion?"

His countenance falls into a stern expression. "Tone down the language and attitude. I did not say you had to like it, only keep it secret. I did not bring you in here for your opinion. I brought you in here to clean."

My brows raise in surprise. Did I piss him off in some way? I know I'm a smart ass sometimes, but I never meant to make him angry.

"Sorry, Doc. I didn't mean to offend you. It's just this stuff," I gesture around the room. "It doesn't seem like you at all. It's all…" I pause, searching for the right word. "Bizarre."

His stern expression melts away as one corner of his mouth quirks up. "Oh? And what kind of things should I have in my private office since you know me so well?"

"I don't know," I huff. "I don't know you all that well personally, only professionally, but you don't seem like someone who is into…well, whatever this stuff is."

Harper chuckles. "What do you think this stuff is?"

Anger rises in my chest, and I ball my hands into fists at my side.

"Why are you laughing at me? This is serious, Harper!"

Harper chuckles again and quirks an eyebrow as he asks, "Why do you think it is so serious? What about me makes you think I would not be into strange things?"

"Well, those books talk about witchcraft," I shoot back, glaring into those entrancing blue eyes. "And, you are not ugly or evil like witches. You help people, and you are..." I gesture toward him. "Well, you are gorgeous."

I cannot believe I just said that.

Harper throws his head back and laughs, the sound filling the space and sending rivulets of desire coursing through my body. Damn, even his fucking laugh is sexy! I let out an enraged yell that sounds a bit like a growl.

"Stop laughing at me!" I say.

Harper catches his breath and stops laughing, but the laughter is still in his tone as he says, "I'm sorry. I can't help it. Those stereotypes always make me laugh."

"Stereotypes?" I ask in a calmer tone.

"Yes, stereotypes," Harper answers. His visage turns serious, even though the laughter still twinkles in his blue eyes, and he continues in an informative tone. "Witchcraft is becoming more accepted. More and more people are coming out of the broom closet, so to speak. We have always been everywhere but were too afraid to come out because of those stereotypes. Don't you ever watch the witchcraft videos on the internet or read the articles?"

I shrug, my anger draining away as curiosity takes over. "No. I don't get on the internet. You know I was not allowed to have television or phones when I was younger, and I was too busy with the restaurant I bought with my father's inheritance when I finally moved out on my own."

Harper nods knowingly. "Oh, yes. That's right. You bought a restaurant because your father always wanted to own one. But didn't You get another inheritance from your moth..."

Harper stops and clears his throat before continuing. "Didn't you want to buy another restaurant Just before you had your breakdown?"

I nod sadly. "Yes, and now my uncle runs my restaurant, and my cousin has control of my accounts. I suppose I will have to wait until after I get out of here."

Harper smiles, but it doesn't reach his eyes. "Well, you should be out of here soon. You are the smartest of all my patients. And, the most stubborn."

I glare at him, but the corners of his mouth twitch as his blue eyes sparkle. It irritates me that he finds my anger amusing, but at the same time, I like it. At least I can say I make him smile.

I shake my head and gesture around the room. "Anyway, tell me about all this. If I am to clean it, I should know something about it at least."

Harper nods with a smile that lights a spark in his sky-blue eyes. "Yes, I agree, and I would love to tell you about all this…*stuff.*"

He emphasizes the word 'stuff' with a sarcastic tone, and I let out a short laugh. "Well, what else would you call it?"

"Tools," Harper answers with a smirk.

I roll my eyes. "Like some kind of carpenter or something?"

"No, like some kind of witch," Harper answers, but the smirk is gone.

I raise my eyebrows. "You're not…? I thought you were just pulling my leg. You really are a…?"

The question hangs on the edge of my tongue, but it will not come out. Harper answers it anyway.

"Yes, I am a witch, and these are the tools of my trade, which is witchcraft." Harper narrows his eyes at me, undoubtedly gauging my reaction.

"Hmm," is all I say.

"Is that all you have to say, just hmm?" Harper asks.

I shrug. "I'll say more when I know more. For now, just show me how to clean this stuff. I'm sure there is more to it than just a soapy rag."

"Indeed there is," Harper says. "Not everything in this room can be cleaned with soap. I will show you how to clean it all as soon as I am done cataloging my files for the day. For now, you can start with the crystals. All you need for crystals is a dry, clean white cloth. Handle them carefully, and don't drop them. You just dry polish them, and they will be fine."

I glance around the room. Crystals? "I don't see a crystal ball anywhere, or any other crystal for that matter."

Harper throws his head back and laughs again. I frown unhappily. He glances my way, sees my angry stare, and stops laughing. "Sorry again. I forget how…uneducated about this you are."

He pauses, glancing my way, but I simply stare expectantly at him. He sighs. "The stones?"

I shake my head with a confused frown. "You mean the rocks?"

"We call them crystals," Harper says.

"Why didn't you say so in the first place?" I say with a smirk. "I will clean the ro…er…crystals while you work."

"Good," Harper says with a smile.

He walks over to his desk, pulls open one of the drawers, and hands me a white cloth. It is so soft, and I bring it to my face to stroke it down my cheek. I close my eyes in pleasure at the sensation.

It is like the softest cloth in the world, thicker than silk and softer than cotton. Where can I get one of these towels? I open my eyes to find Harper watching me with an intense gaze in his crystal blue eyes.

I feel the heat of a blush creep into my cheeks as I clear my throat and straighten.

"I'll just…uh…get to work," I stutter out, my voice wavering.

I practically run to the other side of the room and take down the first rock…er…Crystal, I come to and begin polishing it with the cloth, turning my gaze away from that piercing stare.

I finish that crystal, place it back on the shelf, and pick up the next crystal. I glance out of the corner of my eye toward the desk to find that Harper has begun working on the computer that sits on top of the mahogany surface.

He glances my way as if feeling me looking, and I quickly turn back to the crystal in my hands. I sigh. Naughty thoughts enter my brain, causing my heart to beat erratically and my blood to boil in my veins.

I imagine Harper's hands, those hands that are working furiously over the keys of his computer. I wonder what they would feel like running over the sensitized skin of my torso. I close my eyes, focusing on the sensation of the crystal in my hand.

As I finish the crystal I am working on and pick up another, the sensation of the cloth in my hands and the smoothness of the polished crystals become erotic in my mind.

Is this how soft Harper's skin would feel? I rub my hands over the crystal's surface, noting its silkiness. The hardness that lies under its surface must be how Harper's muscles feel under his skin. What would it be like to run my hands over all that firmness?

My heartbeat speeds up, my breathing coming in short gasps. My skin heats as I imagine Harper lying naked under me as I run my hands over all those smooth, hard muscles.

I fumble the crystal in my hands, coming dangerously close to dropping it. My eyes fly open as I catch it, placing it carefully back on the shelf where I found it and picking up another. I need to pay more attention to what I am doing.

I take a relieved breath, wondering how angry Harper would have been if I had dropped and broken the crystal; if these rocks can even be broken. What kind of punishment would I receive if that happened?

That thought sets off another fantasy: I am bent naked over Harper's knees, my bare ass at the mercy of his firm hands as he spanks me until my cheeks are red.

The sensation of imagining the firm smacks and the sound of his flesh hitting mine sends spirals of ecstasy coursing through my body. I am practically panting like a dog in heat. A low moan escapes my lips, and I slap my hand over my mouth to muffle the sound.

I swallow hard as I place the crystal back on the shelf before I fumble that one, too. I really need a cold shower. This effect Harper has on me is becoming dangerous to my sanity, and it is already on the precipice of shattering as it is.

I chance a glance toward Harper to find him watching me with a look I cannot read on his face. I swallow hard, but I hold his stare. He stands and begins to walk toward me slowly and sensually, or maybe I'm just reflecting my emotions on his movements after all the fantasizing I just did.

All I know is if that look on his face indicates what will happen when he reaches me, then it will be a long night.

I may not survive.

I am not sure I can handle what this man will bring.

CHAPTER 4

Harper reaches me, but he does not say anything. He simply reaches out and gently pulls the cloth from my hand. He folds it and places it on the shelf.

My voice is breathless as I ask, "Was there something else you wanted me to do?"

He only smiles as he reaches for the crystal. My breath hitches in my throat as my heart pounds in my ears. His fingers brush against my hands as he takes the crystal, leaving my nerves a quivering mess of unrequited ecstasy.

"I have changed my mind," Harper says, and his tone is low, deep, and husky, causing shivers of delight to crawl up my spine and wind their way through my veins.

"About what?" I ask breathlessly.

"About having you clean my office. The sight of you standing here handling my…crystals…is too much for me to bear."

I gasp. Am I dreaming? Hallucinating? Fantasizing?

"What do you mean?" I ask. I cannot believe he means what I think he means, so I have to ask.

"I mean, you are a temptation to me, Sophia."

OH…MY..GOD.

What the holy fuck? Is he serious right now?

I blink several times and raise my right arm to pinch myself.

It hurts.

He leans in closer, his breath fanning over my face as he says, "The way you handle those crystals is just…"

I swallow hard, my heart pumping a mile a minute as heat pools between my legs. I tremble slightly as I stare into those intense blue orbs, coming ever closer to my dark chocolate ones.

"It makes me want to…" he says but pauses mid-sentence again. He runs his tongue along his lips sensually.

My breath comes in short, uneven gasps, making my words seem whispered as I ask, "Makes you want to what?"

He smirks, his tone gaining a humorous quality as he answers, "It makes me want to teach you about crystals."

My eyes widen. Was he teasing me? What an asshole! Anger flares, replacing the ecstasy his teasing had triggered.

"You dick!" I cry out as I lean away from him, curling my hands into fists to keep from slapping him in the face.

He laughs as he responds, "Oh, come on, Sophia. I was only teasing you."

"Yeah, well, it wasn't funny," I spit out. "You are my doctor. You should be more professional."

Harper chuckles. "I'm sorry, Sophia, you are right. I can get a bit too playful sometimes."

Harper stops, his gaze turning serious again as he adds, "But only with you."

I let out an angry growl. He is probably only teasing me again.

"I'm going to bed. It's late," I say as I move past him.

Harper catches my wrist before I can get completely around him and turns me to face him.

"I really do want to teach you about witchcraft if you are interested in learning," he says, and there is a seriousness to his tone that belies the smile that spreads across his face.

"Why would I want to learn about your witchcraft?" I ask spitefully.

"Because I think it could help you," Harper says, the smile fading. "I could teach you some exercises, meditation techniques, that could help you deal with your depression and grief."

"You're saying this stuff really works? That magic is real and can magically fix what is happening inside my head?" I scoff and roll my eyes.

Harper shakes his head, his eyes growing serious. "No, that is not what I mean. No one or nothing can magically fix you except for you, but witchcraft can show you the way if you follow the techniques I give you. And as far as magic being real, that all depends on how much you believe and how strongly you can manifest what you want."

"Whatever that means," I say sarcastically, pulling my wrist from his grip. "Goodnight."

"I'm serious, Sophia. Plus, you could spend time with Jeremy."

That catches my attention.

I turn back to him, my eyes narrowing suspiciously. "I thought you said you released him?"

"I released him to my care," Harper answers. "There is a difference. He no longer resides here at this hospital, but in another private facility I own."

"you have your own hospital?" I ask, my eyebrows raising in surprise.

"I do," Harper answers with a smirk. "Though it is not as large as this one. Also, it only specializes in psychiatric cases. It is a mental health hospital.

"How would I be able to spend time with Jeremy?" I asked curiously.

"I would move you to that facility. It is my private clinic, and much like my private office, I want it kept that way. I only chose patients who are interested in learning these techniques that are found in witchcraft. The hospital would frown on me doing that here, so I set up my own facility where I have more freedom on how I practice."

I consider his words carefully. "So, is that place like this one? Are we locked up and trapped in a certain space in the facility, or do we have free reign?"

Harper's jaw twitches as he answers, "It is a long-term facility, so you have a bit more freedom there. But there will still be places you won't be allowed to go. I need some privacy in my own house."

My eyes widen. "This place is your house?"

Then the corners of his mouth twitch, and he gets that teasing glint in his eye. "Yes. So, will you live with me, Sophia?"

I huff in irritation. "You are incorrigible. I will think about it," I say before storming out of the room.

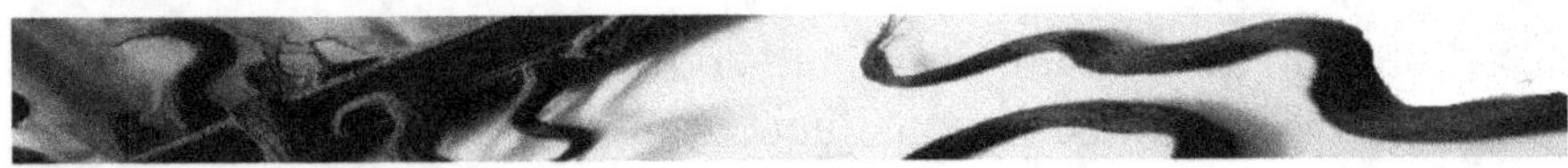

The following day, Harper is called away on an emergency, announcing to the ward that he will be gone for a while. Marcel will be in charge until he returns.

Great.

It is bad enough that I will be without Harper for God knows how long, but I will have to endure it without Jeremy around. Not that I expect him to return. He is probably living his best life over in the other facility.

And I have a chance to join him.

I decide to tell Harper I will take him up on his offer when he returns. In the meantime, I will have to deal.

It is dismal.

How is someone supposed to get rid of their depression when the very place they live (even temporarily) is depressing as hell.

Over the next four weeks, I fall back into my daily routine. I wake up from a fitful sleep, go to the nurse's station and get my pudding and meds for the day, sit in the rec room and wait for the lineup, and then follow the line to the cafeteria to eat breakfast. After breakfast, we have group therapy in the rec room for an hour, free time until lunch, then we do another lineup for lunch.

After lunch are the individual meetings, where Harper or Marcel (However, it is now only Marcel since Harper is gone) meets with each patient on the ward in a one-on-one session. Separately, of course. Those not in session have to do chores until it is their turn.

When the sessions are done, we enjoy some time outside in the courtyard until it is time for dinner, and then after dinner, we have more free time until ten P.M. when it is time for lights out. This is when those who are approved for visitation can receive visitors.

After free time is over and all visitors are gone, everyone shuffles off to their rooms and prepares for sleep. The guard stationed outside the door behind the nurse's station (the door that leads out into the rest of the hospital and freedom) comes in to shut and lock each of the patients' doors.

The harsh, bright fluorescent lights go out, and soft, dim night lights flicker on. That is when the shadows appear. That is why my sleep is so restless.

Although they do not move and come alive like they used to before the medication stopped my hallucinations, they still scare me. They are too much of a reminder of my life before I came here and after my mother died in front of me.

Then we get up and do it all again the next day, except on Sundays when we can do what we want all day long, even though there really isn't anything to do.

BORING.

The weeks drag by miserably as I wait for Harper's return, dreaming of having more freedom and seeing Jeremy again once I am transferred. I wonder about Jeremy being in the new place. Is he happy? Does he like it?

I miss him terribly.

I miss Harper, too.

I wonder where he is and what has kept him away for so long.

Almost a month later, I am helping set up the rec room for group while these thoughts run through my mind. We move the gaming tables back out of the way and set all the chairs in the middle of the room, forming them into a circle. I sit down in one of the chairs when Doctor Harper walks into the room.

It snaps me out of my own head.

Needless to say, I am more than excited to see him. It means I will be getting out of here soon.

His eyes meet mine and I offer him a bright smile. There is a question in his ice-blue gaze. Even though it has been weeks, I remember the question. He wants to know if I have decided to go to his facility and let him teach me witchcraft.

I nod enthusiastically, earning myself a returning smile brighter than my own. My eyebrows raise at the utter happiness on Harper's face. It must have meant a lot to him that I accepted his offer to take me away from here.

And teach me witchcraft.

That is the part I am nervous about. I mainly agreed so I could be with Jeremy again, and so I could get out of this dismal hospital. I am unsure what to expect about the rest, but I will endure what I must. Harper said he thought it would help, and, if nothing else, I trust his judgment as my psychiatrist. If he thinks it will help, I will give it my best shot. I am sure I will be safe. What could go wrong when I am in a facility my doctor owns?

"Good afternoon, everyone," Doctor Harper says as he settles into one of the seats.

"Good afternoon, Doctor Harper," we all say back excitedly.

We all missed Doctor Harper.

"How did everything go while I was away?" Doc asks, but his gaze is trained directly on me.

I feel compelled to answer.

"It was boring," I say flatly, settling back in the seat and crossing my arms over my chest.

Harper chuckles as he responds, "That is better than dramatic, I suppose."

"I wasn't bored," Julia, the lady who lives all the way at the end of the hall, says. "I was fighting with Amy all week. She keeps giving my pudding to Barb."

One of Julia's many afflictions is that she is a pathological liar.

Barb, the older lady who thinks she is a dog, responds huffily, "Dogs do not eat pudding."

"Dogs eat everything," Danny, the boy who commits suicide almost every week, says.

"Not this dog," Barb shoots back, ending her statement with a bark.

"Well, dogs don't talk, either, but you never shut up," Julia says, her voice rising.

"Yes, it makes me want to kill myself," Danny says sarcastically.

"You already did that yesterday," Barb yells.

Harper stands, waving his arms in a calming gesture. "Everyone stop for a moment. Let's go one at a time, shall we?"

Julia and Barb, who had both been leaning forward toward each other, settle back into their chairs. Julia crosses her arms over her chest, mimicking me.

It is another of her afflictions; it is called mirroring.

Barb sticks out her tongue and begins to pant like…well…like a dog.

"Now, Julia, why do you think Amy keeps giving Barb your pudding?" Harper asks.

Julia launches into a lengthy explanation of how Barb tricked Amy by pretending to be Julia, and I zone it all out. I am not interested in listening to Julia's lies, Barb's adventures as a dog, or Danny's last failed suicide attempt. I only want this session to be over so I can talk to Harper alone. I am tired of listening to these people's problems when they seem silly and mundane compared to mine.

I jerk upright in my seat. This was how I felt when my "incident" occurred during another group session. Only, this group was voluntary, and not in a hospital's psychiatric ward.

The session when I had my psychotic break, when the shadows took control. Of course, now I knew that the shadows had been a hallucination and that I had been the one to go crazy on those poor people. How had I become so uncaring and unfeeling toward others?

The memories take over as I zone out completely.

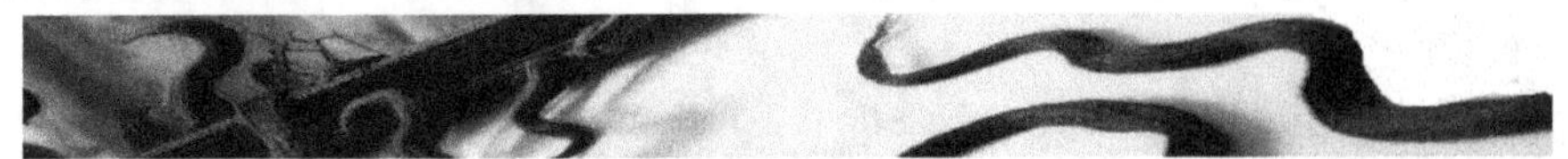

I was sitting with my friend Tamara, back when she still had both eyes and was still my friend. Her black, tightly curled hair was pulled back from her face and set into a curly bun on the back of her head. Her dark brown eyes were almost the same color as her coffee-colored skin, large and round inside an oval-shaped face. Her broad nose flared over her large lips as she scented the air around us.

"Are those doughnuts I smell?" she asked.

"Maybe. They usually bring some kind of snack for us," I answered, smiling at Tamara's excited look at the mention of sweet snacks.

She had always been a sucker for desserts.

"Go get one," I told her laughingly. "Everyone is welcome to them."

She handed me her purse and coffee cup, saying, "Here, hold these. I'm gonna get me one."

I took her things and sat them on the floor beside mine, next to our seats. I looked around at the other faces in the room curiously. No one looked weird or strange. They were all like me, just people looking to unload their problems on other strangers to make them feel a modicum of normality. Strangely, it made me feel better. I did not feel so alone.

"But, they are not like you," The then familiar voice in my head whispered to me. *"They don't have shadows in their heads."*

"I don't want you," I replied silently in my head. *"Go away and leave me alone."*

"We will never leave you alone."

I decided to ignore them and concentrate on enjoying the session and learning as much as I could from others who were dealing with grief like I was.

If only I had known then what I know now.

I would have screamed a warning, telling everyone to stay away from me. I would have gotten up and run to the nearest psychiatric hospital and begged them to take me.

I would not have picked up that pencil and run it through my friend's eye just because she happened to be the one sitting beside me when I finally broke.

I can still feel the helplessness I felt when my hand seemed like it had a mind of its own, when the voices in my head told me what they were going to make me do, and my body complied.

I can still hear them, telling me what boring simpletons the others in the room were, and how none of their grief could hold a match to mine.

I had believed them. Even my mind complied with what the shadows told me.

They made me raise my arm, pencil in hand. They all thought I was raising my hand to speak. When the leader called on me, everyone turned to look at me expectantly.

I shiver as I relive the memory.

I can see Tamara's wide, brown eyes clearly in my mind, staring at me questioningly as I held the pencil up. I can still remember struggling with my own body, unsuccessfully. I can still see the fear on Tamara's face as the pencil rushes toward her eye.

I was sitting too close for her to react. There was nothing she could have done to stop me, and there was nothing I could have done to stop myself.

The memory keeps playing as the pencil penetrates her eye, and I can feel the blood rushing from her eye socket and running down onto my hand.

It felt good, almost orgasmic.

The rest of the room erupts into chaos as I get up from my chair. They will not get away…

NO, NO, NO…

I cannot relive this again. I am not ready. I start to pry myself away from the memory.

"I will always be with you," the voice says as I strain to open my eyes. *"You can go to all the hospitals in the world and take any medicine they give you, but the shadows will always be there."*

Wait…that wasn't part of the memory. The shadows never spoke to me after I ran the pencil through Tamara's eye. They had been placated, so they had remained silent.

Up until I had gone home and tried to take my own life.

My eyes snap open, but I cannot see anything. Only darkness greets me until the shadows begin to fill the corners of my vision.

Their movements are smooth and melodic, like some dark, dangerous predator trying to woo its victim. Something grabs my upper arms, and a frigid cold steals its way into my bones.

They have me in their grasp, trapping me in this nightmare of a place.

Wherever that is. Where is the group? Where is Harper? Why am I seeing shadows again?

They are going to try to take me again, just when I thought they were gone and would never return.

But I thought they had only been a hallucination…

Am I hallucinating again?

One of the shadows moves before me, filling my vision and taking a shadowy human form. Eyes illuminate in the space where its face would be, red and glowing eerily like some phantom light.

It opens its mouth to speak, showing off sharp, shadowy fangs set in a gaping, hollow hole of a mouth that threatens to suck me into its evil oblivion.

"You will be mine soon," it says in a raspy, whispering voice.

The coldness of its grasp and the terror it induces consume me. Its face draws nearer, its mouth opening wide. There are nightmares in that gaping hole, an endless void of a dark place I never want to go. The arctic cold of it rushes into my very bones, threatening to freeze me from the inside out.

Flashing pictures of the blood and gore from that day run through my mind. The ecstasy I felt coils in my bones, torturing me with the memory. The sensation of being sucked into that abyss of a nightmare consumes me.

The evil laugh of the red-eyed shadow man promises to trap me there forever.

Not again.

I cannot relive that day again.

I will die if I have to relive it over and over.

"Someone save me," I mutter, but no sound comes out. It is as if the nightmare has rendered me mute.

If I cannot speak, maybe I can scream.

I slam my eyes shut and let out a blood-curdling scream louder than any I have ever heard.

Not even the day I had mutilated a room full of strangers.

CHAPTER 5

Teh sound rings in my ears as my scream fills the room. The resounding echo runs through me, causing me to grit my teeth against the threat of another scream.

The cold grasp on my upper arms tightens, and it begins to shake me, rattling my bones and tearing the other scream from my throat, this one hoarse and cracking.

"Sophia!" a deep, booming voice calls out in my mind.

No, not in my mind. That voice was real.

"Sophia, calm down," the voice yells.

The sound of that voice penetrates my brain, and awareness fills my thoughts. Slowly, I open my eyes.

Harper's blessedly handsome, angelic face fills my vision. His hands grip my upper arms as he stares into my face. His eyes are tortured with worry, and his dark auburn hair has fallen into his eyes again.

My fingers itch to reach out and brush it back from his face.

The shadows are gone, and the room is bright, as if they'd never been there at all.

They hadn't been there, had they? Am I hallucinating again?

"You fell asleep, Sophia," Harper says softly, piercing me with his worried blue stare.

Oh, thank God. I just fell asleep. The shadows are not coming back.

"I…I'm sorry," I stutter groggily.

He releases my arms and places a hand on my back to help me sit up as I say, "I guess I had a nightmare."

"You had me worried for a second," Harper says. "You said something about the shadows."

I come fully awake as Harper kneels in front of me. I glance around the room at the frightened eyes of the others staring at me.

"I was dreaming of that day," I whisper, knowing Harper will know what day I am speaking of. I did not want to share that memory with the group.

"Okay," he says simply, patting my knee as he stands and moves back to his seat.

"Alright, everyone. Let's call it a day. Julia, I will speak with Nurse Amy about the pudding.

"Barb, I want you to work on your mantra. Remember, you are a person, not a dog.

"Finally, Danny, I want you to write me a paper on constructive ways to gain attention that do not include attempting suicide. Have it ready by tomorrow.

"Group is dismissed."

Sighing with relief, I rise from my chair, but Harper stands in my path before I can walk away. He looks me up and down, one eyebrow raised questioningly.

"Is everything alright with you, Sophia?" he asks smoothly. "Are the nightmares getting worse?"

I put both hands on my hips defiantly and answer, "Yes. They have been getting worse for a while, but you have not been here to help me. I need to get the hell out of here."

Harper sighs. "I'm sorry. Something came up that needed my undivided attention."

'Well, now I need your attention," I say huffingly.

"Someone is in a mood today," Harper says sarcastically.

I growl angrily as I stomp one foot. "Damn right I'm in a mood. You throw me a bone and then run off for an entire month! What did you expect? Not to mention, I just had a fucking nightmare in front of the entire group."

"I understand, but didn't you use your time constructively while I was away?" He asks, cocking his head curiously.

"And how was I supposed to use my time constructively?" I ask cynically.

"Did you ask around or do any research?" He asks, ignoring my mocking tone.

I straighten, my arms falling to my sides. My voice is more serious as I ask, "Research?"

"Sophia, I know you have never spent time on the internet before, but you could have accessed the computer in the rec room during your free time and had someone help you with it. Did you not get curious about…well, about what we talked about?" Harper's tone is filled with disappointment, as if scolding a disobedient toddler.

I frown. I had, in fact, looked up witchcraft online one day while he had been away. However, the overflow of information, along with the contradictions from one site to the other, had been too much for me to take in. I say it aloud.

"It was like falling down a rabbit hole. There is no way someone could learn anything from all that information," I finish with a frustrated shake of my head.

"I suppose it can be confusing if you do not know specifically what to look for," Harper says with a shrug. He turns to stuff papers into the leather satchel he carries everywhere.

He sighs, pushes his hair away from his face, turns back to me, and says, "I will have your paperwork processed in a couple of days. Try to hang in there."

"Fine, I'll start packing then," I say and turn to walk off. Harper's voice stops me, and I turn back toward him.

"Are we just going to ignore your nightmare? Don't you want to tell me about it?"

I frown. "It was just a nightmare, Harper. Nothing to worry about. You know I have them all the time."

He shoots me a worried glance before snapping the flap closed on the satchel. "You had one during a group session when you should not have even been sleeping. You should not be having nightmares at all, anyway. We should discuss that during our one-on-one session today."

"So I'm not leaving today?" I ask, my voice a whine.

Harper stands. "No, like I said, the paperwork will take at least a few days to go through. Be patient. I will see you at your session in an hour."

I let out a moan of frustration, but Harper is already picking up his satchel and walking away. He didn't wear scrubs today. Instead, he wore black dress slacks with a light blue polo that brings out his eyes. I watch his ass in the black slacks as he walks away, thinking how much sexier his ass looks in those than in the unflattering scrubs.

And I get to see him today for my private session, not Marcel.

I am still upset that I do not get to leave the hospital today, but I cannot help but skip as I head toward my room to prepare for my session with Harper.

My one-on-one session with Harper.

How can I stay upset when I have that to look forward to?

I begin rummaging through my drawers for something to wear when I get to my room. My choices are limited. We are only allowed to wear elastic-waisted hospital pants and t-shirts. No jewelry, no makeup, and the women cannot have snaps or hooks on their bras.

I get it. We are all on close watch here, so any sharp thing, even in our clothing, could be used dangerously. They have to take precautions. But, dammit, I would love to have something nice to wear again.

The clothes I came here in were thrown away when I first got here. They were too bloody to salvage.

I would have died had it not been for Harper. He saved my life. I was about to give in to the void, float away into the darkness, and pull the shadows with me, but his voice kept me rooted to the living.

The thought brings the memory to the front of my mind, and I flow into it as muscle memory takes over, allowing me to dress while I reminisce.

The lights are what I remember first. Bright and garish, cutting a slicing path right through the middle of the darkness. They caught my attention and distracted me, so I hadn't realized that my eyes had been blinking rapidly. I was awake and had not even realized it.

Then I remember the voices. There was a lot of yelling. It was medical jargon that most people would not understand, but I caught enough words to know that they were prepping me to give me blood and trying to stabilize me.

The light faded, and faces appeared in the corners of my vision, a sea of worried visages floating around me. But one stuck out from amongst them all. He had been the most beautiful thing I had ever seen and still was.

At the time, I had thought he was an angel coming to take me to my next life beyond, but now I knew what he really was. An earthly angel sent to pull me from the precipice of death.

And he had done it.

His face, his soft tone while he soothed me and asked me if I knew where I was, and the pleading in his voice as he begged me to hang in there had kept me from drifting away into the abyss of death.

Something moves in the corner of my eye, pulling me from my thoughts and returning me to the present. My door slams shut suddenly, causing me to jump and turn at the sound.

Julia stands in the doorway, and the malicious look on her usually solemn face sends slivers of fear skittering through my nerves.

"Hey, Julia," I say carefully, keeping my voice steady and my movements slow. "What brings you into my room?"

Julia looks at me steadily momentarily, and then a wicked smile curves her thin lips. Her brown, frizzled hair sticks out on either side of her head, adding to the crazed look. However, the look in her small, emerald-green eyes scares me the most. It is definitely the eyes of someone insane, and it is directed at me for some reason.

"You stole my pudding and then blamed it on Barb," Julia says, the accusation causing her voice to raise slightly.

I move slowly to the other side of the room, placing my bed between me and the crazy lady. Thankfully, my voice remains calm.

"Julia, we will get in trouble with the door shut."

"I want my pudding!" She screeches.

I make a calming gesture with my hands. "I thought Doctor Harper explained this to you earlier. No one stole your pudding, Julia. You just forget to go get it. Did you forget it again this morning?"

She steps forward, her hands balling into fists at her sides. "I didn't forget. The shadows told me you took it."

Fear races through me, cold and paralyzing, causing my breath to hitch. My voice quivers as I back up a step and hiss, "What did you say?"

"The shadows, they speak to me too, you know." Julia's tone is cold and calculating.

She takes a step toward me as she continues, "They told me what you did to that girl, to those people."

She moves quicker, taking a few more steps toward me as she continues to speak, "Now, you want to do that to us, and I will not let you."

She is almost to the bed now, only feet from where I stand on the other side. I back up even more, but my back hits the wall, and I can go no further.

"I don't know what you're talking about," I lie, and I can hear the terror in my voice.

"Liar!" She screams, then lunges, landing on the bed, stomach down, her head raised, and her arms reaching frantically for me.

Panic seizes my soul as I let out a scream, dodging sideways to avoid her hands. I can see her green eyes, wide and wild, as she grabs for me, growling like a wild animal on the verge of catching its prey.

I scoot sideways, keeping my back against the wall, until I come to the end of the bed, then I dart forward toward the door. I do not dare look back. I make it to the door and grab the handle, preparing to fling open the door, when something hits me in the back with the force of a bull.

I am slammed against the closed door…hard…and the air rushes from my lungs, leaving me breathless and stunned. A hand grabs the back of my head, weaving its fingers into my hair for a better hold, then slams my head into the door.

I had no idea Julia was so strong.

I scream out in pain as my forehead hits the door once, twice, three times until I see stars in my vision. Frantically, I bring my hands up and place them on the door, pushing with all my strength to keep my head from hitting it again.

Julia roars in frustrated anger and kicks at the backs of my legs, trying to force me to fall. Her grip on my hair is so tight and firm that I cannot escape.

I struggle against her grip, and since she has ceased banging my head into the door, I bring a hand up to grab her wrist and attempt to pull her hand away from me. In the same movement, I twist my body around and rotate my shoulder so that I am now facing Julia.

The look in her eyes is frantic, wild, almost not human, and alarm and terror tear through my body. She is feral, kicking and growling, pulling at my hair as I try to pry her grip from my brown locks.

"Let me go!" I scream at her through gritted teeth.

"Not until you are dead. The shadows told me you must die!" Julia screams wildly, her voice rough and scratchy from her growling.

She brings her free hand up, balled into a fist, and pulls it back. It is aimed toward my face. I see all of this too late. There is no time to react.

This is going to hurt.

I shut my eyes tightly, bringing my face down in the hopes that she lands the blow on the top of my head instead of in my face.

No luck.

The punch lands directly on my eye.

Pain explodes through my head, and the stars dance across my vision once again. A cry of pain escapes my lips as my head is jerked back from the force of the hit. Adrenaline pumps through me as I see her cock her fist back for another hit, and I lunge my body forward into hers suddenly.

My shoulder crashes into her stomach, and she staggers back. I grab her around the waist and let the momentum of my tackle keep moving us forward, slamming her back into the side of the bed.

She lands with a loud "OMPH" sound, and her grip on my hair releases. I fall to my knees from the impact, falling back onto my butt and crab-walking away from the feral woman who is now crumpled to the floor and wailing miserably.

Suddenly, the door to my room is flung open, and it almost slams into me in my position on the floor. I manage to move back right before it slams into my side, and it hits the wall with the force of a tank. It would have put a hole in the wall had it not been for the plastic door stopper attached to the baseboard.

I have never in my life been so happy to see Harper. I am always happy to see Harper, but this time I am fucking ecstatic.   Three other men in scrubs and white lab coats come rushing in behind Harper, and I see a syringe in one of their hands. With a cry of relief, I pick myself up from the floor, ready to bolt out the open door and let the medical staff deal with the crazy lady.

At least, I try to pick myself up.

I rise up slightly, and nausea hits me with the force of a storm. It roils through my stomach and up my esophagus, causing me to heave and fall back on my ass. The room spins violently, and I feel myself falling onto my back.

I lay there momentarily, staring up at the ceiling and waiting for it to stop spinning. I hear Julia cry out next to me, and I instinctively flinch away from her, expecting another attack. It does not come. Instead, I feel gentle hands curve around the side of my neck. Harper's face comes into view.

His ice-blue eyes are creased with worry as his other hand comes up to gently stroke my cheek. I am in too much pain to feel anything but relief at his presence. The adrenaline rush leaving my body leaves me feeling shaky and vulnerable, and a lone tear slides down my cheek. It burns along its path.

Great.

I must have minor scratches on my face, even though I do not remember Julia scratching at me since everything happened so fast. It would explain the burning sensation of my tears against my face.

Then, I remember her punching me in the face, and as if on cue, my eye starts to throb.

Double great.

Harper gently prods the side of my face. It must be bruised because a jolt of pain shoots through my head, and I moan miserably.

I can see the medical staff bent over Julia in my peripheral vision since my good eye is pointed toward that side of the room. I see her arms flailing as they try to get control of her, and she screams violently as if the men are trying to hurt her. I know they are not, though.

Finally, the one with the syringe plunges the needle into her ass and pushes the plunger, pulling it back out quickly and dodging the swing of Julia's arm as it comes close to hitting his face. Julia slumps, her screams quieting.

Damn, that medicine worked fast.

Then I see it. The shadows. They drift into the air slowly, like smoke curling up from an open fire, coming from Julia's body! The shadows merge into one big blob, taking the shape of a body floating in mid-air.

The pain in my head is forgotten as horror takes over, snaking its way down my spine and leaving an icy trail in its wake. Red, glowing eyes stare out from the dark shadow body, shining brightly from where its head would be. A dark hole opens where its mouth would be, and the voices fill my head.

"You will never escape."

I open my mouth to scream, but nothing comes out. I can hear Harper saying my name urgently, asking if I am alright. I am paralyzed with fear.

I can't scream, I can't speak, I can't even breathe. All I can do is lay there and stare at the shadow body hovering over Julia, who is now a silent, crumpled heap on the floor.

"Get the stretcher in here, stat!" Harper says, never taking his eyes from mine.

He shines that damn light in my eyes as he repeats my name.

"Sophia. Sophia, can you hear me? Come back to me, Sophia."

Come back? I'm still here. Aren't I?

"You will always be mine," the voice whispers.

"Sophia?" Harper calls again, and I can hear the worry in his voice that matches the look in his eyes.

I want to reassure him, but I cannot. The absolute terror holding my body prisoner won't let me go as long as the shadows are still watching me.

I watch as they float over Julia's prone form, smoky curls drifting from the shadowy formed body as it drifts nearer where I lay on the ground.

"She's going into shock, and she is concussed. Where is the damn stretcher?" Harper shouts.

One of the other three men picks up Julia's prone form and carries her from the room while another turns to Harper and says, "I am sure they will be here soon."

The shadow looms even closer, its red eyes glowing menacingly as a smoky hand reaches out toward me. I suck in a breath and realize I can breathe. My heart stutters and begins to thump hard against my chest. I release the breath, and it comes out in a blood-curdling scream.

They are going to take me again, I know it. The hand looms closer, so close I can feel the iciness of its touch against the side of my face. My scream fades, and I suck in another breath, ready to release another scream.

The scream never comes. The sound fades as unconsciousness threatens to take me away. I hear Harper calling my name, but I don't care. I welcome the looming darkness.

I smile as my consciousness fades away. The shadows cannot follow me into the abyss of oblivion.

The shadows lose again.

CHAPTER 6

My eyes open to sunlight streaming in from my window, and I blink as my vision adjusts to the brightness. I glance around the room and realize I am alone, and my door is shut.

That's weird.

My vision is stilted and weird as if I am seeing out of only one eye, and then I realize I am. My right eye refuses to open. I struggle to sit up and groan at the pain that shoots through my head. I raise a hand to probe my right eye, where the pain is concentrated, but something tugs at my arm. I glance down my body and see the tube of an IV leading to the needle placed in my lower arm close to the bend of my elbow.

I lower my arm back down and use my other hand to probe at my eye, closing my other eye tightly in preparation for the pain. It lances through my head as I touch gently around my eye. It is swollen shut, but as long as I do not touch it, the pain is not too bad. I stop touching my eye and lay back on the pillows.

Memory comes as the pain fades to a dull ache. Julia's assault comes rushing back to me. No wonder my head hurts. I am surprised I don't have more injuries. Or maybe I do. I haven't looked in the mirror yet, nor do I want to. The mirrors are where the shadows live.

The shadows…

Something tugs at the edge of my memory, but it is gone as quick as it came. The sound of a toilet flushing distracts me, and I open my eyes, glancing toward my closed bathroom door.

Someone is in my bathroom. The water in the sink turns on and runs for a moment, then shuts off. I hear footsteps clacking along the tiled floor, then the knob turns.

I suck in a breath. I am more curious than I am afraid, which is strange considering the events that have led to me laying in this bed hooked up to an IV. Shouldn't I be more afraid that Julia will return to finish the job?

My eyes widen as the door opens.

Harper stands in the doorway, drying his hands with a paper towel. He turns to toss it into the trashcan by the door, then turns back to enter the bedroom. His gaze lands on mine and his eyes widen in surprise.

"Sophia."

His voice is laced with so many emotions it is hard to discern them all. Surprise, relief, and do I dare hope for happiness?

Okay, I know I shouldn't read too much into it. Of course, he is happy I am awake. He is a doctor, and I am his patient, so he is supposed to be concerned for my welfare.

Right?

Then why is he looking at me as if his entire world had disintegrated and suddenly came back?

I move to sit up again; this time, my body complies with minimal pain. Harper moves toward me hesitantly, reaching out as if wanting to touch me to assure himself I am really here. My heart flutters, and I brace myself for the heat of his touch.

The door to my room opens.

"Did I hear you say Sophia's name? Is she awake?"

Harper's hand drops away and I swear I note a spark of disappointment shine in his gaze just before he turns toward the visitor. It is gone so fast that I wonder if I imagined it.

Probably.

I did not, however, imagine the familiar voice. I turn toward Jeremy as he rushes into my room and hurries to the side of my bed.

"Sophia, you're finally awake," he says happily as he sits gingerly on the side of my bed and carefully gathers me into his arms, avoiding the tube still snaking from my arm.

The familiar comfort I always get at my best friend's touch envelopes me. It's like coming home.

"I am so happy to see you," I whisper into Jeremy's ear, burying my face into the side of his neck but carefully avoiding my swollen eye. I breathe in his scent, earthy and rich, convincing my brain that he is really here and I am not dreaming.

I glance over Jeremy's shoulder to see Harper watching us with a strange look on his visage.

Anger? Or Jealousy?

Surely not...

I clear my throat and move out of Jeremy's embrace, pushing him back from me so I can look fully at him. His hazel eyes smile into mine as I look him up and down.

His light brown hair is cut in a short shag, with tendrils falling almost to his eyes. I know from experience that it is soft as silk to the touch. His soft features give him a boyishly handsome quality that goes along with his kind and gentle personality.

His nose is straight, his lips full, and his eyes round and heavily lashed. His body is athletically toned and firm, and I admit that I often checked him out when we first met.

He is a beautiful man.

But I don't see him that way anymore. He is my friend. He is the only one I have left.

Jeremy fidgets under my scrutiny. He lets out a nervous chuckle as he says, "Sophia, why are you staring at me like that?"

I laugh, glancing nervously at Harper, who still stands watching us with that unreadable expression.

"I'm just happy to see you, that is all," I answer. "What are you doing here? I thought you were with Harper at his other facility."

Harper steps forward, placing a friendly hand on Jeremy's shoulder, but there is a hardness in his eyes that belies the action. His tone is also friendly, but I hear a slight inflection of anger in its depths.

"I brought Jeremy here for you," Harper says. "I thought it might make you feel safer."

"Doc told me what happened," Jeremy says, taking one of my hands into his. He touches the side of my face gently, causing me to flinch with pain. "That Julia can get a bit crazy sometimes."

"A bit crazy?" I say. "She almost bashed my head in!"

"Why was she trying to hurt you?" Jeremy asks. He traces his fingers gently around my eye, and I hiss with pain. "What did you do to piss her off?"

"Nothing," I say indignantly, turning my face away from his touch. Jeremy drops his hand. "She just came into my room, shut my door, and then lunged for me."

"Did she say anything before she attacked you?" Harper asks, and again, I hear an inflection of anger in his tone.

"She said...," I pause, something niggling on the edge of my thoughts. That same memory trying to climb its way to the surface of my brain.

"What? What did she say?" Jeremy asks, giving my hand a

comforting squeeze.

Memories of her words hit me, coalescing in my mind like a nest of writhing snakes.

"The shadows speak to me too, you know."

The blinding terror comes rushing back, and my heart stops as my breath freezes in my lungs. I swallow hard.

"The shadows," I say, but my voice is barely a hoarse whisper.

I catch the worried frown on Harper's face before he recovers his features and says, "What about the shadows?"

Jeremy squeezes my hand a bit tighter than is comfortable. I welcome the pain. It drives away the fear enough that I can think.

"Julia said she could speak to the shadows, and they told her about what I did to my group," I say, my voice quivering. "She says she saw the shadows, too. How?"

I gaze up at Harper, who gives me a blank stare. I stare back, knowing my coffee-colored eyes are wide with fright. The comfort of Jeremy's hold on my hand calms me enough that I am not frantic, but I am on the verge. Jeremy tightens his hold even more.

I don't know how long I can stand to sit here while Harper stares at me silently. Luckily, I don't have to find out. He shakes himself as if pulling himself from a daydream. His visage falls into a comforting look, and his tone matches as he speaks.

"Sophia, I am sure Julia was just reflecting on what she heard in group. You were talking in your sleep when you had your nightmare about the shadows."

"But what about the other thing? She said they knew about…about…you know." I cannot bring myself to say it.

"You talked a lot. We all heard you say that you were sorry for what you did to your group. You talked about being afraid of the shadows and that the shadows would never let you forget."

I swallow hard. I had been so private about my problems since I had been here. Harper and Jeremy were the only two people here who knew the entire, bloody story.

Or they had been. Now everyone knew, apparently. Thanks to my stupid nightmares. Harper was right. Julia was nothing but an attention seeker and a pathological liar, and she had made up the entire scenario to create drama and bring attention to herself.

But, damn, did she have to hurt me to get it?

The fear leaks away, and I nod in acquiescence. "I guess you're right.”

Still, something nags at the edges of my consciousness. Something important, something frightening. I let it go. I cannot force it to come forward, so maybe if I stop focusing on it, the memory will come back naturally.

“I know I am right,” Harper says, relief reflecting in his tone. The tenseness and anger in his features disappear with his smile. “Now, who is ready to get out of this place?”

Jeremy frowns, his grip tightening even tighter.

“Ouch!” I say, pulling on my squished hand.

Jeremy loosens his grip immediately, shooting me an apologetic look before saying, “Harper, shouldn’t we wait until Sophia is fully recovered before we make the journey?”

Confusion runs through me as I look alternately between Jeremy and Harper. “What do you mean? How far away is this place?”

Harper’s tone is firm as he shoots Jeremy a stern look and replies, “Not far enough away to be concerned. I will send someone in to take out that IV so you can pack your things. We will leave first thing tomorrow morning.”

With that, Harper stalks out of the room, leaving me alone with Jeremy.

He leaves the door open.

“What was that all about?” I ask Jeremy when Harper is out of earshot.

Jeremy’s frown disappears as he turns his attention to me. “Nothing,” he answers, shaking his head as if to clear it. “I’m just tired from the drive over and worried about you.”

“Again, I ask, how far away is this place?” I ask, concern blooming in my chest.

“It really isn’t that far. Only a couple of hours. I’m just worried for you,” Jeremy says with a tight smile.

“Why don’t I believe you?” I say as I look at Jeremy suspiciously.

Jeremy blows out a defeated breath. “Alright, I’ll tell you. But don’t get mad…okay?”

“Why would I get mad?” I ask.

“Because,” Jeremy answers. “You have a crush on Harper, and what I am about to tell you is not exactly flattering to him.”

I roll my eyes. “I do not have a crush on Harper.” My tone turns sarcastic as I teasingly add, “I am madly in love with him and want to have his babies. There is a difference."

Jeremy's lips quirk up in the corners, but he quickly recovers and says sternly, "Be serious for a minute, Sophia. This is important."

"Alright, jeesh. Just spit it out already," I say.

"I don't want you going to that place," he says hurriedly as if trying to say it before he changes his mind.

My eyebrows twist in confusion. "Why?"

"Because Harper is…well, he…oh shit, Sophia. I don't know how to tell you this," Jeremy says. He releases my hand, stands, and begins pacing the room.

I watch him pace back and forth for a minute before asking, "Is he mistreating you, Jeremy?"

"Not exactly," Jeremy says, running a hand through his silky brown locks. "I mean, I am fed, sheltered, safe. But some of the things that happen in that house are…I don't know…bizarre. And most of it revolves around him."

I quirk an eyebrow. "Harper is teaching you witchcraft, Jeremy. I wouldn't expect it to be anything but bizarre. His private office here is bizarre."

"But that's the thing," Jeremy says. "He hasn't even started teaching us yet. We've just been doing exercises like meditation and learning about its history. We haven't done any magic spells or anything like that."

I shrug. "That sounds normal. So what is so bizarre?"

"Take yesterday, for example. We were meditating in group…"

I cut him off. "Group? There are others there, too?"

"Well, of course, there are. Did you think it was just going to be you and me?" Jeremy asks with a smirk.

"No, I guess not. I just hadn't really thought about it," I say. "I'm sorry. Go on and finish."

"We were meditating, and this loud sound made everyone jump. We all asked what the sound was, but Harper acted as if we were all hearing things. He kept insisting that nothing was there and that everything was fine."

I frown. "What kind of noises?"

"I'm getting to that," Jeremy says, his voice lowering to almost a whisper. "It was like someone was trying to scream, but it was muffled. And then it just stopped suddenly."

Jeremy stops talking and shivers. His pacing stops as he stares at nothing as if drifting into a daydream. Concern sears in my gut.

"Jeremy, are you alright?" I ask worriedly.

His gaze snaps to mine as if he had forgotten I was there. He shakes his head as if to clear it. But he does not answer my question. Instead, he continues his story. "It was the next day when we found out about the dead girl. I had only been there for a day, and someone was already dead."

Jeremy looks at me with torturous hazel eyes.

"Oh, Jeremy," I mutter softly.

"They said it was a suicide, but others say it was something else…something bad."

He pauses again to sit on the bed beside me and then continues, "They say she was murdered. Harper came for an extended stay to cooperate with the authorities during the investigation."

So that's what had taken Harper so long.

"What did they find out?" I ask nervously, almost not wanting to know.

"They determined it a suicide, just like everyone said at first. But I am not so sure. Those noises still haunt my dreams sometimes." He looks at me with a haunted look, and my heart goes out to him.

I place a hand on the side of his face and say, "Oh, Jeremy. I am sorry you had to go through that. Are you alright?"

His throat works as he answers, "Yes, I am fine now. I just don't want you to go there. I have a bad feeling in my gut about it."

I remove my hand from his face. "Jeremy, you're just being paranoid. I am sure it will be fine. Besides, I'll have you and Harper there with me."

He grabs my hand and squeezes. "I don't trust Harper, Sophia. Please, just stay here. I'll try to come for visits often."

My frown deepens. "No. I want to go, Jeremy. It isn't just about you. Harper thinks it could help me."

Jeremy sighs, his shoulders slumping in defeat. "Fine, but promise me you will be careful. Promise me you will pay close attention and guard yourself."

I look into his hazel eyes, sincere concern etched into their depths. I say the only thing I can say. "I promise, Jeremy."

He squeezes his eyes shut for a split second, then opens them and pierces me with a strange look. He bends down and places a soft, tender kiss on my forehead.

"Good. I will come back later and help you pack. Get some rest."
And with that, he releases my hand, rises from the bed, and walks out
of the room.

I watch him go, confusion swirling in my mind. A girl had
committed suicide there. We had not lost one person here, not even
Danny, who tried often. What was going on at that place?

It had Jeremy so shaken, and he was one of the bravest people I
knew. It almost made me want to listen to him and not go.

Almost.

CHAPTER 7

Today, I am leaving this place. My heart is light with happiness. Not even the sight of Julia giving me the evil eye look across the table at breakfast can ruin my good mood. I just smile at her as if nothing had happened, even though my bruised and swollen black eye and the giant lump on the side of my forehead are apparent pieces of evidence.

At least I can open my eye today.

I can hear her growl of anger across the table as I smile brightly at her, and then I feel a sharp pain in my ribs.

"Ouch!" I exclaim, rubbing my side and glaring angrily at Jeremy sitting beside me.

"Stop antagonizing her," he hisses as he removes his elbow from my side.

"I'm not. I'm just showing her that she cannot ruin my day," I say indignantly.

"We will be leaving soon, so what does it matter?"

"It just does," I snap back. "Now, let me have my last bit of fun before we leave."

Jeremy shakes his head and chuckles, leaning forward in his seat and digging into his oatmeal and toast. He continues to watch throughout breakfast as I smile at Julia, and she glares back at me while we eat.

By the time breakfast is over, Julia is shaking with rage, but I continue to smile as I leave my tray in the cafeteria window and line up to go back to the rooms. My bag is packed, and I am more than ready to be on my way.

Julia worms her way in front of me during the line-up, pushing Barb to the side and taking her spot. She turns and glares at me. Jeremy, who is standing behind me, steps up beside me and pushes me behind him.

"Don't be starting any trouble, Julia. Sophia has not done anything to you," Jeremy says sternly.

She narrows her beady, green eyes at him. "This doesn't concern you, boy."

Jeremy is taken aback by her brash behavior and angry words. He takes a few steps back, never taking his eyes off Julia's crazy stare. I move with him, taking a few steps into Danny's personal space, who does not complain and only moves to give us more room.

"If it concerns Sophia, then it concerns me," Jeremy responds. "No one is going to hurt her while I am around."

"What are you, her bodyguard?" Julia spats.

"No, I am her b…er…her friend," he tosses back, and I wonder if he almost said brother.

It is certainly how I feel about him. Like a safe, loving, big brother who smells like sunshine and happiness and feels like home at Christmas time.

"A bodyguard isn't going to do any good against the shadows," Julia says, and her tone is dark and menacing. "She will have more than a black eye and a bump when they are done with her."

Rage skitters through my chest, causing my heart to skip a beat, and that now familiar nagging begins in the corners of my mind.

"Stop talking about the shadows," I seethe, leaning around Jeremy's body. "You don't know anything about them."

"I do, too," Julia argues, but her voice is unsure. "I know they are after you."

"You only know that because of my nightmare the other day, and I was talking in my sleep," I shoot back. "And now you are just trying to scare me."

"No!" Julia screeches, her voice rising and echoing through the cafeteria. "I talk to the shadows, just like you! They like me better than you!"

The anger grows inside my gut, twisting and writhing inside me like a nest of snakes. I have had enough of Julia and her lies! I have had enough of all of them. They are all a bunch of crazies, and I am done with them all!

I ball my hands into fists, turning sideways so I can see all of my group that I have lived with…no, not lived with…have been trapped with for the past three months. My voice echoes through the empty cafeteria, louder than Julia's had been.

"Julia, stop using lies to shield the truth. Just admit that you are nothing but a sad child who has done nothing with her life and is now a complete failure, and would do anything to make others suffer just because you suffer.

"And Danny, stop using suicide as a means to gain attention. If you are that hard up for someone to give you attention and fuss over you all the time, then buy a dog.

"Speaking of dogs…"

I turn to Barb.

"YOU ARE NOT A DOG!" I scream so loud that the entire group flinches. They all look at me with wide eyes sat in disbelieving faces.

Even Jeremy.

That stops me.

I swallow hard, taking a deep breath to calm myself and letting it out slowly. My eyes dart away from his. I cannot even look him in the eye as shame fills me.

Then I see it. I see a darkness at the edge of my periphery. It slithers to the front of my vision like smoke from a pipe. It fills the air in front of me, filling out in form and shape until the red-eyed shadow stands before me, staring at me with its glowing gaze.

It looks at me…almost as if….it is proud of me.

I scream.

"What is going on over here?" Harper's voice says from behind me.

He grabs my shoulders, turning me around to face him and pulling me into his arms. It surprises me enough to calm me. Harper has never hugged me.

I glance over my shoulder, and the shadow is gone, but the memory that had been nagging my brain is definitely not. It finally comes to the surface, exploding the memory in my mind of seeing the shadows hovering over Julia's prone body yesterday in my room after she had attacked me. They had formed into a shadow man with red eyes.

And now I have seen it again.

"Julia was messing with Sophia the entire time during breakfast, and Sophia finally had enough and went off on everyone," Jeremy answers Harper. "Well, everyone except me."

"She called me a liar," Julia says.

"She said that I was not a dog," Barb says.

"She told me to buy a dog," Danny says.

Their voices blend together, echoing off the cafeteria walls as everyone tries to speak over each other. Harper's hold on me tightens.

"Enough!" Harper yells into the cacophony.

The room falls silent.

Harper's voice is low and quiet as he responds, "Everyone, go back to your rooms. Jeremy and Sophia, you two come to my private office. I will leave the double doors unlocked for you."

He releases me suddenly, and I almost stumble, but Jeremy is there to catch me. He places a steadying hand on my elbow as Harper walks away from us.

I lean into Jeremy, and he leads me away, out the cafeteria doors, and down the hallway.

"I am seeing the shadows again," I whisper to Jeremy as we walk past my bedroom door.

"What? Tell me." His tone sounds urgent and worried.

I lean into him further so I can whisper without being overheard. I tell him all about the shadowy figure from yesterday and seeing it just now in the cafeteria as we walk slowly through the rec room.

"What does it mean that you are seeing them again?" Jeremy asks.

"What do you think it means'?" I ask sarcastically as we pass the Nurses' station. "It could mean I'm having another episode, or I should ask Harper to check the dosage on my meds."

"You didn't take your meds for two days while you were out," Jeremy says flatly, then adds, "So I think you should speak to Harper about it. It could be just the lack of medication."

"I thought you didn't trust him," I say jokingly, but I am half serious.

"I don't trust him, but what choice do we have? I'm no doctor, so I can't help you, and it's obvious you need help."

"Are you calling me crazy?" I ask, and this time, I am joking.

Jeremy frowns. "I would never call you that."

I laugh. "Lighten up, captain serious. I am only joking."

He stops just beyond the double doors, turns to me, and takes one of my hands into his as he says softly, "Your health and well-being is never something I would joke about."

Since I feel the same about him, I cannot argue. My visage falls, and I mumble, "Sorry. You are right. I do need to talk to Harper."

We turn toward his office, neither of us taking a step toward it. We just stand there quietly for a moment until I break the silence.

"What if he tells me I am having another episode and cannot go to the other facility?" I ask, my voice filled with dread.

"Then I will be glad," Jeremy answers.

I glare at him.

Jeremy huffs. "Sophia, you know I do not want you to go."

I cross my arms over my chest, my glare remaining on my features. "I know. But I still don't understand why."

"I don't know if I will be able to keep you safe," Jeremy answers, and the uneasy apprehension in his tone frightens me.

"What would you possibly have to keep me safe from, Jeremy?" I ask, my tone wavering.

His hazel eyes pierce mine with an intense stare. "From yourself."

"What do you mean by that?" I ask indignantly.

He doesn't answer and only stares at me, then sighs in defeat. "Never mind I said that. Let's just go see what Harper wants."

He turns and walks to Harper's office. I sigh and follow. Jeremy knocks on the office door, and Harper's voice sounds from inside.

"Jeremy?" is all he says.

Jeremy calls out, "Me and Sophia. You asked us to come."

"Yes, I know that," Harper says irritatingly. "Come in."

The door opens, we step in, and then the door slams shut behind us, causing me to flinch violently. I look around the room and am surprised to see Harper sitting at his desk.

The door must be on an automatic mechanism.

Harper's fingers are steepled under his chin, and a worried frown sits on his features. He lifts his chin when we walk into the room and folds his hands onto his desk. He gestures with his eyes for us to sit.

We each sit in one of the leather chairs in front of Harper's magnificent mahogany desk. The skull stares back at us, and it sends shivers up my spine, just as it did the first time I was in this office.

The crystals…I remembered they are crystals and not rocks; yay me!...cast sparkles of light all around the room from their places on the shelves. The cloth I used to polish one of those crystals still sits on the shelf, folded neatly just as Harper had left it that day.

Other than the light of daytime shining from the giant window at the back of the room instead of the darkness of night, the office looks exactly the same as I had left it weeks ago.

"Tell me what happened yesterday and this morning with Julia," Doctor Harper tells me, bringing my attention back to him.

I shrug. "I honestly don't know. She came into my room, accused me of stealing her pudding, then started talking about the shadows.

"It scared the bejesus out of me. I did not know how she could have known about the shadows then.

"She said the shadows wanted me dead, and then she lunged at me. I dodged and ran, but she caught me before I could get out. She banged my head into the door several times and punched me in the eye.

"I managed to struggle and get out of her hold, and then you and the doctors came in and sedated her. I remember trying to get up, but I fell back because of the pain in my head and the dizziness. I don't remember much after that."

I finish my explanation and sit back in my seat. Doctor Harper leans forward, still looking at me expectantly. I frown.

"That is not all that happened," Harper says. "You saw something that scared you. I saw it in your eyes, and you screamed just before you passed out."

"I…don't…," I start to say I do not remember, but Jeremy darts a look my way with a gesture toward Harper.

"Tell him about the shadows," the look says.

I grit my teeth. If this keeps me from getting transferred, I will never forgive Jeremy.

"I am seeing the shadows again," I blurt out quickly.

Harper frowns. "Did they speak to you again?"

"Yes. They said I would never escape," I answer.

Harper does not respond for a long moment, then asks, "Anything else I should know?"

I clear my throat. "They took a form. A human-shaped shadow with red glowing eyes and a black hole for a mouth."

"I see," Harper responds, his tone tight with anger. "And this morning?"

My gaze falls to the surface of the desk. I cannot look Harper in the eye as I answer, "Julia kept looking at me with an angry look, so I smiled back at her. I wanted to show her that she couldn't intimidate me.

"After breakfast, she pushed Barb out of her spot so she could stand in front of me in the line-up. She turned and said some stuff to me that pissed me off, so I said stuff back.

"I was mad and took it out on the others, too. I know I should not have done that, and I'm sorry."

"And?" Harper says through clenched teeth. "Just tell me, Sophia.

Stop making it so difficult to get anything out of you."

Jeremy takes one of my hands and squeezes gently. "Just tell him. I will be right here."

I glance over into his gentle, hazel eyes. His expression is worried yet soft. He gives me an encouraging nod.

I take a deep breath and turn back to Harper. "After you broke up the fight, I saw the shadow in human form again. The shadows looked like they came out of me as if they had been inside me, and then they formed right in front of my eyes."

"So, you are seeing the shadows again, and they are possessing you again?" Harper asks.

"Yes, I am seeing them, but I don't think they are possessing me," I answer and brace myself for Harper's reaction.

I do not know why Harper is so angry. Could it be because I had not told him before now?

I see the muscles in his jaw work as he grinds his teeth together and his blue eyes narrow at me. "It doesn't matter. The transfer has been accepted, so we will go ahead with it. I will up your medication dosage once you get settled in at the new place."

I breathe a sigh of relief, but it is short-lived when I realize something at that moment. I had detected an inflection in Harper's tone as he had spoken. Harper is not angry. Harper is scared. That makes me scared.

"Harper, what is wrong?" Jeremy asks. Apparently, he had caught it too.

Harper blinks several times, and I see his throat work as he swallows. He takes a breath and blows it out quickly before answering, "It is nothing to worry about now. Let's just get on the road, and we can talk about it when we arrive at my place."

Jeremy asks, "So, why did you want to see both of us? Is there something you need from me?"

Harper shoots me a look. "I figured she could speak easier with you in here."

"She is right here," I say, rolling my eyes. "And I can speak just fine all by myself."

"Then why didn't you?" Harper says. "You know you can tell me anything."

I hang my head again. "I know. I was just afraid that you wouldn't let me go to your place if I started showing symptoms again."

"Nonsense," Harper says, and his tone is gentler now. "If anything, I think my facility can help you better than this one, even at your worst."

I pick my head up and smile at him. "Good, because I am ready to get out of this place. I may be psychotic, but I am not insane."

Jeremy rolls his eyes at my joke, but Harper laughs. It makes me smile and chases the fear from Harper's eyes.

"So when are we leaving?" I ask. "I don't want to wait for another second.

"Fine. We will leave now," Harper says as he stands. "I will gather my things while you sign the last of your paperwork. Jeremy, will you please pack Sophia's bag and put it into the transport van? I will tell Amy to let you out of the doors."

Jeremy stands and nods as he says, "I'm on it."

My heart beats excitedly. Finally, it is time to go to the new facility.

I only hope the shadows do not follow me there, but I have a sinking feeling that I have not seen the last of them.

CHAPTER 8

am glad the van has big windows in the back. The view whizzes past as I stare out of it. I chose to ride in the back because it meant I would have an entire seat to myself.

I stretch out my legs, enjoying the extra space and the freedom of being out, even in a van riding down the road. I will soon be at my new home for the next…I do not know how long.

I hope it will only be for a few months.

I hope we get there soon. I am itching to get out of this van and into the sunlight.

Jeremy looks over his shoulder at me from the front seat. He chuckles.

"Are you having fun back there?" he asks humorously.

I do not move from my position as I answer, "Mmmhmm."

Jeremy shakes his head and turns back around. I see Harper's eyes in the rearview mirror looking at me. I raise my eyebrows questioningly.

"What?" I ask.

"Nothing," he mumbles and turns his attention back to the road.

I say nothing and only turn my attention back to the trees whizzing by the window. There are no buildings or stores anywhere. We pass an occasional house here and there, some pastures with cows and horses, and large wheat fields spread out over vast spots of land. We are definitely not in town any longer.

After a while, I start regretting that we did not wait until I was better to travel. My face hurts, and my head is throbbing in time with my heartbeat. It seems like it is taking forever, even though Harper assured me it was not far. What does he call far if not this?

"Is it much further?" I call up to the front of the van.

I can tell from the loose swing of Jeremy's head, rocking back and forth along with the gentle swaying of the van, that he is asleep.

Harper answers, "We should be there in about an hour."

I groan in disappointment. "Are there any gas stations or stores coming up soon?"

Harper's eyes glance my way in the rearview mirror. "There is a rest stop ahead. Do you need to stop?"

I nod enthusiastically. "Yes, please. I really have to pee."

Harper chuckles, and his eyes leave the mirror.

Only a few minutes pass when I feel the van shift. I sit up straight so I can see out of the front windows of the van. We are turning off the interstate, and I can see the lights of the rest stop as we coast down the exit ramp.

"Oh, thank God," I say as I lean between the front seats for a better view.

"You mean thank Goddess," Jeremy says sleepily, looking over his shoulder at me.

His eyes are still droopy from sleep, and his hair has fallen into his eyes.

I nudge him with my shoulder and brush his hair away from his face as I say, "Yeah, whatever. I just have to pee."

Jeremy laughs and shakes his head. It makes me smile, and I am still smiling when Harper comes around the van and opens the back door for me.

"Come on, Sophia. Hurry up and go so we can get home," He says.

His tone sounds tired and just a bit angry, and I wonder why he is so cranky. I cannot read the look on his face, but it is definitely not a happy look.

"What's wrong, Harper?" I ask as I climb out of the back.

"Nothing. I just want to get home," Harper responds, stepping back to give me room to climb out.

My toe catches the runner at the bottom of the open door, and I stumble out of the van. Harper catches me, his arm going around my waist to steady me. I fall into him, both hands going to his chest to catch myself as he leans down so he can tighten his arm around my waist to keep me from falling. My face lands so close to his that our noses are almost touching, and I can feel his breath brush across my lips.

His eyes are so close that I can see the minuscule lighter blue flecks streaking through his darker blue irises. My hands flex at the sensation of his hard chest muscles under my fingers. The feel of his hard body against mine makes me instantly wet, and my inner walls pulse with longing.

Desire curls through me, and I swallow hard, my eyes widening at the sudden, darkly sensual position I have found myself in.

My tone is shaky as I stutter, "I…I…I'm sorry. I lost my footing."

His tone is husky when he responds, "It's quite alright."

My pulse quickens at the feel of his breath on my lips, and my breathing becomes fast and shallow as his head leans a tiny bit closer, if that is even possible.

My voice is barely a whisper as I say, "I really need to go."

"Yes, you do," Harper whispers back, and the sound of his sensual tone sends shivers of pleasure down my spine.

He moves even closer, so close that his lips barely graze mine, like the faintest touch of a fluttering butterfly's wing against my lips, skyrocketing my pulse in my throat.

I suck in a breath, the unexpected touch of his mouth on mine sending shockwaves through my system. Harper snaps his head up suddenly, his grip on my waist loosening.

Had Harper just kissed me? I couldn't be sure. The touch was so light and fleeting that I wonder if I just imagined it.

"Are you going to go to the bathroom or not?" Jeremy asks, opening the passenger-side door of the van and stepping out behind Harper.

Harper stiffens and releases me, stepping aside as Jeremy steps around Harper to stand beside me. He drapes a casual arm around my shoulders and pulls me with him.

"Come on, I'll walk you there. I have to go too," he says, leading me away from Harper.

I glance back over my shoulder, catching a glimpse of Harper's face. He looks…disappointed…but that can't be right. His eyes continue to watch as Jeremy takes me toward the main building where the bathrooms are.

"I'll go get some snacks from the vending machines," Harper calls, then turns and walks toward a smaller building off to the side.

When we are out of earshot of Harper, Jeremy asks, "What was Harper doing creeping on you like that?"

I scoff. "He wasn't creeping on me. I stumbled getting out of the van, and he caught me."

Jeremy's tone is sarcastic as he replies, "Caught you, huh? Because from my point of view, it looked as if he was trying to kiss you."

I shrug. "So, what if he was?"

Jeremy doesn't answer, but he stops mid-stride, forcing me to stop with him since he still has his arm draped around me. I turn with a frown that matches the one Jeremy throws at me as his arm slides from my shoulders.

"I told you, Sophia. I don't trust him," Jeremy hisses under his breath, looking around us as if he expects Harper to be standing right behind us.

"You might not trust him, Jeremy, but I do. The man saved my life, for fuck's sake." I pause to take a deep breath before I get too angry and say something I might regret. I take one more deep breath before continuing.

My tone is softer now, and I gaze at Jeremy calmly. "Look, Jeremy, I appreciate your worry for me. Hell, I was worried sick about you until I made Harper tell me where you were, so I get it. But you don't have to be worried for me where Harper is concerned."

He runs a hand through his sandy locks and blows out a breath. He gazes at the ground momentarily before lifting his hazel eyes to meet mine.

"I may not trust Harper, but I do trust you. If you say Harper is safe around you, then I believe you. However…," Jeremy pauses, taking my hand and pulling me close.

He leans his tall frame down to my shorter one so that his face is even with mine and whispers, "If you ever feel unsafe in this place, just scream my name, and I'll come running."

My eyes widen. "You would be able to come to me?"

Jeremy smiles and nods. "Yes, Sophia. There are no locked doors at this place other than the ones that lead outside. You can roam wherever you want as long as you stay in the house."

"Do we ever get to go outside?" I ask trepidatiously.

Jeremy's smile widens. "Every day, with supervision, and only for an hour or so. Sometimes, we even get to go out at night when we are performing a special ritual or rite."

I frown in confusion. "A what or a what?"

Jeremy chuckles. "You'll find out when you learn more." His face turns serious again, and his dizzying display of emotions confuses me even more.

"Just remember what I said," Jeremy says in a serious tone as he rises back to his full height. "If you feel unsafe or threatened, run and scream my name."

My breathing hitches. I do not know whether to feel happy that we have so much freedom or be afraid that Jeremy thinks I may not be safe. I only nod in response to his statement.

That seems to satiate him. He turns back toward the facility and begins walking again. As he walks away, I watch his tall, muscular form and think how much bigger he seems than when I first met him.

Jeremy was the first person I met after I came out of my three-day coma, spent several hours in recovery, and then was moved to the psychiatric ward.

He was sitting in the rec room, the first room I came to when I entered the psych ward. I had been sent there to wait for a nurse to show me to my room.

He seemed lost, almost afraid, as he sat and stared out the window. I was instantly drawn to the sandy shag of hair and those sad hazel eyes. His boyishly handsome face, rugged and unshaven, was so downtrodden and sad that it made me want to cry for him.

He noticed me when I sat down near him. He instantly rose and came to me, striding like something had pushed him toward me. He introduced himself and started talking to me as if we had known each other our entire lives.

We became almost inseparable after that. We had so much in common and were both suffering through grief. It helped to have someone with me with whom I could relate, and I'm sure it helped him, too.

I remember how lanky he was when I first saw him. Then, after we started hanging out together, he began eating right and lifting weights in the rec room. Now, only a couple of months later, he had filled out to his present athletically muscular form. He looked good, healthier, and definitely happier.

He turns, snapping me out of my thoughts as he calls, "Are you coming?"

I shake my head to clear it and then jog toward the facility, where Jeremy holds the door open for me. I find the ladies' room, do my business, and then meet the boys back at the van in record time. Apparently, it still was not fast enough for Harper.

"What took you two so long?" he asks, his voice laced with irritation.

"I didn't think we took that long," I snap back. "Anyway, we are back now, so stop fussing at us, and let's go."

Harper narrows his eyes at me as if to retort but turns around and starts the van. He pushes the gas, revving the engine several times before putting the van in gear. He steadily backs the van out of the parking spot and then speeds off toward the interstate.

Harper tosses the snacks he got from the vending machine over to Jeremy, saying, "Here, share these with Sophia. That should hold you over until we get there."

Jeremy passes me a bag of chips, a candy bar, and a soda. I eat my snacks as I gaze out of the window, watching the traffic pass us on the interstate. Harper sure drives slow for someone who is in a hurry.

I roll my eyes with an exaggerated sigh and see Harper give me a hard look in the rearview mirror. I have no idea why he is suddenly being such an ass.

I finish the last of the chips and start on the candy bar, taking a long drink of the soda. The fizz stings my nostrils and tickles my throat as I swallow the huge drink. My thoughts wonder to Harper as I eat my candy bar.

I wonder if Harper really would have kissed me if Jeremy had not interrupted. I wonder why the sudden interest. I have long been in lust with Harper and have not been very vague about it either.

I have shamelessly flirted, thrown not-so-hard-to-read hints his way, and I openly watch him whenever he is around. I have made it clear that I find him attractive, but he has never shown any indication that he reciprocated the feeling.

Not that I expected him to.

I have no such expectations where Harper is concerned. He is my doctor, my psychiatrist, and I am his patient. No matter how much I long for him, There could never be anything between us.

Besides, there is nothing wrong with lusting after someone. Especially someone as sexy and exotic as Harper. Who knows? Maybe if circumstances were different and I was not crazy, Harper would reciprocate my feelings.

I am sure I just imagined that he almost kissed me.

Then I remembered the seriousness in Jeremy's eyes as he had warned me to stay away from Harper. Jeremy had said he did not trust

Harper but was vague about why. Did Jeremy know something that I did not?

It could be possible since Jeremy had spent more time with Harper than I had. I did not know, and now I am more confused than ever about Harper.

My eyes grow heavy as I pop the last bite of chocolate-covered caramel in my mouth and guzzle down the last of the soda. Apparently, the caffeine is not going to keep me awake at all. The silence stretches through the van as sleep tugs at me. I keep thinking of Harper's almost-kiss as I settle back in the big back seat and fall into a long-overdue sleep.

CHAPTER 9

"Sophia, wake up. We are here."
Jeremy's voice cuts through my mind, and I wake up blinking rapidly. I rub the sleep from my eyes before sitting up and glancing out the front window.

I gasp.

The bright sun sits low in the sky to the west, telling me it is well past noon. My rumbling stomach tells me we missed lunch, and it could even be time for dinner. But food is the last thing on my mind as I gaze up at the wonder that is Doctor Harper Andrew's house.

The gothic-style Victorian house rises three floors into the blue sky, but even the cheery sky does not detract from the ghostly style. The entire front of the wood-sided structure is graced with an intricately designed, wrap-around porch. The arched windows are large and imposing, with ornately designed frames that match the ornate designs of the gables.

The second floor has a wrap-around, roofed balcony that circles around the cylindrical turret on the left side of the house. The turret rises above the third floor, where the balcony stretches from the other end of the house and stops at the turret. The turret rises above the rest of the house and beyond the main roof. It must have its own fourth floor or even an attic.

The windows of the second and third floors are rectangular, and not as large as the first-floor windows but just as intricately designed. The same designs grace the circular windows of the turret.

The house is dark gray with black trimming, shudders, and roof. The décor is also black, lending to the sinister air of the creepily beautiful home. Even though the sun shines brightly and the sound of birdsong fills the air, the ambiance is eerily foreboding, like the scariest of haunted houses.

The house is beautiful yet aesthetically creepy.

I shudder as I stare out the van's window, hesitant to leave the comfort of my seat. Jeremy is already out of the van and reaching for the back door's handle. My heart thuds in my chest as I continue to stare at Harper's house. Jeremy opens the door.

"This is where we are going to live?" I croak nervously.

Jeremy gives me a weird look, one eyebrow quirking as he answers, "Yes. Why? Is something wrong?"

I turn my gaze to Jeremy.

"Is something wrong?" I repeat sarcastically. "Have you seen the house?"

Jeremy makes a sound deep in his throat, similar to my scoffs but throatier. "What's wrong with the house?"

"It's the creepiest house I have ever seen!" I exclaim.

"I get that the house is a bit…eerie…but it is my home," Harper says as he comes around to our side of the van. "It has been in my family for generations."

"I can tell," I say. "It looks ancient."

"The inside is very modern, I assure you," Harper says, and I hear the pride in his tone.

"Is the inside as scary as the outside?" I ask.

"It depends on what you call scary," Jeremy answers. "I call it romantic."

I quirk an eyebrow at him. "What do you mean romantic?"

"I mean, most of the house is lit by candlelight or firelight from the fireplaces. It's romantic," Jeremy says.

"More candles?" I moan, turning to Harper. "Don't you believe in electric lights?"

Harper chuckles. "You don't think candles are romantic?"

"Not particularly," I answer. "I like being able to see."

"There are electric lights if you prefer," Jeremy says. "But most of the other residents like the dark."

"Well, I don't, for obvious reasons that I should not have to explain, especially to the two of you," I quip.

Jeremy's face falls, and he flinches visibly. "I did not think of that, Sophia. I am sorry. We will turn on the lights."

My face softens, and I smile. "Thank you, Jeremy."

"Let's get you inside so I can show you to your room and get you settled," Harper says, moving to the back of the van and opening the double doors. "You will feel better after you have eaten."

Jeremy offers me his hand.

"I hope the food here is better than it is at the hospital," I mumble as I take Jeremy's hand and exit the van.

Harper pulls out my suitcase, which is filled with my regular clothes, and walks up to us.

Doctor Harper had been thoughtful enough to stop by my house and let me pack clothes so I would have more to wear than hospital garb. Not only was I happy to wear real clothes again, but I had been happy to see that my home was still intact and not taped up like some big crime scene.

Someone had cleaned up, too. Probably Uncle Vinny. I couldn't imagine Mia would do anything nice for me.

Harper let me borrow his phone, and I called Uncle Vinny. He had been so excited to hear from me since I had not been allowed to contact anyone at the hospital, and Uncle Vinny had been told he was not allowed to visit for the first six weeks.

It was standard policy for the mental ward at this facility.

However, as of yesterday, the six-week period was officially over, so he could visit me at the new place. He told me the restaurant was doing fine, which was not a surprise since it was the only Mexican restaurant in Daisville, Kentucky. He had also paid my rent for the next six months. I had nothing to worry about.

I hadn't bothered to call my ex-best friend, Tamara.

She definitely hated me now. She and Mia probably had some sort of Sophia Hate Club going, which probably included everyone who had been in my survivor's group that day.

"I hope you don't mind being on the second floor," Harper says, pulling me from my thoughts.

I shake my head to clear it. "No, I actually prefer it."

He smiles as he carries my suitcase up the short walkway to the house.

He glances over his shoulder and says, "Good. Come, let's go inside."

I swallow and follow Harper. There isn't much to the tiny piece of land in front of the house. The short but wide driveway stops not far from the house. A concrete walkway is attached to the end of the driveway and runs down the middle of the front yard, dividing it into two halves. To the right is a large tree, its branches reaching out toward the second and third-story windows.

To the left is a small flower garden set up against the house, surrounded by landscaping timbers. The flowers are bright and cheery, but they do nothing to alleviate the foreboding feeling in my gut.

The entire front yard is surrounded by a tall fence. The chainlink ends at the sides of the house and continues with a wooden privacy fence that disappears to the back of the house. I wonder how big the backyard is.

Harper opens the gate to the walkway leading to the front steps with its intricately decorated, gabled roof. I had never seen a set of outdoor stairs with a roof before, except in pictures. Small pillars hold up the roof at the bottom of the stairs, and two gargoyle statues stand guard in front of the pillars.

I stiffen as I pass between them, expecting one of them to spring to life at any moment. I laugh inwardly at my silliness. It is like I am a small child again, running from the boogie man under my bed. They are just statues, dammit.

I blow out a breath as I begin my ascent up the short expanse of stairs. I climb up and onto the concrete porch, marveling at the baroque railings of the stairs that match the rail that runs the length of the porch.

The front door is stunning with its large lion's head door knocker and fancily designed peephole. The door is black to match the trimming of the rest of the house. The door handle and the intricately designed metal around the peephole are gold. Above the peephole is a stained glass window set into the door, and the designs in the glass are breathtaking.

I gaze in awe at the front door and wonder how I can be so consumed with the beauty of the place and yet filled with dread at its menacing ambiance. Harper opens the door and gestures for me to go in. I start forward, and a hand at the small of my back causes me to jump around and squeal. I had almost forgotten about Jeremy.

"I am sorry, Sophia. I didn't mean to scare you," Jeremy says, and I can tell from the twinkle in his eyes and the thin set of his mouth that he is holding back laughter.

I glare at him and hiss, "Are you trying to give me a heart attack?"

"Oh, come on, Sophia. I promise, I really didn't mean to scare you. I thought you knew I was behind you," Jeremy said, but I could still hear the laughter in his tone.

I shake my head and turn back to the door. "You are such an ass," I mumble.

I hear Jeremy snicker behind me. Harper ignores us and continues to lead us into the house. I step inside right on Harper's heels, then pause to check out my surroundings. I gasp.

The foyer is bigger than the entire psych ward at the hospital! The floors, the sweeping staircase, and the grandiose trimming are all done in very dark mahogany wood, stained in the darkest color possible.

The walls are black and decorated with various paintings all along its surface. The ceiling is black like the walls, and a huge, lavish chandelier hangs in its center. The curtains that cover the floor-to-ceiling window on the back wall are a dark royal purple, like the stair runner and huge circular rug that takes up most of the floor.

The vast staircase takes up the left side of the room and curves gently up to the open second-floor landing. I crane my neck to look up and discover that the stairs do not go any further than the second floor. There must be another set of stairs somewhere else on the second floor that leads to the third floor.

"How do you get to the third floor?" I ask curiously.

"Why do you want to go to the third floor?" Harper asks suspiciously, which only serves to pique my curiosity further.

I turn my gaze to him, gesturing toward the staircase as I speak. "I'm only asking because the staircase only goes up to the second floor. I was only being curious."

"There's nothing on the third floor except storage," Jeremy says, stepping up beside me. "No one goes up there."

"I never said I wanted to," I respond in a frustrated voice. "I only asked how to get up there."

"There is a set of spiral stairs that goes up to the third floor in the turret. Happy?" Harper quirks an eyebrow and smirks at me.

Like an adult, I stick my tongue out at him.

"Come on, kitty cat. Let's get you to your room and out of my hair," Harper says.

"Kitty cat?" I ask.

"Yes, because curiosity killed the cat," Harper responds as he heads toward the staircase with my suitcase still in hand.

Jeremy snickers, and I glare at him before following Harper up the stairs. I glance back longingly at the door in the grand foyer's right-hand wall before being dragged away. I did not even get a chance to discover what was behind it.

It is okay, though. I will probably be here a while, so I will have more time later to explore. Maybe I'll even go up to the third floor.

I hurry after Harper and soon realize I am no longer in the best shape. By the time we reach the second-floor landing, I am breathing heavily from the exertion.

I really need to exercise more. The staircase, while definitely wide enough for three people abreast, wasn't even that extensively tall. We only climbed one floor, for goodness' sake.

I pause at the top to catch my breath, keeping an eye on Harper as he continues past the landing and turns a corner to the right. I scramble after him and find him standing at an ornate wooden door at the end of a short corridor. He pauses before turning the knob and looks at me.

"This will be your room," Harper says.

The strange look on his face and the husky tone of his voice cause goosebumps to form along my skin, and I shiver. The heavy feeling of malice that had permeated my skin as soon as I laid eyes on this house flares in my gut as I draw closer to Harper and the room.

"It seems a bit…lonely," I say, looking around the small hallway. That is the only door down this hallway.

"My room is in the next hallway," Jeremy says from behind me. "All the rooms have their own hallways on this floor."

"Oh," I say as I move forward.

Harper opens the door for me, the hinges creaking eerily. It opens slowly, revealing the room in pieces. The first thing I notice is the floor. It is covered in black, super plush carpeting that looks like I could sink into it.

I spot the bed next, covered with a silky, royal purple canopy that matches the comforter and pillows. It looks enormous, a queen maybe, and I delight in the thought that I will have all that room to stretch out in tonight.

It beats the teeny-tiny little beds they had us sleeping on at the hospital. I'll bet that bed is way more comfortable, too.

The door opens further to reveal a beautiful chestnut armoire that is the same wood as the four large posts of the bed. I see something, some type of frame, standing beside the armoire. The tiny hairs on the back of my neck stand at attention as the object is revealed as the door swings open all the way.

The ornate décor carved into the chestnut wood of the frame

matches the décor carved into the armoire's doors. I look around the rest of the room to see if there is any other furniture in here that goes with the bedroom set, but the bed, armoire, and the fucking mirror is all there is.

A fucking mirror.

CHAPTER 10

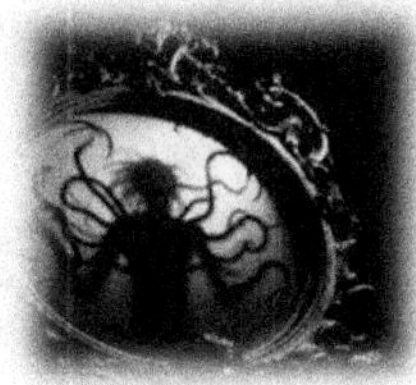

I turn angry, haunted eyes to Harper.

"You are giving me a room with a full-length fucking mirror?" I ask in disbelief. My heart races in my chest as my body trembles.

"I thought it would be… therapeutic," he says with an undertone of mystery.

I raise my eyebrows at him. "Therapeutic? You think it is therapeutic to put my worst fear in a room where I am supposed to sleep?"

Harper smirks. "Yes. You get over your fears by facing them. Just stand in front of it for at least a few minutes before bed, then you can cover it for the rest of the day and night."

The thought of looking in that mirror terrifies me. My trembling grows worse, to the point that my teeth are chattering. I look behind me for Jeremy, but he is not there. Panic threatens to choke me, and I jump violently when a hand touches my shoulder.

"Sophia, it's only me," Harper says, and the sound of his voice calms me a bit.

"Jeremy went to his room," Harper adds as if reading my mind.

"I don't think I can do this," I say, my voice quivering. "I wanna go back to the hospital."

Harper steps closer, clasping my chin between his finger and thumb and raising my face toward his. His breath brushes across my lips as he speaks, causing tendrils of longing to skirt through me and mix with the panic.

"Just give it a chance, please, Sophia," Harper says, and the pleading in his voice melts me. The fear begins to drain away as I stare into his sky-blue eyes.

My voice is barely a whisper as I reply, "I'm too afraid."

"I'll be right here," Harper says. "I'll stay with you this time and help you cover it afterward."

I swallow the lump in my throat as he leans even closer. His lips barely brush against mine as he whispers against my mouth, "Please, Sophia?"

How in the hell can I say no to that?

His lips press closer to mine as he releases my chin and trails his hand to the back of my neck. He presses me closer, and then he is kissing me.

Harper is kissing me!

My heartbeat skyrockets, and my breathing becomes hurried and ragged. I am putty in his hands. The surprised passion that flows from his lips touching mine completely erases the panic and terror from my mind.

His kiss grows more insistent, more….just more. His tongue probes my lips, and I part them, allowing him entry. The sensation of his tongue swirling through my mouth sends tendrils of electrifying desire coursing through my veins.

I moan against his mouth and bring my arms up to wrap them around his neck. I want him…no…, I need him closer. The desperation for more heats my skin to a fever pitch and sends a torrent of fire into my groin.

He breaks the kiss to nibble my earlobe as he whispers, "Will you try for me?"

What?

The aching want for him muddles my mind so that the words do not register. All I can think of is the feel of his lips on my skin, my hands exploring the hard, cut muscles of his back and arms, and the sensations swirling through my body.

His hands trail down my torso and land on my hips, and then he begins moving, taking me with him as he nibbles on the sensitive spot below my ear. We go deeper into the room, the darkness closing around us when the door slams shut.

I gasp and pull away from his hold, but his hands tighten on my hips, and he pulls me back in. Panic sets in as shadows dance from the minuscule light coming in from the curtained window. Fear mingles with desire, and the sensory overload is too much.

I push against his chest, but he grabs me roughly by the shoulders and turns me around.

"Harper, stop," I say, my voice anxious. "Let me go. I need out of this room!"

He ignores me, pulling my back into his chest and wrapping one arm around my upper chest and shoulders. I struggle against his hold, but it is too strong.

I am trapped.

For one lucid moment, I wonder why on Earth I would struggle against a hold that I have dreamt of being in since I first laid eyes on my sexy doctor. Isn't this exactly what I wanted? Harper was actually showing an interest in me, and I was trying to get away from him.

Was I insane?

Wait…yes, I was insane. I was not struggling to get away from Harper. I was struggling to get away from the dark, the shadows. Harper would not hurt me.

Would he?

My breathing is ragged, my heart threatening to beat out of my chest. He holds me tight even though I stop struggling, and I wonder if he can feel how hard my heart beats. I can feel the rigid muscles of his chest against my back, and I concentrate on that. It helps chase the panic away. His lips brush across the back of my neck, and I hear his whisper as he continues to move us through the shadows.

"I'm right here, Sophia. I won't let anything happen to you."

I believe him. That is until we stop, and I see what is before us. My eyes widen with terror as I stare into the mirror, the shadows writhing around its reflection in tendrils of darkness. I open my mouth, but Harper clamps a hand over it, stifling my scream.

His hold tightens even more until I almost cannot breathe. I watch his reflection in the mirror with terror-filled eyes, and his gaze locks with mine. He smiles a slow, devious smile.

"Relax. We won't hurt you."

We? Who is 'we'? And why is Harper looking at me like that?

It does not take long for me to discover the answers.

The writhing shadow tentacles come for me, shooting out of the mirror and dancing around me. They begin touching me, stroking along my arms and slithering into my hair. Harper's blue eyes crinkle with delight as he watches them caress my skin and play in my hair.

Harper's hold tightens when I start struggling again, and now I really cannot breathe. My lungs scream for oxygen, and my heart pounds so hard it hurts. I try to drag a breath in through my nose, but it is not enough to satiate my need for air.

I stop my struggles to make eye contact with Harper, begging him with my eyes to let me go. I try to put the panic and need for air into my eyes, and, finally, his arm loosens, allowing me to breathe deeper through my nose. My lungs quiver with relief.

I do not struggle again, afraid that the next time Harper holds me too tightly, I will suffocate. The panic from being touched by the shadows threatens to overwhelm my senses as the tentacles of darkness move closer to my breasts.

I see the panic in my too-wide eyes in my reflection through my periphery. My gaze is still locked on Harper's in the mirror's reflection. His lust-filled eyes follow the tendrils as they continue to caress me, one brushing the edge of my breast and another reaching up to flick the nipple of the other breast.

A scream catches in my throat as electrifying sensations crash through me, and I am not sure what I am feeling right now. I know in the front of my mind that I should be feeling terror, revulsion, and panic. However, the currents that flowed through my body when the tendril touched my nipple felt very much like arousal or lust.

The dark desire in Harper's eyes fills me with a keening hunger so intense that I can almost taste it. Is it this yearning that is fueling the stimulation? It has to be. I refuse to accept that I am turned on by a bunch of writhing tentacles of shadows that previously tried to take control of my senses and lead me to hurt people.

I suck in a sharp breath as Harper's hold disappears, and his hands come around my body to take the place of the tendrils. My breasts fit into his large hands as if they were made precisely for Harper's hold. He pinches each nipple between his thumbs and forefingers, rolling and pulling lightly through my clothes.

I throw my head back against his chest, closing my eyes and moaning his name. The sound echoes through the room as the walls of my inner core tighten, longing to be filled. Something touches my thigh. My head jerks back upright, and my eyes fly open.

The shadows still playing in the mirror thicken, turning into a swirling darkness like a dense fog. They undulate together, twisting and writhing until they take on a shadowy form with glowing red eyes.

My mouth opens in a silent scream.

The figure steps out of the mirror, piercing me with a fiery red stare as its shadowy fingers stroke my hips and thighs. I flinch away from the touch, melding myself into Harper as tightly as possible. I am pressed so hard against him that I can feel his erection against my back.

My heart launches into a pounding irregular rhythm at the feeling, even as my breath seizes in my lungs with horror at the sensation of the shadow man touching me.

Harper leans down and whispers against the back of my neck. "Why do you flinch away from me, Sophia? I know you want me."

I swallow hard and gasp as Harper's hands leave my tits to run down my torso and stomach. They stop just short of where I want them to go, where the shadow man's hands are moving toward.

"I do want you," I reply, and my voice is barely a whisper. "But I am afraid of the shadows."

"Why? They are only part of me," Harper says. "Let me play with you…let us play with you."

That cannot be true. This cannot be happening.

The shadows came from me, didn't they?

Or did Harper have his own set of shadows?

The shadow man's hand cups my sex, and a tendril of shadow that I can only describe as a shadowy finger wafts through the barrier of my pants and enters me. I cry out, half in fear and half in desire, as the tentacle of darkness curls inside my core and touches all the right spots.

"No," I gasp. "Please."

"Your mouth says no, but your body says yes," Harper responds,

Then, Harper and the shadow man demonstrate just how much my body says yes as Harper plunges his hand into my pants and joins the shadow man in violating my entrance with his fingers.

Sweet ecstasy fills every nerve as Harper's fingers work inside me, coming out and plunging back in with such veracity as the shadows swirl around the sensitive bud just above my entrance. Together, they bring me to orgasm in no time.

I scream my pleasure through the room as my body bucks against Harper's hand. I ride out the orgasm, and when it is over, he pulls his hand away as the shadows dissipate around me. I am left a trembling mess of useless flesh in Harper's arms.

I am disgusted with myself. How could I possibly have an orgasm when I am being raped? Harper is why. My lust for him knows no bounds, apparently.

Harper spins me violently around and pushes me to the bed. I land on my back on the soft mattress. I turn my head to the side, and the mirror catches my attention, the mirror's angle giving me a perfect view from where I lay on the bed.

The writhing mass of shadows that still play with the reflections in the mirror follows Harper's reflection as he comes closer to me. His large hands grasp my hips and hold me there as the mirror shadows play with my reflection's hair and stroke my stomach.

I gasp at the sensation of the touch. I can feel them touching me, even though they only touch my reflection in the mirror! Harper's reflection turns its head toward me even though Harper does not move. It smiles deviously and winks at me. Fear crashes through me, mingling with desire as I watch Harper's reflection run his hands along my inner thighs.

Harper's hands, the Harper that is above me, do not move and only hold tightly to my hips, holding me down on the bed. However, I feel the reflection's hands touching me, stroking up my thighs until they come to the apex, where my entrance throbs with horrifying ecstasy.

Every part of my mind screams with terror while my senses and my body writhe with intense longing, and I am left torn into a tattered mess of confusion on the bed. Harper holds me down while the reflection and the shadows violate me, stroking every part of my body while masterfully working my clit until sheer pleasure engulfs my fear.

Pressure builds inside my core as my inner walls throb with desire and the need to be filled. The pressure of Harper's hands holding me to the bed loosens as he allows me room to writhe and dance on the bed. Soft moans escape my lips, and my gaze is plastered to the reflections in the mirror.

I watch as Harper's reflection and the shadows skillfully stroke my skin, intensifying the pleasure I feel from the feathery touches of hand and tentacle. Harper's reflection begins taking off his clothes as the shadow man forms again, but this time, he is outside the mirror.

My eyes widen as he approaches the bed, blocking my view of the mirror. My heart threatens to pound out of my chest as I look up and notice that Harper is entirely, gloriously naked above me, even though he has not let go of my hips.

He is as glorious as I imagined he would be.

"Yes, Sophia. That's it. Writhe for me, baby," he says huskily as he pulls my hips down toward the edge of the bed. "I am going to take you now, and my shadows will make you scream for me as I cum inside you."

My heart skyrockets, and my breathing is so fast that I am practically panting. The shadow man grabs my wrists and pulls my arms up, then pulls the hem of my shirt up and over my head and arms. My breasts spill free from my bra as the shadow man rips that away as well. Harper pulls my pants and panties past my hips and down my legs so forcefully that the movement jerks my body. He tosses them to the side carelessly.

I begin to struggle with terror, my body fighting against the violation of being forcefully undressed. I have already been violated, but Harper had yet to actually fuck me. Now, with him naked above me, the possibility is becoming a reality.

I fight against his hold, but tendrils of dark shadows snake around my wrists and ankles. The tendrils around my wrists pull my arms down, trapping them to the bed on either side of me. Then, Harper grasps my hips, pulling me close to him where he stands by the bed. My lower legs dangle over the side of the bed, and the tendrils wrap around my ankles, pinning my legs in place.

I scream and thrash, but more tendrils wind their way around my torso and waist, stopping my thrashing and minimizing my movements. I cannot thrash, I cannot move my arms or legs, and I cannot sit up.

I am effectively trapped and naked under Harper's muscular body and the shadow man's imposing form. I shudder, the mixture of lust and fear coursing through me is too much to bear. The shadow man plays along my breasts with his whispy shadow fingers as Harper grasps my hips once more and places the head of his cock against my entrance.

"Please," I whimper, grabbing onto the sheets in panic. "Please stop."

"Oh, baby, I know you really don't want me to stop," Harper says above me. "I will not stop until you drown in pleasure and scream my name to the heavens."

His fingers dig into my hips, and I scream in ecstatic terror at the sensation of Harper's cock pressing into my entrance, violating my walls with his massive girth. I can feel my pussy stretching to accommodate him, my insides quivering with every delicious inch that works its way inside me. Shadow fingers pinch my nipples, and I scream again, half from fear and half from pleasure.

"Say my name, Sophia," Harper says, his voice strained as he pushes deeper into me.

"Please," I whimper again as pressure builds and builds in my core, and Harper's massive cock penetrates me even further.

The shadow man leaves my breasts, leaning over my body to reach my clit. The shadowy tendrils of his fingers stroke and pull at the tender bud and the sensitized flesh around it as Harper buries himself all the way inside me.

"Say it!" Harper demands, pulling himself almost all the way out and then slamming back into me. The shadow's touches become more pressurized as Harper finds a slow, sensual rhythm, and my insides throb around his slow-moving member.

"Please, stop this," I say, my voice trembling with a mixture of…well…everything.

"You do not mean that," Harper says as he continues to move in and out of me. "Cum for me. Cum for me and scream my name."

His rhythm grows faster as the shadowy fingers continue to stroke my clit. The pressure of pleasure builds and builds, even as fear and anger build in my chest. The melding pot of emotions coalescing inside me only intensifies, feeding upon each other as Harper and the shadow man rape me.

I am angry that Harper is taking me against my will, shattering my dream of him wooing me and declaring his love for me. I am terrified of the shadows, horrified that they are helping him take advantage of me. And I am dying with the need for release. I am mortified at the passion and ecstasy burning through me without my permission, but it is there all the same.

That sweet, blissful pressure builds in my core, threatening to spill me over the edge, no matter that I did not ask for this. It is coming no matter what. Harper's massive member drives in and out of me, creating sweet friction against my walls. The shadow fingers roughly massage the spot above my entrance, causing the pressure to spill over in one long, crashing, intense wave of fierce, hip-writhing pleasure.

I scream Harper's name, then scream my pleasure over and over as it dances through me, shuddering my walls around Harper's cock as he buries it inside me and stills, allowing my orgasm to roll over us. I scream his name again as the orgasm ebbs, the waves leaving me a shuddering mass on the bed.

"Oh, yes, that's it, baby. Scream for me," Harper pants, his voice strained.

He begins to move again, his rhythm fast and uneven. The shadow fingers slide away, leaving me with only the sensation of Harper's cock driving into me over and over. His breathing grows ragged, and his fingers dig deeper into my hips, causing me to hiss and cry out in pain.

"Harper, please!" I scream, but that only drives his rhythm faster, and that pressure begins to build inside me again.

No…not again. My traitorous body heats with the desire for another release as Harper fucks me hard and rough, pounding into me as his fingernails dig into my flesh. My hips rise of their own accord, giving a better angle for Harper to drive even deeper into me.

"Sophia!" Harper yells, and the sound of my name being called in such an ecstatically pleading tone drives me over the edge.

My walls throb as waves and waves of pleasure crash through me again. I scream out in ecstasy, and Harper simultaneously moans his pleasure. I feel his cock throb inside me. He pulls out and shoves back into me one last time before a hot flood of liquid shoots inside me.

Harper's screams of pleasure mix with mine as the shadow man laughs maliciously. Harper's orgasm ebbs along with mine. He shudders over me as his arms tremble with the effort to keep his weight off me.

The glowing red eyes of the shadow man dance in my vision as he leans over me, the vicious laugh playing through my mind.

"Again," a whispery voice says in my head. *"I want more."*

Harper's eyes open, staring down at me in an icy blue swirl of lust and desire. My eyes widen as I feel his member stiffen again inside me, and his hips start to move.

"As you wish," Harper says, smiling evilly down at me as he fucks me again.

The shadow man's laugh peals through my head, and I look helplessly up at him. His form has grown more corporeal, and I can now tell it is definitely a he.

His massive shadow cock throbs as he watches Harper fuck me. He moves toward me slowly, his tentacles of darkness writhing from his sides, reaching for me as he slowly strokes his shadow cock.

His wispy voice plays through my mind. *"I am going to fuck your pretty mouth now. Open wide, baby."*

I watch in horror as the shadow man brings his cock closer to my lips while Harper drives into me, jerking my body with every thrust.

"No! Please, no!" I say, but it is no use.

The tentacles hold me prisoner as Harper fucks me, and I am helpless against the assault. I will not be able to escape the violation of my mouth.

I open my mouth, but it is not in surrender.

I scream…

And scream…

And scream until a shadowy yet solid, huge cock is shoved deep into my throat, hushing my screams and choking me into oblivion.

CHAPTER 11

"Sophia!" Jeremy's panicked voice calls out to me. Hope floods my veins. Jeremy is here. He will rescue me.

"Jeremy, help me," I try to cry out, but I remember the cock shoved in my mouth.

Then, suddenly, I realize that I am no longer being violated. No shadow man is hovering over me with his cock in my mouth, and Harper is nowhere to be seen.

In fact, nothing can be seen. It is complete and utter darkness. My eyes are closed. Was I asleep?

"Sophia, wake up!" Jeremy calls out again. "I am right here."

Yes, I was asleep, and Jeremy is trying to wake me. My sluggish brain refuses to come to alertness, and sleep threatens to drag me back down into the dream.

Into the nightmare.

It was all just a nightmare.

My heavy eyelids refuse to open, even though the panic in Jeremy's voice squeezes my heart like a vice. I want to let him know I am awake and okay, but I cannot.

"She won't wake up," I hear him say, his tone filled with fear and worry.

"At least she stopped screaming and thrashing," Harper's voice says.

My heartbeat speeds at the sound of his voice. Whimpers of fear escape my lips as I try and fail to scramble away from that voice. The remnants of forced, yet mind-blowing, orgasm cause tremors to shudder through my body from the memory of Harper's violation. My body jerks violently, and hands grab my shoulders and hold me down.

"Harper, pull over now! I think she's having a seizure!" Jeremy's voice has risen to a panicked pitch, and I can hear the terror in his tone.

"Sophia, please wake up," Jeremy says in a quieter voice. The sheer desperation and pleading make me want to hold him close and reassure him, but I cannot get my body to cooperate.

Besides, it would be a lie. I am not okay. My body is acting on instinct. Has the nightmare made me afraid of Harper, whom I would have never been afraid of otherwise? Or, was the dream…no, nightmare…a conception of my fears of Harper's witchcraft stuff combined with Jeremy's warning of Harper? Had I let Jeremy and my own asinine fears manipulate me into thinking that something was wrong with Harper?

That thought makes me angry at myself for being so gullible and angry at Jeremy for causing me to doubt Harper. The anger helps, giving me the strength to break free from the hypnotic hold of the nightmare. My mind clears, and I am finally able to open my eyes.

The relief in Jeremy's hazel eyes is the first thing I see. My gaze narrows in anger, causing the relief in Jeremy's gaze to turn to confusion. He flinches away from me.

He must have climbed into the back seat sometime during my nightmare because he is sitting on the large backseat beside me. The van stops suddenly, and I am thrown sideways. Jeremy reaches out and catches me, steadying me back on my seat.

"Sophia, are you okay?" he asks softly.

"I had a nightmare," I say through gritted teeth.

The relief returns. "Oh, is that all?"

"Is that all?" I repeat, my voice rising in agitation. "It was horrific and terrible, Jeremy. And it was all your fault!"

Jeremy frowns. "How was your nightmare my fault? I was in the front when you started kicking and screaming, and I climbed back here to wake you up. I never touched you before that."

"It was what you said to me before," I pause, flicking my gaze toward the front where Harper sits. I lower my voice. "It freaked me out and caused me to have a nightmare."

Jeremy's frown deepens as he follows my gaze. He leans close to me, and his voice is a whisper as he asks, "You mean about me not trusting him?"

I back away from Jeremy's nearness and nod my head. Jeremy's shoulders sag. He looks at me with such regret that guilt over my ire engulfs me.

"I did not mean to cause you grief," he says lowly, casting his hazel-colored gaze to the floor. "I just want you to be safe. I always want you safe."

The defeat in his tone melts my anger, and I sigh in resignation. "I know, Jeremy. It's just that…well…it was a horrible dream. It scared me. A lot."

Jeremy's eyes raise to meet mine. "I will always be here to protect you, Sophia. You have no reason to be scared or nervous as long as I am around."

I smile. "Thank you, Jeremy."

"You don't have to thank me, Sophia. I do it because I love you," he says. He reaches out and brushes the backs of his fingers across my cheek tenderly.

I throw myself against him, winding my arms around his neck to hug him. I bury my face into his neck, breathing in his familiar scent like I always do when I hug him.

He smells like earth and musk and…well, like Jeremy.

He smells like home.

He embraces me, returning the hug as I respond, "I love you too, Jeremy. You are my best friend."

Jeremy's hold loosens, and I hear him sigh. I pull away and look into his face, but I can't read his expression. He runs a hand through his light brown hair, a look of sorrow swirling in his amber eyes. I start to ask him what is wrong when Harper's voice booms through the van.

"Is everything alright back there?" he bellows. "How is Sophia?"

Jeremy clears his throat and answers, "Everything is fine. Sophia just had another one of her nightmares."

Jeremy's tone is flat and dull as if it is no big deal.

"So, she's not having a seizure?" Harper asks.

"No, she is fine," Jeremy says.

He turns away from me and climbs back into the front seat. I stare after him in confusion. What had I said or done to cause that reaction?

I turn my gaze to the rearview mirror and lock gazes with Harper. Looking at the reflection of Harper's sky-blue eyes reminds me of the reflection in my nightmare, and I shudder. Harper arches an eyebrow quizzically.

"Are you alright, Sophia?" he asks, and I can hear genuine concern in his tone.

I should not be afraid of Harper. It was only a dream. It was a terrible, horrifying dream, but a dream nonetheless. I take a deep breath and steel myself against the involuntary fear creeping into my bones.

It was just a dream.

"I am fine," I say resolutely. "It was just a dream."

It was just a dream.

I repeat the mantra silently as I turn away from Harper's questioning stare and gaze out my window. The sun still shines high in the sky. We have to be almost there. Harper had said that it was not too far away, and we left right after breakfast. It must be past noon already.

The van rumbles to life, and Harper veers back onto the road. The three of us are silent, uncomfortably silent. Jeremy keeps darting glances at me over his shoulder, and Harper sneaks a few quick looks in the rearview mirror. They both think I do not see, but I do.

I see them in my periphery. I see the worry in Jeremy's hazel gaze, but I cannot read Harper's looks. I continue to stare out my window and decide to ignore them both. It makes for a boring ride, but thankfully, it only takes another 30 minutes.

It was a long, uncomfortably silent, boring 30 minutes.

The van finally stops, and I turn my gaze to the front window and stare in absolute shock at the house. It is the same house from my nightmare! The only differences are that this house is white with black trim, which gives it a cheerier ambiance, and it does not have a pair of gargoyles guarding the steps.

If the inside looks the same, I will lose my shit.

The back door slides open and Jeremy holds his hand out to me.

"Come on, scaredy cat. Don't you wanna see your new home?" he says.

The name is frighteningly familiar, but at least it was not Kitty Cat like the nightmare. Still, what the fuck?

"Scaredy Cat?" I ask, quirking an eyebrow.

"Because you always have scary nightmares," Harper answers.

I groan. "Are you two going to start calling me that all the time now?"

Jeremy smiles slyly. "Probably. Now, come on! I'm tired and hungry."

I huff as I take his hand and allow him to help me from the van.

Harper comes around from the back of the vehicle carrying my suitcase. He still wears his unreadable mask as he approaches.

"I will show Sophia to her room. Get cleaned up for lunch, and tell Chef Amelia to have an extra place set at the table. We will meet you in the dining room," Harper says to Jeremy.

Panic seizes my heart, and I grip Jeremy's hand tighter. Jeremy glances down at me quizzically, and I try to communicate with my eyes.

"Don't leave me alone with him," they say, but I doubt Jeremy will understand. After all, did I not fuss at him earlier for not trusting Harper?

"I would like to come with you," Jeremy responds, and I let out a relieved breath.

"Then who will let Chef know to set the extra place? You want Sophia to be able to eat lunch, don't you?" Harper says in a condescending tone.

Jeremy releases my hand, but I am reluctant to let him go. He turns to me, turning his back to Harper and embracing me in a hug.

He whispers very quietly, "Sophia, are you sure you are alright?"

I take a breath to tell him no and ask him not to leave me, but the mantra repeats in my head…

It was just a dream…it was just a dream…it was just a dream.

Suddenly, I feel silly. So what if the house looks like the one from the nightmare? It is just a coincidence. Maybe I caught a glimpse of a pamphlet on the place while I was cleaning Harper's office. After all, this is his private facility, so he probably has advertisements about it all over his office.

Yes, that has to be it.

I return Jeremy's hug and whisper back, "I am fine. I'm just tired from the long drive."

He pulls out of the hug and catches my gaze. His eyes roam over my face searchingly. "Remember what I said at the rest stop?"

I nod. "If I need you, just call your name."

"Yes. Always remember that, Sophia," Jeremy says.

He releases me, turns, and walks toward the house. I watch until Harper's hand on my back startles me, and I flinch.

"Come, let's go inside," Harper says.

His touch sends electric currents shooting through my veins, and I do not know if it is the normal longing that I feel when he touches me or the fear leftover from the nightmare. Either way, I do not want him touching me right now.

I turn so that his hand falls away from my back, and then I sidestep to put some distance between us. Harper gives me that questioning look again, but I act casually as I follow him toward the house.

He doesn't say anything as he leads me up the steps, across the porch, and to the front door. I sigh with relief when I see that this door is nothing like the door in my dreams.

Even better, when we step inside, the cheery, bright foyer is not a foyer at all. Instead, the entire front room is set up like a reception area. Comfortable furniture is placed strategically throughout the room. A large reception desk takes up most of the right side of the room, and an arched doorway on the right wall behind the desk has signs that say 'kitchen and classrooms'.

Another arched doorway on the opposite side of the room has a sign that says 'living areas', so I assume the bedrooms are that way.

There is a staircase like the one in my dream, but the wooden railing is not as dark, more like a bright cherry-colored wood instead of the dark mahogany. A floor sign sits beside the staircase. It reads, 'office space' in big, bold letters. Harper does not lead me toward the staircase, and my nervousness and fear melt away.

I am being paranoid. This is nothing like my dream. It was just a dream.

The smiling woman behind the reception desk greets us as we draw closer. Harper smiles brilliantly and says, "Nurse Cora, this is Sophia. She will be staying with us a while."

Harper lays a file he had been carrying tucked under his arm on the desk's surface. Nurse Cora nods and takes the file, turning her megawatt smile on me as she says, "Hello, Sophia. It is nice to meet you."

"Likewise," I say, returning her smile.

"If you need anything during the day, just come out here and let me know. I will do my best to accommodate you any way I can," Nurse Cora says to me as she lays some papers and a pen on the desk and scoots them toward me. "Please fill these out, and if you have any questions, do not hesitate to ask me."

"Nurse, my patient has been on the road for some time," Harper says as he scoots the papers and pen back toward Cora. "How about I send her to you tomorrow to sign all her admittance papers after she has had a good night's rest."

"Yes, of course, doctor. That would be just fine. I'll just get her bedclothes together. What color would you like, dear?"

I blink a couple of times. "Color?"

Nurse Cora smiles at me patiently and answers, "Yes, dear. What color sheets and stuff would you like for your bed?"

"I…uh…I don't really know. What colors do you have?" I ask.

"Give her the blue," Harper answers for me, and I glare at him.

He shrugs. "What? I know your favorite color is blue, and we have blue."

"Maybe I wanted a different color," I quip. "How do you know I want blue?"

"What color do
 you want, then?" Nurse Cora asks softly.

I turn to her. I really want to pick another color just to be a pain in Harper's ass, but then I would have to live with it on my bed the entire time I am here. Do I really want to punish myself just so I can annoy Harper? And why do I suddenly want to annoy him? I really need to get some uninterrupted sleep. I am turning into a grumpy monster.

I sigh in resignation and say, "I suppose I will take the blue."

Harper smirks as Nurse Cora turns to a door behind the desk. She opens it and steps in. I strain, trying to capture a glimpse of the room behind the door, but I am too late. Nurse Cora closes the door.

"What's back there?" I ask Harper as we wait for Cora to come back out.

"Tsk, tsk, Scaredy Cat. Nothing that concerns you other than the bed set she is bringing you," Harper answers teasingly.

"If you keep calling me Scaredy Cat, I will eventually show my claws," I say sarcastically.

"Maybe I like claws," Harper quips back.

Is he flirting with me?

Surely not.

Nurse Cora comes back through the door carrying a pile of folded blue linens. She lays the folded bedclothes on the desk and scoots them to me.

"There you are, dear," she says with a smile. "You have sheets, a pillow and pillowcase, a soft blanket, and a comforter. Have a good night, and I will see you first thing tomorrow to complete your admittance paperwork."

"Yes, Nurse Cora," I say automatically.

Nurse Cora scoffs. "We are not that formal around here, Sophia. You can just call me Cora."

I smile as I take my pile of bedclothes from the desk. "Thank you, Cora. I will see you in the morning."

"Come, Sophia. Let's get you settled into your room," Harper says.

I expect him to turn toward the staircase, but he turns toward the arched doorway on the opposite side of the room instead. I scramble after him as he leads me down a large hallway with multiple doors on both sides. Another hallway leads off to the left further down. Doctor Harper turns there and goes down that hallway.

This one is much like the other, except there are only three doors, two on opposite sides and one on the end. Harper leads me to the one on the end and opens the door. He steps inside, and I follow.

I gasp delightedly.

The room is massive, with a sitting area on one side of the great space and a large bed on the other. A small bedside table sits beside the bed, and a dresser sits along the wall opposite the bed.

It has no mirror.

The floor is lush, navy blue carpeting that matches the trim along the lighter blue walls. The ceiling is stark white, with a blue ceiling fan light over the living area and a softer light fixture in the bedroom area.

The sitting room features a small sofa, a recliner, and a television. I have my own television! A tiny table sits beside the recliner, and a coffee table is placed before the sofa.

The furniture and window dressings are done in shades of blue, with splashes of orange thrown in here and there, bringing respite to all that blue. The wooden bedframe, dresser, and tables are all light oak. It is a beautiful room and no mirrors to be found.

"Do you like it?" Harper asks.

I turn to find him studying me with those hypnotizingly blue eyes and that unreadable expression.

I smile wide as I answer, "I love it. Much better than the dull hospital room."

I see a flicker of relief pass through Harper's gaze, but it is gone in a heartbeat, and I wonder if I imagined it. Why would he care if I like my room or not?

"Good," Harper says. "I will put your suitcase down here, beside the bed. The bathroom is through that door.”

Harper points to a door I had not noticed on the back wall between the sitting and bedroom areas.

Harper continues, “I will meet you at the cafeteria. Just follow the signs once you get to the reception area. Don’t be too long. Lunch will be ready soon.”

I nod, and Harper leaves, shutting the door behind him.

He shut the door…

We can shut our doors here?

This place is going to be awesome!

I lay my bedclothes on the big bed, smiling as I notice the quilted mattress topper and even more fluffy pillows. The bed looks inviting and comfortable, and I know it will look even more so once I get it made.

I turn toward the door to the bathroom. I wonder if it is as inviting as this room. The remaining nervousness fluttering in my stomach from the residue of the nightmare flitters away as I step into the decadent, luxurious bathroom.

There isn’t a mirror in here, either.

The black and white tiles that cover the floor and halfway up the walls are shiny and clean. The sink, toilet, and tub are all black with gold-colored metal knobs and trim. The shower stall features dual shower heads, plus a rain shower installed on the ceiling.

I could get used to this!

I turn the water on in the shower and adjust the temperature. Water runs from every shower head, cascading down the shower walls and running straight down from the rain shower fixture.

I stare at the falling water longingly. Just a quick shower should be fine, right? I quickly undress, step into the shower, and close the glass door. It is heavenly. I could absolutely get used to this!

I quickly realize that a quick shower is next to impossible in this bathroom. If I do not shower and get out fast, I will luxuriate in here too long and miss lunch. Therefore, I clean up rapidly and step out of the water, vowing to take a nice, long shower before bed.

There is a small door beside the toilet, and I open it, searching for a towel. Sure enough, a large linen closet lies behind the door with enough towels to keep me in linen for a long time.

And they are large, fluff oversized towels. Just the way I like them.

I leave the bathroom and spot my suitcase by the bed where Harper said he would leave it. I walk over to it and lift it onto the bed. Someone knocks on my door.

"Sophia, are you in there? Lunch is almost ready," Jeremy calls through the closed door.

I clutch the fluffy, luxurious towel I found in the bathroom closet around me and head for the door. I open the door for Jeremy and pull him inside, shutting the door behind him.

"Hey, Jeremy," I say as I turn to him. "Perfect timing. Can you help with my hair?"

He is staring at me with an expression I cannot read, his hazel eyes darkening to a startling amber. The muscles in his jaw work as if he is clenching his teeth together, and I see his throat bob like he is swallowing something.

"Sophia…" My name is barely a whisper on his lips.

My brows knit together with worry. "Jeremy, are you feeling alright?"

Jeremy blinks a couple of times and clears his throat before answering. "Sorry, I am just tired. I would be happy to help with your hair."

"I'll just get dressed and get my brush," I say.

"Yeah, you do that," Jeremy says after clearing his throat again. "I'll wait over here in the sitting area."

He turns away from me and walks over to the sitting area. I watch him walk away with a worried frown still on my face. Jeremy is not acting like himself and hasn't since he came into my room after Julia's attack back at the hospital.

I shrug and turn toward the bed. He will tell me what is wrong if he wants to. Either way, it is not my business to know. Besides, Jeremy has always told me everything, so I am sure he will tell me soon.

I rummage through my suitcase until I find my favorite pair of jeans and the black, loose-fitting gypsy top my mother bought me right before she died. I grab my lacy bra and panties and a pair of socks. It will feel great to be in my own clothes again.

I hurry to the bathroom to change, taking one more quick glance over my shoulder. Jeremy sits in the recliner, staring out the window on the back wall of the sitting room. His face is twisted into thoughtful lines, and I wonder what he is thinking about. He seems so…lonely.

Just like the first time I ever saw him.

He is still sitting there when I leave the bathroom, fully dressed and ready for my hair to be brushed.

I pad across the floor, my bare feet silent on the plush carpet. I catch Jeremy's attention by handing him the brush, and he startles. He stares up at me somberly but smiles as I kneel in front of him. I return his smile before turning around and sitting on the floor between his legs.

This will probably be just as therapeutic to him as it will be to me. It has always relaxed him to brush my hair. The sensation of the brush running through my hair also relaxes me.

Jeremy's fingers follow the strokes of the brush, massaging my scalp with gentle rotating motions. I sigh contentedly and let Jeremy work his magic. This is the reason I always ask him to help with my hair.

Well, this, and because I can avoid looking into a mirror if someone else fixes my hair.

The sensations cease, and I am disappointed that it is over so soon. It would be nice to feel Jeremy's fingers massaging my shoulder and back. It would relieve some tension and possibly help me sleep more easily.

I turn to beg Jeremy to give me a shoulder massage, and Jeremy's face is suddenly right in front of mine. He had slipped from the chair and knelt beside me while I was distracted by thoughts of a nice massage. The brush lies loose in his outstretched hand, and his startled hazel eyes meet mine.

His throat works as he swallows, and I hear a slight quiver in his voice as he says, "I was just leaning down to give you your brush. I'm sorry if I startled you."

His breath brushes across my face, and I smell minty toothpaste mixed with Jeremy's earthy scent. My stomach twists with a new sensation that causes my heart to palpitate rapidly. I have never had this kind of reaction to Jeremy before.

He is my best friend.

I keep telling myself that as a lump forms in my throat, and I swallow it down before I reply, "You didn't startle me. I was just turning around to ask if you would give me a shoulder massage."

Jeremy blinks a couple of times before nodding. "I can do that. It may help you sleep."

I laugh nervously and say, "That is exactly what I was thinking."

He smiles softly, and my heart stutters. What the hell is wrong with me? Why am I so nervous around him now when I have never been before?

And why is Jeremy suddenly sexy as hell sitting there on the floor beside me?

CHAPTER 12

"*H*E IS MY BEST FRIEND,*" I tell myself firmly. Jeremy has always been my friend, nothing more. I have never felt anything more for him, so I do not understand where these sensations are coming from now.

It is probably from stress. I have been having a lot of nightmares lately. Also, I am tired and hungry. After the massage, we will eat lunch, and I will feel better.

"Yes, that is it," I decide. *"I just need a massage, food, and rest."*

"Come here," Jeremy says in a whispered voice, beckoning me to sit on the floor before him with my back to his front. His hazel eyes swirl with a heat I have never seen in them before, bringing out the jade-colored flecks in his irises.

I take a calming breath and move to sit where he indicates. His legs outstretch on either side of mine, pinning me between his legs. I flinch when his hands curl across my shoulders.

I feel his hot breath brush across the sensitive skin behind and below my ear as he whispers, "Relax, Sophia."

It is hard for me to relax at first, the memory of the dream threatening to overwhelm me with panic. I force myself to relax and endure his touch. This is Jeremy, not Harper. I take a deep breath and lean into Jeremy's hands.

His fingers begin kneading my shoulders, gently at first. The feathery touches send shockwaves of yearning through my system, and I gasp. There it is again. That feeling of longing…

For Jeremy…

What the hell?

Then, his fingers dig in, massaging the tension and tightness from my shoulders, moving up my neck, then back down to my biceps. It distracts me from my thoughts and forces me to focus on the sensations.

It hurts, but it feels good at the same time. I can feel my muscles soften, the rigid tension of stress disappearing with Jeremy's magic touch. I groan in satisfaction, leaning my head back on Jeremy's shoulder and closing my eyes. I feel the heat of Jeremy's breath on my cheek as I settle in.

I am lost in the divine sensation of his touch and the comforting heat of his breath. All the tension is gone from my shoulders and upper arms, and my muscles feel like liquid under his ministrations.

His working fingers move down my arms, and he picks up my hands and begins massaging gently, running his magic fingers over the backs of my hands and taking the palms with his thumbs.

"Jeremy," I breathe, his name a plea on my tongue. "That feels so good."

"You want more?" he asks in my ear.

"Yes, please," I answer.

He plays along the backs of my hands for a second longer, then drops my hands and leans forward. His arms reach past my shoulders as his chest molds into my back. My head falls forward, but I do not open my eyes. I feel his hands on my thighs and upper legs, just above my knees, as he begins to methodically massage the taunt muscles there.

I moan in pure ecstasy from the complete and udder bliss of his probing hands and fingers. I am lost in the sensations. I can feel the worry and anxiety from the past few days draining away as Jeremy's hands continue to knead away the tightness in my muscles. My head hangs limply, and Jeremy's face is beside mine.

He turns and kisses my cheek softly before saying, "If you lie on your stomach, I can give you a full body massage."

"That sounds heavenly. Let's go to the bed," I say.

"Are you propositioning me? I never said I would give you a happy ending," Jeremy says, giving me another soft kiss on the cheek.

My eyes fly open, and I look over at him. The humorous smirk on his lips makes me smile.

"You would if I asked you to," I tease.

The humor melts from his face, and his hazel eyes bore into mine. "I would do anything for you if you asked me," he says, and there is no teasing in his tone.

I had been so lost in the sensations of the wonderful massage, and the euphoric feeling had made me bold. I suddenly realize that I had just been too bold.

I swallow hard as Jeremy's gaze flicks to my lips, and before I can say anything, he is kissing me. The feel of Jeremy's lips on mine does not startle me as it should have. Instead, the pure pleasure of it mixes with the rest of the euphoria still swirling inside me, sending shockwaves of need through my entire body.

Most surprising of all is that I am kissing him back, and I like it. His tongue swirls along my bottom lip, begging for entrance, and I give it. My tongue dances with his, and I lose myself in the entrancing kiss.

My muscles tense, and all Jeremy's work is undone, but for a different reason than stress. The frustration and overwhelming sexual tension hit me like a tidal wave, threatening to spill me over the edge. I am suddenly reminded of my nightmare, and the intense pleasure that ran through my body unbidden as I was being violated comes to the forefront of my mind.

But this is different.

Instead of some dark, forbidden ecstasy that fills me even though I don't want it to, this desire is warm and welcoming and makes me want more. It feels safe, not intrusive. It feels comfortable, not like it wants to tear me apart.

And there is no fear.

I want to give in to it so bad, especially since Jeremy's kiss becomes more insistent. His hands run up and down my arms as he kisses me, and my hands dig into Jeremy's thighs as I hold myself in this awkward position.

Jeremy must read my body well because he breaks the kiss and leans back against the recliner.

"We need to get up off the floor," Jeremy says breathlessly, but he wraps his arm around my shoulders and pulls me close to his body as if afraid to let me go.

"I can't get up if you hold me so tightly," I say, my voice as breathless as his.

"I'm afraid," he says, his voice quivering.

"Afraid of what?" I ask.

"That you will be angry with me for kissing you, and you will run away from me. I don't know what happened, Sophia, honestly. We were teasing each other one minute, and the next minute I was…"

"Jeremy!" I call loudly, interrupting his tirade.

He stops speaking, so I continue, softening my tone as I reply, "I am not mad. I kissed you back in case you didn't notice, so I cannot be mad at you. I'm not going to run away."

"Okay. I believe you. What now?" He asks cautiously.

"Now, we get off the floor and move to the bed. Then, you will behave and give me that massage you promised me," I answer.

"With the happy ending?" he asks teasingly.

"Don't push your luck," I say, wriggling from his hold.

He laughs and releases me, rising before I can and offering me a helping hand. We move to the bed and I lay on my stomach on top of the soft mattress with its quilted top. I had not yet had a chance to put the bedclothes on, so I lay on the bare mattress.

Jeremy climbs onto the mattress beside me. He climbs on top of me, sitting with his knees on either side of me and his buttocks on my lower back. He starts at my shoulder blades, massaging and working the muscles along my upper back.

I turn my head to one side, place my arms over my head, and relax into the mattress. Jeremy's body is a comforting weight over me. He leans most of his weight on his knees as he moves down my body with his hands and fingers.

Eventually, he ends up at my upper thighs, massaging my lower back with his expert touch. He works my muscles into submission as if he is a puppet master and I am his puppet. I am a quivering mass of relaxation when the massage is over.

It was way too soon.

I startle when I feel Jeremy's hands move to my ass and give a slight squeeze.

"How about that happy ending?" he asks, and I hear the laughter in his tone.

I slap at his hands. "Get off me, you perv!"

He laughs, slaps my ass, then rolls off the bed and dodges my furious kicks at his retreating figure. I roll onto my back, flinging my arms out to my sides as I groan in satisfied ecstasy.

"That felt so good," I say just as my bedroom door is thrown open, and Harper walks into the room.

The unadulterated fury on his face startles me, but it disappears so quickly that I wonder if I imagined it. His eyes are unreadable, his face a mask of unemotional boredom, when he comes up to the side of the bed where I lay sprawled out like a starfish underwater.

"What felt good," he asks nonchalantly, but I catch the slight inflection of…something…in his tone.

I am not sure what it is. Anger? Disappointment? Sadness?

"Don't you knock?" I ask indignantly.

"This is my house. You are my patient. I don't have to knock." He pauses, giving me a questioning look, adding, "Now, answer the question."

"I gave her a massage," Jeremy answers from the other side of the room. "To help her relax. She has been under a lot of stress lately."

"We have professionals here that could have given her a proper massage," Harper answers.

Yes, that is definitely anger in his tone.

"I asked him to," I say, sitting up and swinging my legs over the side of the bed. "I wouldn't feel safe letting a stranger touch me, especially after my last nightmare."

Jeremy's gaze swings to mine, giving me a questioning look. Harper narrows his eyes.

"You never told me about your nightmare," Harper says, and it almost sounds accusatory.

"That's right, I did not. I have not told anyone, and I do not want to talk about it now, either," I retort.

Harper flinches as if I had hit him, but he quickly recovers. "What has gotten into you, Sophia?"

I quirk an eyebrow in confusion. "What do you mean?"

"For the past few days, you have reverted back to how you were when you first came to the hospital. Guarded, secretive, and…Well …scared and angry."

"I told you, Harper, that the shadows were back," I say, my voice barely a whisper. "You said we would deal with it later, but it is getting worse, and you have done nothing to deal with it."

Jeremy's eyes narrow as he comes up beside me. "She did tell you. I was there, remember?"

Harper takes a deep breath and lets it out slowly. Some of the angry tension leaks from his eyes, and he runs a hand through his dark hair. "You are right, Sophia. You did tell me. And I told you that we would start you on new medication when we got here. I have already spoken to Nurse Cora about your new medication regime, and we will start it tomorrow after you sign your admittance papers," Harper says.

I stand from the bed, linking my hand with Jeremy's, saying, "Good. I am sorry I snapped at you. I am just hungry and tired, so can we go to lunch now?"

Harper glances at our joined hands, and his gaze hardens. His tone matches those icy blues as he looks toward Jeremy and says, "I give you certain freedoms here with a great amount of trust. Don't betray that trust and make me have to take those freedoms away."

Harper turns and leaves the room, leaving the door open. I frown.

"What was that about?" I ask Jeremy.

"I don't know," he answers, shaking his head in confusion. "If I didn't know any better, I would swear he is jealous."

I scoff. "Yeah, right. Harper wouldn't care if I slept with every male in the place."

Jeremy's hand tightens in mine. "I would. I would mind very much."

I look into Jeremy's boyishly handsome features. His hazel eyes darken to an amber shade as he returns my stare. His sandy brown locks fall into his eyes, and I automatically brush them away and run my hand through the silky locks.

Just as I have done a hundred times before.

Jeremy's gaze softens, his eyes closing momentarily as if cherishing the feeling, then opening again to gaze into my eyes with such longing that I suck in a breath.

I frown. Is Jeremy developing feelings for me? Or were they always there, and I did not pay attention?

"You know I would never do that, right?" I say to him.

Jeremy nods. "I know, Sophia. You are not that kind of woman. Now, let's go eat."

I am not that kind of woman. He is correct, but I came close to being that kind of woman when the shadows had me. He knows the horrid stories of my past. I told him everything, or at least everything I could remember, and he has never judged me for it. Instead, he defends me, physically as well as mentally. And he never asks for anything in return.

Had he always been in love with me? My mind races to this morning in the van, just after the nightmare. He had touched me tenderly and told me he loved me.

He had told me, just like he tells me all the time. I just have not listened. I took it the wrong way, as I always have since we have known each other.

It is almost surreal that I have discovered the depths of Jeremy's feelings for me, and now I am left with the daunting task of asking myself if I feel the same.

I had always thought I was helplessly in love with Harper. Now, I am not so sure. My feelings for him have dimmed dramatically since that dream.

That dream.

The memory of it haunts me. I feel a soreness down there as if it had really happened. It makes no sense. Maybe it is a placebo effect.

No matter the reason, it terrifies me. Harper has noticed that something is wrong. I brushed it off with him earlier, making it sound like it was all in his head.

But I know it is not. I am different around him, and I wonder if I will ever be the same around him again. Maybe I should just tell him about the dream. Surely, he would understand.

I sigh as I walk down the hallway beside Jeremy, still holding his hand. Something has changed between us this day, and it saddens me to think that we will never be the same to each other again.

I will no longer be hopelessly in love with Harper, and Jeremy will not be my best friend. I suppose Harper will only be my Doctor, but what will Jeremy be to me now? I only hope that we remain friends of some kind, no matter what happens.

It scares me to think that I could lose Jeremy. It scares me more to think that I may never lose him, that I am just as in love with him as he is with me.

The thought that I may feel the same fills me with terror…

Am I in love with my best friend?

I hope not…and yet, I hope so.

CHAPTER 13

Harper is nowhere to be found when we make it to the large dining room that is converted into a lavish cafeteria. The circular dining tables are made of wood, not the cold steel tables like in a regular cafeteria. The chairs are wood to match the tables. There are four tables in the room, each with six chairs.

The tiled floors are a beautiful shade of green with golden swirls throughout. The pattern is lovely. The walls and ceiling are white, and a lavish crystal chandelier graces the ceiling in the middle of the room.

An arched doorway with wooden, saloon-style doors leads into what I assume is the kitchen where they cook the food. My stomach rumbles just thinking about it, and then growls ferociously when the smell of food hits my nose as we draw closer into the room.

Either we are the first ones here, or everyone else has already eaten and left because the room is blissfully empty. That is fine. I did not feel like meeting new people today, anyway. I just want to be alone with Jeremy. We have some talking to do.

Jeremy leads the way, pulling me along with him by our still-joined hands. He does not speak as he leads me to one of the tables, pulling a chair out for me. I sit, and Jeremy helps me scoot my chair in, and then he sits in the chair beside me.

"The others should be along soon," Jeremy says, glancing around the room. "When everyone gets here, they will begin serving the food."

I turn my head to look at him, raising my eyebrows questioningly. "Serve the food? You mean we are served here like we are in a restaurant?"

Jeremy chuckles. "Sort of. The Chef plates the food and sends it out to us. Depending on who has kitchen duty, that person passes it out. We have to take our own plates to the kitchen where that same person washes the dishes."

"Kitchen duty?" I ask, my eyebrows rising even further.

"We are given chore lists at the beginning of the week. We all do our part here," Jeremy says.

"It is so different here," I say.

Jeremy shrugs. "It takes some getting used to."

"And when will we start our lessons on witchcraft?" I ask, and I hate how fearful my tone sounds.

Again, he shrugs. "I was here about a week before I got my syllabus."

"Syllabus?" I squeak.

"Are you just going to sit there and repeat everything I say in a questioning tone?" Jeremy asks humorously.

I do not laugh. "Are we at a private mental facility or a school? Why do we need a syllabus?"

He holds up his hands in a surrendering gesture. "Alright, you are in no mood for joking. Message received."

He sighs, running a hand through his sandy brown locks before continuing. "This place is both. We check in at the nurse's station every morning for our meds, and we have group sessions and one-on-one sessions just like at the hospital.

"The difference is that our group sessions are tied in with our classes, and one-on-one sessions are once a week. The rest of our time is spent however we want. Our classes consist of learning skills to help us reintegrate into society when ready, and we have the witchcraft classes.

"We have schedules we must follow just like the hospital, but we are not locked in one space. As long as we attend meals and classes, the rest of our time is free to roam the entire facility except for the turret. That is Doctor Harper's private living quarters."

Jeremy folds his hands on the table as he finishes, gazing at me calmly. I blink several times, absorbing everything he said and processing the information in my mind. Other than the witchcraft classes, it sounds rather ordinary here.

Well…ordinary for someone in college…not necessarily for someone in a mental facility.

I do not know what I expected, but it was not this.

I am beginning to question why I was so nervous to come here. I think I am going to like it here.

"Are you going to tell me about your dream?" Jeremy asks softly.

The abrupt subject change catches me off guard. I whip my gaze to him, my eyes narrowing.

"Why do you want to know?" I ask. "Didn't you hear me tell Harper I did not want to talk about it?"

Jeremy smiles. "Yes, but I am not Harper. You will tell me."

I quirk an eyebrow. "And, what makes you so sure of that?"

He reaches over and takes my hand into his. He looks straight into my eyes, his visage falling into serious lines.

"Because you trust me more than you trust him. No matter what you say, I know it is true."

"You seem to think you know me better than I know myself," I say sarcastically.

He leans toward me, his face coming mere inches from mine. His breath trails along my lips as he whispers, "Because I do."

Nervous little tendrils play inside my stomach at the memory of those lips on mine. I close my eyes as Jeremy's free hand cups my cheek. His fingers wrap around the nape of my neck, and he draws me to him.

The touch of his lips is electrifying. I suck in a breath as tendrils of longing course through me. I lose myself in the sensations of his lips and hands on me, his smell of earthy musk assaulting my nostrils, and the sweet taste of his tongue swirling with mine.

The kiss ends abruptly, leaving me feeling bereft and unsatisfied. I open my eyes, blinking rapidly with a questioning look. Jeremy's gentle hazel eyes stare into mine with pure adoration.

"Tell me," he whispers. "Let me carry your burden."

I don't know if it is the after-effects of his gentle kiss or the intense look in his eyes, but I have the overwhelming urge to tell him. I open my mouth to speak, but Harper enters the room and steals my attention. I sit up quickly, pulling away from Jeremy. He releases my hand and sits up as well.

Harper's icy blue gaze sends shivers down my spine when he spots me. He looks so…angry? Then, it is gone. Like always, I only get glimpses and flashes of his mood before he dons the unemotional mask he has been wearing these past few days.

"There you are," he says to me, the gentleness in his tone belying the anger I saw in his eyes just seconds ago. "Everyone else has already had lunch, but Chef has prepared something special for the two of you."

Harper smiles and motions toward the swinging doors. I look that way to see a woman come through the doors with two plates in her hands. Her eyes narrow, assessing me as she comes closer to the table. I raise my eyebrows, challenging her look with one of my own.

"Sophia, this is our chef, Amelia. Amelia, this is our newest patient and student, Sophia," Harper introduces us.

Amelia smiles, but I can tell it is fake. I instantly do not like her. I am shocked at my reaction. I do not even know this woman, but a twisting sensation in my gut screams at me not to trust her.

"Hello, Sophia," she says, her voice dripping with mock saccharine sweetness.

She places the plates down in front of Jeremy and me. I do not even look at my plate. I don't even know if I want to eat it since it was made '*especially for me*' by this woman.

I give Amelia the same look she gave me when she entered the room, looking her up and down with narrowed eyes. Her round, dark eyes are almost the same color as mine, but with more black than brown. Her nose is small, with thin lips that are painted a shade of pink. Her dark hair is tied in a ponytail at the nape of her neck, with a few wisps hanging loose on either side of her oval-shaped face.

She is tall and appears thin and willowy. Her chef coat and pants hide most of her body, making it hard to tell if she is as tiny as the loose-fitting clothes make her seem. I must admit, she is pretty, even if that makes me want to tear that wonderfully straight, silky-looking hair out of her head.

I smile my sweetest smile and reply, "Hello, Amelia. It is nice to meet you."

"The pleasure is all mine," Amelia says, still feigning sweetness. "I see you have met our Jeremy?"

I frown in confusion, glancing from her to Jeremy in turn. "I have known Jeremy for a while now, so, yes, I have met Jeremy."

She looks at me, really looks at me, and her face turns sour. Her tone is condescending as she replies, "You must be one of the nut jobs from the hospital that Jeremy came from."

Jeremy stands, his hands balled into fists at his side. His hazel eyes flash with anger. "Sophia is not a nut job."

Amelia rolls her eyes. "Whatever," she says and then turns to Harper. "Are you going to tell Jeremy the good news?"

Jeremy frowns. "What good news?"

Harper shoots Amelia an angry look and says, "I may change my mind if you keep up with that attitude."

Amelia huffs. "Fine, fine. I apologize if I offended anyone. Now, can we tell Jeremy what we have planned?"

Amelia looks absolutely delighted, Harper looks bored, and Jeremy looks downright suspicious.

"Tell me," Jeremy says, narrowing his eyes at Harper.

"Wouldn't you like to eat first?" Harper asks.

Jeremy shakes his head, sitting down and glaring at Harper expectantly. "No, tell me now. What is Amelia talking about?"

I watch the exchange curiously. I would also like to know what she is talking about, especially if it involves Jeremy.

Harper sits across from us, but Amelia leans against the table beside Jeremy. She crosses her arms over her chest and smiles deviously.

"I have the roster ready for the full moon ceremony," Harper says. "You had expressed interest in becoming more involved in the ceremonies since you have moved up to the second tier in classes."

Jeremy nods. "I remember that conversation. If possible, I would like to be in the circle, or at least narrate the ceremonies. I just want to be more involved."

"Well, I gave you a role in the full moon ceremony this weekend," Harper says with a nervous glance at me.

I quirk an eyebrow, but he quickly looks away.

"What would you like me to do?" Jeremy asks.

"I want to draw down the moon, but we need massive amounts of energy for that. Therefore, I want to do an energy-building exercise during the ceremony, and that is where you come in."

Jeremy frowns in confusion. "So, you want me to build energy?"

"Yes, but we will need a lot of energy. More than you could produce by any simple act such as meditating," Harper says. "I need sexual energy since it is among some of the most powerful energies, so I need a sexual rite to gather energy. Several other couples are performing the rite, along with you and…"

"And me!" Amelia interrupts. She moves closer to Jeremy.

"I will be your consort," Amelia says seductively, interrupting Harper. She runs a hand through Jeremy's silky locks as she gazes at him with lust-filled eyes.

White-hot rage bubbles in my core, and I grit my teeth to keep from saying anything. The sight of this vile woman touching Jeremy sickens me. What is a sexual rite anyway? Is it what it sounds like?

What the hell kind of practice is witchcraft?

Jeremy jerks away from her touch, and I smile in satisfaction. His eyes are filled with disgust, which makes me smile even wider. Jeremy doesn't like her either, which makes me strangely happy.

I am not ready to explore the reason why I got so jealous of this woman touching Jeremy, nor am I ready to think about why it makes me happy that he doesn't like her. I push these thoughts to the back of my mind and focus on the conversation at hand.

"I am not going to be Amelia's consort," Jeremy says through gritted teeth. "If that is your only role for me, then I will not attend as a participant."

"You have never had a problem raising energy for me before," Harper says smoothly.

Has he done this before? Suddenly, I don't feel so good. Amelia smirks at me, and a stab of jealousy twists my gut. I don't give her the satisfaction of seeing me upset.

I smile innocently as if I don't have a care in the world about the conversation. I pick up my fork and twirl it around on my plate just to have something to look at other than her triumphant smirk.

"You have never asked me to raise sexual energies before," Jeremy responds. "I have only ever meditated to raise energy. I refuse to participate in sexual rituals."

"Come on, baby," Amelia says, sitting beside Jeremy. She places her hand on the table next to his. "No one else has ever refused to be my ritual partner."

How many "partners" has she had, I wonder? Not-so-nice names flash through my brain as I continue to push the food around on my plate. I really am hungry. Maybe it wouldn't hurt to take a tiny bite.

"I am not having sex in front of people," Jeremy says, scooting closer to me.

"We can put a curtain up and give ourselves privacy if you are shy," Amelia says, moving her hand closer to his.

"Let me reword that statement," Jeremy says. He wraps an arm around my shoulder and pulls me close before continuing, "I am not having sex with you."

I drop my fork. Is he insinuating that he would have sex with me? He had kissed me earlier, and we may have gone further had we not been interrupted, but saying it aloud makes it more real somehow.

My eyes widen as I glance over at him. He glares at Amelia, the anger burning in his eyes turning them into molten gold. Harper's eyes are shards of icy blue rage, and it is directed at Jeremy.

Things are about to go to hell…or whatever place of punishment they believe in.

Amelia stands, glaring over Jeremy's head at me. "You would have sex during a ritual with this welp? She doesn't know a thing about magic."

Jeremy swivels, placing me at his back, and then stands facing Amelia. The anger radiating from him is so palpable that it makes the air hard to breathe.

"I never said anything about having sex with anybody," he seethes.

"The ritual is not literal," Harper says through gritted teeth. "You would not be having sex. Energy is raised by the emotions involved, not the literal act. I would never force someone to have sex if they did not want to."

I will not think of the dream, I will not think of the dream. The mantra plays in my head as I peek around Jeremy's body at Harper. He had forced me in that nightmare.

I shift my gaze to Amelia to gauge her reaction to Harper's words.

The smugness on her face falls, but she lifts her chin anyway and says, "Even so, you cannot do the ritual with her because she doesn't know the first thing about witchcraft or drawing energy."

"She may not know anything about magic and witchcraft, but she is the only person in this place I would even consider being intimate with, literal or metaphorical," Jeremy seethes.

He could not have made it any clearer than that. Jeremy definitely would touch me and have sex with me. Do I want him like that? My body certainly does. It reacted to him earlier, even if it wasn't the wild, soul-wrenching, terrifying sensations that Harper raises in me.

Harper…

I glance over at him, and the pure anguish in his eyes as he looks my way tears my heart from my chest. Why is he looking at me like that? Besides a few bouts of teasing, which I never took seriously, and the one almost-kiss that I am not even sure happened, Harper has never shown an interest in me.

Even when I flirted mercilessly, made it clear I was interested, and pretty much threw myself at him, he kept me at arm's length.

Then, there was the dream.

I don't know if I can ever stand Harper's touch again without the memory of the dream wreaking havoc on my emotions, despite his words that he would never force someone. I will never be able to be with Harper, even if he were suddenly interested in me.

Harper slaps his hand on the table hard, causing us all to flinch. His tone is laced with suppressed fury as he says, "Enough of this! Jeremy, you are the one who asked for more. I gave you more. Work it out."

Jeremy's eyes widen in surprise, but Harper continues before Jeremy can say anything. "Sophia, when you are finished eating, I need to speak with you in my office. Jeremy can show you the way."

Harper stands with one more pointed glance at me, then turns and walks out of the room. Amelia stands as well, brushing her hand along Jeremy's shoulder and shooting me a look of triumph.

"I'll see you this weekend, lover," she says before turning and retreating to the kitchen.

Jeremy sighs, running a hand through his hair and blowing a breath through pursed lips. He turns a defeated gaze my way.

"Sophia, I am so sorry Amelia treated you that way," he says.

My heart softens. "Why are you apologizing for someone else's actions?"

He takes my hand and pulls me close. "just know that I will never touch her, no matter what Harper says. I will find an alternative."

I shrug, lowering my eyes with a tight smile. "It's alright. I mean, we are just friends, right? You don't owe me an explanation."

He tugs on my hand gently. "Sophia, look at me."

The tender way he says my name causes my heart to stutter. I raise my eyes to his, staring into the amber depths.

"How can you say that after the kiss we shared? I only want you, Sophia," Jeremy says.

My breath hitches. "Jeremy, you have been my best friend for so long that I don't know how to think of you as…as…"

Jeremy cuts me off. "As your lover?"

My eyes widen as I nod. Jeremy's dark, seductive look as he brings my hand to his mouth shoots my heart into overdrive. He brushes a kiss across the back of my hand as he gazes at me with a look that would put a porn star to shame.

"Come to my room later, and I'll show you how," he says.

My mouth goes instantly dry as he pulls me closer, staring at my lips like they were his last meal. I swallow hard as his mouth claims mine, and he kisses me as if his life depended on it.

Surprisingly, I kiss him back with as much fervor, grasping a handful of his silky hair and pulling him closer. He wraps an arm around my waist, sliding me out of my seat and onto his lap. I straddle him, wrapping my legs around him and trapping him to the chair.

He sucks my bottom lip into his mouth and nips it gently, eliciting a gasp and pleasurable moan from me. His hands dig into my hips as he pulls me tight against his body. I writhe at the sensation of his hardness pressing against my center. The only thing keeping him from entering me is our clothing.

"Does that feel like we are just friends?" he whispers fiercely against my lips, then delves his tongue into my mouth.

I don't stand a chance. I am putty in his arms. This definitely does NOT feel like we are just friends.

"Jeremy," I whisper when he finally releases my mouth from his assault to kiss his way down my neck.

"Yes, always say my name like that," he says against my skin as he rocks his hips up, pressing himself harder against me.

I gasp his name like an urgent plea, breathless and filled with desire. "Jeremy!"

His hands dig into my hips as he rasps, "I changed my mind. Say my name like that."

I arch my back and throw my head back, pressing myself against his raised hips. His lips continue their assault on my neck, dipping lower and kissing the spot between my breasts.

God, I want these pants off. I want his pants off. I want his cock inside me now…

Wait…

What am I saying?

This is Jeremy, not Harper.

Harper…

The nightmare crashes through my consciousness, ravaging my mind with the memory. My heart races with terror as my breathing grows ragged. The panic that held me frozen in its clutches consumes me again, and I push against those hands that have me trapped against a body that threatens to violate me again.

My eyes widen in terror as I lift my head and glance wildly around the room, searching for the shadows that are coming for me. I know they are there, waiting for their chance to trap me and help Harper rape me again.

No.

Not again.

I am blinded by the terror that crawls its way up my throat, leaving my body in a horrific scream that is stifled by the sound of my name being called by a familiar voice.

"Sophia! Sophia, I am sorry. Please, come back to me," the voice says.

I know that voice. The pleading tone pierces my heart with its intensity. It helps me focus and brings me back to myself. It's the voice of safety…of home.

I am sitting back in my seat when I come back to myself, with Jeremy kneeling in front of me. His worried stare pierces me as he holds my hand tightly.

"Jeremy?" my voice is breathless.

"Yes. I'm here, Sophia. You started struggling, so I let you go and helped you back to your seat. What happened to you?" his voice is calm, but I can hear the undertone of anxiety and worry.

"It's the nightmare," I say, and then I tell him everything. I spare no detail.

When I am done, Jeremy's eyes are filled with rage. His hands are fisted on the table, his knuckles white from holding so tightly. He closes his eyes for a moment, takes a deep breath, and blows it out slowly.

He opens his eyes, and his tone is eerily calm as he says, "Let's go see Harper."

Oh shit…

CHAPTER 14

"It was just a dream, Jeremy," I say, fearful of the anger flashing in his hazel eyes. What will he do to Harper when we reach his office?

"There are things you do not understand, Sophia. Things that you cannot understand yet. But don't worry, I will protect you." Jeremy's tone frightens me.

"Protect me from what?" I say, dread causing my voice to quiver.

"From falling into his trap," he says.

My heart thumps erratically. "What trap? He is our doctor, Jeremy. You're being paranoid."

Jeremy's gaze saddens, and he looks at me with something akin to pity. "I was once like you. Innocent, gullible, and naive. I am not paranoid, Sophia."

I swallow hard. Even though my mind says Jeremy is being irrational, my body seems to believe some type of danger exists. My heartbeat quickens, my breathing is shallow and fast, and my mouth goes dry. I have an overwhelming desire to run from this place and never look back.

Am I letting Jeremy's paranoia influence me, or is there something I do not see here?

Besides the shadows, that is. I have a dreadful feeling that I will always be stuck with the shadows. I just have to learn to control them.

Jeremy touches my face, gently cupping my cheek in his palm. "You're afraid. Good. It keeps you sharp, and you must be sharp right now."

"Jeremy, please just tell me what you think is wrong," I say pleadingly. "It was just a dream. I don't think Harper would really do that."

Jeremy sighs, running a hand through his hair. "I don't know how to explain it to you. It would require you to have some sort of understanding about what we do here.”

“So, let me gain understanding,” I say. “I wanted to come here because Harper offered to teach me about witchcraft. So, let me learn and come to my own conclusions.”

Jeremy gazes at me thoughtfully for a moment before replying, “Alright, Sophia. Have it your way. Just make me one promise.”

I quirk an eyebrow. “What kind of promise?”

“Promise me you will stay sharp, pay close attention, and don’t let Harper talk you into doing anything that makes you uncomfortable.”

I nod. “Okay, I can promise that.”

Jeremy grasps my hand tightly as he continues. “And, if you ever find yourself in danger…”

I interrupt him. “I know, I know. Scream for you, and you will come.”

Jeremy smiles. “Exactly. I will always protect you. Now, tell me something truthfully.”

I raise my brows questioningly. “What?”

“Tell me the real reason you wanted to come here,” he says.

I grin mischievously. “How did you know I wasn’t being truthful?”

He scoffs. “Because I know you better than you know yourself. I know you would have been…reluctant to learn about something like witchcraft.”

I huff. He is right, even if I do not want to admit it to myself. Maybe he does know me better than I know myself. I shrug and tell him the truth.

“I was reluctant at first, but then Harper told me you were here. I was ready to leave that place and be with you. I was sad when I realized you were gone.”

Jeremy’s eyes widen in surprise. “You wanted to be with me?”

I let out a breathy titter, the laughter coloring my tone as I reply, “Of course I do. You will always be my best friend, no matter what we become to each other in the near future.”

The corners of his mouth lift into a happy little smile, crinkling the edges of his hazel eyes. “So, there is a chance we can be more?”

The words that had tumbled out just seconds ago replay in my mind. Had I really said that? I did not want to give Jeremy false hope, but my mouth had reacted without my brain’s consent.

Did I really want more with Jeremy, or was I leeching onto him for all the wrong reasons? I did not want to start something with him only to find out later that I was just scared or lonely or that I just wanted an ego boost because my self-esteem was shit.

I take a deep breath and decide honesty is the best route right now. I don't want to hurt Jeremy, but I especially don't want to lose my best friend.

"I don't know, Jeremy. But I am willing to try. I just cannot make any promises right now. I don't want to chance losing you."

Jeremy's smile falls, but his gaze has no anger or sadness. Only a silent acceptance and a bit of determination.

"I can accept that. But know this, Sophia. I will never stop, never give up. I will always be here, waiting, hoping, and when you are ready, I will treat you like the goddess that you are."

His words melt my resolve, and I smile widely. "You think I am a goddess?"

He returns my smile, bringing my hand to his soft lips and replying, "Baby, I know you are."

He kisses my hand lingeringly, closing his eyes as if relishing the sensation. He releases me and opens his eyes, desire swirling in their golden depths. I love the way his eyes change depending on his mood.

Happiness courses through me, and I can't help the wide smile that plasters to my face.

"Now, let's go see Harper. I want him to see how I can make you smile," Jeremy says, his eyes darkening with renewed anger. "And I am going to talk to him about that ritual. There is no way I will do…that…for him."

That makes me happy, too. The smile remains on my face as he stands and reaches for me. He laces his fingers with mine and pulls me to my feet. My stomach growls loudly, and I place my free hand over my stomach.

Jeremy halts, turning back to me with a worried frown. "I forgot you haven't eaten yet. We spent too much time talking, and now the food is cold."

I suspect the food would not have been that good, anyway. But I don't say that. Instead, I say, "Maybe some hot food is left in the kitchen?"

"I doubt it," Jeremy says disappointedly. "Amelia always puts everything away before leaving the kitchen."

"Are there sandwich supplies in the kitchen?" I ask hopefully. "We could make something to tide us over until dinner."

"I am sure I can scrounge us up something," Jeremy says, turning and leading me toward the kitchen instead of the exit.

An hour later, I am fed, and my stomach is happy. We are sitting at the same table as before, only this time, we have eaten, and no one bothered us. We ate in silence, casting casual glances toward one another as the minutes ticked by.

I have a feeling Harper will be angry with me when I finally get to his office. Jeremy missed a class, so he will probably be in trouble, too. I look down at my empty plate and sigh.

"Do we have to go?" I ask dejectedly.

Jeremy's tone is not any perkier as he answers, "I am afraid we do. I have to tell Harper that I missed my Tarot class."

"Tarot?" I ask.

"Yeah, as in Tarot cards. Don't tell me you have never heard of Tarot cards. Did you grow up under a rock?" Jeremy says, but his tone is humorous.

I poke him with my elbow. "Don't make fun of me. I was never allowed to read, watch, or listen to anything *"worldly,"* as my mother put it. Especially not about anything that had to do with magic. That was strictly forbidden."

"Your mother was Mexican, right?" Jeremy asked.

I nod. "Yes, she was. Why should that make a difference?"

"Because," Jeremy says. "Most of the Mexican population is Catholic with strong ties to indigenous practices, both of which dabble a bit in some form of spiritual magic or another. Therefore, I am surprised you know nothing about magic."

"What a stereotypical thing to say," I tease.

"Well, am I wrong?" he quips.

"Actually, yes," I say. "My mother was not Catholic, nor did she practice anything indigenous. She was a Jehovah's Witness. She did not believe in getting involved with worldly things. We were not allowed to have things such as television, computers, phones, or anything connecting us to the media or the outside world.

"Our lives were focused on Bible studies and converting others. We were homeschooled, so we only associated with other children of our religion. So to say I was sheltered is an understatement."

"Wow," Jeremy says dryly. "I'm surprised you know anything at all. How did you ever make it?"

I roll my eyes, but a smile raises the corners of my lips. "Stop teasing me. You already knew some of that story."

Jeremy smiles. "Alright, I'll give you a break. It isn't your fault that you were sheltered. Did you ever have any type of fun?"

I shake my head. "Nope. No sports, no playdates, no birthday parties. We never even celebrated holidays. Of course, it is hard to shield a kid from *everything,* especially since most holidays are so commercialized. Mom had to go shopping for groceries. So, we all knew what Christmas, Easter, and Halloween were, but we were not allowed to speak of them or own anything associated with them."

Jeremy frowns in confusion. "Wait, I thought you were Christmas shopping with your mother when she…When she passed?"

I nod. "Yes, I was, but she was only shopping for food for her bible study. She never forced her religion on me after I was old enough to make my own decisions, so after I moved out of the house, I never went to church anymore. I started celebrating holidays that I had always missed out on."

"So, you have never studied any other religions or beliefs?" Jeremy asked curiously. "Not even after you moved out?"

"No," I answer. "I never felt drawn to search. I believe something is out there making the universe work and the world turn. But I never felt the need to try to find it. I was too busy setting up my restaurant, and then after, I was too busy running it."

"Okay, that makes sense. But, didn't you at least watch television or get on social media or the internet after you moved out?" Jeremy asks.

I shrug. "I got a cell phone to keep up with my friends and workers. I even talked Mom into getting a landline so I could keep up with her, too. But, no. I never watched television or got on the internet. I hired a public relations advisor to take care of advertising for the restaurant, so I never needed to get on social media. Besides spending my days at the office taking care of inventory and paperwork, I was still an introvert. I guess old habits die hard."

"So, how do you feel now?" Jeremy asks.

"I don't know," I say, frowning thoughtfully. "I have not thought about it. I am willing to learn, though."

"I hope you feel something for it," Jeremy says. "I may not trust Harper, but I love his teachings. I feel a connection to the world and everything in it, and it feels amazing."

"It sounds amazing," I say forlornly. "I hope I feel that, too."

Jeremy leans into me, his voice a whisper as he says, "You will. I have faith."

"And I have faith that Harper is not going to be too angry that we are so late," I quip.

"You have a warped sense of faith," Jeremy quips back.

Sighing, I get up from the table, picking my plate and glass up to take back to the kitchen.

"Here, let me get these," Jeremy says, taking my plate and cup. "Wait here while I put these away, then we will walk to Harper's office together."

"That would be best since I don't know my way there," I say with a shrug.

"You'll get to know your way around in no time," Jeremy says with a wink.

I snicker and shake my head at him as he disappears through the swinging doors, leaving me alone in the dining room/cafeteria.

Leaving me alone…

I glance around the room nervously. There is nothing other than the beautiful oak tables and chairs and the lavish chandelier that hangs from the ceiling. The bright colors of the room hide no shadows that I can see, particularly since the bright sunlight streams in from the glass doors on the opposite side of the kitchen.

I glance out those doors, not having noticed them before now, and suck in a breath at the spectacular view. The courtyard is wonderfully aesthetically pleasing. The gazebo in the center is draped with vines of pink, red, and white roses. Rows of paths flow from that center, one of them leading right to this door. The others lead off into various other places in the garden.

Flowers of all colors and variations grace the garden beds, flanked by benches where one can sit and enjoy the colorful courtyard's scents, sounds, and sights.

Birdbaths and feeders provide sustenance to the beautiful birds that grace the gardens, and various sizes of birdhouses are hung strategically throughout, providing housing and shade.

The entire courtyard is bright and cheery, and I long to walk outside and sit on one of the benches. I could bask in the sunlight and not be afraid of ever-pressing shadows coming alive around me.

"No shadows will torture me out there," I say cheerily, my voice echoing eerily through the empty room.

"We are inside you. You will never be rid of us," the voices ring in my mind.

My heart skips a beat, but I ignore the voices. Giving them attention just gives them power, and I have given enough power to them. It is time to take some back. Harper's new medicine regime will remove the voices and shadows.

A movement in the corner of my vision catches my attention. I turn my head to look in that direction, and something white flashes across my line of sight. It was too fast to discern what it was, and I see nothing else in the room. Whatever it was is gone now.

Frowning in confusion, I looked around to see where it could have gone. It did not move close enough to the exit to be able to have gone out of the room, and it was nowhere near the kitchen either. It was more like in the middle of the room, and nothing is there except for another table like the one I am standing beside.

I move around the table, ducking low to look under the other table. It is the only place it…whatever it was…could have gone.

There is nothing there.

The fine hairs on the back of my neck and arms stand on end as a chill runs through me. My fight-or-flight instinct kicks in, filling me with an overwhelming urge to run from the room and not stop until I reach safety, wherever that may be.

I force myself to stay put, glancing toward the swinging doors where Jeremy had disappeared only minutes ago. How long did it take to put dishes away?

My heart thumps hard and fast inside my chest. My breath catches, then turns shallow and ragged. A sense of foreboding overshadows the cheeriness of before as I nervously take another quick glance around the empty room.

Nothing.

There is nothing there, and now I begin to feel silly. It had probably been a trick of the light. Perhaps a bird had flown past the glass doors, and the sunshine had reflected off its bright feathers and caused a flash in the room. And now I am standing here scaring myself over nothing.

I scoff at my silliness and take a deep, calming breath. I walk up to the glass doors and look outside one more time. There are birds in the garden, so I convince myself that my theory had to be correct.

My reflection in the glass catches my eye. I have avoided mirrors like the plague since I have been at the hospital, so I barely have a chance to see myself.

The shadows had first come from the mirror.

My eyes widen in surprise at my appearance. My dark brown, almost black eyes shine with renewed vigor. The dark circles that had rimmed the delicate skin underneath them when I had been hospitalized are gone. I trace the lines of my prominent nose, high cheekbones, and full cupid-bow lips. My face has filled out and no longer has that skeletal look from being undernourished, sleep-deprived, and overly stressed.

My slightly dark skin looks whole and healthy once again. My hair is longer than it has ever been. The deep auburn curls that frame my face and flow over my shoulders look shiny and healthy.

My body looks much healthier than when I first came to the hospital.   My hips have filled out, my arms and legs are meatier, and my boobs are slightly bigger. The sight gives me a renewed sense of self-confidence.

"What are you staring at?"

Jeremy's voice coming from behind me startles me, and I squeal as I twirl around.

"Jeremy, you nearly scared the life out of me! You are too quiet!" I exclaim, clutching my chest where my heart threatens to beat out of my chest.

Jeremy snickers before responding, "I was not that quiet. What had you so distracted?"

"The garden is beautiful," I responded.

Even though I knew I was giving a misleading answer, it was still the truth. I did not feel like launching into a lengthy explanation of how I came to be looking at my reflection in the glass, nor did I want to embarrass myself by admitting a flash of light had scared me enough to have me nearly running.

"Yes, it is," Jeremy says. "Maybe I can take you for a walk after seeing Harper."

"If he doesn't take our privileges away for being late," I say.

Jeremy scoffs. "He won't. We do not get privileges revoked here. We get extra chores as a consequence for breaking the rules."

"I hope you're right," I say. "Because I would love to go sit in that garden."

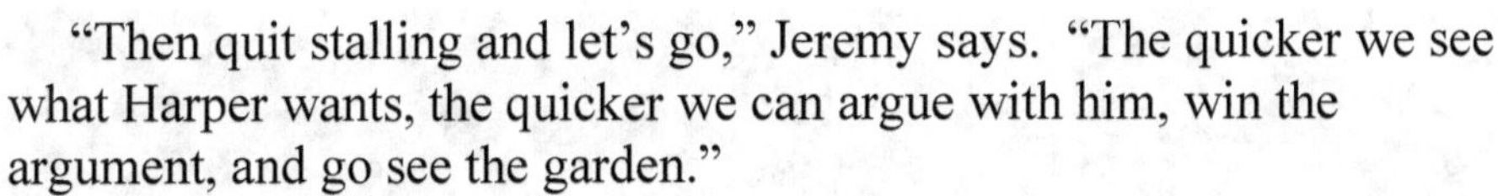

"Then quit stalling and let's go," Jeremy says. "The quicker we see what Harper wants, the quicker we can argue with him, win the argument, and go see the garden."

That makes me laugh as I follow Jeremy out the door with a more confident stride.

Maybe I will even ask for a new mirror.

arper's office is almost identical to his private office back at the hospital. I look around at the crystals on the shelves, and my face heats at the memory of polishing crystals with Harper.

The day he had teased me into thinking he was going to kiss me.

The day he had offered to bring me here.

I was angry at the first memory but smiled at the latter. I could never regret the actions that brought me here, especially since I had been reunited with Jeremy.

The office was on the second floor, which set my nerves on edge when I had realized where we were going. It turned out that I had nothing to worry about. It was nothing like my nightmare up here. There were not multiple hallways, and there was not a bedroom with a mirror.

Or, at least, I had not been taken to one.

The open landing curved around to one side where a set of double doors stood, but they had been closed, so I did not know what was behind them. There was a hallway that led from the other side of the landing, but it only led to Harper's office at the end. There were three other doors on both sides of the hallway, but I had no way of knowing what was behind those doors.

The décor was bright, with marble floors and beige walls that matched the swirls in the marble. White crown molding graced the edging around the ceilings that matched the molding at the edges of the floor. It was beautiful, and I could not help but stare as we had traveled down the hallway to Harper's office.

Now we are standing inside the office, impatiently waiting for Harper to end the phone call he had been on when we entered so we can find out what he wants.

He had looked annoyed when we had come in, and now he keeps darting angry glances toward Jeremy. His gaze softens when he looks at me, telling the person on the other line that he will call them back later.

He hangs up the phone, steepling his fingers as he pierces me with a look.

"Thank you for bringing Sophia to me, Jeremy," Harper said, darting another angry glance toward him. "You can return to your classes now."

"I'm not leaving here until we come to an understanding about the ritual," Jeremy says sternly. "Like I said before…"

Harper stands, interrupting Jeremy's tirade. "Look, Jeremy, I am sorry about that. I have been under a lot of stress lately. This facility is still new, and the grants I need to keep it running are hard to get. I should not have taken it out on you, and I am sorry."

Jeremy's gaze turns hopeful. "So I don't have to raise energy with Amelia?"

Harper shakes his head, his eyes filled with regret. "No, Jeremy. You don't have to do anything you do not want to do. I understand that you are not ready for that phase in your studies yet, and I am sorry I tried to force it on you."

Jeremy frowns. "Wait, Harper, I am ready for the next phase. I just don't see why I have to…"

Harper interrupts Jeremy again, holding up a hand to silence Jeremy's rant. "No, no. You were right, and I was wrong. I admit it. Now, go back to your classes."

"Harper, that's not what I meant…"

"Now!" Harper's tone is forceful, leaving no room for argument. The devastating look on Jeremy's face fills my heart with sorrow for him, and a bit of anger rises in my gut at Harper.

"Wait, Harper," I say, stepping forward and taking Harper's focus from Jeremy. "Jeremy is ready to step up in his studies. Just because he is uncomfortable with intimate situations in a public setting is no reason to hold him back."

Harper's gaze narrows on me, and the warning in his tone sends shivers down my spine. "Sophia, you should not comment on situations you know nothing about. I am still your doctor, and you are the patient. I invited you here to learn something new to help you, but that does not mean you no longer have to complete your original program. Now, sit down so we can start your private session while Jeremy returns to where he is supposed to be."

I open my mouth to argue, and at the same time, Jeremy takes another step forward.

Harper's voice stops us cold, and his tone freezes us in our tracks. "You both heard me. Now, do as I say, or, Sophia, you can go back to the hospital, and Jeremy, you will have extra chore duty for the rest of your time here. The decision is yours."

The line is drawn. Harper is still in charge, and Jeremy and I are nothing more than his patients. Nothing has changed other than a new setting with new faces.

Oh, and I am no longer picking out names for mine and Harper's love children.

Or dreaming of where we will live after we are married.

In fact, I don't like Harper very much anymore. I used to trust Harper, lusted after his scorching hot body, and even thought I might be in love with him. What had changed?

I watch as Jeremy's shoulders slump in defeat. He looks at me, his hazel gaze filled with an apology as he turns for the door.

"I'll see you at dinner," he says softly. "Remember what I said."

I nod. "Bye, Jeremy," I say as I watch him walk to the door and leave the room, closing the door soundly behind him.

Harper gestures to one of the chairs in front of his desk. "Please, sit."

I sit.

"Tell me, Sophia. What do you think of the place so far?" Harper asks as if the last five minutes never happened.

"Well, I haven't really had a chance to explore yet," I answer, then tentatively add, "But I don't like Amelia. She seems mean."

Harper chuckles. "She can be a bit snarky, but I know someone else like that." He looks pointedly at me with a smirk.

I point to myself with an innocent expression and mouth, *Who me?"*

Harper laughs, but my laughter is forced. I look down at my hands clasped together in my lap and sigh.

"Sophia?" Harper says my name with a questioning tone. "Are you going to tell me what is wrong with you? You haven't been the same since we piled into the van this morning."

I swallow hard and shake my head. I am still not ready to open up to Harper about the nightmare or about the sense of wrongness I have felt since I got here.

"Okay, you don't have to talk. I am sure you will feel better after your new meds kick in in a few days. In the meantime, I want you to explore the facility and study your syllabus. You can go to the classrooms on your syllabus, meet the teachers, and even sit in on a class or two."

I nod, keeping my eyes down. I pick at my nails. I used to keep them trimmed before I was committed. They used to be healthy, slightly long, with a beautiful French manicure. I used to get a monthly mani-pedi at my local salon…

"Sophia! Are you listening to me?" Doctor Harper says a bit loudly, shaking me out of my thoughts.

I glance up to see Harper shaking a stack of papers stapled together at me. I reach for the papers as I answer, "Yes, go meet with teachers, explore, and study my syllabus. I take it this is my syllabus?"

The distressed look on Harper's face eases. "Yes, it is. Look it over and tell me what you think."

I take the papers and look them over. There are only three classes: The first class is something called Dialectical Behavior Therapy, then there is The History of Witchcraft, and finally, a class called Re-entering Modern Society. Each class is only an hour long.

"I am only taking three hours' worth of classes daily?" I ask.

"Yes, is there a problem?" Harper asks.

I frown. "What is the rest of my schedule like? What time is breakfast, lunch, and dinner? What time am I to report to the nurses' station every day? When…"

"Sophia," Harper says, interrupting my questions.

I stop speaking and look up at Harper. His blue eyes pierce me with an amused look.

His tone matches the look in his gaze as he says, "This is a long-term facility. It is not as structured as the hospital. You will have more free time, so learn to use it constructively. Your free time is spent however you choose."

I take in a breath and nod. "Okay, so when do I have my therapy sessions?"

"The first class of the day is a therapy class," Harper says. "It will be considered your group sessions. Your individual sessions will be once a week on Saturdays, so they will not interfere with your classes," Harper answers.

"What about my meds?"

"You can visit the nurses' station anytime after breakfast and before ten a.m."

"What time is that, and the other meals?" I ask.

Harper smiles softly. "Breakfast is at seven a.m., lunch is at noon, and dinner is at seven p.m. You can take anything from the community kitchen if you would like snacks in between. Any other questions?"

"Yes, will Amelia be in the community kitchen?" I ask nervously.

Harper lets out a bellowing laugh, rising from his seat and coming around the desk to sit in the chair beside me. He turns my way, still laughing and speaking between guffaws.

"I think you and Amelia got off on the wrong foot. She is a patient here like you."

"She doesn't seem very nice," I mumble.

Harper's laugh subsides as he places a finger under my chin, forcing my gaze away from my lap. My eyes meet his. The laughter still shines in his blue orbs, but his visage falls into softer lines. His softness and humor put me at ease. This is the Harper I grew to know and trust at the other facility. I relax somewhat and feel the relief in my neck and shoulders.

His tone matches his features as he says, "Give her another chance, Sophia. She was a great chef before she was institutionalized, so I thought you two would get along. She knows a lot about the restaurant industry."

"Yes, well, she seemed very," I pause, trying to find the right word. "Unhinged. She did not like that I knew Jeremy, and Jeremy did not like her either."

Harper sighs. "Jeremy. That is another problem. Were you aware that he suffered another episode after coming here?"

I narrow my eyes at Harper. "How could I know that? You wouldn't let me have any contact with him."

"That is true. I just didn't know if he has told you since you have been back in contact with him."

I shake my head. "No, he never told me."

Harper's eyes stare into mine, a look of compassion falling over his visage. "I am sorry, Sophia, but he did. His paranoia has gotten worse, and I am afraid he may be hallucinating again."

I stare at Harper suspiciously. "I admit that Jeremy has seemed more paranoid than usual, but that does not mean he is hallucinating again, nor would it explain his reaction to Amelia."

Harper sighs. "Amelia tried to help him when he first arrived, but he was convinced she was trying to hurt him somehow. She has become fond of him like you were. Maybe you could explain to her that you and Jeremy are good friends like they are. That may smooth things over between you two."

I start to open my mouth and tell Harper that has changed.

At least, I think it has changed.

Jeremy has made it clear that he wants more from our relationship. I am just not sure what I want yet.

I start to tell Harper all of this, but something in my gut stops me. The words get stuck in my throat, and something freezes my tongue. I think back to the scene in the dining room/cafeteria.

I remember the anguish on Harper's face as Jeremy had made it clear that I was the only person he wanted intimately in this facility. Harper had seemed angry, jealous even.

Even Jeremy had said Harper seemed jealous. Maybe Jeremy was right. But why? What does Harper want from me?

My suspicions rise as the nightmare plays through my head yet again, and I become tense and quiet. Harper grasps my chin again. I take a shuddering breath and turn my eyes away from Harper's.

"Sophia," Harper whispers my name, and there is such sorrow in his tone that my gaze turns back to his again.

His eyes are tortured, searching mine fervently as he says breathlessly, "Please, tell me why you are pushing me away. Why don't you trust me anymore?"

The desperation in his tone, the helplessness in his blue eyes, and the way his hand drops in defeat when I tear my chin away from his finger almost breaks me. I almost tell him about my nightmare.

But I don't. Something tells me to keep my mouth shut, so I do.

Harper moves closer to me, his face so close to mine that our noses are almost touching. I suck in a breath, the panic closing my throat and freezing the breath in my lungs.

"Tell me what I can do to make you trust me again," he whispers, his breath caressing my lips in a soft, almost-kiss.

"Harper, please," I say, my voice a breathless whisper. "I can't…"

Fear courses through me, eliciting a tiny whimper from my mouth as Harper's lips press against mine. He cups my cheek in his large hand, angling my head so my mouth slants over his. His tongue glides across my lips in a silent plea.

Panic grips my chest, freezing me in place under Harper's touch. The memory of the nightmare fills my mind as his lips assault mine. But this is no dream. This is real. Harper is actually kissing me.

Harper is kissing me!

The familiar sense of longing that usually runs through my body with Harper's nearness is absent. I wait for the intense desire that should be coursing through my veins about this time, but it does not come.

The fear overrides it all. The memory of the nightmare is too overwhelming.

My eyes dart nervously around the room as Harper's tongue continues to beg my mouth for entrance. There are no mirrors in here. That should have lent me some comfort, but it doesn't.

Finally, my frozen muscles unclench and act of their own accord. I jerk away from Harper's hold, pulling my face away from his and leaning back as far as I can in my seat. The breath unfreezes in my lungs, and I take in deep, panting breaths as I lean as far back in the seat as I can.

"What the fuck are you doing?" I say between gasps of air.

Harper looks stricken as he stands and backs away from me. "I am sorry, Sophia. I don't know what came over me just now."

I don't know what to say. I simply glare at him as I hunker in my seat. I try calming my frazzled nerves and thumping heart by concentrating on my breathing. I take a deep breath in and count to ten as I breathe out slowly.

"Say something, please," Harper says as he backs away from me, his tone desperate.

I start to open my mouth to scream at him again, but the words get caught in my throat. Something slithers from the edges of Harper's form, catching my attention in my peripheral vision. My gaze slants to the movement to see the slithering tentacles of shadow emanating from Harper's sides.

My eyes widen as dread rockets through me, and I scramble from my seat. I back slowly toward the door.

"Leave me alone!" I scream at them as I continue to back away.

"I am not going to touch you again, I promise," Harper says, holding his hands in the air in surrender.

I did not answer. How was I supposed to tell him that he had shadows leaking from his body? I need to get out of here. I need to find Jeremy. He had said if I screamed for him, he would come.

Well, I definitely need him now.

I turn and charge for the door but freeze suddenly before I get there. The shadow man stands between me and the door, his eyes glowing with that eerie red light. He drifts toward me menacingly.

I open my mouth to scream, but a hand goes over my mouth, silencing me. An arm slides around my waist, pulling me back against a rigid body. I can only assume it is Harper. There is no one else in the room.

Except for the shadows slithering from his body and the shadow man blocking the way to the door.

I struggle against his hold, but it is no use. He is too strong. Fear grips me, lending strength to my struggles. I dig my nails into the arm at my waist and rip into the skin, hoping to draw blood. Harper hisses into my ear, a pain-filled sound that sends a thrill of satisfaction coalescing with the terror fluttering inside my stomach.

"Sophia, calm down!" he exclaims in my ear as his grip on my mouth slips.

"You said you wouldn't touch me! Let me go!" I shout back.

"I will if you promise to stay and talk to me," Harper responds.

I do not listen, mainly because the shadow man draws ever closer. It reaches out a dark hand to me, opening that dark abyss of a mouth.

I scream.

It startles Harper, and he releases me suddenly. I dash for the door but the shadow man blocks my way, sidestepping quickly and reaching his hands out to me.

I freeze. I do not have room to escape. I begin to back away, looking over my shoulder at Harper, who stands a little behind me. He watches me with fear and worry in his sky-blue eyes, but he makes no move to capture me again. I return my focus to the shadow man in front of me.

Darkness closes on the edges of my vision, billowing out in a dark display of cloudy, black smoke that wafts into the room. I know it is coming from me. The shadows are trying to possess me again. I can feel the press of their presence against my back.

Strangely, it does not fill me with terror as it always had before. The shadow man before me scares me more than the shadows wafting behind me. My eyes grow wide with horror as he drifts ever closer.

"You see the shadows again, don't you?" Harper asks. His tone is not hurried or panicked. Instead, he sounds sad and defeated.

"Don't you?" I ask, pointing in front of me at the shadow man.

"No, Sophia, I do not. They are figments of your imagination," Harper answers. "You could walk right past them if you wanted to."

I shake my head in denial as I say, "No, they are real. He is real."

Harper's tone falls even lower as he responds, "No, Sophia. There is nothing there."

"Do not worry," The shadows around me whisper to me. *"I will protect you from the shadow man."*

"Who will protect me from you?" I ask aloud.

"I am not going to hurt you, Sophia," Harper answers as if I was talking to him.

I ignore him.

"You don't need protection from me. I would never hurt you," The shadows say as they drift around me in smoky waves.

"Yeah, you only want me to hurt the people around me," I mumble.

"What did you say?" Harper asks.

Still, I ignore him.

Suddenly, the shadows surrounding me coalesce before me in a dizzying display of twisting, writhing puffs. I can feel them brushing against my body, caressing me with their terrifying, icy touch. The sensation leaves me nauseous.

Finally, it stops, and the cloud of darkness before me is thick enough to block out the sight of the shadow man. The cloud of darkness continues to writhe and twirl, forming shapes and patterns before settling into a final form.

I gasp.

It is another shadow figure, but this one is definitely female. Her eyes shine with a diamond-like white light that pierces the glowing red eyes of the male figure before her.

"I only did what was necessary to protect her. One day, she will see that," The shadow man says as he stares down the shadow lady.

"Maybe, but she does not see it now. She fears you, so I will protect her from you." The shadow lady replies.

"What the fuck?" I squeak.

"Sophia?" Harper says uncertainly.

I glance over my shoulder at him. He looks my way with wide eyes, and I swear he looks as if he sees the shadow lady before me because his eyes dart back and forth between her and me. He catches me looking at him and focuses his attention on me quickly. It all happened so fast that I wonder if I imagined it all.

His flat tone shows no signs that he saw anything as he says, "Sophia, let me take you to the nurses' station. I can give you a valium to help you rest. You will feel better after a good nap."

The shadow lady hisses at the shadow man before she turns to me. *"Do not be afraid, Sophia."*

What the fuck is happening right now?

Confusion wracks my brain. Harper holds his hands out to me, but I turn and back away, shaking my head. Coldness envelops my back, and I jerk away from the freezing touch of the warring shadows. I turn, angling myself so I can see the shadows and Harper at the same time.

I need to get out of here.

"You can leave. I won't let this evil spirit have you," The shadow lady says, glaring at the shadow man.

Evil spirit? Is she talking about Harper or the shadow man? Or maybe both?

I glance toward Harper, who continues to move toward me with his hand held out to me. The look in his eyes begs me to trust him, but I no longer do. I need to be away from him.

Oddly enough, I believe the shadow lady. I turn trusting eyes to her, and she nods, gesturing toward the door. She turns toward the shadow man, opens her mouth, and screams a warning.

The blood-curdling sound sends chills up and down my spine. It is the eeriest sound I have ever heard. I don't stick around long enough to see the shadow man's reaction.

I turn and bolt for the door, running full-out down the hallway toward the staircase. I scream as loud as I can, screaming Jeremy's name all the way to the bottom of the stairs. I see Nurse Cora staring at me from behind the desk, her eyes wide with confusion and worry.

I skid to a stop, trying to remember where my bedroom is. Thank goodness for the signs. I turn toward the archway with the sign pointing to the living areas. I start to run, but…

It is down the hallway and then…Did we make a left at some point? I remember that we made a turn, and then it was at the end of a hallway.

It has been a long day, and I do not remember which way to go. I hear thundering footsteps from above and from the archway behind the reception desk with the sign pointing to the classrooms.

I breathe a sigh of relief when Jeremy comes thundering down that hallway, his visage twisted into a mask of intense worry and dread. The lines of his boyishly handsome face smooth with relief when he spots me.

I imagine what a sight I must seem, standing in the middle of the reception area, glancing around in a panic with too-wide, frightened eyes, screaming for him as if the devil was after me.

The devil in question comes charging down the staircase, shouting toward the reception area. "Cora, I need ten milligrams of Aripiprazole, stat!"

Cora disappears behind that door behind the desk, supposedly to do Harper's bidding. Jeremy reaches me, pulling me behind him and taking up a protective stance in front of me. He glares at Harper as Harper reaches the bottom of the stairs.

"You are not going to give her that injection," Jeremy seethes.

"Mind your business and return to class, Jeremy," Harper says.

A flash of white catches my attention. I see four large men in white lab coats coming through the door behind the reception desk where Nurse Cora had disappeared just seconds ago. They are the biggest nurses I have ever seen.

Had Cora sent them?

Were they even nurses?

I am usually no coward, except when it comes to the shadows, but these guys are enormous. If Harper wants to inject me with that tranquilizer and asks those men to help, he will succeed.

And I do not want to be tranquilized and have another nightmare.

"Don't let them give me that injection," I tell Jeremy. If anyone can stop them, he can. Maybe not physically, but Jeremy has a way of talking us out of things.

"You heard her," Jeremy says threateningly to Harper. "I am not returning to class until I know she is safe."

The four men in white take up positions behind Harper, settling into threatening stances as they stare menacingly at Jeremy and me. A tiny whimper of fear escapes me. Why am I being such a coward?

"I would never hurt my patients," Harper says.

"She does not want that medication," Jeremy says. "You cannot force her to take it."

Harper's eyes narrow to slits. "You cannot stop me. You are a patient here.”

“I can report you,” Jeremy says confidently. “Unless she is posing a threat to herself or others, you cannot give her meds without her permission.”

“She was causing a disruption in this facility,” Harper says.

“She is not causing a disruption now,” Jeremy says. “She is calm, and she is telling you she does not want meds.”

The muscles in Harper’s athletic jaws work as he grits his teeth. “Fine. But Sophia needs to finish her session with me.”

I start to come out from behind Jeremy and tell Harper I am not going anywhere with him when a motion at the top of the stairs draws my gaze. I suck in a breath.

The shadow woman stands at the top of the stairs, reaching for me as she stares down at me with her glowing, diamond eyes.

“What the hell is that?” Jeremy mumbles under his breath, but I hear it all the same.

I move beside Jeremy, looking up into his eyes and following his gaze. He is looking right at my shadow lady!

“You see her, don’t you?” I whisper to Jeremy.

His gaze flicks to Harper, who seems oblivious to our whispered conversation as he looks at me expectantly. Then Jeremy’s gaze finds mine as his eyes grow wide with horror.

“Her?” He asks shakily.

“Yes, the shadow lady. You see her. Please, tell me you see her,” I say, my tone pleading, even though part of me hopes he doesn’t see her.

That would mean I was not crazy, which is a good thing.

That would mean the shadows are real, which is not such a good thing.

“I do see her,” he says, his whispered voice shaky. “Your shadows are real, after all.”

Well, fuck.

CHAPTER 16

My heart races inside my chest as I realize Jeremy can see the shadows, too. Surely, if Jeremy can see them, everyone else can. So why hadn't Harper seen them in his office just now?

Or any other time they had shown themselves while I had been in Harper's presence?

"How can you see them when no one else can?" I ask Jeremy, still whispering softly.

"Maybe I really am having an episode," Jeremy says softly.

I gaze up at him in confusion. "I thought you faked the episodes so you could stay."

"I thought I did, too," Jeremy says in stunned fright as he continues to stare up at the shadow lady.

"Sophia," Harper calls out. "Are you going to come finish our session?"

My gaze switches to Harper's stern expression, and I flinch. He looks angrier than I have ever seen him. The men at his back look ready to take on a semi-truck. I glance up to the top of the stairs at the shadow lady. She is still shaking her head rapidly.

"Don't go with him. He wants to control you," The shadow lady says in my head.

Like she has a right to talk. The shadows want to control me, too. So why are my instincts telling me to trust the shadow lady?

I am so confused. I do not know what to do. My gaze flits between Harper and the shadow lady as my heart drums in my chest. My breathing is ragged, and a slow trembling starts in my hands. The need to run overwhelms me, but I do not know which way to go.

My muscles twitch, and I decide to take a chance. Looking toward the arched doorway on the opposite side of the room, I bolt. Arms and legs pumping, I run as fast and hard as possible, skidding around a corner and down another hallway.

I was sure that was the turn that leads to my room. I hope I am going the right way. I see the door at the end of the hall, and I go for it. My breath comes fast, but not fast enough to feed my oxygen-starved lungs. I feel like they are going to burst inside me at any minute. My heart pounds so hard it might tear itself from my chest.

I ignore my name being called from multiple places as I continue to run. I reach the end of the hall, crash through the door, and realize that Jeremy is on my heels. He tumbles into the room behind me just before I slam the door. Quickly, I shut and lock it.

I look at Jeremy, and he looks at me. Neither of us says anything as we catch our breaths. I look around and am happy to realize I had been right.

This is my room.

I hear footsteps down the hall just before the doorknob rattles. A growl of frustration comes through the locked door.

"Sophia, let me in," Harper's voice calls through the door.

"What the fuck?" Jeremy asks in a low voice, between gasps of breath. "Why did you run like that? I was handling it."

"I don't know," I answer, just as breathless. "I just got overwhelmed. Everything was happening too fast."

"What made you run from Harper in the first place?" Jeremy asks.

I take a few more hurried, deep breaths and answer, "He kissed me, and it scared me. Because of the nightmare, I think. But then this shadow man came out when I ran from Harper and blocked my way to the door. The shadow lady came out and said she was there to protect me. I was so confused…"

Jeremy interrupts my tirade. His eyes grow dark, swirling with the color of rich chocolate as he says, "Back the fuck up. Say that again. I don't think I heard you correctly because I swear I thought you said that Harper kissed you."

"That's what I said," I respond.

"That son of a bitch," Jeremy mumbles and reaches for the knob.

"No!" I exclaim, grabbing Jeremy's hands. "Please, just don't."

"He doesn't have the right to touch you," Jeremy seethes through gritted teeth. "I will have his job…"

"Jeremy!" I exclaim, interrupting his tirade. "Please, don't make it any worse than it already is! I'm already going to be in trouble."

"Hell, no, you are not," Jeremy argues. "If he tries to give you or me extra chore duties, I will not hesitate to retaliate."

I scoff. "Are we just going to ignore the fact that I am seeing shadows again, and now you can see them too? Besides, what are you gonna do? File him to death? You are a medical secretary. Well, that is if you still have your job."

"Oh, I still have my job, Sophia," Jeremy says. "I will always have my job. And, no, we are not going to ignore the shadows. We are just not going to talk about them right now."

"Fine, we won't talk about the shadows now. But how can you be sure you still have your job?" I ask as Harper bangs on the door again.

"Sophia, come on out, please. I just want to talk to you." Harper's tone is low and calm.

Jeremy lets out a disbelieving scoff at the door before he answers me. "There is something you don't know about me, Sophia, something I never told you."

"You're gonna play let's-reveal-all-our-secrets right now?" I ask incredulously as another loud knock sounds on the door.

"Jeremy, if you don't get back to class now, there will be consequences," Harper's stern voice calls through the door.

"Give us a minute!" Jeremy calls at the door. "I'm trying to calm her down!"

"You got five minutes, then I'm coming in. I've already sent for the keys," Harper calls back.

Jeremy turns to me. "I haven't told anyone what I am about to tell you, so you have to swear you won't tell."

I nod. "I promise."

Jeremy sighs and runs a hand through his light brown hair. He moves away from the door and begins pacing as he speaks.

"I know I will always have my job because the psych wing we were in before we came here is named after my father," Jeremy says hurriedly, as if afraid he would lose his nerve if he spoke slowly. "I will always have a job because I own half of that hospital."

My eyes widened in surprise. The Oakes and Dane Medical facility is Kentucky's most famous and medically advanced, privately owned medical facility. This, and the privacy it afforded me, was the reason I had chosen that hospital when I was court-ordered to be hospitalized. I did not need to go to the state hospital. I could afford a private one.

Don Oakes, who was part owner of the facility, was the most famous surgeon in Kentucky before he was killed in the fire that took both of Jeremy's parents from him.

Jeremy Oakes…For fuck's sake, the wing that the psych ward was located on was the Don Oakes wing! And everyone knows that Don Oakes was killed in a fire along with his wife. Their son was the only survivor.

Why didn't I make the connection?

"Why didn't you tell anyone?" I ask as I stare at him incredulously.

"I never wanted to be treated differently," Jeremy explains. "I knew I would be if everyone knew who I really was. I just wanted to get help for my condition without people giving me special treatment because of who my father is…er was.

"Harper and Marcel knew, but none of the other hospital staff did. No one but him, and now you, knows here, and I want to keep it that way. But if Harper continues to mess with you…"

Jeremy stops mid-sentence and turns to me. His glare is murderous as his hazel eyes flick to the closed door, and his tone is laced with fury as he continues.

"I will single-handedly end his career."

"Jeremy, it isn't that serious," I choke out as my throat tightens with nervousness.

"The hell it isn't," Jeremy says harshly, turning those rage-filled amber eyes to me. "I told you, Sophia, I don't trust him. There have been things happening here that you wouldn't understand. I don't have time to explain now, but promise me you will not be alone with him until I figure this out."

"But how am I going to do that when I have to have private sessions with him once a week?" I ask.

"You won't have to. I will call Marcel. She can come here and do your sessions once a week," Jeremy answers. "I will make Harper agree."

"You told Harper and Marcel. Why did you not trust me with this?" I ask, a bit of hurt in my tone.

He crosses the room back to me, cupping my cheek in his hand and staring down into my eyes with his pleading hazel gaze.

"Marcel already knew," Jeremy says softly. "She knew my parents. Same with Harper. I will explain everything, but we have no time right now."

I look up at him. This man has been my best friend for several months. I told him everything about myself, but what had he really told me about himself? Do I really know him? Can I trust him?

As if reading my thoughts, Jeremy pleads softly, "Please, Sophia. Just trust me."

Jeremy owns the hospital we were in…Jeremy is rich…beyond rich…Jeremy is…I don't know who he is anymore. My brain processes this as I stare into those swirling golden depths.

But all I see is Jeremy.

Jeremy, the man who saw me sitting alone in the rec room on my second day in the psych ward, and came over to sit with me so I would not be alone.

Jeremy, the man who fixed my coffee just right every morning because he knew the hospital coffee was horrible and I could not drink it black.

Jeremy, the man who was just as broken as I was but still managed to smile for me every day and made me smile as well, making us both feel better every day.

My face is still cupped in his hand, and he softly brushes his thumb along my cheek to capture my attention. He brings his face close to mine, his warm breath blowing across my frozen lips as he asks, "Do you trust me, Sophia?"

I do, I decide. Just because I have new information about the man I have come to know doesn't mean I shouldn't trust him. He is still my Jeremy.

I swallow hard and nod.

"Good. Now, stand aside and let me deal with this."

His hand slides away from my face, and he steps back. I step aside so he can open the door. Harper charges in, but Jeremy puts a hand up, stopping Harper from advancing further into the room.

"Not so fast," Jeremy says firmly. "Tell the brute squad to go away. They are no longer needed."

"I don't think so," Hulk number one says, ducking so that his head does not hit the door frame as he squeezes his bulking form into the room.

"Harper," Jeremy says in warning, wrapping an arm around my shoulders and pulling me behind him.

Harper sighs, brushing his dark, auburn bangs from his eyes as he turns to the hulking man. "Go back to your stations, all of you."

"But boss…," The brute argues.

"I said go!" Harper says firmly.

Hulk number one backs out of the room, joining Hulk number two, three, and four in the hall. He gestures with his arms as he tells them to go back, and they all turn and exit down the hallway.

Harper looks around Jeremy's body at me. "Sophia, I only want to talk to you."

I step to Jeremy's side. "So, talk."

"Alone," Harper says, shooting an angry glare at Jeremy.

Jeremy tenses, but I cut him off before he can say anything.

"No. After what just happened, I would feel more comfortable with Jeremy here," I say, crossing my arms over my chest.

"Sophia, I really did not mean to…" His gaze flicks to Jeremy, then back to me. "I was unprofessional, and it was wrong of me to do what I did. Please, forgive me."

I shrug nonchalantly. "I forgive you, but I will not trust you again."

Harper sighs, grasping the bridge of his nose between his thumb and forefinger. He squeezes his eyes shut momentarily and holds that stance for a long moment, during which time Jeremy moves me gently as far away from Harper as he can.

Harper looks up, dropping his hand to his side as he says, "Sophia, I really don't know why I did that, but please don't shut me out. It won't happen again. I promise."

"Damn right, it won't happen again," Jeremy says. "Marcel will take over her private sessions, and you will never be alone with her again."

Harper narrows his gaze on Jeremy. "You are just a patient here. You have no right to give me orders."

Harper's gaze flicks to me, and Jeremy puts his arm around my shoulders as he says, "She knows. I told her."

Harper's eyes widen in surprise momentarily, then narrow on Jeremy again. "So, she knows. However, you are not at the hospital any longer. This is my facility. I am the owner here."

"That may be, but I could have your license revoked over touching her like that, and you know it," Jeremy says. "Don't think I won't carry out my threats if you continue to mess with Sophia."

Harper's jaw clenches as he stares Jeremy down, but Jeremy does not budge. Finally, Harper eases his stance.

"This isn't over," Harper says, but his tone has no fire. "I will earn back your trust, Sophia. You will see Jeremy's true colors, and then…"

"Not another word," Jeremy interrupts through gritted teeth. "Stop trying to manipulate her, and get out."

Harper reluctantly turns to leave, shooting me a mournful glance over his shoulder. I watch his form as he stalks out the door, closing it softly behind him.

I collapse, all the fear, frustration, confusion, and stress draining from my body all at once, leaving me a mess of jumbled nerves and slack muscles. Jeremy catches me, draping an arm around his neck and helping me to the chair in my sitting room. I fold into the chair with a sigh of relief. Jeremy sits on the floor before the chair and gazes up at me with those intense hazel eyes.

"I'll call Marcel first thing in the morning," Jeremy says softly. "Are you okay with that?"

I only nod.

"Do you want to talk about it?"

I shake my head.

"Sophia, I know you have questions. Go ahead, ask me anything."

I take a shaky breath and ask the first question that pops into my head. "How is it that you can see the shadows?"

Jeremy's head dips as he chuffs raggedly. "I thought you might ask me that, but I didn't think it would be your first question."

I rise up and sit on the edge of the chair to see him better. He lifts his eyes to mine, and I gasp at the color. Never before had the green in his hazel eyes come forward, but it did now. His irises glow a jade color with golden flecks throughout.

"Your eyes," I whisper breathlessly.

Jeremy smiles weakly. "They are green, aren't they?"

I nod.

"That's the color they turn when I am scared," He says in a low tone.

I frown. "Why are you scared?"

"I am afraid you will no longer love me when you hear the answer to your question," Jeremy confesses.

My frown deepens. I slide from my seat, kneeling on the floor before Jeremy. I place my hands on his and gaze into those beautiful jade-colored eyes.

"Jeremy, what could be so bad that you think I would no longer love you? I don't even think that is possible. I cannot promise I will not be angry, but I will always love you, whether as my friend or as…"

I stop, the words getting caught in my throat. The question of whether or not I am willing to go further in our relationship is still up in the air, and I do not want to give him false hope.

But it is too late. I know he caught the unsaid words at the end of my sentence because his visage grows hopeful, and he smiles softly.

"As your lover?" He asks, the hope in his eyes leeching into his tone.

I start to pull back my hand, but he grasps my wrist and tugs gently. "No, please don't pull away. You know I would never force you to do anything you don't want to do."

"I know you wouldn't," I respond, scooting closer and resting my hand on his knee. "And I could never hate you, so answer my question."

He takes a deep breath and says, "Okay. I will tell you."

I hold my breath, waiting for the explanation as Jeremy prepares to answer my question.

"I can see shadows because I am an umbrakinetic witch," he says.

I stare at him in confusion, so he elaborates.

"I can control, create, and manipulate darkness and shadows. At least, I am learning to do that. That is what I am learning here."

Fear pulses through me as his words penetrate my brain and sink in. I swallow hard, my eyes going wide. My sweet Jeremy can control the thing that I fear the most.

Jeremy takes another breath and adds, "So, I may have accidentally created that shadow lady due to my overwhelming desire to protect you. I swear, Sophia, I didn't know. I would never scare you like that on purpose."

So that was why Jeremy had been horrified when he saw her and why the shadow lady felt different than the other shadows…

Jeremy had been protecting me all along.

CHAPTER 17

Jeremy squeezes his eyes shut as if dreading my reaction to his words. I stare in astonishment. Every time Jeremy had told me he could protect me from them, he had been telling the truth. He had created the shadow lady, and she had protected me from the shadow man.

And Jeremy had not even known.

He opens his eyes, and the resigned look in those hazel depths melts my heart. Did he think I would be mad at him for protecting me? If anything, his overwhelming urge to protect me at all costs erases any other doubts I had about my feelings for him. Who am I kidding? I want him.

I may not have realized it before because my temporary, erotic transference-induced longing for Harper obscured my desire for Jeremy. Still, it was always there, hiding under the surface. I just never paid any attention to it until I had to be without him.

I lean forward, balancing my weight on his knees and placing my lips against his. I kiss him softly, feeling the sparks of desire run through me as my lips touch his. I hear his sharp intake of breath as he gasps in surprise, and I smile against his lips.

"Sophia," He whispers longingly against the kiss, and I am suddenly in his arms. My legs are bent at the knees and rest on either side of his legs, effectively straddling him.

I press closer to him, deepening the kiss. My lips part to invite his tongue entrance to my mouth, and he obliges, stroking my tongue with his in an intimate, hot dance. I thread my fingers through his fine, silky hair and press even closer to him.

He growls deep in his throat, grasping me on either side of my hips and digging his fingers into my flesh. White-hot ecstasy soars through my veins, lighting me on fire from the inside out. I moan against

Jeremy's lips as the sensation melts me.

I feel the fluttering of my womanly walls as an overwhelming need to be filled by him overtakes me. I can feel his hardness for me through his pants as I rock my hips forward, pressing into him hard as my hands grip his shoulders.

Jeremy breaks from the kiss, and we both pant breathlessly. I can feel our hearts beating against each other through our pressed-together bodies. Jeremy nips my bottom lip, then flicks his tongue out to lick where he bites. I moan in ecstasy.

"Sophia," Jeremy growls my name. His voice is rough with desire. "I don't know if I will be able to stop if we keep this up."

"Then don't stop," I say, running my hands down his back to feel the sleekness of his athletic muscles under my palm. I see his throat work as he swallows hard.

"There is more I need to tell you, Sophia. I want you to have full disclosure before we go any further," Jeremy says breathlessly.

"Can't you disclose everything after?" I ask disappointedly. I grind my hips into his groin to accentuate my point. The fiery longing twists my gut as I feel his erection against me through my jeans.

I should have worn a skirt today.

Jeremy's eyes squeeze shut, and he growls as I grind against him. "Sophia, please. That's not fair."

"I don't feel like being fair. I feel like being fucked," I say. I grab one of his hands from my hip and place it on my breast, pushing against his hand as I feel him tense.

"Yes, touch me, Jeremy," I say sultrily, throwing my head back and letting out a sensual moan.

That seemed to do the trick.

I hear him growl, feel his hand squeeze my breast, and then his lips are on my neck. He devours me, licking and nipping at my neck, earlobe, and down to the top of my breast. Electric currents of desire run through me at every touch of his teeth and tongue.

The hand that plays with my breast pauses, and I whimper, which turns into a gasp when that hand grips the hem of my top and rips it over my head. Jeremy pulls back, and I raise my arms so he can pull my shirt all the way off, leaving only the lacy white bra underneath.

I reach around to unclasp my bra and let it fall from my shoulders. My breasts tumble free from their prison, and I watch Jeremy's throat work as he swallows.

His lust-filled eyes roam over me as he breathes, "You are beautiful."

He cups one in his hand, bringing it to his lips and sucking the hardened nipple into his hot, wet mouth. I throw my head back and bask in the attention he laves onto my nipples and breasts, licking and sucking each one.

His cock throbs against me, and suddenly I want us both naked. I raise my head up to fumble with the buttons on Jeremy's shirt, wanting desperately to rip it off him and feel his skin on mine. Heat builds inside my center, causing my walls to quiver with longing. The intensity of my want for him grows unbearable.

"Jeremy," I say, my voice a plea as I undo the last button and tear his shirt open, pushing it over his shoulders and dragging it off him.

I lunge for him, craving that skin-on-skin contact, crushing my breasts against his chest as I nibble along his jawline. His skin is hot under my tongue, the earthy scent of him filling my nose. The sensations send a burning need coursing through my center.

"Fuck, Sophia, we are going too far," Jeremy moans as I slide my hands up over his torso, relishing the feel of his hardened abs and chest.

I ignore him as I lick, kiss, and suck my way down his body, following the path of my wandering hands. Jeremy grips me under my shoulders and hauls me back up, bringing his face close to mine as he tries to catch his breath.

"Sophia, I want you more than anything, but I have to tell you this first," Jeremy says through gritted teeth. "I don't want to lose you because…"

I put a finger over his lips to silence him and say, "You are not going to lose me, no matter what you have not told me yet."

"Goddess, Sophia, I don't know what I would do if…" Dread laces his tone, and he squeezes his eyes shut.

"Jeremy, I will always be your friend," I say comfortingly. "Even if this doesn't work out, I will never abandon our friendship."

"And you won't accuse me of lying by keeping things from you?" Jeremy asks worriedly.

I cup his face with my hands and answer, "I will acknowledge responsibility for you not telling me and not accuse you of keeping things from me."

I bring my face even closer to his, so close our noses are touching, and whisper sultrily, "Now, stop talking and fuck me."

"Fine, but you better be prepared for the ride, darlin'," Jeremy drawls in his best cowboy impression.

I laugh, but he wastes no time.

Jeremy slips his hand between our bodies, dipping into the waistband of my jeans. His other hand grasps the back of my head, his fingers capturing my hair as he balls it into a fist. He captures my mouth with his, ceasing my laughs and swallowing the gasp that escapes from my throat.

I run my hands down to his shoulders and hold on.

His hand, the one he plunged into my jeans, plays along the top of my lacy underwear as he holds my head still with the other hand and kisses me breathless. I moan in ecstasy against our joined mouths. I rotate my hips forward to give him better access, and his fingers dip into my panties to graze the top of my folds.

Sparks of pleasure rocket through my system as I cry out against our joined mouths. Jeremy releases my hair and pulls his hand from my pants, but he keeps my lips trapped by his as his tongue dances with mine. He uses both hands to undo the button and zipper of my jeans.

I rise onto my knees so he can pull the jeans down, then squirm out of them until they lay in a heap beside us. We never break the kiss. I start fumbling with his jeans, but he stops me with a hand on my wrist.

He breaks away from the kiss to breathlessly say, "No, not yet. Lie down on your back."

I am dying with need, but I do as he says. He watches me as I lay back on the carpet, gazing up at him with a sultry look. His hazel eyes swirl with a deep, golden color as he looks me up and down.

I am panting with desire as Jeremy hooks his fingers into the tops of my panties and begins to pull them down. The longing in his golden gaze intensifies as my nakedness is revealed. My sensitized skin heats, prickling with fiery need as my panties are flung across the room.

He rises onto his knees as he stares down at me, and his eyes glow molten gold. His gaze travels up and down my body, becoming more heated the longer he lingers.

Then, his visage grows tortured, and he whispers roughly, "Sophia, do you trust me?"

I frown in confusion; the burning hot need cooling with growing concern. "Of course I do, Jeremy. What's wrong?"

"The thing I needed to tell you," he says, closing his eyes tightly before continuing, "It wants out."

"What?" I ask in confusion. "Jeremy, tell me what's wrong."

Jeremy's eyes open, and I gasp at the solid jade color radiating from his irises. "Nothing is wrong, Sophia. Don't be afraid."

His tone is soft and calming, but it still raises goosebumps along my naked skin. The heat of desire mixes with a spark of fear, but I don't have an overwhelming urge to run.

On the contrary, the fear makes the desire more intense, and I squirm with the sensation. Then, the fear grows as I see something dark and cloudy rise behind Jeremy.

My eyes widen, and I rise up on my elbows. "Jeremy!" I cry out in warning. "The shadows! Behind you!"

"Don't be afraid," Jeremy says softly, and his eyes glow brighter green.

"But you are afraid," I say. "Your eyes are green."

The shadows continue to writhe around him, and I start to squirm backward on my elbows. But the calmness of Jeremy's tone stops me as he says, "I'm afraid you will hate me when you see…"

Jeremy shakes his head, staring down at me somberly as he adds, "Just watch, please."

So I do.

Curiosity takes over the fear as I watch the cloud of shadow proliferate, coalescing around Jeremy's body as it slides down toward the ground. It billows out when it touches the carpet, then gathers into a swirling vortex of darkness beside Jeremy.

The vortex grows, rising above Jeremy's head as he remains kneeling, taking on a human form. Fear blossoms along my skin, rising goosebumps along my arms, but my stomach still quivers with the need to be touched by the man kneeling over me.

The mixture of fear and longing is heady, taking over my body with an intense desire more vital than any sensation I have ever felt. The shadow man looks at me, and I gasp at the violet-colored, glowing eyes. They are terrifying yet beautiful at the same time.

"Jeremy, what the hell?" I ask, but my tone is more surprised than horrified.

"You said you wouldn't be mad at me, Sophia," Jeremy says as the shadow man moves beside him.

"I know, but this? You know how I feel about the shadows."

"Do not be afraid of this shadow," Jeremy says. "This one is mine.
He won't hurt you any more than I would."

Jeremy's shadow man kneels beside Jeremy as if he were his mirror
image instead of his shadow. The ultraviolet glow of its eyes is
soothing, not the horror-inducing red glow of the other shadows.

It reaches for me, but the recoiling sensation I expect does not
come. Instead, I feel a peace come over me, unlike anything I have
ever felt. The intense desire is still there, along with an inkling of fear.
Still, the peacefulness overrides everything as the shadow's hand
caresses my naked stomach.

My skin quivers at the touch as heat flows over me, and I gasp.
The climax that had been building before the shadow appeared starts
building again, filling me with a longing desire that threatens to burn
me up.

This is not the freezing numbness of the shadows that fill my
nightmares. This is the heat of a blazing sun that fuels my fantasies.
Jeremy smiles down at me as his shadow strokes the skin of my
stomach, building the tide of longing in my core.

"Jeremy," I cry breathlessly, still propped on my elbow as I gaze
down my body at Jeremy.

"I am here, love," He says, bending down and joining his shadow.
He blows along the skin of my navel, hot and sultry, causing me to cry
out in pleasure at the blissful sensation. Then, his shadow strokes that
same spot, spreading heat with its touch.

Jeremy trails kisses across my stomach, then begins to travel down.
His shadow's fingers follow the path. I suck in a breath, my eyes
going wide as I watch Jeremy's mouth graze the delicate sprinkling of
hair that covers my mound.

"Jeremy," I plead as he gently nips the top of my folds.

My cries of pleasure intensify as his shadow's fingers swirl around
the spot where Jeremy's teeth are. Then I cry out in pleasure as
Jeremy's tongue dips into my folds, swirling around the sensitive bud
between them.

His shadow moves above him and spreads my legs, its fingers
digging into my thighs as Jeremy's tongue tortures my clit. I throw
my head back as the pleasurable sensations threaten to rip me apart.
My eyes flutter into the back of my head, and I am lost to the
sensations of Jeremy and his shadow.

The nightmare of Harper and his shadows threaten to come to the surface of my mind, stealing the pleasure I am feeling from Jeremy and his gentle, violet-eyed shadow.

Jeremy's shadow does not hold me down but helps me writhe as he strokes the sensitized skin of my thighs. Jeremy's tongue strokes and loves me instead of forcing entrance as Harper's violating dick did to me.

This is not the rape of my nightmare.

Jeremy makes another long lick up my entrance and swirls around my clit, causing the heat building in my center to build even further. It threatens to spill over in a white-hot rush of magma that will consume me in its tide, helping me forget the nightmare and concentrate on this dreamy fantasy. One more lick, one more touch is all it would take to spill me over that edge, but suddenly, Jeremy and his shadow stop.

His wet heat is gone from my pussy, and the gentle hold is gone from my thighs, leaving me trembling with unshed release and longing for the tide to spill over. I whimper at the loss.

"Please, don't stop," I beg as I raise my head and open my eyes. The shadow is gone.

"I don't plan on stopping," Jeremy says as his hands move up my thighs where the shadow's fingers had played. One of those hands moves to my pussy, spreading my folds wide as he dips his head back down for more.

This time, his tongue dips inside me, entering my center as my walls suck him in. I scream out in pleasure as my walls quiver with need. Jeremy's tongue dips in, then pulls out repeatedly until I feel like exploding.

"Jeremy, please!" I cry out as I squirm under his tongue's assault.

Just as I am about to blow, Jeremy stops again. I moan in frustration. The torture of being brought so close to climax and then being denied is too much. I glance down my body to see Jeremy climbing me, and I watch him move sensually toward me.

He forces me back until I am lying flat again, and he puts his face close to mine. His eyes devour me, filled with need and longing so intense it makes me gasp.

His tone matches his visage as he rasps, "You taste so good, baby. Here, have a taste."

He falls on me, kissing me…no, ravaging me with his mouth, and I can taste myself on his tongue. I whimper and reach down, grazing over his hardened member as I fumble with the button on his pants.

I have been naked under him long enough. I need him naked above me. I need to feel his nakedness against mine. I need him inside me. Now.

Our kiss becomes urgent, as if we are trying to climb into each other's mouths. Tiny little whimpers are coming from my mouth, coalescing with his pleasurable moans as I fumble with his pants. Finally, I get his pants open and release my prize from its prison.

I moan with utter ecstasy as my hand wraps around his massive, hard cock. I can't even get my hand all the way around it. I moan again at the thought of all that gloriously hard muscle forcing its way into my tight, wet pussy. My walls pulse at the thought.

I cannot hold my hand very tight because of his girth and our positions, but I move my hand up and down that long shaft anyway. I stroke up and down as I flick my wrist to move my hand around simultaneously. I find a nice, steady rhythm as I feed at his mouth and writhe under him.

"Fuck, Sophia, that feels so good," he rasps against my mouth. "I won't last long if you don't stop."

"I want this inside me," I say as I stop stroking and tug gently.

"As you wish," he whispers.

He positions himself, using one hand to place the head of his shaft against my entrance. He eases the head inside me, and I cry out. My walls quiver as my pussy sucks at his cock. He balances himself with both hands on either side of my head as he eases in a bit more.

"Fuck, baby," Jeremy whispers roughly. "You are so fucking tight."

"More," I whimper, bringing my legs up to wrap around his thighs.

He pushes deeper inside me, building the pressure with each delicious little inch. Deeper and deeper he pushes, slowly, torturously, until he is buried at the hilt inside me, and my walls throb around his cock.

My sensuous little whimpers are kissed away as Jeremy leans down and captures my mouth again, rocking his hips against me while he is buried inside me. The friction against my clit builds that heat closer to the edge, then he pulls back until only the head is inside me.

Jeremy pulls back from the kiss and gazes down at me. The look of sheer pleasure in his golden depths almost does me in. I suck in a breath as he eases back into me, holding my gaze as he buries himself to the hilt again. My eyes flutter as he rocks against my clit again.

"Keep your eyes open," Jeremy demands huskily. "I want to see them while I fuck you."

"Then fuck me," I say breathlessly.

"Hang on, baby," He growls. I dig my heels into Jeremy's ass, drive my nails into his muscular shoulders, and hang on.

Then he fucks me.

His cock drives into me over and over as his hips pump mercilessly. The walls of my pussy throb from the abuse, building a heat so intense that I am afraid I will melt into the carpet. The heat builds hotter as he pumps harder and faster, and I am not sure I will survive when the molten heat spills over and consumes me.

My eyes widen, holding his gaze as his cock pumps in and out of me faster and faster, and I scream his name until my voice is ragged and broken.

Jeremy's moans become louder as his eyes glow with heat, his lids drooping as his rhythm stutters. I can tell he is close, but I am closer. The heat slams into me as it spills over and consumes me, and the walls of my pussy milk his dick as the orgasm rolls over me. My eyes flutter close as I ride it out, reveling in the blissful sensations.

Jeremy continues to fuck me as my orgasm subsides, causing the pleasurable sensations to continue. The heat builds again, quicker and more intense this time, as Jeremy drives himself to the hilt inside me and grinds himself against me.

"Fuck, you feel so good, fuck, Sophia!" he cries as my pussy milks his dick while he grinds against me one last time. Hot liquid spills from his dick and fills me inside.

His massive member throbs erratically inside my throbbing pussy while he cums, and it drives me over the edge again. Or maybe it is the same orgasm. I am not sure as my pussy throbs even harder than before, and we ride our orgasms together. Our voices coalesce in the room as we scream out our pleasure.

Finally, the orgasm subsides, and Jeremy pulls out slowly. He collapses beside me, breathing heavily as his body goes limp. Neither of us moves as we relearn how to breathe. We can only lay and bask in the aftermath of our lovemaking.

"Sophia?" Jeremy whispers weakly. "Are you mad at me?"

I laugh derisively. "Did that feel like I am mad at you?"

"No," He answers, and I hear the smile in his tone.

"Sophia?" he calls again, his tone stronger this time.

"Yeah?" I answer, still smiling.

"I love you."

My smile widens. I answer with no doubt, no fear, and the absolute truth.

"I love you too, Jeremy."

CHAPTER 18

A loud voice booms from somewhere in the room, startling me from my afterglow-basking. I hurriedly scramble to my feet and run around, gathering my discarded clothing as the voice fills the room.

"All patients, report to the dining room for dinner. Remember, clean hands, happy tummies. Dress appropriately."

Jeremy slowly rolls to his side, laughing as he says, "Calm down, Sophia. It is just the intercom. All the rooms have one."

I spin around to fuss at him for laughing at me, but the sight of Jeremy lying there naked stops my heart.

His sandy brown hair is adorably mussed, with parts sticking up and pieces plastered to his forehead. His eyes are back to their normal hazel, swirling with the afterglow of great sex. His smiling lips are swollen from my kisses, and the skin of his boyishly handsome face is flush from exertion.

His athletically toned muscles ripple as he props himself up on one elbow, the other arm draped over his washboard abs. My gaze travels lower to the v-shaped curve under his navel that leads to his groin. Even soft, his shaft is long and wide, the tip touching the floor as it hangs limply.

He is like a Greek God, a vision of smooth skin and toned muscle that sets my core on fire with want. My knees almost buckle with the remembered sensation of his skin against mine and the memory of being filled by that massive cock.

"If you keep looking at me like that, we are going to miss dinner," Jeremy says seductively as he pushes himself to a sitting position.

I swallow hard.

That position does not help matters. His legs are crossed in front of him, his massive member nestling into the pocket of his large balls. I force my gaze up to his face, and I inhale sharply at the intensely seductive look in his hooded eyes.

"I could say the same to you," I say, my voice rough from

screaming.

Jeremy runs a hand through his hair, taming the tendrils that were sticking up, and lifts himself from the floor. He stalks over to me, his movements smooth and graceful. I feel like prey as his predatory eyes look me up and down. His flaccid cock swings back and forth mesmerizingly as he stalks closer.

I back away, holding one hand up to fend him off. "Please, Jeremy, put your clothes back on and stop looking at me like that."

"You are the one looking at me like you want to eat me," Jeremy says huskily as he continues toward me.

That image flashes through my mind as I gaze down at his not-so-soft-anymore penis. I gulp as the image of that shaft of hardened muscle penetrating my lips plays vividly through my brain. I can almost feel his engorged cock pushing its way toward the back of my throat so intensely that I almost gag.

I suck in a breath, his semi-hard dick jumping as he draws closer. His chest grazes my hardened nipples, and my gathered clothes fall back onto the floor. I fall to my knees.

A surprised groan escapes Jeremy's throat as I take him into my mouth. He is still somewhat soft, so I greedily suck while I can before he becomes too big for me to take him all.

I feel him grow inside my mouth as I suck until he becomes too large, and I have to pull away. I take the extra length into my hand, cupping and gently squeezing his massive sack with the other hand. I fuck him with my mouth and hands, stroking, sucking, and licking as I find a rhythm that has him moaning with pleasure.

"Fuuuuck, Sophia, don't you dare stop," he rasps breathlessly as I enjoy the sensation of his hard dick pumping in and out of my mouth.

He begins to rock his hips in time to my rhythm. The head of his cock hits the back of my throat with every thrust, and my hand holds the extra length. Still, it is not enough to take all of him. I have to open my mouth almost too wide to take all that girth, but the sensation is amazing. The feel of his soft sack filling my other hand is heavenly.

He fists his hand in my hair and forces me to stop with his dick planted in my mouth, all the way to the back of my throat. My lungs scream for air, and my throat begs for closure. I start to gag, and then he releases me suddenly. I pull in a long string of air through my nose, let it out, and pull in another large breath just before he sinks into my mouth again.

After another fight for air, he pulls himself all the way out, leaving me whimpering for another taste. I release his balls as he kneels down, forcing me down to my hands and knees before him, his hard cock bobbing up and down in front of my eyes.

Scorching heat flows through me from my hips, and I whip my head around to look behind me. Jeremy's shadow is there, grasping my hips with his hands and piercing me with its purple-glowing gaze. I gasp as I feel something against my entrance, but Jeremy's hand in my hair turns my head back around to his bobbing cock.

"I'm going to fuck you with my shadow while you suck me, Sophia," Jeremy rasps. "I shouldn't take all the pleasure. I want you to feel good, too."

"Okay," I answer weakly, my pussy already pulsing and begging to be entered.

My eyes grow wide as I feel the push of his shadow's dick against me from behind as Jeremy's dick begs entrance to my mouth. I open wide, and he plunges into me from both sides. I scream around his dick as his shadow's dick plows into my throbbing pussy.

Jeremy uses his hand in my hair to help me fuck his cock with my mouth as I get lost in the sensation of being fucked from behind simultaneously. The orgasm doesn't take long to build, and in only minutes I am screaming my release around Jeremy's dick pumping in my mouth. The sensation of the shadow man's dick inside my pussy fades along with my orgasm, but the vibrations of my screams must have done something for Jeremy.

I hear his rasping voice say, "fuck, I'm not gonna last."

Then, I feel his dick throbbing as it hits the back of my throat, and his tangy, hot seed shoots into my mouth. I swallow, fast and hard, taking him all down my throat as he screams his release. He holds onto my hair tightly, holding me against him until his own orgasm fades and my lungs scream for air.

He releases me, and I pull away, gasping for oxygen as he collapses to the floor. I collapse beside him.

"Last call for dinner," The voice over the intercom says.

"Shit," Jeremy curses. "I don't know if I can stand for a while yet."

"If we keep this up, we won't be able to stand up for days," I say humorously.

"But it will be worth it," Jeremy chuckles.

"We can't stay here all night," I say seriously. "I need sustenance after that workout.”

“Okay, okay. I’m getting up,” Jeremy groans. “But I want more of that later.”

“Honey, I want more of that for the rest of my life,” I say jokingly, but I am only half joking.

Jeremy shoots me a serious look with those intense hazel orbs. His tone is just as serious as he says, “I would be happy to deliver.”

I gulp.

Jeremy turns away to find his clothing, and I do the same, trying not to think about Jeremy’s cock and his promise to fuck me forever.

Another quickie in the shower and thirty minutes later, we enter the empty dining room and groan in disappointment. We missed dinner. Unfortunately, that only leaves us with one option.

We have to ask Amelia for some food.

Great.

“Do we really have to eat?” I moan. My stomach answers me with an angry, loud rumble.

Jeremy laughs. “Your stomach says we do. Besides, Amelia isn’t that bad. She is just delusional.”

I roll my eyes. “Really? I couldn’t tell.”

“Smart ass,” Jeremy says as he slaps my ass.

I yelp and swat back at him, but he is too fast. He dodges my feeble attempts at retribution and ducks into the kitchen through the swinging doors.

We are laughing as we burst through the doors, but our laughter fades at the sight of Amelia waiting on the other side, narrowing her almost-black eyes at us.

Her hands are on her slim hips, which are cocked to one side in an angry pose. Her tight-fitting, white cotton jumper leaves no room for doubt about her willowy figure. The wide bottoms flare around black leather heels that look like boots. The loose cotton cardigan that hangs off her shoulders is black as well.

Her dark brown hair cascades over her shoulders and down her torso, a curtain of silky strands that reach her waist and contrast sharply against the white of her outfit. Her eyes are dark and fiery as they dart over Jeremy and me, and if looks could kill, I would be dead.

Jeremy steps forward, placing himself between me and the angry cook. “Amelia, we missed dinner. Is there any food left?”

“Not for you,” she hisses. “You missed lunch and didn’t even eat when I made you something special. Why should I give you dinner to waste as well?"

"So, you would let us go to bed hungry?" Jeremy asks.

"Is it my fault you missed dinner?" she asks. "Why did you miss, anyway? Harper was looking for you both."

"We got…uh…distracted," Jeremy answers. "What did Harper want?"

"How am I supposed to know? I told him I hadn't seen either of you, which I hadn't. He seemed very tense and angry when you never showed up for dinner. Are you two in trouble?"

Jeremy feigns innocence, raising his hands in a surrendering gesture as he says, "Would I cause trouble? Come on, Amelia, you know me better than that."

"Yeah, I thought I did, but then you chose that tramp over me," she spat, gesturing toward me with a wave of her hand.

Jeremy takes a threatening step forward. "Watch it, Amelia. Don't speak about Sophia like that."

"Did you fuck her?" Amelia asks, crossing her arms over her chest. "I bet you did."

I hear Jeremy growl deep in his throat, and I place a calming hand on his shoulder. "It's okay, Jeremy. She doesn't bother me."

Amelia leans sideways, glaring at me around Jeremy's body as she says, "He's pretty good in the sack, isn't he?"

White-hot anger slices through me, and I curl my hands into fists. Okay, so she does bother me.

She bothers me a lot.

"Don't listen to her, Sophia…," Jeremy says, but I am already moving around him and heading toward Amelia.

Her eyes widen and she backs away from me, but I am too fast. I am lost in my anger as I grab her by her hair and smash my fist into her face. I hear a satisfying crunch as my fist connects with her nose, and she squeals in pain. Hands grab at me, but I shrug them off and cock my fist back for another blow.

The anger consumes me; it all happens so fast that I have no time to think about my actions or pay attention to the buzzing in my brain. I become the rage as I move to hit her again, but she blocks the second blow and retaliates.

She twists around in my grasp and punches out, landing a blow to my abdomen. The air is knocked out of me as her fist connects with my stomach, bending me over as I struggle to breathe. Her knee connects with my face, and blood sprays across her lovely, white pantsuit.

Satisfaction courses through me at the sight of her now-ruined white clothes. I ignore the pain of her assault and stand straight. Blood pools into my mouth, pouring from my nose. I glare into her angry, black gaze and spit my blood into her once-beautiful-but-now-ugly-broken-nose face.

"Sophia! Stop this now!"

Chills climb up my spine at the threat in that tone. It is furiously murderous, and it is not Jeremy.

It's Harper.

Oh, fuck.

Darkness pools in my peripheral vision, and I gasp as I watch it coalesce around me. It swirls around the corners of my eyes.

I also hear Amelia gasp, and my attention turns back to her. She backs away from me, her hands in front of her, palms facing me as if warding me off. Her eyes are wide with terror, showing too much white, and I can see her hands tremble.

I hear the sounds of a struggle behind me: grunts of pain, the slap of fists hitting solid muscle, and angry cries of strain. I turn to see the Hulks struggling with Jeremy, two of them holding him while another approaches with a syringe filled with something yellow.

Jeremy's eyes lock with mine, and a knowing resignation and flash of terror flow through his gaze.

"Sophia, run!" he cries just as the needle pierces his skin, and he lets out an unearthly cry of rage, terror, and defeat.

Shadows flow from his body, swirling in a vortex of angry darkness as the shadows still surging around me move to join it. The two billows of shadow meet and merge between me and Jeremy as I watch his body go limp and his eyes close.

"No! Jeremy!" I cry out.

The shadows swirl together, dancing around each other as they form into two shadow beings, the diamond-eyed shadow lady and the violet-eyed shadow man. Their eyes glow with dazzling lights as they open their mouths and scream at each other.

I cover my ears, the sound deafening, like a million banshees screaming in the still night. Jeremy's order for me to run plays in my head, but I am frozen by the eardrum-busting scream of the two shadows.

Finally, the sound stops. I look around me to find that no one else had been affected by the screams.

Except for Amelia.

She hunkers on the floor, both hands over her ears. I glare at her, but her eyes widen as she stares at the space behind me.

I whip around, following her gaze, to see the fourth hulk I hadn't seen moving menacingly toward me while the other hulks are carting Jeremy away.

"Jeremy!" I call out, but he can no longer hear me. He is unconscious.

"Where are you taking him!" I shout at the giant of a nurse as he moves toward me menacingly.

"Somewhere safe," Harper answers as he comes into view, stepping out from behind the nurse…if he is a nurse.

"Let him go!" I scream as I back away from the hulk. "Leave us alone!"

"No one is going to hurt you, Sophia," Harper says as he pats the air in a calming gesture.

I glance quickly toward the shadows still fighting in the middle of the room. The violet-eyed shadow is reaching for the shadow lady menacingly, and I wonder why Jeremy's two shadows are fighting each other.

The shadow lady desperately tries to dodge the shadow man's grasp but is not fast enough. He starts to fade as if he is being sucked away. His form dissipates from the bottom up as he clings to her. A wail of despair fills the air as the diamond-eyed shadow lady tries to wrest away from the disappearing shadow man form.

A wave of sadness hits me harder than Amelia's fist in my gut. I can feel her sorrow, and I suddenly understand. She is feeling my sorrow. She does not want to leave me, but she has no choice. She must go back to where she came from, but she does not want to go.

I bend over as if I had been physically hit, groaning in agony as the sadness consumes me. My wail permeates the air, coalescing with the shadow's cries. She drifts toward me, pulling away from the shadow man's dissipating hand and reaching for me. She has free reign now that the shadow man has completely faded, but she is also fading.

I reach back for her with a cry of despair. As our fingertips touch, she begins to dissipate just as the purple-eyed shadow man had. I feel her sadness combine with mine as she dissolves into nothingness. Large hands grab me roughly, pulling me into a massive, unyielding mountain of muscle and holding me there.

"Noooo," I wail miserably as I feel the bite of a needle in the flesh of my hip. I scream in agony as my world spins. Darkness closes around the edges of my vision, and it is not the darkness of the shadows. The shadows are gone.

Harper's face comes into view, and terror settles in the pit of my stomach, nauseating me with its intensity. Not all of the shadows are gone. The evil shadow man with red glowing eyes is here. He stares at me from above Harper's head, his menacing laugh rolling through me as I begin to fade from consciousness.

I try to fight the drugs from taking me out, and the horrified panic helps me momentarily. I struggle against the massive hulk of a man who holds me prisoner, grunting and screaming in anger.

"What did you do to me?" I wail.

"Sophia, please calm down," Harper says as the shadow man laughs evilly behind him. "You are safe, I promise."

But I am not safe. The red-eyed shadow man reaches for me, and I know I am doomed. His icy touch claims my soul, freezing the breath in my lungs and stopping my heart from beating.

I lose my fight with consciousness and slip into the void of the shadow man's icy hold. His abyss of a mouth opens, and I am consumed.

All I know now is darkness.

CHAPTER 19

A m I dead? That is the question I ask myself as I slowly become aware. There is no sensation at first, as if I am drifting in a sea of nothingness in the void of nowhere. No sound, no light, no feeling in my body; nothing is here.

I begin to panic, and my heart races in my chest. I am relieved to feel the beating of my heart. It is something, at least. All I see is darkness, but it is hard to tell if my eyes are even open. I blink several times, or at least I think I do.

I take a deep breath and am relieved to discover I can breathe. I try to move my limbs, but it is hard when I cannot feel them or my body. My brain is confused about where to send the signals.

I run my tongue along the inside of my mouth and feel that. Tentatively, I stick out my tongue and run it around my lips. I taste salt, and my lips are moist with…water, maybe?

I don't know where I am or what is happening, but at least I know I am not dead. But why can I not feel my body? Or see? Or hear? Did something happen to me? Did Harper do something to me?

Fear grips me in its cold embrace as I remember the shadow man laughing as I drifted out of consciousness. Have the shadows taken over my body? Is that what is happening? Am I in some kind of prison inside my own body?

Questions swirl around my mind, causing terror to rise inside me. I whimper with anxiety and try to call out for help.

"Please…somebody…anybody…help!" I pause between each word, but I cannot even hear my own voice other than the echo of it inside my own head. It sounds like I am shouting underwater.

No one is here. Hell, I don't even know where "here" is. I begin to cry, tears streaming down from the corners of my eyes. I feel the wetness running down my face, pooling toward my ears. From that sensation, I can tell I am lying on my back, even though I am lying on nothingness. At least I can now tell my brain where my body is so I can try to move.

I wiggle my fingers and am satisfied to feel my fingertips brush my palms as I make a fist. I rub my fingertips with my thumb, and it feels…gritty…yet soft at the same time. The sensation is bizarre.

It helps. The panic that had been welling inside me ebbs as I continue to stroke my fingertips. I wiggle my toes, and I feel that, too. I take in another deep breath. My heartbeat and breathing slow, and I feel calmer.

"Hello?" I call out, and my voice is amplified inside my own head. "Anyone out there?"

Suddenly, I see something. A tiny spark of purple ultraviolet light shines over me. It is dim at first but becomes brighter gradually as if allowing my eyes to adjust.

Finally, I can see somewhat in the dim light. I am in some sort of box or machine. There is no room for me to try to sit up and get a better look at my surroundings. But at least I can see now.

There is a glass window in front of me, but it is tinted with black film. That must be why the light is so dim. I try raising my arms, and it works. I can see my arms rising above me, and I place my palms against the…ceiling?..door?...Lid? Whatever it is that I am in to try to open it.

I push up, but I only accomplish pushing my body down. What the hell? I look down the length of my body to realize that I am floating in a dense, filmy, watery solution of some kind. My nakedness is covered by a simple, black one-piece swimsuit.

Fear courses through me as I wonder who changed my clothing and whether or not I had been violated while doing it. I focus on my body, specifically my groin area, and all I feel is the delicious soreness that proves Jeremy has claimed me as his own.

I raise my head, and my ears pop. My ears were under that dense water. That explains why I couldn't hear.

Air rushes over me suddenly, and I look up to see the top opening. The gentle purple light is gone, replaced by bright fluorescents hanging overhead. I turn my head away, shielding my eyes from the violation of my sensitive orbs.

"Sophia, how are you feeling?" a familiar voice asks.

A voice that I am slowly learning to hate.

"Like shit," I snap as I blink rapidly, trying to force my eyes to adjust to the light.

Harper sighs disappointedly. "Please don't be angry with me. I am only trying to protect you."

"Bullshit," I say as I flounder in the dense solution, trying to get my bearings enough to sit up. "Where am I? What have you done with Jeremy?"

"Jeremy is safe," Harper says. "He is medicated, relaxing, and sends his regards."

"Liar," I exclaim as I finally sit up. "Jeremy would be fighting to get to me if he were conscious. Where is he?"

I look around curiously. The thing I am sitting in seems to be some kind of futuristic metal pod. I wonder what this murky solution I am sitting in is.

"Jeremy is no longer your concern," Harper says firmly. "Your concern is to get better, and the only way you will do that is to forget Jeremy and learn to trust me again.

"Jeremy has been a terrible influence on you. He is not conducive to your recovery. Therefore, I am separating you two until you can make a sound decision where he is concerned."

"You can't do that!" I exclaim. I glance over the sides of the pod, looking for a step or ladder where I can get out of this thing.

Harper grunts, crosses his arms over his chest, and responds, "I can, and I did. You will not see Jeremy again until you complete your program."

I huff in irritation, pausing in my mission to get out of the pod to sneer. "You are just jealous because I fucked him and not you."

Harper moves so fast that I do not even see it. One minute, he is standing by the pod, and the next, his face is before mine, so close our noses almost touch.

He glares at me, showing teeth as he hisses, "Sophia, I don't care who you fuck. I am here to do a job, and part of that job is to care for your mental well-being, not to be your boy toy or eye candy."

"Fuck you!" I cry out, anger and indignation twisting my gut in knots.

"No thanks," Harper shoots back.

Suddenly, I feel like crying and I don't know why. I don't care what Harper thinks of me anymore, so why did that remark hurt me? A lump forms in my throat, and tears prick the backs of my eyes. I blink rapidly to keep them from falling.

Harper backs away and pierces me with a stern look, which

matches his tone as he says, "You are in the turret. This is my private domain. This machine is a sensory deprivation tank that is very helpful for calming violent people such as yourself. I thought it would help you.

"From now on, you will stay in the turret with me. You will not be allowed to go into the rest of the house. You will take mealtimes with me, live with me in the extra bedroom, and take classes with me.

"You and I will be joined at the hip for the next six weeks, or until I think you are ready to be placed back with people again.

"I know I promised you some freedom, but you have proven that you cannot be trusted on your own. In just the few hours you have been here, you have disrupted classes with your hallucinations, had sexual intercourse with another patient, which is highly against the rules, and gotten into a physical fight with another patient.

"Had I known you would act out this bad, I would not have invited you here."

By the time Harper is done, the tears are sliding down my face and dripping from my chin. I sniffle as I wipe the tears away with the backs of my hands. Fear, anguish, and misery weigh on my chest, making it hard to breathe. I take in short, ragged breaths as sobs threaten to escape my throat.

Harper's visage softens. "Sophia, don't cry. I am sorry to be so hard on you, but you left me no choice."

I sniffle again as I gaze over at him. I tense, expecting to see his shadow peeking around his shoulder, but I see nothing. Harper doesn't seem evil or scary or as if he wants to hurt me in any way. In fact, Harper seems very…reasonable.

Still, Jeremy is not here, and the fear that Harper may have done something terrible to him rips through me. I will not feel safe or trust Harper in any way until I know Jeremy is safe.

"Can you just give me some kind of proof that Jeremy is okay and safe?" I ask, my voice wobbly with tears.

Harper smiles softly. "I can do that. Come, I will take you to see Jeremy."

That is incentive enough to grasp Harper's offered hand and allow him to help me out of the sensory deprivation tank. How in the hell had they gotten my unconscious body into this tank anyway?

Then I remembered the four hulking nurses I didn't think were nurses, and my own question was answered. Had they undressed me, too? The possibility makes me shudder in disgust.

Harper mistakes my revulsion as he pulls me into his arms and drags me from the tank. He sits me down on my feet and says, "I am sorry I had to touch you."

I stumble as he releases me, my muscles flaccid from being unused for Universe knows how long. Harper catches me, bringing me back into his arms and trapping me against his chest.

"You may have some imbalance for a while after being in the tank," Harper says as he holds me close. "It is normal."

My traitorous heart flutters in my chest as he stares down at me. His sky-blue eyes pierce me with a look I cannot read. I glare at him and push against his chest.

"Let me go," I say sternly.

"Not until I know you are steady on your feet," Harper says.

"I'm fine, now let me go," I reply.

Harper sighs and releases me, holding out a hand in case I stumble again. I sway for a moment but then stand firm. I glance around the room curiously.

The tank thingy seems to be the only thing in the room. There is only one door and a giant window on the opposite wall. Chills crawl up my spine when I realize the window is mirror-tinted.

I eye the giant window/mirror warily, and my voice is shaky as I ask, "Can I see Jeremy now?"

"This way," Harper says, holding the door open and gesturing for me to go before him. "Go down the hall; it is the first door on your right."

I take a tentative step forward. Is he really letting me go to Jeremy after his speech about keeping me to himself?

"Go on," Harper says at seeing my hesitation. "I'll be right behind you."

I guess he isn't letting me go alone. Fine. I sigh in defeat and walk out the door into the hallway with Harper close behind me.

My nerves are stretched taut with worry. What is Jeremy going to do now? Will he be able to get us out of this situation? Surely he can. He owns half of the hospital. Maybe he can get us sent back there and request a different doctor.

I know he will be furious with worry when he finds out what Harper has planned. Jeremy had warned me to stay away from Harper as much as possible and not to be left alone with him. He had even suggested bringing Marcel in to do my one-on-one sessions.

He would never let Harper take me away from him.

My heart flutters with anticipation as we come to the first door on the right. I smile widely, flinging the door open and preparing to leap into Jeremy's arms.

But Jeremy is not here.

Instead, the room is empty, save for a couple of office chairs on wheels and an entire wall of televisions. No, scratch that. Those are not televisions. They are video monitors, each showing a different area of the house.

I frown in confusion. "Where's Jeremy?" I ask suspiciously.

"Right there," Harper answers, pointing to one of the monitors.

I move slowly toward the monitor Harper points at, staring at the screen with wide, nervous eyes. The picture on the screen comes into focus, and my hand goes over my mouth to stifle the scream of rage that threatens to burst forth from my lungs.

The room is solid white, the walls covered with cushioned foam that matches the ones placed all along the floor. Jeremy lies in the middle of all that white, bundled up and struggling in a straight jacket. He is facing the camera.

Apparently, the video has no sound because I can see his mouth opening and closing in silent screams. His jade-colored eyes are wide and filled with rage. His hair is a mass of tangles on his head, and his features are flushed from the exertion of his struggles.

Pure, white-hot fury coils in my gut. I spin on Harper with my hands balled into fists at my side. My rage is a palpable thing, pulsing the air in front of me in an almost touchable inferno of destruction.

I see a flash of fear in Harper's eyes as I stalk toward him, but he recovers quickly with a blank look.

"Let…him…go!" I pause between each word for emphasis, spitting them out through clenched teeth. I jab my pointer finger into his chest when I reach him.

Harper's eyes blaze iceberg blue. He stares menacingly at my finger, then turns his icy gaze to mine. "I will do no such thing. He is a danger to my staff, my place, and himself. He will stay where he is until he calms. I assure you, he is in no danger."

I let out a rage-filled scream of frustration and turn back to the screen. I could never read lips, but I can clearly see my name on Jeremy's lips as he screams over and over. My heart clenches with anxiety and fear for him, and I choke on the tears that threaten to come again.

He is calling for me, and there is nothing I can do. Why doesn't he call his shadow for help? I don't know, and there is no one to ask. The helplessness consumes me, and my shoulders drop in defeat. There is nothing I can do.

"Come on, Sophia. I'll show you to your room," Harper says, motioning for me to follow.

I sigh in resignation and follow Harper out, darting one last glance at the monitor.

"I will find you somehow," I tell Jeremy silently, even though I know he cannot hear me. "And when I do, we are getting out of here."

CHAPTER 20

Two weeks later, I am sitting in my bedroom pondering over the last couple of weeks. This room is not nearly as big or cozy as my other room, and the comforter and bed sheets are a dull gray instead of the bright blue I had picked out. I have to share a bathroom with Harper, and I have to wear hospital scrubs again.

I have free roam of four rooms: my bedroom, the bathroom, the dining room, and the living room, all of which are Harper's private quarters. The door that leads to the spiral staircase, which leads down to the bottom floor and out of the turret, stays locked at all times.

Only Harper has the key.

The door to the kitchen is locked as well. If I want to eat, I am at the mercy of Harper's schedule. If I want to watch television, I must wait for Harper to be here and ask for the remote. If I am bored, I have books that I can read and classwork I can study.

Harper is in control of my entire schedule. He brings me my meds every morning. He teaches me lessons from my classes every day. He is in charge of when I have free time. Once a week, he takes me to the balcony to get some sunshine and vitamin D. That is considered my therapy time.

Other than those interactions, Harper has pretty much ignored me. He only speaks to me when he has to, and when he does, it is with indifference.

Gone are the days when we teased each other mercilessly, and I miss the easy camaraderie I used to have with him. I am supposed to be afraid of him, according to Jeremy, but now I wonder if Harper was right. Maybe Jeremy really did have an episode. Harper no longer seems dangerous to me, and I wonder if he ever was or if it was Jeremy's paranoia combined with my hallucinations.

I have not seen the shadows since Harper has been giving me the new medications. But what of Jeremy's claim that he could control the shadows? Was that part of his paranoia? It is a possibility that I must consider if I ever get to see him again.

Today, Harper will start me on my lessons on witchcraft. I will be reading about it to start off. It sounds boring, but Harper says it is necessary.

I will also be doing some exercises along with the readings, but nothing ritualistic yet. I gave Harper a tough time and almost backed out of studying witchcraft altogether when he told me I would have to do shadow work. I didn't understand what it was, but the name scared the hell out of me.

When he explained that shadow working was simply getting to know myself and tapping into my subconscious mind, I agreed to try. What could go wrong with simply getting to know oneself better?

The first exercises are simple meditations. Harper downloaded a guided meditation called 'Taming Your Inner Demons' that we will start today.

I don't know how I feel about that, considering what my inner demons are. But maybe when he starts teaching me about his passion, we will recover some of what we used to be to each other.

Whatever that was.

Right now, I am nothing but a prisoner in Harper's house.

Maybe I should feel lucky. At least I am not in a white room, tied up in a straight jacket like Jeremy. But I don't feel lucky. I feel like I lost my lover and my best friend. And the best friend I used to have isn't my friend anymore.

But today I am happy. Harper has been keeping me updated on Jeremy's condition, even though I can tell it irritates him to do so. He told me yesterday that Jeremy will be released today and is doing much better.

He will not be allowed to come see me, nor even know where I am, but at least I know Jeremy is okay. Maybe when we are both straight in our own heads, we can see each other again. Maybe he will even still want me.

At least, I hope he will.

Thoughts of Jeremy bring back the memories of the last day we spent together. I can still feel the sensation of his lips on mine and the dance of our tongues inside my mouth. I miss the feel of my skin against his and the sight of Jeremy lying on the floor naked.

I lie back on the bed, remembering the feel of his weight on top of me. My skin heats with the memory of our lovemaking. My pussy walls pulse with the memory of his massive cock pumping in and out of me, and I stifle a moan of pure ecstasy.

My hips buck of their own accord, and I close my eyes and lose myself in the sensations the memories are eliciting from my body. I run my hand up and down the smooth, heated skin of my torso, remembering the ministrations of Jeremy's mouth all over me.

I run one of those hands down to the waistband of my hospital scrubs, pushing past the elastic and dipping fingers into my panties. My heart pumps erratically in my chest, and my breathing becomes ragged.

The memory of Jeremy's mouth on my pussy has me writhing on the bed, and I dip a finger between my folds to rub the stimulated bud where his tongue had been. A whimper of pleasure escapes me as I feel the build-up of an orgasm.

I continue to relive the sensations of that day as I bring myself to the brink of pleasure with my fingers. I plunge two fingers inside my heated, wet pussy and feel my walls quiver around them. With my free hand, I grab one of the pillows on my bed and cover my face.

I pump my fingers in and out of my entrance, paying extra attention to my clit with my thumb. I pretend it is Jeremy's enormous cock that is probing in and out of me and his fingers rubbing pleasurable circles around my clit.

The orgasm rolls over me, my pussy milking my fingers as I plunge them deep inside myself and hold them there as I cum. I scream my pleasure into the pillow as I writhe and buck against my own hand. Waves of pleasure crash through me, building to a crescendo and then fading away, leaving me trembling with aftershocks.

I pull my hand from my pants and rest it beside me as I pull the pillow from my face. My heart pumps rapidly in my chest, and my breath comes in short, quick pants. It wasn't as intense as the real thing, but it quells my craving for now.

The sound of clapping startles me, and my eyes fly open to see Harper standing over me, clapping his hands together.

"Bravo, Sophia. Thanks for the show," he says, his blue eyes sparkling with humor.

I pull the pillow back over my face and cringe, my skin heating with embarrassment.

"Don't you know how to knock?" I cry out through the pillow.

"What did you say? I can't hear you because you have a pillow over your face," Harper says humorously.

I raise up and throw the pillow at him, growling in mock anger as he dodges it.

"I said, don't you ever knock?" I repeat.

"Not in my own house," he answers as he bends over and picks up the pillow. "And not when the door is unlocked."

The sight of his ass bent over causes my heart to flutter, then a stab of guilt freezes it. What is wrong with me? I just got myself off to memories of Jeremy, and now I am staring at Harper's ass as if it is my next meal.

Harper turns with his ass sticking up in the air and pierces me with those blue orbs as if he knew I was staring at his ass.

"Enjoying the view," he says with a smirk, and I turn my gaze away quickly, my face heating up again.

I am mortified, but then I realize what is happening.

Harper is teasing me. Never mind the fact that I feel like dying from embarrassment because he caught me pleasuring myself and then caught me staring at his ass. Despite that, my heart soars with happiness over his teasing.

Does this mean Harper and I are friends again? What of Jeremy? I push the thoughts aside and decided to just enjoy the moment like I learned to do in my mindfulness class.

Harper's eyes glitter with mischief as he stands back up. He raises his arm with the pillow in his hand, and I see what he is about to do. I raise my arms to block, protecting my face from the onslaught I know is coming.

Sure enough, the pillow blasts into my defending arms and bounces back onto the bed beside me. Harper laughs when I glare at him in mock fury as I sit back up.

"You do have a lock on your door, you know?" Harper says with a chuckle.

"I kind of got caught up in the moment," I say as I stand. "If you will excuse me, I need to use the restroom."

Harper bows with a flourish and a wave of his hand. "Of course, my lady. Anything for you after that performance," he says, and I laugh despite the heat creeping back into my cheeks.

Again.

It feels good to be playful, though, to laugh and smile again, and to feel clear-headed again. The embarrassment is simply a slight annoyance. I will gladly endure it to have things back to normal with Harper.

I wash my hands and clean myself up, putting on a fresh pair of underwear and pants. I brush my hair and glance quickly in the mirror at my handiwork. I have gotten used to Harper's mirror in his bathroom. I do not look into it much other than to quickly check my reflection. But I am comfortable with its presence now and happy to put my dark, auburn locks into some semblance of a style. It falls in waves over my shoulders and down my back.

He even gave me some makeup to wear when I am in the mood. The black eyeliner and copper eyeshadow he picked brings my coffee-colored eyes out wonderfully. My cheeks are filled out, lending prominence to my high cheekbones. The red lipstick looks lovely on my full, cupid-bow lips.

Harper was considerate enough to take the mirror off the dresser in my bedroom so that I would not have to look into a mirror more than necessary. He had only kept the mirror in the bathroom because he needed it. I have learned to deal with it.

Mirrors are not as scary as they used to be anymore.

I leave the bathroom to find Harper standing in the hallway waiting for me.

"Are you ready to begin?" he asks.

I frown. "Right now? I haven't even had my meds yet."

"Yeah, about that," Harper says with a quirk of his eyebrow. "I have decided to change your medication routine."

My frown deepens. "But I have been doing so good on the meds you have me on now," I complained. "I am even able to look in the mirror again."

Harper's eyebrows raise. "Really? And how do you feel about mirrors now?"

I shrug. "I am still a bit wary but doing much better."

"All the more reason to change. If you are doing better, then I feel you can begin the process of weaning off of them."

"Shouldn't I continue to take them for the rest of my life?" I ask confusedly.

"Not necessarily," Harper answers. "Your condition was temporary. You do not have a permanent condition like, say…Danny, for instance. He has chronic depression along with borderline personality disorder. His condition is treatable with meds, but he will have to be on them for life.

"In your case, however, you had a temporary psychological breakdown, but you never had anything wrong with you before that. Therefore, you only have to take meds until your condition improves."

"So, how do we do this?" I ask curiously.

"I take you off them gradually. We will start with cutting back on your dosage and then go from there," Harper answers. "For today, we will skip the morning meds and only take the afternoon meds and your sleeping pill. We will see how it goes over the next two weeks and then change accordingly."

I groan. "How long is it going to take? I have already been here for two weeks. Now, you want me to stay another two weeks?"

Harper gives me a look I can't read as he answers, "Sophia, this is just the first round. You will have to go at least three rounds to be off the medication."

I do the math in my head, then gasp in horror. "You want me to stay another eight weeks? That is longer than my original program was supposed to be."

Harper runs a hand through his hair as he says, "This is detrimental to your program, Sophia. I just want you to be healthy."

"Do I have to be locked up the entire time?" I ask.

Harper answers, "That all depends on you. For now, however, it is time for your first lesson."

I sigh in defeat and reply, "Fine. Let's get this over with."

"Well, don't sound so enthusiastic about it," Harper scoffs sarcastically.

"You can't expect me to be excited to face my inner demons, Doc," I say sarcastically.

"Once you learn to control them instead of them controlling you, you will be on the road to a mentally healthier you," Harper says, sounding like a commercial for a psychiatrist's office.

"Is that going to be your new motto?" I say snarkily.

"Don't be cute," Harper says. "This is serious. I want you to really try, Sophia."

I huff. "Alright, alright. I will try."

"Good. Now, follow me. We are going upstairs." Harper's tone is mysterious, causing me to be instantly suspicious.

He had never taken me upstairs before. I had only been on this floor of the turret while conscious. I am curious to see what is up there.

I follow him toward the door that leads to the spiral staircase. I wonder fleetingly how easy it would be to run away as soon as Harper unlocks that door. I dismissed the thought almost as quick as it came. The door leading out of the turret at the bottom of the stairs is probably locked as well.

It would be a futile effort.

Harper unlocks the door, and we start up the stairs steadily. An open doorway at the top of the stairs leads into darkness, and my mind prickles with nervous energy. I take a deep breath to calm myself. Harper pauses at the doorway to reach in and turn on a light.

The stairwell is bathed in light emanating from the open doorway. Harper is standing with his back to the stream of light, gazing down at me with his hand outstretched. The light radiates around him, making him look like some kind of reaper reaching to take my soul away.

It is debatable which place I would go to.

I take his hand, and he pulls me up the remaining steps and into the room. I immediately begin to look around. We are in what seems like a rounded attic. Stacks of boxes line the walls, circling around a few haphazard stacks that sit in random spots.

An old, ratty sofa sits in the middle of the room, its covering faded and torn. I can't tell what color it used to be, but I estimate it had been some shade of yellow due to its current mustardy color. Despite its condition, it is clean. In fact, the entire space is dust-free, and the air isn't stuffy or moldy as I would expect from an attic.

The bright lights hanging from the ceiling reflect off something in the back behind the sofa. It draws my attention as I move further into the room. My brain makes sense of what I am seeing, and my heart ceases to beat.

I thought I was doing better about mirrors, but there is something about this one that I do not like. It gives me the creeps despite its beauty. The gilded frame of the fancy, floor-length mirror is beautifully patterned in graceful swirls and lines. The surface of the mirror is clean and free of scratches. It appears to be an antique, but it is well-preserved.

Chills run down through me, massaging icy fingers down my spine as I draw closer to it. Something in the glassy, clean surface stirs.

Probably my reflection, I assume, but its movements are not in sync with mine. Maybe it is Harper's reflection as he moves through the room behind me.

My heart takes up a speedy rhythm in my chest as my breaths come in short, quick gasps of air. The fear tearing up my nerves intensifies as I draw closer. Finally, I can see what is reflected in the mirror, and I scream in horror.

Floating in the mirror, staring back at me with glowing red eyes, is the evil shadow man.

I swing around to run, my heart threatening to burst from my chest and run into a solid wall of muscle. Harper stands there calmly, a hand on each of my shoulders. His thumbs rub gentle circles as he locks his blue-eyed gaze with my dark brown one.

"Sophia, I need you to stay calm," he says soothingly. "I need you to take a deep breath and not panic."

My eyes are wide as I hold his gaze. Every muscle and nerve in my body is stretched taut with anxiety. But I do not panic. I hold Harper's gaze, taking deep breaths and blowing them out slowly like he taught me to do.

When I feel like I can speak without my voice wobbling, I say calmly, "I saw a shadow in the mirror. I still need my medication."

"No, Sophia, you do not still need your medication," Harper says.

He pauses, his eyes roaming over my face as if gauging my reaction.

"How can you say that?" I ask, gesturing behind me. "I see the shadow. He is right there in the mirror."

Harper takes a deep breath and says, "You see the shadow not because you need medication but because the shadows are real."

CHAPTER 21

Time seems to stand still as I take in Harper's words. I stand frozen with my mouth hanging open as I stare into his face. Had Harper really just said that?

"What the hell do you mean the shadows are real?" I ask.

"Shadow working is all about getting to know our inner selves, making peace with our inner demons, and exposing the parts of ourselves that we keep hidden in our subconscious minds," Harper explains.

I laugh derisively. "This has nothing to do with metaphorical inner demons. There is an actual shadow man in the mirror. I am seeing shadows again, Harper!"

Harper turns me around to face the mirror despite my struggles. He holds me firmly, gesturing toward the mirror, saying, "You do not see shadows. Sophia, meet your inner demon."

I watch my reflection as my almost-black eyes widen in fearful surprise. The shadow takes a menacing stance as it stares at me with its glowing red eyes. It bows as if bowing to a queen, and chills run down my spine.

I back up as far as Harper will let me go. My back is against his steely chest, his arms wrapped around my shoulders. His hold is strong like a vice, yet gentle and not suffocating. It helps me stay calm and think without panicking.

I gulp and say, "You mean we all have shadowy demons inside us? I thought the term 'inner demon' was just a metaphor."

"For most people, it is," Harper says. "But for some of us, we must work harder since our inner demons are real. Thankfully, most of us with a literal inner demon also possess the skills to control them."

My gaze shoots to Harper's in the mirror. "Well, I don't. My inner demons, which I assume were the shadows, always controlled me. Besides, this one is yours."

I gesture as much as I can in Harper's hold toward the shadow, still standing in the mirror with his red eyes glowing in my direction.

Harper chuckles dryly. "No, that one is yours, my dear. My demon does not have red eyes."

"My shadows never took on a form. They just floated around like black clouds and talked to me in my head," I said. "I didn't start seeing this shadow man until I got to the hospital."

Harper's hold tightens, and he places his chin on top of my head as he locks eyes with me in the mirror. I hate that look in his eyes. He looks at me as one would look at a child who doesn't understand anything yet.

"A person's personal demon appears and takes its form when the person gives it enough power. Before the demons have a form, they are nothing but shadows."

"None of this makes sense," I say, my voice rising with irritated apprehension. "I couldn't have given that thing power. The shadows were never there before…before my mother…before she died."

"People with real demons are born with them, so they were always there. Like most people, you did not pay shadows any attention or even notice they were there."

I scoff and say, "I think I would have noticed a shadowy demon hanging around."

"As I said before, they don't appear as shadow people right away," Harper says. "They are simply regular old shadows until they gain enough power to gain a form."

"But how did I give mine power?" I ask anxiously. "How can someone give something power without even knowing it exists?"

Harper's arms tighten as his muscles grow taut. "They play with their owner's minds and force them to give over power."

"How?" I ask.

He answers my question with another question. "Did you ever have random intrusive thoughts? Did that nagging voice in your head ever ask you to do something so vile that you would never dream of doing it? Have you ever been so angry that you felt like you would blow, and your thoughts churn and churn, making it worse?"

I shrug as much as Harper's hold allows. "Yeah, but those kinds of things happen to everyone."

"How often did those things happen to you?"

I pause to think. "I had intrusive thoughts a lot. I just ignored them or laughed them off. Every time I was angry, I had churning thoughts. I assumed it was my mind's way of dealing with negative emotions.

Also, everyone has that voice in their heads. Mine is just more evil than others."

Harper shakes his head and says, "None of that is normal, Sophia."

"But I never acted on any of those thoughts or listened to that voice," I say defensively. "And I eventually learned different techniques to calm myself down before the angry thoughts began."

Harper nods approvingly. "And that's why the demon never surfaced. It only started gaining power after your mother died, and everything aggravated you and pissed you off to the point that you forgot your coping techniques. You lashed out, you lived in depression, and you let the voices have free reign without shutting them out. Your anger gave your demon power.

"It gained enough power to show itself, and then it grew more aggressive in its efforts to gain more power by appearing to you and making you think you were losing your mind. It forced you to start spending more time in your depression, staying in the dark and living in the past, giving it even more power.

"You then tried to come out of the dark and cure yourself of your depression, which pissed it off. It talked you into hurting people even though you did not want to, even though you blamed it on your demon. You tried to kill it by killing yourself, but you were only giving it more power.

"The violence of the act gave it power. Your constant state of regret gave it power. Your anger gave it power. You eventually gave it enough power to take this form, despite my efforts to keep it dormant with medication.

"I should have known I could not keep it dormant forever. I knew it kept gaining power by those nightmares it was giving you. I thought I could keep it dormant long enough to teach you about it and help you control it. That's why I invited you here.

"However, when I invited you to come here, I didn't know it had already gained the power to take on that form. When you told me about your dream and seeing the shadow man the day we left the hospital, I knew I had to act fast.

"Then, Jeremy turned you against me, and we have wasted precious time. Now, it is perilously close to gaining enough power to take you over entirely despite having you on the highest dosage of the medication that usually keeps these fuckers at bay.

"If I don't teach you how to control it soon, it will take you, and you will be lost in the darkness of your own subconsciousness forever while this fucking demon lives your life."

Harper's tone had grown more aggressive as he spoke until his voice quivered with dread. He still holds me in his arms, but his chin no longer rests on my head. He holds my gaze in the mirror, and his look is…worried…Not angry, but worried.

I keep my attention on Harper, ignoring the narrowing of my shadow man's evil gaze and the threatening movement toward the mirror's surface.

Had I really given it that much power?

I swallow hard. My voice is raspy as I reply, "I didn't mean to. I didn't know…I didn't think…I didn't mean to."

"I know, Sophia. I know," Harper says, his tone tortured. "But now you know why I took you from Jeremy. I am not being cruel. I just need you to trust me, to let me help you."

"You lied to me," I say, trying to sound brave despite my voice wavering. "How can I trust you?"

"How did I lie to you?" Harper asks innocently.

"You told me you couldn't see the shadows," I seethe. "Even after I told you I could see them, you pretended you couldn't. You could have told me all this before, but you didn't. You say time was wasted because of Jeremy, but it was your fault, too."

Harper sighs in defeat. His arms release me and falls limply to his sides. I immediately move behind him, shielding myself from the terrifying shadow's gaze.

Harper turns around to face me, his eyes tortured and his tone pleading. "I know, and I was wrong. You have to know that everything I did, and still do, was to protect you. I admit I made some wrong decisions, but I am trying to rectify them."

I frown and cross my arms over my chest but do not say anything. I am pretty sure the look I shoot his way says it all.

Harper sighs, running his hands through his dark auburn hair. "I am sorrier than you know. But if you let me teach you, I will tell you everything from now on."

He gazes at me expectantly, and when I still do not answer, he simply says, "Please."

It was the please that was my undoing. That one word held so much hope, so much angst, so much pleading that I could not possibly stay angry with him, even if he told a thousand lies.

Besides, it would only be giving my demon more power.

I take a deep breath and let it out slowly. "What do I need to do?"

"All I ask is for your trust and forgiveness," Harper answers hopefully.

"I do forgive you," I say. "But it will take time for me to trust you again."

I see the hurt in Harper's eyes. I feel horrible for causing that hurt, but it cannot be helped. I am not going to lie to him to save his feelings.

"I understand," Harper says solemnly. "Will you at least work with me so I can teach you to control your demon?"

"I will try," I say.

"That's all I ask," Harper responds. "I will do my best to earn back your trust."

"You can start by letting me go and letting me see Jeremy again," I say hopefully.

"Sophia, I can't do that. Don't you see? He will only try to turn you against me again," Harper says, his anger rising.

"Maybe if you tell Jeremy the truth too, he will understand and not be suspicious of you anymore," I say convincingly. "He may even be able to help."

Silently, I wonder if Jeremy's ability to control shadow would help with inner demons, but I cannot ask Harper. That is Jeremy's secret to tell.

The corners of Harper's mouth turn down in an angry scowl. "I'll think about it, Sophia, but I don't trust Jeremy just like he doesn't trust me."

My frown matches his as I fist my hands and balance them on my hips. "What is it with you two? Why can't you get along?"

"It's complicated," Harper says, then adds, "And personal. Please, don't make me tell you."

I quirk my eyebrow. "I won't, for now. Eventually, though, you will have to tell me."

"And why is that?" Harper asks, his blue eyes turning the shade of storm clouds.

"Because, whether you like it or not, Jeremy and I are together. If you want me to trust you, and you want to continue to be my doctor and help me, then we will have to work this out."

Harper's jaw ticks as his eyes darken with rage. He moves closer to me until he is looming over me. I swallow and try to back up a step, but he catches me around the waist and pulls me into his body.

I catch myself against his chest, my palms pushing against a wall of hardened muscles. I struggle, but his arm tightens around my waist, and he uses his free hand to grab the hair on the back of my head, forcing me to hold still or pull my hair out.

His tone is livid as he asks, "You really did have sex with him, didn't you? You didn't just tell me that to make me jealous."

My heart beats furiously in my chest, and my breathing comes in short gasps as I struggle against Harper's hold. The nightmare comes tumbling back into my mind. My struggles become frantic as pure adrenaline and terror take over.

"Tell me the truth," Harper yells, his hot breath fanning my face as he brings my face close to his.

"Please, not again," I cry, pounding my fists into Harper's hard chest.

He lifts me off my feet, and I kick frantically, trying to connect with any part of him. But he holds me too close, and the angle is wrong. I only succeed in taps to his shin, which does nothing to make him let me go.

"What do you mean not again?" Harper asks, his tone slightly calmer. "I'm just asking you a question."

"Please, let me go," I cry weakly as I give up my struggles.

It's no use. He is too strong. I begin to tremble as I dangle in his hold, bracing myself for what Harper will do to me. Surprisingly, his hold loosens. He lets go of my hair and lets me slide down his body until my feet hit the floor.

"I'm not going to hurt you, Sophia," Harper says, his tone calm and even. He stands over me as if afraid I will bolt, but he makes no other move to touch me again.

I back away, giving him a wide berth as I move away from the damn mirror.

"But I am interested in why you think I would hurt you," Harper continues. "Just because I am angry that you and Jeremy had sex does not mean that I would hurt you."

My entire body trembles violently as the fear and adrenaline fade. I take a deep, calming breath as I continue to back toward the door. Harper watches me with weary eyes, but he makes no move to chase me.

"Tell me, Sophia. What has Jeremy told you about me that makes you fear me so?" His tone is gentle now.

I gulp. "Jeremy didn't tell me anything. It was…"

I stop suddenly. I came so close to telling Harper about the nightmare just now.

Maybe I should tell him. What could it hurt? Jeremy knew, so why not tell Harper?

"It was what?" Harper asks. "Please, tell me, Sophia."

"Fine. I'll tell you," I say, throwing my hands in the air surrenderingly. "But can we move away from the fucking mirror?"

"Why?" Harper asks. "He is gone now."

My gaze jerks to the mirror, my eyes wide, and my eyebrows raised. Harper is right. The shadow man…er…demon is gone. The only thing in the beautiful mirror's glassy surface are reflections.

"Where did he go?" I ask.

"Back inside you," Harper says. "You stopped paying attention to it, so it left. But it will be back, make no mistake. Now, please tell me why you are so frightened of me."

So, I do. I tell him all the horrible, gruesome details of the nightmare. When I am done, Harper stares at me with a look I cannot read.

"Sophia, you have to know I would never do anything like that to anybody, especially not you," Harper says ruefully.

"I want to believe you," I say. "But I have felt off ever since coming here. Then, Jeremy says he doesn't trust you, which gives me more reason to doubt you. And to top it all off, you separated us, and now I find out you have lied to me the entire time I have been under your care. What am I supposed to think or believe, Harper?"

"I can prove that the dream would never happen," Harper says.

"How?" I ask.

"First, you must promise you won't run away," Harper says.

I frown suspiciously. "Why should I promise that? What are you going to do?"

"Nothing that will hurt you, I promise." He says, and the sincerity in his sky-blue gaze makes me believe him.

I sigh. "Fine. I promise I won't run away."

"Good." Harper pauses, rubbing his hands together nervously as he takes a couple of calming breaths.

"The reason that I know the dream will never happen," Harper says.

"Is because…"

Harper pauses again, and I see his throat work as he swallows hard.

"Oh, for fuck's sake," I say frustratingly. "Just tell me already. I promise I won't run, and I won't get mad."

"Alright, alright," Harper says, running a hand through his auburn hair. "The reason I know the dream would never happen is because I have a demon, too."

My eyebrows raise so high they threaten to get lost in my hairline. I hold his stare for a heartbeat, and my visage twists in confusion.

"How does that prove that the dream wouldn't happen? If anything, it only proves that it would since a demon helped you rape me," I say.

"Not if my demon is the proof," Harper says nervously. "Not if I can show you that my demon is not the one that raped you."

I am even more confused. "What?"

Harper gestures toward the mirror as his eyes flash triumphantly. "My demon could never be the demon from your dream because my demon is female."

My heart ceases to beat, and time stands still. It is like moving in slow motion as I turn toward the mirror. I watch as the terrifying shadows slither from it.

The familiar swirling of the shadows commences, and I watch them take form. After a moment, the shadow lady with the diamond-colored eyes forms before me. I swear I see a shadowy smile stretch across her face like she is happy to see me. She waves …actually waves…at me as I watch her with my mouth hanging open.

"This is my demon," Harper says proudly. "And my demon would never hurt you when she has spent the last few weeks protecting you, even from your own demon. I am sure you have seen her around."

Well, hell…

CHAPTER 22

My brain buzzes with confusion. Jeremy was wrong. He did not accidentally create this shadow lady. She is not even a shadow at all. She is a demon. Harper's demon.

Harper has a demon. Wait…does Jeremy have a demon? He is an umbra-whatever that controls shadows, but is his violet-eyed shadow really a demon?

"Why do you look so confused?" Harper asks as I continue to stare at his shadow lady.

"I just didn't know she was an inner demon. I thought she was Jer…," I stop when I realize I had almost told Harper Jeremy's secret.

Scrambling for another explanation, I blurt, "I thought she was...um…I just…she told me not to go with you out in the hallway when I ran away from you. And I saw her again when you took Jeremy and me from the cafeteria. She seemed…sad."

"I said not to go with him, meaning Jeremy. It is not my fault you assumed wrong," The shadow lady's voice rings in my head. *"Also, I was sad because your demon took me out, and I could no longer protect you. I will have words with that bastard when I see him again."*

I throw my hands in the air in surrender. "Great, now I'm hearing your shadow…er demon…in my head too."

Harper sighs, gripping the bridge of his nose between his thumb and forefinger.

"There is much you need to learn," He mumbles.

I cross my arms over my chest. "Then teach me."

"Do not listen to them," The now-familiar voice of my demon whispers through my mind. *"Jeremy is stronger."*

I wait for the familiar tingle of fear that usually accompanies the voice of what I now know is my demon, but it does not come. Instead, I feel…

What do I feel?

Rage…

Burning, hot, fiery rage simmers under my skin, threatening to consume me in its burning fury. My hands ball into fists at my sides as my blood boils, pumping through my veins like lava.

I am tired of these fucking shadows and demons, and I am especially fucking tired of these overbearing men.

Harper takes a tentative step toward me, then pauses and looks toward the shadow lady. He frowns as if concentrating. His head whips back toward me, and his blue eyes fill with anxious worry.

"Sophia, is your demon speaking to you now?" He asks.

I do not trust myself to speak right now, so I only nod.

"What is it saying?" Harper asks.

"HE says I should not listen to you," I say through gritted teeth, emphasizing the gender of my demon. "And that Jeremy is more powerful than you and your demon."

Harper quirks an eyebrow. "Didn't we just talk everything out? Are we going to go down this road again? You should not let your demon manipulate you."

The anger bubbles inside my chest. "You are the one who has me locked up. You are the one who is keeping me away from Jeremy. You are the one manipulating me into thinking that you care!"

Harper flinches. "I do care, Sophia. Why would I risk sending you my demon to protect you if I didn't?"

"How do I know she was protecting me? For all I know, you sent her to keep me away from Jeremy," I say harshly.

"Jeremy is only using you," Harper retorts. "You don't know who he really is!"

"Really?" I say, sarcasm dripping from my tone. "Well, then, why don't you tell me?"

Haper growls and answers, "You wouldn't even know what I was talking about if I did tell you. You have not had any training yet."

I cross my arms and glare. "Try me."

Huffing, Harper stalks toward me and says, "Fine."

He stops inches in front of me, his stormy blue eyes filled with rage as he spits out, "He is an umbrakinetic, a person who controls shadows, and demons are simply another form of shadow."

I am slightly surprised that Harper knows Jeremy's secret, but that realization does nothing to deter the rage swirling inside my gut.

Without thinking about what I am saying, I yell, "I already knew that, you moron!”

Harper’s eyes grow wide, and then he frowns. “Jeremy told you that?”

“Yes,” I snap. “He tells me everything, unlike some people!”

“He told you he can control demons?” Harper asks sarcastically.

I start to answer, and then I stop. Jeremy had not told me he could control demons, only shadows. However, did Jeremy know that my shadows were really an inner demon?

“He didn’t tell me he could control demons, only that he could control shadows,” I say, my voice calmer. “But that doesn't mean anything. He probably didn’t know my shadows were actually an inner demon.”

“Oh, he knows,” Harper seethes. “Regrettably, I told him before I found out I couldn’t trust him with you.”

“But I told Jeremy that I saw shadows, so as far as he knows, I do not know about my demon yet,” I argue. “Maybe he was controlling my demon all along to protect me.”

Harper shakes his head. “No, love. He cannot control personal demons. Only the demon’s owner can control them. He is manipulating you for other reasons.”

I shrug angrily. “What reasons?”

Harper answers darkly, “He wants your demon, Sophia. He cares nothing for you.”

“I thought you said he couldn’t control my demon,” I say triumphantly. “You lie so much you contradict yourself.”

“I am not lying,” Harper answers calmly. “I said he could not control your demon. I never said he couldn’t take it. You have a powerful demon, Sophia. Many umbrakinetics would risk much to have him.”

“How do you know?” I ask irritatingly.

“Because I am an umbrakinetic as well,” he answers. “And if I was power-hungry like most, I would want your demon.”

I huff, “Fine, you can have my fucking demon! Jeremy can have it! Someone, please take it because I do not want it!”

“Sophia, he is part of you. No one could take him unless you are dead, and then he would have to be bonded to the person’s demon that takes him,” Harper says patiently.

I stare at Harper in confusion for a heartbeat, and then my brain catches up to the words Harper is saying. My head begins to shake back and forth.

"No, that cannot be. Why would my demon tell me to trust him? My demon won't let me die," I say.

"Your demon won't let you die because it would die, but if he was bonded to another demon, then he wouldn't," Harper says, his tone calm. "Untrained inner demons don't care about their owners. They only care about power; demons are more powerful if bonded, especially with another powerful demon. Jeremy's demon is powerful."

"How does a demon bond with another?" I ask, but deep inside, I know the answer. Still, I have to know if my instincts are correct.

"Demons will bond if their owners are lovers. They bond through sex, but only if the demons participate."

Fuck.

I swallow hard and ask, "Would both demons have to participate?"

Harper takes a deep breath and fists his hair with both hands. "Oh, goddess, Sophia, please tell me you didn't."

"Only his demon participated," I say shakily. "Mine never appeared during…during the act."

Harper releases his hair and runs his hands down his face as he mutters, "Thank the Goddess."

"So, what would Jeremy get out of it if our demons did bond and I died?" I ask carefully, dreading the answer yet needing it anyway.

"The demon would essentially become Jeremy's demon, which would make him powerful as hell," Harper answers. "There are not many umbrakinetics with two demons.

"The ones that do have two demons gained their second demons when the loved ones they were bonded with passed. They did not manipulate to steal more power; they inherited it.

"But Jeremy is after power. He doesn't care about you. He only cares about stealing your demon. He will kill you if he bonds your demon with his."

"Harper lies," My demon whispers in my mind. *"Harper is the one who wants to steal me from you. Jeremy wants us to join with him to protect us from Harper."*

Confusion swirls within me, and I do not know who to trust or what to believe.

"Think about it. I showed you that dream as a warning."

"You made me have that dream?" I ask indignantly. *"So it's your*

fault I am afraid to be touched…and you helped…what the fuck?"

"It was only a dream, Sophia. I nor Harper did that to you. I was only showing you a possibility of what could happen…"

"But, how do you know?" I ask my demon aloud, interrupting his explanation as my temper grows.

"Because Jeremy's demon told me," He answers.

"How do you know you can trust it?" I ask. "How do you know the stupid demon isn't lying to you?"

My demon does not answer me. Good. I did not want to speak to it any longer.

Harper grabs me gently by my upper arms and shakes me slightly to get my attention.

His tone is soft as he says, "Sophia, don't listen to your demon. You have to control him. If your demon takes over, he could force you to bond him with Jeremy's demon, and then Jeremy will kill you to take him."

I shake my head. "That cannot be true. Jeremy could never hurt me. My demon trusts Jeremy, not you."

"I told you, Sophia, your demon is untrained. It only seeks power. It does not know you well enough to love you yet." Harper's tone is patient, kind even, and it pisses me off.

He sounds so…condescending…as if he is talking to a child. The anger that had begun to fade rages once more, building to a dangerous level.

"You cannot trust your demon any more than you can trust Jeremy or his demon," Harper adds, and I explode.

"That's a lie!" I scream. "Jeremy is in love with me, and we will be together when we get out of this place!"

Harper scoffs. "Don't be so gullible and naive, Sophia. It does not become you."

I let out an enraged squeal and try to pull away from this infuriating man.

His grip on my arms tightens as he says, "Your anger is not good. Your demon is manipulating you into feeding it power through negative emotions and actions. It feeds off high emotions and great acts, but positivity will also feed it. You will have a more compliant demon if you feed it positivity."

I continue to struggle as I yell, "Fine, I am positive that I hate you right now!"

"Sophia, you promised you would try," Harper says patiently, tightening his hold even more.

"And you promised to tell me the truth!" I scream.

Harper huffs. "I am telling you the truth!"

"No!" I scream as I struggle.

Harper does not answer. He only holds me tighter, pulling me to his chest, wrapping his arms around me, and waiting out my struggles.

And I struggle.

Hard.

But it does not matter. Harper's hold is too strong for me to get away. The struggle is more internal than physical. I struggle with the nagging thought that Harper might be right. I struggle with the infuriating reasoning behind it. And I struggle with the idea that I am gullible and naive, just as Harper said.

But I have never been in a relationship. I have never had a man show interest, or I never noticed if they did. I was always too busy proving myself, proving that I was intelligent, brave, and capable enough to make it on my own.

Especially after the fight with my mother when I announced I was moving out, and when she had told me that I would never make it without her.

And now, here I am without her.

Literally.

And I am not thriving. Hell, I am barely surviving. She had been right all along. That, more than anything, pissed me off enough to, strangely, calm me down and make me think.

My struggles slow as I continue to think.

Jeremy never showed any interest in me before. I was just simply his friend. Had he only started showing interest after I told him about the shadow man? I tried to remember but couldn't.

Mainly because I did not want to. I did not want to have doubts about Jeremy. I did not want to have hard feelings toward Harper, either. I didn't want any of this, but I had no choice.

I had a stupid demon inside me, and it was my responsibility to control it before it made me hurt anyone else. I had to get a grip before someone else lost an eye. If Harper could help me do that, I needed to let him.

My struggles cease, and I take a breath as another emotion grips me. My chest tightens, and tears prick the backs of my eyes. A sob escapes my lips as my muscles relax, and I lean my head into Harper's rock-hard chest.

Harper holds me while I cry out my frustrations. He holds me while I let go of old illusions. He holds me while I weep over Jeremy and what could have been if only we were ordinary people with typical problems.

Minutes pass, or is it hours? It could be days for all I know. I lose all sense of time and space. When I finally come back to myself, I am being held in Harper's grip.

One arm is under my head, the other under my knees. He holds me like a baby resting in his arms, and we are moving. I don't know where we are going, nor do I care. I am too tired and emotionally wrecked to care.

The sounds of Harper's steps are magnified as he walks through a hallway, and the sound echoes off the walls. A door creaks open, and darkness envelops us for a heartbeat before the light shines brightly through my closed eyelids.

I moan, the light burning my tear-soaked, sensitive eyes despite them being closed. I feel Harper's muscles tense.

"Sorry, dear," Harper whispers, then darkness envelops us again.

My back hits something soft and Harper's arms slide out from under my head and knees. I whimper at the loss of the comforting touch, the cold seeping into my bones.

"Please," I say, my voice barely a whisper. "Don't leave me."

"I had no intention of leaving," Harper says.

I am covered with something thick and warm, and then Harper's arms are around me again, pulling my back to his front. He spoons me in his embrace, tucking me against him firmly.

"Sleep now. I'm here," He whispers softly.

I sigh contentedly, warm and snuggled in his arms. I don't care that I shouldn't be in Harper's bed. I don't care that my world has shifted, and I should be upset about it.

I don't care about anything except the overwhelming sense of peace and warmth that envelops me as I drift off to sleep, surrounded by the comfort of arms I do not know I can trust.

But damn, do they feel good.

CHAPTER 23

I wake in darkness, suffocated in someone's embrace. I do not know where I am as I come to full wakefulness, then memory comes slowly back.

Harper.

We had a horrendous fight, and I ended up being carried away in his arms. He took me to bed and tucked me in. He is still here. He stayed with me, holding me while I slept.

How sweet.

If only I could believe he was sincere.

My thoughts turn to Jeremy. Was he sincere? I wish I knew. I wish I knew who was telling the truth and who was only playing with my emotions. Maybe it would be better if I swore off both of them.

Harper was supposed to teach me how to control the shadows. I would at least let him do that much. I did not want to live in darkness inside my own head for the rest of my life.

I hear Harper snore. He is still asleep, and I really need to pee. It is still dark in the room, but I don't know if it is because it is late or because the curtains are closed.

Either way, I do not want to wake up Harper.

Holding my breath, I slowly slide out from under the arm draped around my shoulders. At the same time, I pull my legs from under Harper's leg. When I am free, I roll away to the side of the bed, drape my legs over the side, and carefully rise to a standing position.

I hear a snort and a grunt, and then Harper rolls over to his other side. I stand there, still holding my breath as I wait. Harper commences snoring, and I blow out the breath I was holding and sigh with relief.

I try not to think about how adorable it is that Harper snores as I practically run out the door and take in my surroundings. Thankfully,

Harper had taken me to my bedroom, which is closer to the bathroom than Harper's bedroom. I would have pissed myself if I would have had to come all the way around the circular hallway from Harper's room.

I make it into the bathroom, hurriedly pull down my scrub pants, settle myself on the porcelain throne, and sigh with ecstasy as I relieve myself. I had made it just in time, and the release of my overly full bladder almost felt better than an orgasm…

Almost…

With my bladder now empty, I have an overwhelming desire for a shower. I pull the biggest towel I can find out of the linen closet on the back wall of the bathroom and set it on the vanity sink.

The circular-shaped shower stall calls my name as I turn around and turn on the hot water. I barely turn on the cold. I want it as hot as I can stand it.

I open the medicine cabinet above the sink and pull out my toothbrush, toothpaste, floss, and mouthwash in preparation for a good mouth scrubbing.

I close the medicine cabinet door and glance away quickly. I do not want to look in the mirror today. It is bad enough that I am standing in front of it. I look down at the sink, concentrating on pulling out a sizable amount of floss and looping it around my thumbs.

I turn away from the mirror and begin flossing when the lights flicker on and off, followed by an electric buzzing sound. The lights flicker again as the buzzing grows louder, and then the lights go off altogether. The buzzing stops.

Fucking great.

There is a small, round window in the bathroom that is high up on the circular wall above the toilet, which sits behind a divider wall beside the shower. Thankfully, the sun is out, and light streams from the tiny window, so I am not thrown into total darkness when the lights go out.

A tiny thrill of dread snakes along my spine, but I shrug it off. I am getting better about being in darkness. Besides, there is still enough light that I can see well enough to find my soap, shampoo, and conditioner. I am fine. I will wake Harper afterward so he can fix the lights.

I finish flossing and pick up the toothbrush. I slather it with toothpaste and begin brushing. Something catches my gaze, and I mistakenly glance over to the mirror. My eyes lock on the reflection of movement behind me.

My heart races as I spit out the toothpaste to avoid choking on it. I wipe my mouth quickly as the movement draws closer, and then I let out a shaky laugh when I realize what is moving behind me.

The steam rises from the top of the shower, billowing in frothy clouds up and over the shower doors. It looked like shadows floating around in the darkness, which kicked up the fear fluttering in my chest.

"Fucking shadows and demons," I mutter as I shake my head at my own reflection.

I was tired of this…

I was tired of constantly being afraid of everything around me. I was tired of being confused about everyone around me and not knowing who I could and could not trust. I was tired of being ignorant while everyone else was informed.

I was fucking tired.

I turn my back on my reflection and undress. A shiver of cold runs through my body but is quickly warmed when I open the shower door and am surrounded by warm, moist steam. I step into the water and sigh delightedly.

The hot water is heavenly.

I stand there for a long moment, enjoying the ecstasy of the hot water warming my skin and the steam heating my lungs as I breathe it in. I have been cold for so long that it feels nice to finally be warm, even if it is only on the outside.

I still feel a chill that will always be there, deep inside my bones.

"Sooophiiiaaa…" My name is whispered ominously in the dark room, the sound coming from all around me as if carried in the steam.

As fear flows through my veins, a sprinkling of goosebumps breaks out all along my flesh. The fine hairs along my arms and the back of my neck stand on end, and my breath freezes in my lungs. My heart pounds against my chest, ringing in my ears like the beating of a bass drum. My eyes go wide in the darkness of the shower as the hot water runs down my back.

The water is not warming me now. The icy terror that runs through me is too cold.

"Sophia," The whispering voice calls again, deep and baritone, like rumbling thunder. *"I am coming for you."*

I open my mouth to scream, but no sound comes out. I take in a deep, gasping breath as my lungs work again, but all that comes out is a squeak of terror, working its way around the gigantic lump in my throat.

Something cold caresses my arm, and I flinch away from the touch. Another squeal of terror escapes my mouth as I move to the other side of the shower out of the spray of water.

That was a mistake.

My demon stands in the water, staring out of the spray with his red eyes glowing through the darkness like a beacon. His shadowy smile is malicious, almost victorious, as I huddle against the slick, tiled, rounded side of the shower wall.

Something slithers behind me, wiggling and inserting itself against my back, between me and the shower wall. I try to scream, but icy hands clamp down on the top of my head, holding me like a vice. It freezes the scream in my throat and paralyzes me.

I am frozen in place. I cannot move, I cannot scream, and the horror that fills me causes my entire body to tremble violently. The sensation of the hands on my head terrifies me, but not as much as the sensation of the fingers.

It feels like they are piercing through my skull and stroking my brain. My senses shut down suddenly. I am still paralyzed, but now I cannot see, feel, or hear anything. It is like I am back in the sensory deprivation tank. However, instead of floating in nothingness, I feel like I am being pulled from reality.

Random pictures and flashes of light play in my mind as I am sucked through time and space.

I see my mother lying on the cold ground as her life bleeds away from the gunshot wound in her chest. She had been caught in the crossfire during the mall parking lot shooting. We would have still been inside and safe had I not insisted we hurry and leave.

Why had I been in such a hurry?

I see the faces of those people, the ones from that fateful group meeting. I had been telling the group how angry I was that the shooter had shot himself because I wished it had been me who had beaten him with my bare hands for killing my mother. My demon had been pissed that I was finally seeking some way out of the dark depression I had fallen into after my mother's death, so he saw to it that I got my wish.

Only, it was not the shooter that I had beaten with that folded metal chair. I remember the feel of the cold steel in my hands and the satisfaction I felt after every contact of the metal against flesh.

I see my friend Tamara's horror-filled face as I hover over her with the pencil in my hand. The mutilation of her eye had been the start of my rampage and the end of my life as I had known it.

I see Harper's heartbreakingly handsome face as he shines that stupid penlight in my eyes, telling me to follow his finger as he examines me for…I don't know what for. I watch his mouth move as he talks to me, but I hear nothing.

I am nothing. I am an empty shell of a person who had just beaten four people and mutilated the person who had been my friend for years.

And, finally, I see Jeremy coming toward me with that smile that makes my heart turn somersaults inside my chest as I wait in the empty community room for the nurse to show me to my room.

He holds his hand out to me, and I take it. He pulls me down the hallway to his room and shuts the door.

Wait…

We are not allowed to shut the door. We will be in trouble.

"Wait, Jeremy, we can't shut the door!" I say. Then my brain wakes up, and I realize…

I can speak…I can move…and I am…

Where am I?

How did I get back here?

Jeremy says nothing as he turns the lock, and then he turns to me with that smile still on his face.

"Jeremy?" I say, my voice shaky with fear. "What the hell is going on? How did we get here? How are you here? How…"

Jeremy interrupts my tirade. "Sophia, stop. Your body is not really here."

My breathing is fast and ragged, and my heart threatens to beat out of my chest. How can I not be here when those sensations are so real?

"Am I dreaming?" I ask breathlessly.

Jeremy looks thoughtful for a moment before answering, "Kind of. It is like a dream, but everything that happens here is real. You can experience everything your body does, and your body can experience everything you do."

"I'm confused," I say, my tone filled with fear.

"This is a different dimension where shadows roam. Your soul, the part of you connected to the shadows, is here while your body is back there. He brought you here."

Jeremy points to a corner of his room behind me. I turn to look where he is pointing and gasp. His violet-eyed demon stands in the corner, shrouded in darkness and shadow. It gives me a slight nod, then dissipates into the drifting shadows.

I turn back to Jeremy. My voice is biting when I ask, "What is going on?"

Jeremy moves closer to me, his hazel eyes looking me up and down as he answers, "I just needed to see you to make sure you were okay."

He pauses and moves closer still. His gaze moves to mine, his eyes tortured as he continues, "Goddess, Sophia, I missed you so much. It was pure hell not knowing what had happened to you."

He is close enough to touch me now, but he makes no move to do so. He runs his hand through his silky, sandy locks and blows out a breath. "I am a shitty boyfriend. I couldn't even protect you. But I swear I am working on getting you out of there."

I back up a step and ball my hands into fists at my side. "Don't bother," I say firmly. "I am fine where I am."

Jeremy frowns in confusion. "You can't mean that, Sophia. Fuck, did Harper tell you some bullshit about me?"

I narrow my eyes. "No, Jeremy, Harper told me the truth. Well, mostly. I don't know about the rest."

Jeremy's eyes go cold, turning a shade of green I have never seen in his eyes before. His jaw tenses as he asks, "What did that son of a bitch tell you?"

"He told me about my demon," I answer through gritted teeth, watching the guilt fill his visage before continuing. "He said you knew about it…but you didn't tell me."

"He made me promise not to tell you. Dammit!" he pauses, punching the air with a fist as he turns away. "He set this up! He did it to make me look bad! And I stupidly fell for it."

Jeremy bows his head, his shoulders slumping in defeat. His tone is filled with regret and sorrow as he says, "I'm sorry, Sophia. I should have told you anyway."

"Why didn't you?" I ask, not showing an ounce of remorse.

"Harper said he could help you," Jeremy explains. "He told me if you knew too soon, it would just freak you out and give your demon more power over you. Then everything happened, and there was no time. I tried to tell you, but you wouldn't let me. You said…"

"Oh, hell no," I interrupt, shaking a finger at him. "Don't put this off on me. You had plenty of opportunity to tell me something like this. But you didn't. You and Harper let me go on believing that I was some kind of crazy person seeing shadows everywhere. Well, I am done with both of you!

"I will let Harper teach me how to control this damn demon. Then, I am going to complete my program so I won't be in trouble with the law. Finally, I will return to my restaurant and my life and hope I never hear of shadows, demons, or umbra…whatevers….again!"

I am raging when I get done, and Jeremy stares at me as if I have grown another head. His eyes are wide, and his mouth is hanging open. He blinks several times before drawing in a breath and letting it out slowly.

"It's obvious that you are mad at me…"

I cut him off before he can continue. "Mad? No, I am not mad…I am fucking furious! I am tired of being afraid. I am tired of not knowing who to trust. I just want to go home!"

"Sophia, please cal…"

"Don't you dare tell me to calm down! Just make your demon take me back or wake me up or whatever he needs to do! Do you know what I went through to get here? I had to relive everything all over again!"

My breathing is ragged, and the room spins when I am done. My fists are so tight that my palms sting from the bite of my nails. My chest heaves as I try to calm my breathing.

Jeremy takes a slow step toward me as he says, "Oh, I see. I understand why you would be upset about that."

"Upset? Upset? Jeremy, I am way beyond upset. I am absolutely livid."

"I forgot that happens when you are dragged through your own head into your subconscious. But it had to be done to bring you into this dimension. I am sorry."

Jeremy backs away from me and sits on the bed. He places his head in his hands and sighs defeatedly. "I knew Harper would turn you against me."

I advance on him, one hand on my hip and the other still pointing my finger at him. "Don't blame this on Harper. This is no one's fault but your own. You could have told me, Jeremy. And I don't want to hear Harper told you not to. Since when have you ever listened to Harper?"

"I did at first," Jeremy says, his tone laced with regret. "He said he would help me, and when I told him about you, he said he would help you too."

Jeremy pauses, raising his head from his hands and piercing me with his hazel gaze before continuing, "He had me convinced he wanted to help us. Then he brought me here, and I caught him talking to his demon about you. I didn't hear most of the conversation, but I didn't trust him after that."

He stands and moves closer, running his hand through his hair. "Then I found out Harper had invited you here. I created a diversion to keep him here, away from you. It didn't work. He hired those brutes to watch us so he could return to the hospital. When I found myself in the fortunate position of being able to see you before you came here, I tried to talk you out of coming, but…'

"Wait, wait," I interrupt. "So when Harper left and stayed away for an entire month because of some emergency, that was you?"

Jeremy shrugs sheepishly and answers, "Well, yeah. I was trying to keep him away from you until I could find out what he wanted with you."

"What did you do that kept him busy for a month?" I ask suspiciously. "You told me he was cooperating in a murder investigation."

"Well, yeah. Do you know how hard it is to make a suicide look like murder?"

I back away from him. "Jeremy, you didn't," I say shakily.

He waves a hand in the air dismissively as he moves closer. "That doesn't matter right now. The point is I brought you here to warn you. I am doing what I can to get to you, but…"

I narrow my eyes, holding up a hand to ward him off and interrupting him again. "No, Jeremy. I am tired of being in the middle of your and Harper's fight. Whatever you two have against each other, you need to work it out between yourselves."

Jeremy huffs in frustration and replies, "Sophia, I fear that Harper wants to steal your demon. You are in danger."

I cross my arms over my chest, my tone derisive as I say, "Yeah, that's the same thing Harper says about you."

Anger passes through Jeremy's gaze. "Of course he says that. Do you really believe I would do that?"

I sigh defeatedly. "Jeremy, I don't know what to believe. Both of you have lied to me and kept things from me. Neither one of you will tell me the whole truth. I think the best thing for me is to learn to control this thing and get on with my life."

He takes another step toward me, reaching his hand out to me as he says, "Sophia, please…"

But I do not give him a chance to finish. "No, Jeremy. I am done. Now, have your demon take me back."

Jeremy's visage changes. His eyes grow dark, like the darkest green of a stormy sky. His tone is angry when he snaps, "No."

I back up another step. "No? What… are you going to leave me stuck in some kind of dreamland?"

"No. I'm going to leave you stuck inside this dimension, which is nowhere and everywhere at the same time. Only demons can bring you here and take you back. Your body will be in a coma, and when Harper takes you to a hospital, I will find out where your body is and let you return with me there."

I step back one more time, and my back hits something solid. My voice wavers as I say, "You can't do that."

Jeremy smirks triumphantly. "Yes, I can. You're stuck here, love, until I decide to let you go."

"Stop playing around and take me back, Jeremy. I'm not kidding around," I say sternly.

"Neither am I," Jeremy says darkly, his smirk turning sinister. "I am not going to let Harper have you. I will protect you no matter what."

"I don't need your protection. I can handle myself. I know what it takes to bond a demon, and I simply won't let Harper do anything," I say, pressing myself against the wall.

"He could take you by force, you know. Don't you remember your nightmare?" Jeremy moves closer, the evil smile still playing on his face.

"I'm coming," A tinny female voice in my head says. I know it is Harper's demon. I have heard her voice enough to know it by now.

"Hurry," I tell her in my mind.

Aloud, I say to Jeremy, "Yes, I remember the nightmare. He looked at me like you are looking at me now."

Jeremy chuffs out a malicious snicker. "You are rather infuriating at times. I would love to bend you over my knee and spank your naked ass right now, but I would never do it without your consent."

A sudden rush of longing shoots through me as I imagine that scenario. Me naked, bent over Jeremy's knee. The sensation of his hands on my ass, the sound of flesh hitting flesh, the sting of pain mixing with the pleasure…

Maybe I could stay a bit longer.

NO!

I refuse to let myself get distracted by either of these sexy, possibly evil men right now. I need to concentrate on learning how to control this fucking demon, not how many ways I can fuck Jeremy or Harper.

"There it is," Jeremy says, bringing his face close to mine and whispering the rest of his statement. "There is that look I love seeing on your face. The look you get when you know I am getting ready to make you feel good."

I roll my eyes. "We have only had sex one time…well, a couple of times…but it was all one session. We haven't been together enough for you to know my looks."

"Maybe we need to remedy that," Jeremy says against my mouth as he kisses my lips softly.

The rush of longing grows into a whirlwind of want and need. He cups my cheek with his palm, slanting his head to the side to deepen the kiss. I am frozen to the spot. Partly because there is a wall at my back, but mainly because I do not know how to react.

I still want him, even though he may be using me. I still ache for him, even though he might want to kill me and steal my demon.

What the fuck is wrong with me?

Thankfully, I am saved from having to assert my willpower to break away from the kiss by Harper's demon. I feel the grip on either side of my head and gasp at the sensation of fingers entering my brain.

I hear Jeremy's scream of fury before I am ripped away from the kiss and thrown from reality. Just like in the shower, I am transported back through space and time, only this time, the pictures fly by too fast to see or feel anything.

Thank goodness for small miracles. I don't think my frayed nerves could have handled living through those scenes again.

The only sensations that assault me as I fly back into my own head are relief at not having to deal with Jeremy any longer and dread at seeing Harper again.

Because I know he is there, waiting for his demon to bring me back to my body.

A fluttering sensation alights in my stomach, making me nauseous. I feel as if I am freefalling for an instant in time. It is over almost as quickly as it had begun, and then I am lying on my back with water cascading over my face.

"Sophia! God, Sophia, please, please, wake up. Dammit, Jewel, hurry up and bring her back!" Harper's voice sounds panicked and hurried.

Who is Jewel?

"She is back, master," The tittering tones of Harper's demon says.

Harper's overwhelmingly relieved voice responds, "Thank the fucking universe. Thank you, Jewel. You have done well."

"My pleasure, master," The demon says.

Jewel.

That must be her name.

Do demons have names?

My eyes flutter open to see Harper's worried expression staring down at me. He shuts off the water and then turns back to me.

"Sophia, are you alright? Did that bastard hurt you?"

"I'm fine," I answer, my voice sounding hoarse and scratchy. "How long was I out? And how did you know where I was?"

"You were out for about an hour, and your demon told my demon where you were," Harper answers, the relief evident in his tone.

I must have looked hopeful at that statement because Harper adds, "Don't read too much into it. He only told Jewel so he could gloat about it."

Figures.

"Come on, I'll help you up and get you a towel," Harper says.

And then I realize…

Harper is standing over me, and I am lying on the shower floor…

Soaking wet and…

Completely…fucking…naked.

Well, shit.

CHAPTER 24

Harper's demon stands behind him, her diamond eyes shining like a beacon. Harper turns away and grabs my towel from the sink, giving me a clear view of the medicine cabinet's mirror. My demon smiles back at me from the mirror's reflective surface.

A thrill of fear runs through me. I am naked. Harper's demon and my demon are present. If there is ever a time that Harper has the chance to bond my demon with his, it would be now.

He could force me like he did in my nightmare, and I would be powerless to stop him. I do not know how to control my demon, Harper's demon would do anything he told her to do, and Harper is much stronger than me.

I would not stand a chance.

But Harper is a perfect gentleman. He turns back to me with my towel in his hands, holding it out to me as if he were holding my coat. I stand carefully in the wet, slick shower and curl into the offered towel.

Harper wraps it around me and tucks the corner in, securing the towel just above my breasts. It hangs well past my sex, almost to my knees. I have never been more thankful for giant towels.

He retrieves a second towel and instructs me to bend over with my hair hanging over my head. He wraps the towel into a turban, bundling my hair into it and securing it to the top of my head. He produces a brush from the sink drawer and then motions me toward the door.

"Let's go to the sitting room, and I'll brush your hair for you," He says softly.

His tone is calm and gentle as if he is trying to tame a wild animal. He follows me as I walk down the circular hallway to the sitting room. The room is bright from the sunlight streaming in through the sliding glass doors that lead out onto the turret's open-air balcony.

The tufted, nineteenth-century French-style loveseat in the center of

the room is bathed in the light, bringing out its burgundy and tan
colors. A matching ottoman sits at one end of the sofa, creating an
inviting place to sit. Other pieces of nineteenth-century French
furniture are placed strategically in the room, surrounding the sofa as
the main centerpiece.

The plush carpet of the circular room matches the burgundy color
of the sofa, and the walls are painted to match the tan color. The fancy
crown molding all throughout the room is burgundy as well.

It is a beautiful room, classy and inviting, like its owner. Said
owner strolls over to the sofa, sits on the tufted surface, and places the
ottoman before him. He pats the seat and gives me a suggestive look.

I walk slowly to the ottoman, never taking my eyes from Harper's.
His visage is serene, his blue eyes striking in the light. He smiles that
dazzling smile that used to light me on fire from the inside, and I melt.

Apparently, that smile still works.

I sit before Harper on the ottoman facing away from him and sigh
with ecstasy when his hands go to work on my hair. He massages as
he brushes, running his fingers all along my scalp as the brush runs
through the locks.

His touch relaxes every nerve in my body until I am putty in his
hands. He delicately runs the brush through my hair until every tangle
is tamed, and my hair hangs down my back in soft, wavy elegance.

Suddenly, a memory pops into my head, reminding me of another
time when a man was brushing my hair. My skin heats with the
recollection, and I squirm on the ottoman. It felt wonderful at first, but
now it has become dangerous with the surface of that remembrance.

I clear my throat and say, "Umm, Harper, I think that should be
enough."

I reach back for the brush, and he pulls it through my hair one last
time before laying it in my hand.

"Are you feeling better?" Harper asks as I take the brush.

I nod vigorously. "Yes, thank you very much."

Harper frowns as he looks me up and down. "What's wrong,
Sophia? What happened while you were away?"

"I don't really want to talk about it right now," I say softly, and I
hate how my voice quivers.

I feel Harper's presence behind me when he rises from the loveseat.
He walks around the ottoman until he is in front of me, then kneels
into my line of sight. The look in his sapphire eyes constricts my

heart.

He looks so…utterly defeated….like his entire world crumbled before his eyes. He opens his mouth to speak, and, mother of God, if his voice matches that look…

"Sophia, I don't know how to make you trust me again, but I cannot stand you hating me anymore."

Fuck.

His tone matched the look.

My chest tightens, and tears sting the back of my eyes. My voice sounds choked as I speak around the lump in my throat. "Harper, I don't hate you. Just because I don't trust you doesn't mean I hate you."

"But you don't love me anymore," He says, and my heart sinks down to my toes.

What the ever-loving-fuck?

"Harper, when did I ever tell you that I loved you, and what the hell does that have to do with me trusting you?" I ask in confusion.

"You used to be head-over-heels in love with me," Harper says with a sad little smirk. "You would tell me anything back then, even things you did not want to talk about to others. I felt like your superhero, your protector. It was the most wonderful feeling in the world, and I took it for granted.

"Now, I feel like the annoying fly in your face that won't leave you alone unless you go get the fly swatter, and then it only comes back to bug you again when you put the fly swatter down."

I cannot help the laughter that bubbles up in my chest. My voice is filled with it as I respond, "Harper, you won't even go away if I had a hundred fly swatters."

The helplessness in his eyes dissipates a bit, and the corners of his mouth lift slightly. "No, I suppose not. I am very hard to get rid of."

"You don't say?" I say sarcastically.

The tiny smile I had managed to put on Harper's face fades. "Seriously, Sophia. I am putting myself out there in hopes you will want me again. I am making myself vulnerable to you, and I never make myself vulnerable to anyone. I can't afford to. I am a psychiatrist, and because of that, I have to be strong all the time for everyone. But for you, I will fall on my knees and beg like a pathetic dog if it will make you feel something for me again.

"I am so sorry I took you for granted. I am so sorry I did not tell you the whole truth. I am so sorry I handled this badly. And I am especially sorry that I did not tell you that I loved…love…you too. I am sorry for it all. Just please, please, give me another chance.”

I can barely believe what my ears are hearing. Does he expect me to believe and forgive him just like that? Wasn't he the one that called me naïve and gullible, and now he wants me to just fall at his feet with his confession of love?

Besides, I just got done telling myself that I was done with these two sexy, possibly evil men. But maybe I can have a little bit of fun first. After all, Harper used to tease me all the time.

It would be amusing to tease him for a change.

I quirk an eyebrow, trying to mask what I am really feeling. "So, do it," I say nonchalantly.

Harper frowns. "Do what?" He asks.

"You said you would beg me like a pathetic dog," I say, standing from my seat and folding my arms over my chest. "So, do it."

Harper stands as well, as his frown deepens. "I pour my heart out to you, and all you got out of that entire speech was how I said I would beg like a pathetic dog to get you to give me another chance?"

"Uh-huh. So, do it." I say with an indifferent shrug.

"You are serious?" Harper asks, raising his eyebrows.

"Yep," I say, not backing down. The utter confusion on Harper's face threatens to bring out my laughter, but I keep my features neutral.

"If that's what it will take, then fine," Harper says, and he drops to the floor.

The man actually gets down on all fours and looks up at me with a pathetic look on his face. He rises onto his knees and positions his hands in front of him in a mock-dog-begging pose.

"How is this? Do you think this would pass Barb's inspection?" He asks humorously.

I lose it.

Laughter bubbles up from deep inside, shaking my belly as I let it out. I have not laughed like this in so long. It feels strange but good. Harper joins me, laughing so hard that he cannot get up from the floor.

He captures my hand and pulls me down with him. I am laughing too hard to resist, so I tumble to the floor beside him, clutching my towel to me to cover my nakedness. Hell, he has already seen me anyway. But still, I hold the towel tightly.

I lay in a useless heap on the floor as the laughter renders me helpless. Harper falls down beside me, his deep baritone laugh sending shivers of delight all through me.

I admit, it feels good to be laughing with Harper again.

It feels great that I exist to him again.

It feels amazing that he actually reciprocated my feelings all that time.

If he is telling the truth.

My laughter fades as sadness engulfs me again. Harper's laughter fades as well, and he sits up to find me watching him.

"I like seeing you laugh," I tell him when he shoots me a questioning look. "I haven't seen you laugh in a while."

"It has been a while since you were happy," Harper answers. "I am happy when you are happy."

I frown. "Harper, you can't keep saying stuff like that to me."

"Why not?" He asks.

"Because it isn't true," I say. "And if it is true, why would you wait so long to tell me? When you love someone, you tell them, especially when you know the person loves you back."

"Not everyone can be that brave," Harper says. "Besides, I wasn't completely sure if you loved Jeremy or me. I wasn't ready at the time to have my heart crushed."

"Ha!" I cry victoriously. "I knew you were jealous."

"Fine, you got me. I was jealous." He pauses, piercing me with a serious look as he continues, "Now, I am just scared for you. I am not being jealous when I say I no longer trust Jeremy."

"Yeah, well, he doesn't trust you either, so the feeling is mutual," I say bitterly. I sigh defeatedly and add, "I wish I knew which of you I can trust."

"That's an easy answer for me," Harper says with a smile and waggle of his eyebrows.

"So I should trust Jeremy, then?" I ask innocently.

"That's not funny," Harper scoffs. "Seriously, Sophia, at least let me start teaching you to control your demon. I would rather lose you to Jeremy than to your demon."

"I already told you I would let you teach me," I tell him. "What more do you want from me?"

His eyes turn dark as a seductive look crosses his features. He scoots...no sensually crawls...over to me, causing my heart to jump into my throat. He stops just before me, placing his face close to mine.

His tone is intensely erotic as he says, "I already told you what I want."

I swallow hard, clutching the towel so hard my knuckles ache. How the hell am I supposed to swear off these men when they continue to be frustratingly sexy and irresistible?

My voice is shaky as I answer, "How do I know you don't just want me for my demon?"

"I don't care about your demon, Sophia. I only want you. I will never bring my demon out or ask you to bring yours out other than to protect you or give you a lesson if that is what it will take."

I search his eyes for any tell that he is lying, but I see none. His eyes are serious, seductive, and just a tad bit hopeful. It breaks my heart to see it because I don't want to break his heart.

"What if Jeremy offers me the same thing?" I ask.

A spark of anger flashes in his eyes, but it is gone as quickly as it came. He ignores the question and reaches for me, pulling me to him before I can protest.

He is too quick for me to pull away as he captures my mouth with his. This is nothing like I have shared with him before. The few almost-kisses and the one soft press of his lips on mine did not even scratch the surface of this.

This was…mindblowing.

The feel of his mouth on mine in an actual, real kiss was nothing short of epic. His lips fit against mine so completely that it is as if his lips were explicitly made for kissing mine. His tongue probes my lips, and I open for him.

He slides his tongue in my mouth, swirling it around mine in a sensual dance that pulls a moan from my throat. My heart races, my breathing is ragged, and the raging inferno inside me threatens to burn me up if Harper keeps kissing me.

But he doesn't.

Harper breaks from the kiss and says breathlessly, "The next time Jeremy uses his fucking demon to pull you away from me, you ask him if he would really be willing to have a relationship with you without the demon bond. Good luck with that."

And with that, Harper rises from the floor and stalks away, leaving me a writhing, frustrated, horny mess on the floor.

Fucking men.

"You have to name your demon," Harper says the next day as we move out onto the balcony of the turret.

The sun is shining, and the air is crisp and cool. Autumn has come, and the garden is bursting with all the wonderful reds, golds, and oranges the season brings, and we have a perfect view of it from up here.

However, I am not enjoying that view. My view is much better.

Harper's dark, auburn hair shines in the sunlight, revealing the red color in his dark locks. It contrasts nicely with his blue eyes, which are the same color as the sky today. He sports a three o'clock shadow on his strong muscular jaw that perfectly matches his rugged blue plaid shirt and jeans.

He looks delectable, and I sigh as I enjoy the view of his ass when he pulls two folding chairs up against the railing so we can look over and down at the beautiful garden.

It looks very nice in those jeans, but sadly I can not concentrate on the feelings that looking at Harper's fantastic ass inspires. Instead, I sit down to look over the balcony and am reminded of the day Jeremy was supposed to take me to the garden.

The day we were separated, and I came here.

He was going to show me the garden, and I was looking forward to enjoying a lovely kiss with him.

With kisses on my mind, my thoughts move to the kiss Harper and I shared yesterday on his living room floor, and my sadness vanishes.

I wonder which of my men would get to kiss me in the garden?

Oh, hell, did I really just ask myself that?

"Sophia, don't make me kiss you senseless again," Harper's voice cuts into my thoughts.

What did he just say?

"What did you just say?" I repeat the question aloud.

"I was trying to get your attention. Apparently, that worked,"

Harper says.

"I was just thinking about a kiss in the garden," I say dreamily, propping my elbow on the railing and my chin in my hand.

Harper narrows his eyes at me. "Are you just trying to distract me by offering to kiss me if I take you down to the garden?"

"Hmm…maybe…is it working?"

"No. Sophia, we are supposed to be working on your studies," Harper says frustratingly.

"Fine, if I name my demon, can we go?" I beg.

"The name you give your demon is important," Harper says. "Names have power, so you must give it a name that will match the personality you would like it to have."

"It already has a shitty personality," I complain.

A growl permeates from my right, and I look over at the decorative, fancy floor-length mirror that Harper had moved down here from the fourth floor of the turret. My demon's red eyes glow, flashing angrily at me from the mirror's surface.

"Because it is untrained," Harper responds, shooting the demon an angry glare.

I stick out my tongue at it while Harper's back is turned and then say, "Alright, so I guess the first thing I need to ask myself is what kind of demon I want to have."

Harper nods. "Very good. Yes, that is exactly what you should ask yourself first."

I shrug. "I have never thought about it. I have always wished it would go away, not what I wanted it to be or what its name should be."

"That is why you must change how you think of and interact with your demon. If you accept and interact with him, he will be easier to train," Harper says.

"Yo, Harper!" A voice calls up from below. "You up there?"

I peek over the railing to see Amelia waving her arms up at the balcony. I narrow my eyes. What the hell does she want?

Harper leans over the railing. "I'm here. What's up, Amelia?"

"I need to speak with you in private about something I saw," She calls out, and I can tell she is trying to be as quiet as possible.

"Can it wait?" Harper asks. "I am teaching a lesson right now."

"It can wait til after the lesson, but I need to tell you ASAP," She answers.

"Alright," Harper replies. "I'll be down right after I am done."

Seemingly satisfied, Amelia turns and goes back into the building.

"If you need to see to that, I don't mind," I say. "Besides, it will give me time to think of a name for my asshole demon."

I perk up, and before Harper can say anything, I add, "Hey, can I call him Asshole?"

Harper rolls his eyes. "No, you cannot call him Asshole."

Another growl comes from my demon.

"Stop antagonizing him," Harper says sternly. "That is no way to make friends."

"I antagonize you all the time, and you love me," I quip with a smirk.

Harper's gaze turns dangerous, his sapphire eyes darkening with barely contained lust. That look makes my knees weak. Dammit, why do I open my big mouth before I think?

"One of these days, I will show you what consequences you will get from antagonizing me." He pauses to rakishly look me up and down and then adds, "Fuck around and find out."

He accentuated the word 'fuck', and my pussy is automatically wet as its walls flutter deliciously. That is why I open my big mouth. I love Harper's teasing, even though I know I am playing with fire.

Dammit, I should not even be playing with him. Guilt stabs through me as visions of the day I spent with Jeremy float through my mind. I am supposed to be in love with Jeremy. However, the more time I spend away from him, the more I realize that maybe I was wrong.

"If you would let me bond with Thorn, you would not have this problem," My demon says from the mirror. *"Jeremy would be able to find us and set us free."*

My gaze flies to his. "Is that the name of Jeremy's demon?"

Shit. I said that aloud.

Harper's gaze narrows, the lust vanishing as if it had never been there. "Your demon knows the name of Jeremy's demon?"

"Obviously," I say dryly.

"Don't you dare tell him," My demon says, flashing his eyes at me menacingly.

I smirk viciously at him and turn to Harper. "His name is Thorn."

"Fucking Bitch."

"Stupid demon."

"Names have power," Harper says, interrupting my argument with my stupid demon. "It is dangerous for someone else to know the name of your demon unless that person is someone you explicitly trust, or you may find your demon controlled by someone else."

"But I thought you said no one else could control my demon?" I ask worriedly, my playfulness diminishing.

"Normally, yes," Harper says, going into teacher mode. "But there are some spells that could give a person temporary control over another's demon if they knew the name."

I glance toward the mirror, smirking maliciously. "So, if I name my demon and give you the name, you can control him for me?"

"Hypothetically, yes, but I have never tried the spell myself," Harper says.

His back is to the mirror so my demon does not see the sneaky wink Harper throws my way before he adds, "Hurry up and pick a name so we can try out the theory."

"I will kill you and then haunt you in the afterlife," My demon says, and I am surprised to hear a modicum of humor in the tone.

Is my demon actually joining in on our teasing?

I turn to Harper with wide eyes. "My demon just teased me!"

Harper quirks an eyebrow and turns to the mirror.

The demon crosses his shadowy arms and looks away. *"Don't get used to it."*

Harper turns back to me. "That's a good sign, Sophia. Keep up the good work.

I shrug. "I don't know what I did."

"Your demon is much like a child. If you're happy, then it is happy. It will learn by watching you, so if you are angry and negative all the time, it will be too."

I look at the mirror where my demon still stands, arms crossed. What name would go with his personality yet give an insight into what I want him to be?

Then something comes to me, and I turn to Harper. "You let me know your demon's name."

"Yeah, I did," Harper says with a soft smile. "What of it?"

I smile back. "Nothing. It's just...I just didn't think you would trust me that much."

Harper's smile widens, and his voice goes low as he responds, "I trust you with that, Sophia. I know you would never hurt me."

I do not know how to respond to that, so I just stare into those hypnotizing blue eyes as my heart flutters with contentment.

Harper suddenly gets up from his seat and holds his hand out to me. "Come on. You're going with me."

I raise my eyebrows curiously. "Where are we going?"

"With me to see Amelia. I thought you might want to leave the turret for a while."

I ignore Harper's hand, jumping up excitedly and letting out a happy little squeal.

"BUT," Harper shouts as his hand drops.

I stop and give him my full attention. I'll agree to anything to get out of here, even for only a few hours.

"You will stay glued to my side. You will not interact with anyone. If you see Jeremy, you will ignore him. Am I clear?"

I nod enthusiastically. "Absolutely. No talking to anyone, and stay glued to your ass. Got it."

"I said, glued to my side," Harper corrects me. "Don't touch my ass unless you mean it."

"Whatever," I say sarcastically. "Let's go!"

Harper shakes his head at me and chuckles. "Aren't you forgetting something?" He asks.

I frown, confused until Harper gestures with his eyes toward my right side.

Oh yeah. My stupid demon.

I turn to the mirror, gesturing with my arm as I say, "Come on, asshole. Let's go."

My demon harumphs and poofs into smoky shadows, drifting around the balcony as he dissipates, leaving the mirror's surface shadow-free.

Harper smiles proudly and then turns to leave the balcony. I race to follow after him. I hope I get to see Jeremy. Even if I can't speak to him, at least I will get to see him and see that he is okay with my own eyes.

My heart races as we approach the door at the bottom of the stairs leading out of the turret. Harper unlocks it, and we step out into freedom. I had been unconscious when I was brought here, so I look around curiously at my surroundings. Suddenly, I remember this hallway.

This is the hallway Harper led me down on our way to the turret after I had left the sensory deprivation room and the room with the monitors.

The one where I watched Jeremy struggle in the straight jacket. I had vowed to find him somehow and get us out of here. I had broken that promise.

Did I even want to keep it anymore?

Harper is not the monster Jeremy seems to think he is, or if he is, he has yet to show his true colors. Harper seems to be trying to help me, just like he told Jeremy he would. Maybe Jeremy will see that, too, and he and Harper can learn to get along somehow?

Yeah, right. And pigs will learn to fly, and hell will freeze over. They will never get along because they both say they want me. The only problem is, I don't know which one actually wants me and which one only wants my demon.

Hell, maybe they both want my demon. Just because Harper is teaching me to control my demon does not mean he is only doing it to help me. He could only be trying to teach me for his own benefit so he wouldn't be stuck with an untrained demon when he steals him.

Or maybe I'm paranoid like Jeremy.

I shake my head to clear it of these thoughts as we pass the room with the monitors. I notice that one of the monitors is dark as if turned off. Harper does not say anything, so I keep walking as well. Then we pass the room with the deprivation tank, and I know we are almost out.

My heart pounds with excitement, and I almost stumble in my haste to reach the end of this hallway. Harper pulls a little card from his pocket and slides it into a mechanism on the wall beside a set of double doors at the end of the hall.

The doors open wide, and we step out of the hallway and into another hallway. This hallway is narrow and long, curving to the left and heading straight down to another single door. There are various rooms on either side of this hallway as well, but I do not take the time to ask about or glance at them.

Harper pulls out a key for the door at the end of the hall, unlocks and opens it, and gestures for me to go ahead of him. I go through the door and gasp in surprise. An answering gasp comes from beside me as I turn to face Nurse Cora.

"Is your curiosity appeased?" Harper asks with a smile, gesturing around the nurses' station.

We had come out of the door behind the counter, the one Nurse Cora went through to get my bedclothes when I had first arrived. Harper had teased me for being too curious when I had asked where the door led.

I laughed delightedly and ask, "Yes, but where do you store the bedclothes? I don't remember seeing any on our way here."

Nurse Cora answers, "The door you passed on the right just before you came to this one is a large storage room."

I nod in understanding. I remember seeing the door. I am about to comment when Harper shoots me an annoyed look, reminding me that I am not supposed to interact with anyone, so I do not respond to Cora's comment. Instead, I move closer to Harper and stand there with my hands behind my back.

"Do you know where Amelia is, Cora?" Harper asks. "I just saw her out in the garden, but I don't know where she went."

"She was with Jeremy last I saw her," Cora says.

Harper glances at me, but I do not react. I do not want Harper to see how much that statement affected me. I don a mask of indifference, but I am screaming with rage inside.

Jealously swirls within me like a tornado, fierce and destructive. It takes everything within me not to jolt away from Harper, track down Jeremy, and break Amelia's pretty little neck.

"Sounds like a fun time. Let's do it," Asshole whispers in my mind.

I really need to give him a name. I can't keep going around calling him asshole.

Or maybe I can.

"I am not literally going to break anybody's neck. It is just a figure of speech," I answer the fucker.

Fucker. That's a good name.

"Come on, Sophia. Let's go find Amelia," Harper says.

He leads the way, and I follow. He heads toward the cafeteria first. The cafeteria is empty, but Harper calls out anyway.

"Amelia, are you in here?"

His deep baritone voice echoes off the empty walls. No one answers. Harper heads for the kitchen, but a loud boom reverberates through the room just before he gets to the swinging double doors. The lights flicker threateningly, and then the sound of pouring rain fills the cafeteria.

Harper rushes to the glass doors with me right on his heels. The courtyard is drenched by the sudden afternoon rain. It pours in torrents over the gardens, and lightning flashes across the sky. Another rumble of thunder, this one low and growling, vibrates in the room. The lights flicker again, and this time they stay out.

"Fuck," Harper exclaims, running a hand through his hair. "I'm going to have to start up the generators. Can I trust you by yourself for a minute or two while I do that?"

"I'm not going to run away if that is what you're asking," I say with an eye-roll.

"Okay, just stay here and don't get into any trouble. And if you see Amelia, tell her to wait here with you."

"Okay, Dad," I quip, rolling my eyes again.

Harper moves fast, causing me to gasp loudly as he pulls me up against him and brings his face close to mine.

His breath is hot on my face as he whispers, "Baby, if you want to call me daddy, you have to wait until we get back to the turret. Now, sit still and wait for me, or I will punish you like the bad girl you are."

He does not wait for me to give him a witty reply, as if I could have given him one after he so effectively rendered me speechless. I couldn't move if I wanted to after that statement.

Harper turns and stalks out of the cafeteria, leaving me alone with my thoughts and my throbbing pussy.

CHAPTER 26

I sink down into one of the chairs at one of the four tables, propping my elbow on the table and my chin in my hand. I stare out into the room, staring at nothing as I dissolve into my own head.

The room is a bit dim without the lighting but probably would be more so if not for the glass doors that let in the light. Even though it is a rainy afternoon, there is still a tiny bit of light.

My head buzzes with a myriad of emotions as my mind switches between Jeremy being with Amelia and Harper's last words to me. Those two men and their demons are going to be the death of me if my own demon does not drive me crazy first. Oh…wait…he already did that. That's the entire reason I am here.

The dimming of the light in the room catches my attention, and I turn to the window. Frowning, I watch as the outside world grows dark. It is as if the window is being tinted right before my eyes. The room goes dark, almost totally dark, but there is enough light to make out the shapes and shadows of the table and chairs.

The storm must be getting worse.

My heart flutters. I am getting better with darkness, but the last time a room went dark on me, I was mentally dragged away. My body cannot help but respond. Goosebumps break out all along my arms, and my heartbeat gets faster.

"Sophia, hide. NOW." The voice of my demon rages through my brain, startling me and causing me to flinch violently.

I do not question it. I look around hurriedly for somewhere to hide as my heart pounds against my chest. A thunderous sound, like pots and pans falling to the floor, explodes from the kitchen, driving me into action. I dive under a table. It is not the most obscure place, but I have no other option. If only there was a tablecloth that would hide my presence under the table.

Thunder from the storm rumbles again, vibrating the floor with its power. The room lights up with flickers of light but is cast into darkness once more when the lightning dissipates.

I feel the presence of something beside me, and I start to scream, but the sound of my demon's voice in my head freezes the sound in my throat.

"Do not panic, do not make a sound, and do not move," My demon says.

Shadows coalesce around me, and I recoil at first. But I listen to my demon. I take a deep breath, forcing myself to remain calm as the shadows curl around me, surrounding me in a curtain of shadow and obscuring me from view.

"Thanks," I say in my head.

"I might hate you, but I am not going to let anything happen to you," My demon says.

I roll my eyes. *"Whatever. You never seemed to care before."*

"No one was trying to kill you before," He whispers, and the fear that had been swirling inside me rages into full-blown terror as the crashing sounds coming from the kitchen get louder.

"Who is trying to kill me?" I ask, and even my voice in my mind is shaky.

"No one yet, but if you are found, they might," My demon answers mysteriously.

Suddenly, someone comes running full-out through the swinging kitchen doors. I cannot see who it is because of the darkness in the room, but I can tell it is female from the ample breasts that bounce as she runs. I can see the whites of her too-wide eyes as she chances a look over her shoulder mid-run. She dodges a table but catches a chair with her thigh, and she goes down, her hair flying out in a flowing silk curtain.

The hair gives her away. That has to be Amelia.

Another body comes crashing through the doors, swinging the doors out so violently that one of them falls from the hinges and crashes to the floor. It splinters into pieces. The person is wearing all black, obscured by the dark room, making it impossible to identify them. I cannot even see their face because of the mask they wear.

They come to a stop when they see Amelia fall, and they begin a slow stalk toward her as she struggles to get up off the floor. An evil laugh freezes the breath in my lungs as Amelia's blood-curdling scream fills the room.

I start to come out from under the table. Amelia needs help. I do not care that I hate her, and fuck being afraid. I go on my hands and knees and start to crawl out.

"I don't think so," My demon says, and the shadows around me become solid tentacles, wrapping around me and holding me in place.

They are surprisingly gentle but firm enough that I am trapped and cannot move. I start to scream out, to maybe pull the stalker's attention away from Amelia. But my demon's voice once again deters my actions.

"The shadows that hide you are soundproof. No one will hear your screams."

Fuck. I am rendered helpless, and all I can do is watch as the mysterious figure stalks closer to Amelia's prone form.

Amelia finally scrambles to her feet, but the figure is upon her, grabbing her by her throat and slamming her up against the wall. She cries out in pain, gripping the figure's wrist in an attempt to pull the hand from her neck.

"I will teach you to mind your own business and keep your mouth shut about things that do not concern you," The figure says menacingly.

The voice is muffled by the mask they are wearing, so I cannot tell who it is by the sound of their voice. It could be anybody. I can tell it is male, however. I can also tell from the tone that he definitely means Amelia harm.

I struggle again against the shadows that hold me, hidden and frozen in a soundproof place. Despite the raging terror that spirals in my gut, I want desperately to help Amelia. Regardless of the fact that I am jealous as hell of her and even hate her a little bit, I do not want her hurt or possibly dead.

"Please, I didn't tell anyone," Amelia whimpers, her voice choked and raspy from the man's hold on her neck.

"Liar!" The man shouts, moving his face close to hers. "I heard you in the garden."

"No, I didn't tell him. I swear I wasn't going to tell him that," Amelia says. "I...i...it was about something else!"

The man lifts Amelia off her feet by her throat. Her feet dangle in the air as she attempts to kick out, but her kicks are feeble. He holds her there until her face turns a sickly shade of blue.

I struggle, raging against the inability to help her. *"Let me go! She is dying!"*

"No. You will die too if he finds you, and then I will die," My shadow answers me.

Fear mingles with the anger inside me. My heart is pounding, my breathing ragged, and a cold sheen of sweat breaks out along my forehead. My sobs are muffled by the shadow, and my struggles are fruitless, so I return my attention to the struggle across the room.

The man lets Amelia go, and her body slides down the wall. She takes in gasping, raspy breaths of air as she holds her ruined neck.

"Please, let me go," she wails, and I can tell by her hoarse, cracking voice that her throat is damaged and she is crying. "I promise I won't say anything to anybody."

"Too late," the man says. "You already tried. You know too much."

He grabs her by her beautiful, silky hair and slams her head into the ground. I hear a loud crack, and Amelia lets out a wail of pain. The bright sheen of blood radiates through the dark room as it pools on the floor around her head. Amelia begins to cry, great wracking sobs that echo through the cafeteria.

Tears stream down my face as I cry along with her, but my cries are muffled by the shadows. I cry out in rage at my inability to help, I cry out in anguish for Amelia, and I cry out in fear that I might be next if this man discovers me.

The man is not done with her yet. He climbs on top of her, pinning her to the floor with his thighs on top of hers. Some of the shadows surrounding the man begin to move, and I gasp silently in horror. Are the shadows moving with the light, or is this person controlling the shadows?

My heart sinks in my chest, and nausea hits me like a punch to the gut. I take a second look at the body, the shape and form. The figure's build is too small to be Harper's, with his bulking biceps. But Jeremy…

No, it can't be…

The nausea grows, causing me to heave, and I almost throw up. I wail in utter agony and denial, but there is no denying that this man's frame and build are close to Jeremy's athletically muscled form.

I refuse to believe it. I refuse to give in to the insistence in my gut until I see the face behind that dark mask and know for a certainty that it is Jeremy.

The tendrils of shadow that writhe around the man shoot out toward Amelia's struggling form. They wrap around her wrists and pin them to the ground above her head as Amelia screams, but the sound is raspy and low because of her ravaged throat.

"There is no one around to save you, Amelia. You should have kept your mouth shut," he says, and my heart sinks even more.

The man's accent matches Jeremy's.

But many people have that accent, my heart argues, refusing to comply with my brain's thoughts. But there is no mistaking the inflections of his tone, the same as Jeremy's when he is angry.

Then I see what the man is doing, and I scream in outrage, even though it carries no sound.

The man is stripping off Amelia's pants, dragging them off her as she struggles, cries, and screams against the shadow's hold. My eyes widen as the man wrestles with the fly of his pants and then lays on top of Amelia.

"What's wrong, baby?" He asks derisively. "You didn't complain last night when I fucked you senseless."

His ass raises into the air while he positions himself. Then he lets out a grunt of pleasurable victory as his ass thrusts downward. Amelia screams in pain.

"Please, stop," She wails.

"That's right, scream for me whore," the man says as his ass comes back up in the air, then savagely thrusts back down again.

Amelia screams.

And I scream.

"What's wrong, bitch? I thought this is what you wanted?" The man sneers as he thrusts into her again.

"Please," Amelia whimpers between cries of pain and the figure's brutal thrusts. "Please, stop. It hurts. Please."

"You are a whore, and this is how you fuck a whore," The man says, and then he violently fucks her. He fucks her hard, fast, and viciously as Amelia screams out under him.

I hear his satisfied grunts, the sound of flesh hitting flesh, and Amelia's grunts and moans of pain as the man violates her. I squeeze my eyes shut against the sight of his ass pumping furiously up and down, but my eyes have already seen it. I will never be able to forget it.

I sit and cry in frustration, anger, and fear, covering my ears with my hands to block out the sounds. The shadows holding me writhe around me as if they are caressing me, and a whisp of shadow brushes against my cheek, drying my tears.

"Stay strong, Sophia. Harper is on his way."

My eyes fly open. That was not my demon's voice. The shining, diamond-colored eyes of Jewel, Harper's demon, fills my vision.

Those eyes. I bet that is why he named her Jewel.

Her tone is comforting, and her shadowy features match that tone. Her face blocks out the sight of the rape happening across the room before me, and her soft hum fills my head and blocks out the sounds.

"Please, tell him to hurry," I silently implore her.

She smiles sadly and nods.

Her head turns toward the violence, and I see utter helplessness and sadness enter her eyes. *"I am sorry, Sophia, but you must bear witness so you can tell Harper exactly what happened."*

She moves aside, and I automatically look across the room.

The man has obviously finished his dirty deed and is now atop her, pulling something out of her mouth. I squint, straining my eyes to see what he is doing, and then I retch violently when I realize.

Oh, God, no.

He grasps her tongue, pulling it out of her mouth as far as it will go as Amelia lays there and cries out in pain. He holds something in his other hand, high over his head.

My eyes widen, and I shiver in revulsion at the figure's evil laugh, and Amelia's screams grow louder.

"This is what you get when you don't keep your mouth shut," he says, bringing the knife down. Amelia's tongue separates from her body. I throw up.

Amelia begins choking on her own blood as it pours out of her severed muscle. The evil bastard holds it in the air with a whoop of triumph and then throws it to the side like someone's dirty laundry. Amelia screams out over and over in pain until I hold my ears again.

The man grabs her by her hair and repeatedly bashes Amelia's head against the ground. The dark pool of blood on the ground grows, and Amelia's cries cease. The side of her head caves in, and her eyeball rolls across the floor toward my hiding spot.

I scream, "No…no, please!"

But all the begging in the world cannot stop the inevitable, horrifying fact that this evil man has viciously raped and brutally murdered poor Amelia, and Harper will be too late.

Suddenly, the lights flicker back to life, and the man jumps, looking around as if caught in the act. I am more thankful than ever for my demon's shadows as they hide me from the figure's evil glare as he scans the room. I silently vow never to fear the shadows again unless they belong to this evil freak.

I can see him more clearly now, and there is no more room for doubt. His body type undoubtedly matches Jeremy's, and I can even see some sandy hair peeking out from under the mask.

No, I still refuse to believe it until I see his face, but the figure leaves the mask on.

Satisfied that no one is around, he focuses on his task, slamming Amelia's head into the ground one last time with a satisfied grunt, causing some pieces of her brain to scatter onto the floor along with the blood.

He rises from the floor, grasping both of her legs, one in each hand, and drags her across the ground toward the kitchen. The shadows follow in her wake, lapping up the blood and gore and leaving the floor clean of evidence.

My horrified heart beats furiously. I have never seen shadows eat blood and body parts. My shadows never did that, even when I had left my own bloody mess.

"You did not kill anyone," My shadow explains. *"I would not drink blood from living people, nor would I eat body parts."*

"Some of us would not drink blood or eat body parts at all because we are not evil," Jewel says, and I know it is directed toward my demon.

"Give me time. I am still learning," My demon says. *"But I have a feeling that I am not going to be evil either after seeing that."*

"Acts such as that give us power, but it is the wrong kind of power. I would teach you the difference if you listen," Jewel says.

"I will listen to you," My demon says.

Even through all the violence I just witnessed, all the terror that has settled into my pounding heart, and all the misery at the horrifying event that just took place, I smile.

Maybe there is hope for my demon after all.

CHAPTER 27

By the time Harper shows up, I am trembling uncontrollably from the wracking sobs taking over my body. My vomit is still pooled on the floor by my head, and the sharp tang of it still violates my mouth.

The shadows from my demon have released me from their hold, and I lay curled on the floor in a fetal position, with my arms wrapped around my knees. The raping murderer and poor Amelia are long gone.

I still refuse to think of the man as Jeremy.

Harper's gentle hands roll me over, and I look up into his remorseful gaze.

"It will be okay," He whispers as he kneels and picks me up from the floor.

He pulls me close to his body with one arm under my neck and the other under my knees. I lay my head against his chest, and he carries me out the glass doors and into the garden, planting soft kisses on my forehead as he walks.

The rain has ceased, and the sky is a bright blue again. Birds chirp cheerily, unaware of the violence that just happened in the cafeteria. A helpless, miserable sob escapes my throat, and Harper's arms tighten around me.

He finds a bench and sits down, settling me into his lap with one leg over each of his, effectively straddling him. He grasps the back of my head and brings it down to his chest. I let him, resting my check on Harper's solid chest. My arms curl up to my chest, and I fist his shirt in my hands.

Harper wraps his arms around my shoulders, pulling me even closer into him as if he is trying to absorb me. He holds me, and I let the tears fall. My hold tightens on his shirt as I cry my fear and anger away.

This is twice that I have broken down in Harper's arms. This is the second time that I have let him hold me. This is twice that I have cried over the loss of my friend and lover.

Because even though Jeremy is still out there somewhere and still thinks we are together, I have given up hope for a relationship with him. There are too many secrets, too much suspicion, and I cannot even honestly say I know him all that well.

Not to mention the fact that he may have just raped and killed someone, even though my stubborn heart refuses to believe it.

Harper lets me cry for a while and then lifts my chin with his finger, forcing me to look up at him.

"I have the authorities looking for Amelia," he says, but the hopelessness in his voice tells me that he knows it will be too late. "You need to tell them what you saw."

I shake my head and stutter, "I c..c..can't. Not Yet, p…p…please don't make me."

"Alright, you are safe, you don't have to now. It can wait," Harper says consolingly, pushing my head back down to his chest.

"Amelia…the…that m…m…man. He…he had on…couldn't see his face…Oh, God," I manage to blurt out before I am a sobbing, uncontrollable mess again.

Harper holds me even tighter, kissing the top of my head and stroking my back in comforting, soothing circles.

"You're safe, you're okay. I got you," Harper whispers repeatedly as he rocks me back and forth consolingly.

Eventually, my sobs quiet to tiny little hiccups. I take a deep breath, the scent of earth, rain, and flowers assailing my nose as I breathe.

I bury my face into Harper's chest, breathing in the scent of musk, fabric softener, and…mint? I rise up to gaze into Harper's eyes, the same color as the sky.

"Do you have mint in your pocket?" I ask, my voice scratchy from all the tears.

Harper smiles, pulling a small tin from his shirt pocket, opening it, and offering me a small, round mint. I pop it in my mouth, and I instantly feel better. A light breeze blows across my face, cooling my skin and drying my tears.

He lowers his head to gently kiss my cheek, then raises his head to stare into my eyes again. He kisses the other cheek and then brushes his lips across mine ever so gently.

"Better?" he asks, his voice deep and soothing.

"Mmmhmm," I answer, not trusting my voice to sound normal right now if the tightness of my throat is any sign.

Harper cups the side of my face, rubbing comforting circles over my cheek with his thumb.

"You know I would never let anything happen to you, don't you?"

I nod and attempt to sound normal as I answer, "I am beginning to, yes."

My voice is scratchy and hoarse, and I sound like shit. My throat burns with the effort to speak, but seeing the smile spread across Harper's face is worth it.

"Does this mean you trust me again?" he asks.

"Don't push your luck," I answer hoarsely, but the smile I give back to him belies my words.

Harper chuckles and pulls my face toward his. He brushes another light kiss across my cheek. I chew up the mint, the clean taste filling my mouth and ridding it of the awful taste. I swallow, and it burns my throat going down.

I flinch in pain, and Harper frowns. "What's wrong?"

"My throat just hurts," I answer. "It burned when I swallowed the mint, but on the bright side, my mouth feels better."

Harper laughs and says, "Smells better, too."

I make a face at him, and he chuckles as he brushes another kiss along my lips.

"Tastes better, too," He whispers against my mouth.

I sigh and press against him harder, deepening the kiss. I still hold his shirt fisted in my hands, and I use it to pull him closer. A satisfied hum rises from my chest, vibrating our lips and causing me to shudder.

It runs through me, chasing the darkness, grief, and terror from my soul. A burning need rises in my gut, engulfing my veins with its fiery heat. The longing to touch and be touched overwhelms me, and I press even harder into the solidity of Harper's body.

My arms let go of his shirt to wrap around his shoulders, pressing my breasts into the hardened muscles of his chest. My tongue runs along his lush lips, begging entrance.

A deep, low, rumbling growl vibrates from Harper's chest. His hand goes around to the back of my neck, stroking my nape with his thick, lithe fingers. His other hand wraps around my lower back, pulling me to him even tighter. His lips open, sucking my tongue into his mouth. His tongue swirls around mine in slow, languid circles.

This is what I need, what I want. The swirling heat of desire licking through my veins is what I need to chase away the horror of today. I need something to distract me from remembering the terror, and Harper is the perfect, toe-curling distraction I need.

I lose myself in his kiss, the pressure of his hands on me, and the feel of our bodies pressed together. My heart speeds up, and my breath comes in short, shallow pants. Desire engulfs me as a burning need to have more grows inside me.

A soft, erotic moan escapes me, pulsating against our lips. Harper groans as he strokes my tongue with his, and then he suddenly pulls away.

Our breaths mingle together, rapid and panting, and I look questioningly into his flushed features.

"Why did you stop?" I ask breathlessly.

I see Harper's throat work as he swallows and answers my question with a question. "What are we doing, Sophia?"

I smirk, quirking a brow as I answer, "I thought it was obvious. Don't tell me you are a virgin."

Harper chokes on a laugh and says, "I'm serious, Sophia. You know how I feel, but I don't think it would mean the same to you."

The laughter fades, and Harper's visage turns serious as he adds, "I do not want to just be a comfort fuck for you, Sophia. I want to make love to you, and I want you to make love to me."

I stare into his sapphire eyes and swallow hard. His words sink into my befuddled mind, and I remember what Harper was to me before all the mistrust and confusion.

He was the sunshine during my darkest times. He was my confidant when I had secrets I needed to share. And he was my safe place when I needed somewhere to run.

What had changed? Did it ever change?

No.

I had a nightmare that scared me.

I had Jeremy whispering doubts in my ear.

But I never stopped feeling those things for Harper. The feelings were just buried under all the suspicion and pain. He was still all of those things and more to me. Despite it all, he still is.

Suddenly, all those things are not enough anymore. I want Harper, all of him, right here, right now. I want to feel our naked bodies pressed together, be lost in the vortex of erotic ecstasy as it overtakes us, and give myself over to the sensation of Harper pressing himself inside me. I want to give myself to him completely and take everything he has to give me, not just physically.

I am ready to give him my heart.

I have wanted him for so long, and I am tired of denying myself. Harper has had every opportunity to take advantage of me if he wanted to, but he did not. If I do not start trusting him now, I never will.

"Sophia, please say something," Harper whispers, his tone a mixture of fear, hope, and desire.

My voice is thick with unrestrained desire as I respond, "Make love to me, Harper."

"Sophia."

He told me names have power. The way he whispered my name showed me how true that statement was.

It held all the restrained emotion he had for me, all the heartache and pain, and all the love and joy rolled into one intimate whisper that leaves me trembling with desire.

He cups my face in his hands and brings my face close to his, capturing my lips in the most erotic kiss I have ever experienced. His lips fit perfectly with mine, moving in sync with our heartbeats. His tongue dances in my mouth in long, languid strokes that promise intense pleasure. He sucks my bottom lip into his mouth, nipping gently before swiping it with his tongue and releasing it to continue the knee-weakening kiss.

The kiss becomes more when Harper's hands stroke down my face, across my shoulders, and down my sides, leaving fiery heat in their wake. He grasps the hem of my shirt, bringing it up to slide his hands under it so he can stroke my bare skin.

A thrill of desire shoots through me, and I gasp at its intensity. I moan in pleasure as his hands stroke the bare skin of my stomach, sides, and back while he continues the mind-melting kiss. I lean further into him, pressing myself as close to him as possible.

We are both breathing heavily and droopy-eyed when Harper breaks the kiss to pull my shirt over my head and toss it aside. I was not wearing a bra today, so my bare breasts are there for his taking.

He sucks in a breath as he stares down at them.

His voice is strained with desire as he rasps, "Goddess, you are so beautiful, Sophia."

He releases his hold on me to run his hands down my breasts, pausing to pinch the nipples between the thumb and forefinger of each hand.

"Jewel, give us cover," Harper rasps as his hands run down my sides to grasp my hips.

I gasp as a sudden cloud of darkness rises from the earth below us, swirling and coalescing around us. It envelops us, creating a small space of privacy around the bench and tiny flower garden where we sit.

Harper pulls my attention back to him when he sucks one of my hardened nipples into his mouth, grazing lightly with his teeth and then soothing with his tongue.

I gasp with delight, arching my back and leaning forward to give him better access. He laves my nipple with tongue, teeth, and lips, then turns to the other breasts and gives it the same attention.

Flaming need coils in my veins, pumping through my body with the ferocity of a tidal wave. Pressure builds in my groin, intensifying the longing.

I fumble with the buttons of Harper's shirt, my fingers shaking with impatience as I try to get his shirt off. I am overwhelmed with the need to feel his bare skin against mine. Finally, I get the shirt off and groan in utter pleasure as I run my hands over the solid muscles of his chest and abdomen and then his shoulders and back.

Harper lets out a pleasurable growl from deep in his chest as he plants kisses all along my neck and shoulders. He holds me steady with one hand on my lower back as his other hand travels down my stomach and slips into the waistband of my pants.

I moan with pleasure as his hands slip inside my panties, and his fingers find my folds and dip inside. He swirls his fingers around the sensitive bundle of nerves above my entrance, building the pressure inside my groin even more.

I rock my hips forward and throw my head back, reveling in the sensations Harper's fingers elicit from me. My fingers dig into his shoulders, holding tight as Harper takes me to the very edge of the precipice of pleasure.

"Harper," I say with yearning as his fingers slip inside my entrance. He swirls them around, touching all the right spots before pulling them back out and repeating the process.

"Goddess, you are beautiful," Harper says with a sigh as he watches me while he plays with me. "I want you so bad."

I rock against his fingers, moaning my pleasure as my eyes lock with his, and then I respond, "Then take me, please, Harper."

He growls again before taking his fingers from me. He grasps my hips and stands me up so he can pull my pants down. I am in only my lacy panties now, which are right in front of Harper's eyes since I am standing and he is still sitting.

His eyes darken with a desire that makes me quiver with longing as he brings his mouth to my panties and blows his hot breath on me. I throw my head back and moan, loving the feel of his hot breath through the cloth.

He hooks his fingers in the waistband of the delicately laced underwear and pulls them down to my knees. He doesn't even take them all the way off before grasping my hips and pulling me forward.

He pulls me close to his face and plants kisses across my stomach, paying extra attention to my belly button. Then, his lips travel down to the apex of my thighs, and licks one long stroke up my folds.

I cry out and thrust my hips toward his face as I grasp his hair in one hand and balance on his shoulder with the other. He licks again, this time pushing inside my folds and swirling around that spot. He stops there, swirling around and around that bundle of nerves until my legs quiver and I moan his name.

He adds his fingers, pushing into my entrance as he continues to assault that spot with his tongue. The heat inside my core builds to a dangerous level, and my hand tightens in Harper's hair.

"Close, I'm close," I breathe as my hips automatically move from the sensations.

Harper stops his ministrations with his tongue to whisper against my pussy, "Go, baby. Let me taste your juices."

He pushes his tongue back inside my folds and begins to pump in and out of my entrance with his fingers. The sensation drives me over the edge, and I throw my head back and scream my orgasm into the air.

My pussy walls milk his fingers with the pulsing of my pleasure, and his tongue laps around his fingers, licking me clean. His tongue and fingers keep driving the orgasm through me until my knees go weak, and I cannot hold my stance any longer.

Harper pulls his finger out so he can grab my hips to steady me. He helps me take off my panties and shoes and then lowers me so that I am straddling him again. I rock against him, and the roughness of his jeans driving over my sensitive heat almost causes another orgasm.

"Fuck, you taste good," Harper says as he lavishes kisses over my neck and shoulders.

"And you feel so good on my fingers," He adds between kisses. "I cannot wait to be inside you."

He fumbles with the fastening of his jeans, and I let go of his hair to help him. Together, we release his cock from its prison, pulling his jeans down past his hips. I wrap my hands around his member and stroke up and down, but Harper stops me with a hand on my wrist.

He moans a tortured sound that comes from deep inside his chest. "Please, don't do that. I won't last, and I want to feel my cock inside that delectable pussy."

I don't answer. Instead, I plant my feet on the ground so I can raise up and, with Harper's hand still on my wrist, help him guide his cock to my entrance. I lower myself and let his massive member slide into my hot pussy, relishing the feel of Harper's cock filling me.

My moans of pleasure coalesce with his as I lower myself all the way down, his girth stretching my walls deliciously. I go down even further until I am sitting fully in his lap, sheathing Harper's member to the hilt inside my core. He is almost too long in this position. The head of his muscle bumps my cervix, shooting a sharp pain up through my stomach. I hiss in pain and pull up a bit.

"Are you alright, baby?" Harper asks, piercing me with his worried gaze.

"You're a smidge too big," I say with an embarrassed chuckle.

He scoots back on the bench just a hair, then pulls my hips back down until I sit flat on his lap again. With the angle changed, it is a perfect fit.

"Problem solved," he moans through gritted teeth as I begin to move my hips, grinding my clit against him.

I begin a slow, torturous, steady rhythm, going up and back down, then rotating my hips to grind before repeating the process. The delicious pressure begins to build again, racing heat through my body.

Pulses of pleasure run along my nerves as I continue to ride Harper, digging my fingers into his shoulders for balance. His fingers dig into my hips as I ride him, and his moans become louder as his breath hitches unevenly.

"Baby, I'm not gonna last much longer," he rasps out breathlessly before lifting me off him.

I whimper in protest, but he says, "Easy, tiger. Just changing the position. I want to make love to you, baby."

I swallow hard as he lowers me to the ground gently. I expect my back to hit the ground, but it lands on something heavenly soft instead. I glance down to see a cloudy bed of shadow under us, and my eyebrows raise in surprise.

However, Harper does not give me time to comment on it as he kicks off his shoes and wiggles the rest way out of his jeans. He positions himself between my thighs, and I wrap my legs around him, resting my heels on his ass. He reaches down to place the head of his cock against my entrance and then lowers himself into me inch by delicious inch.

I throw my head back and moan, relishing the feel of all that hardness sinking into my slick pussy. Harper lies on top of me, keeping as much weight as possible off me by balancing on his elbows. He pumps his hips slowly, moving his cock inside my pussy in a toe-curling rhythm that has me trembling with the need for release.

He lavishes kisses along my neck and chin as he makes love to me. He captures my lips with his and delivers another one of those marvelous kisses as his member moves inside me.

The pressure builds torturously slow with his gentle thrusts and heart-melting kisses. Our moans of pleasure vibrate against our lips, sending delicious tendrils of electric desire coursing through my veins.

"Sophia, you feel so damn good, baby girl," Harper whispers against my lips. "Goddess, I love you.'

I do not even think about what he says, and my response is automatic.

"Harper," I whisper back. "I love you, too."

The confession slips, coming from some carnal knowledge deep inside my gut. I had not even meant to say it. My eyes widen as I realize what was said between us.

Harper raises his head to stare down at me, and the utter happiness radiating from his sapphire eyes fills my heart to bursting. I had not meant to say it, but I did mean it.

With every fiber of my being.

I love this man.

I see Harper's throat work as he swallows and a single happy tear rolls down the side of his face. He stops, sheathed as deep inside me as he can go in this angle, and gathers me close to his body.

He buries his head in my neck and whispers against my ear, "I love you so damn much, Sophia. So damn much."

And he begins that delicious, slow rhythm again.

This time, the pressure builds faster with the knowledge that Harper loves me just as much as I love him. I lose myself in the pleasure as our release comes simultaneously, and we ride our orgasms into a pleasurable world of love and wonder, safe inside the bubble our demons had created for us.

CHAPTER 28

“*T*he ground was too hard,*" My demon says in my head. I had asked him why he had made the shadowed bed for me.

"Since when do you care?" I ask silently.

"Since now. Just shut up and enjoy it, " My demon answers.

I roll my eyes and look up into Harper's face. "He says he made us the bed because the ground was too hard."

"I think he may be growing up," Harper says with a chuckle. "You are going to have to name him quickly."

"I have been thinking about it," I answer. "I like the name Lucien. It's French. It means light, elegance, and ethereal."

Harper smiles as he stares down into my eyes, causing his eyes to sparkle like sapphires. "I like it. Do not tell anyone his name."

"I like it, too," Lucien says.

I smile. "He likes it."

"It is a lovely name, " Jewel says.

"Jewel likes it, too," I say.

Harper's smile fades slightly as his eyes go unfocused. I frown.

"Harper, is everything okay?" I ask worriedly.

"Jewel was speaking to me, and I was answering her," Harper says.

"Is that what I look like when I talk to Lucien?" I ask.

"Yes," Harper says.

"Well, what did she say?" I ask curiously.

Harper laughs. "You are too curious sometimes."

I shrug. "You never know unless you ask."

"Just be sure you want to know the answer before you ask," Harper quips.

"Well, I do want to know," I say.

"I am not sure I want to tell you right now," Harper says, worry shining in his eyes. "It might piss you off or cause you not to trust me again, and after what we just shared, I am feeling a bit insecure."

I frown. "Harper, I told you how I feel. I may have kept it bottled up, but you always knew. You told me yourself that you knew I loved you."

"But I wasn't sure if you were IN love with me. There is a difference, you know," Harper says.

I roll my eyes. "Alright, yes, I am head-over-heels in love with you and want to have your babies. Now, tell me what Jewel said."

"Woah, slow down, hot rod. I never said anything about babies," Harper says with a bit of panic.

"Oh my God, I'm kidding," I say in exasperation, then quickly add, "But not about the being in love with you part."

Harper's eyes soften as he brushes his hand over my cheek. "I know, baby girl. I was just playing along."

He softly kisses my mouth, then deepens the kiss when I flick my tongue over his lips.

"For fuck's sake, I will tell you since Harper is a giant pussy."

I almost choke as I break apart from Harper's kiss to laugh.

Harper frowns. "What?"

"Since Lucien finally has a name, we would like to know if you would let us bond," Jewel says.

"I promise, it was our idea. Harper does not even want to ask because he is afraid you will think…well, you know," Lucien adds.

I smile and sigh blissfully as I look at my sexy doctor beside me propped on his elbow. He really loves me. I can understand why he was hesitant to ask what Jewel and Lucien wanted him to ask.

He had promised me that he would not bring his demon out during intimacy so I would not think he was using me for my demon. But Harper had kept his promise. We had just had the most mind-blowing sex…er…made love, and the demons did nothing but hide us and make us comfortable.

Harper looks delectable lying there beside me. His soft cock beacons me, and my mouth waters with the desire to take him in me while he is soft.

A momentary bout of guilt stabs me in the gut when I think of the last time I did that, but I quickly brush it away. Jeremy will never have me again. I will never be able to trust him the way I trust Harper, and I will never let him make me doubt Harper again.

Harper is still frowning when my attention slips back to reality, and I smile apologetically.

"I'm sorry, I zoned out on you for a minute," I say.

Harper's frown deepens. "What were you thinking about?"

I smirk, raising my eyebrows and looking pointedly down at his still-soft cock. "I was thinking I am hungry and in the mood for..."

I pause and waggle my eyebrows.

Harper's frown disappears. "Oh. Well, baby girl, I have plenty of meat for you." he rolls onto his back, places his hands behind his head, and says, "Help yourself."

"Mmmm," I hum as I roll onto my side. "This is going to be a good meal."

I go up onto my knees, throwing one leg over his and straddling him at the knees. I do not want to waste time with foreplay because I want him while he is still soft. I love the sensation of a nice cock hardening inside my mouth, and Harper has the nicest cock in the world.

Just before I take him into my mouth, I say, "Oh, and our demons would like to join, too."

I lean down and gather him into my mouth before he can respond, suckling his softness gently as I cup his balls in my hand.

I hear him hiss with pleasure and groan softly before he says, "Fuck, that is not fair."

"What is not fair," I say around his cock.

"Son of a bitch, Sophia. That feels too damn good, and I am too sensitive right now," He says with a groan. "Didn't anyone ever tell you not to speak with your mouth full?"

"Mmmm, you taste good," I say seductively around his cock, and smile when I hear the groan come from Harper again.

"Goddess, Sophia, please stop…or don't stop…fuck I don't know." Harper says, his voice strained with pleasure.

I have pity on him and let his cock fall from my lips. It is semi-hard now. I rise back onto my knees, balancing myself with my hands on his thighs.

"What do you say, Harper. Do you want to let our demons bond?" I ask.

Harper's breathing has become ragged from my ministrations, and I watch his throat work as he swallows rapidly. "You aren't mad about it?"

I shake my head with a chuckle. "No, I am not mad. Besides, it was their idea, not ours. I think Lucien might like Jewel a bit."

Harper smiles. I am totally in love with that smile. In fact, it just might be that smile that caused me to fall for the man.

"I think Jewel likes Lucien, too," Harper says.

"Then I say we let them," I say with a shrug.

Harper sits up, grabbing my hips and pulling me up his thighs until my body is pressed into his. He cups my face in his hands, forcing me to look directly into his crystal-blue eyes.

"Sophia, you have to be sure. If they bond, we will be bonded as well." He pauses, giving me a serious look as he adds, "And not necessarily as lovers. If we ever split up, we will still have to keep each other close for our demons. You will be stuck with me forever."

I grasp his wrists and give him a serious look back as I say, "I am totally, completely, and utterly in love with you, Harper Zane Andrews, and I would be honored to be bonded to you forever. And we are not going to split up."

He raises his eyebrows in surprise. "I didn't know you knew my middle name."

I glance down guiltily as I say, "I might have accidently-on-purpose looked at my files while your back was turned, and your full name was listed on there as my doctor."

He chuckles, kisses me firmly, and then says, "I love you, too, Sophia Jade Boralis. Let's bond our demons."

"I think I was in the middle of something," I say mischievously, glancing down at his soft cock. He had lost the semi-hardness of earlier, and my heart fluttered at the thought of feeling it grow in my mouth again.

Harper smiles contentedly and lays back, gesturing before placing both hands behind his head. "Be my guest, my lady."

I return to my earlier position, suckling his soft, yet still large, penis into my mouth. The sensation is heavenly. I roll him around in my mouth with my tongue as I suck, and it does not take long for him to start growing in my mouth.

His pleasurable moans make me writhe atop him, sending tiny thrills of sensation through my veins. I moan around his almost-too-big cock, causing Harper to cry out and thrust his hips upward.

It sends his cock deeper into my mouth, and he is big enough now to reach the back of my throat. I pull up and grasp the extra length with my hand, stroking up and down as I suck on the head.

"Goddess, Sophia, don't you dare stop," Harper rasps, grasping the back of my head.

He fists my hair into his hand as I take up a steady rhythm on his cock, stroking up and down with my hand and following with my mouth. I flick my tongue along the sensitive stretch of skin on the underside of his head as I come up and then suck him back down to the back of my throat as I go all the way down, touching my lips to my hand.

Harper begins to move, thrusting his hips up and down as he moans his pleasure. He uses his hand on the back of my head to guide my strokes as he makes love to my mouth.

"Fuck, Sophia," Harper rasps, and I can tell by his shaky voice and the wrinkling of his balls that he is dangerously close.

He grasps my hair and pulls, pulling me off him as he grasps my wrist with the other hand to stop its motion.

"If you don't stop, I'm going to go in your mouth," Harper says.

I swallow hard. "Okay. That would be okay."

He shakes his head and says, "No, not this time. This is for the demons."

He gestures with his head, his eyes following the gesture. I look over my shoulder to see the two shadows slowly approaching one another.

"We must wait for their release before we can enjoy our own," Harper says.

"Oh," I answer as I let go of his cock.

"Turn around," Harper says gruffly, and I comply.

I straddle him backward, my front facing his feet. He grasps my hips and guides me backward up his legs until I am positioned over his throbbing cock. He guides me down onto him, and I moan as all that delicious cock sinks into me.

The position is different, so it touches unfamiliar places inside my pussy. The sensation is unusual. The pressure that builds is lower in my stomach rather than deep in my core, and it is sharper in its intensity. It grows to an almost painful tension, and when it spills, it rides through me more like a running river than an ocean tide. My walls flutter instead of throb, and a sweet-smelling liquid seeps from my pussy and spills over Harper's dick.

I moan Harper's name as I ride out the pleasure, and the sensations are over almost as quick as they came. I had never experienced an orgasm like that one before. It was shorter, faster to come, and not as intense, but still pleasurable.

Harper sits up behind me, keeping me impaled on his dick as he places his face next to my ear.

"That was just the tip of the iceberg, baby girl. I'm gonna make you so wet that you will need a raincoat," Harper whispers.

I moan and rotate my hips, wrenching an answering moan from Harper. His fingers dig into my hips, stopping my motions. One hand trails to my pussy, and his fingers massage the bundle of nerves above my entrance while his cock is still buried inside me.

I throw my head back on his shoulder and moan in pleasure as it sends electric sparks of sensation coursing through me. He pulls his knees up, digging his heels in for leverage, and begins to pump his hips up and down.

The sensation of Harper's cock creating friction over that unusual spot in my pussy again, and the feel of his fingers playing with that familiar bundle of nerves above my entrance, brings me to the brink of another orgasm.

The building of this one is shooting sensations from my groin and all throughout my body, crashing through me in waves of pleasure so intense that my entire body shakes violently. I am screaming Harper's name, writhing and digging my fingers into Harper's thighs as I ride the sensations he is creating.

His hot breath flows over my ear and across my cheek as he breaths hard and fast, moaning with pleasure every time he thrusts his cock up into my pussy. The heat of his breath and the vibrations of his moans over my skin tips me closer to that delicious edge, and I writhe again as my fingernails dig into the hardened muscles of his legs.

Harper hisses in pain, then moans in pleasure as he wraps an arm around my stomach, holding me tight as his hips thrust harder and the fingers of his other hand swirl deliciously faster. His rhythm falters, and his moans become shouts as he continues to pound into me.

My body trembles violently with the crashing waves of ecstasy riding through me, and I still have not gone over the edge. My vision goes black as my eyes flutter into the back of my head, and I fear I might pass out from pleasure.

"Almost," Harper rasps through gritted teeth. "They are almost there."

I open my eyes and raise my head to see the shadows, and my eyes widen in surprise. They have taken on a more solid form. They look like people with very black skin, shining eyes, and black hair.

They could pass for humans if not for the eyes.

Lucien is fucking Jewel from behind, grasping her hip in one hand and holding her by the hair with the other. Her body jerks with every thrust of Lucien's hips, and she hangs onto the bench in front of her for balance.

The sight of them fucking is oddly exciting. I watch in fascination as Lucien pounds into her over and over, and with every thrust, my pleasure builds even more.

Finally, he sinks himself to the hilt and stops. Jewel throws her head back in a silent scream, and Lucien's mouth also opens. They keep their screams silent, but I can tell they are screaming their pleasure to the heavens.

Harper's fingers on my clit press more firmly, and his rhythm quickens as he thrusts into me. My head falls back onto Harper's shoulder again as a crashing wave of pleasure, more intense than all the others, runs through me, melding with the pressure building in my core. Finally, that pressure spills over and through me.

It is the most intense orgasm I have ever experienced.

My screams ride in the air with Harper's as he shoves his cock in my pussy one last time, reaching his climax with me. My walls throb and shudder simultaneously as molten hot waves crash through me. That liquid heat spills from my pussy again, drenching Harper in slick, sweet-smelling wetness. Spasms wrack my body as multiple waves of pleasure ride through me.

I can feel Harper's cock throb inside me as his climax releases his juices. His hot liquid shoots into my core, melding with the juices pouring out of my pussy.

The orgasm rides us long and hard, and I feel as if I will die from pleasure. My spasms fade with the orgasm, leaving me quivering with delicious little aftershocks. My breathing is ragged, my heart pumping fast, and my legs feel like they will never work again.

Something clicks inside my chest, shooting a shard of radiating pain through me. It is the strangest sensation like someone just pierced my heart with a pin. I grab my chest and yelp with pain, and Harper does the same.

Our bodies are still melded together as the pain subsides, and a burning sensation grows from the spot where the pain started. It consumes me from the inside, but it does not hurt. It is more of a comforting burn, like the heat from a campfire on a cold winter's day.

Harper holds me tighter to him, sliding his fingers away from my pussy to wrap his arm across my stomach. His other arm is still wrapped around my midsection, and he squeezes both arms around me tightly.

The burning sensation dissipates, melting into my heart and settling there. Harper lets out a long, shuddering sigh of contentment.

"It is done," He breathes into my ear. "We are bonded for life."

And I could not be happier.

CHAPTER 29

My eyes flutter open to see our demons sitting on the bench, holding each other as they ride out the aftermath. Lucien raises his head to look at me, and I gasp.

His eyes…

His glowing red eyes have changed to a shade of blue that almost matches Harper's eyes, only they glow with an eerie light that has my heart jumping in my chest.

"Why are you looking at me like that?" Lucien asks me.

"Your eyes," I answer. *"They changed."*

"Jewel told me that may happen," He says. *"It means I have changed. Harper will tell you about it."*

The demons fade, returning to the familiar shadows as the aftershocks and sensations fade. Harper's cock goes flaccid inside me, and I gently ease myself off and collapse to his side.

"I don't know if I will be able to make it back to the turret," I say with a satisfied smile. "I don't think I can walk yet."

"I will carry you," Harper says humorously.

"And what will you say happened to me when Cora asks?"

Harper shrugs and answers, "I will tell her I made mad, passionate love to you, and now you are paralyzed with pleasure."

"How about we just sit here for a minute and wait for my muscles to work?" I say with a laugh.

"That sounds like a plan," Harper says, falling back onto the soft shadow bed with his arms flung to his sides.

I lay beside him, throwing an arm across his chest and cuddling into his side. I lay my head on his outstretched arm and sigh contentedly.

"So what do the eye colors mean?" I ask as I play with the light sprinkling of hair on his chest.

"Eye colors?" Harper asks blankly.

"Lucien's eyes have changed," I answer in explanation. "They are no longer red. He told me you would tell me about it."

"Hmm," Harper hums reflectively. "What color are they now?"

"The same as yours, only they glow," I answer.

"Good. That is very good."

I slap his chest. "So, stop being cryptic and tell me what they mean."

Harper chuckles and says, "Alright, I will tell you."

I raise up on my elbow and lean into him. I run my hand along his chest, reveling in the solid feel of his muscles as I bring my hand close. I kiss his hard chest and rest my chin on my hand.

Harper props his head up with one hand behind his head. He wraps the other arm around my shoulders, stroking my hair that lays down my back in soft waves. He looks into my eyes, and his blue orbs radiate pure love and happiness.

I smile at that look. "Tell me."

"The first color of any demon is red. Red means that the demon is newly formed and untrained. Then, the color can go two ways from there."

Harper clears his throat, his visage falling into severe lines as he looks at me and asks, "Are you sure you want to know?"

I raise my chin off my hand to nod my head. What could be so bad about demons' eye colors to cause that look?

Harper takes a breath and says, "If the demon's eyes change to shades of purple, that is a bad sign. That means that the owner does not have complete control over the demon. The demon will fight to take over sometimes, but the owner is strong enough to fight it off.

"Most of the time, the owner is immoral, which leads to the demon being evil as well. Naughty demons do not work well with their owners.

"Other times, it could be a sign of bad training, and the owner will have to work twice as hard to tame the demon. This circumstance is very rare, which usually means the demon is exceptionally strong."

"So, is that why you thought Jeremy's demon was powerful?" I ask when Harper pauses. "You thought he was improperly trained?"

Harper nods. "Yes, I do...well did. At first, I did not think Jeremy was a bad person. Jeremy was so charismatic and charming that I could not think of him as immoral. The only explanation I could think of for Thorn's purple eyes was that he was simply too powerful for

Jeremy to train alone, so I offered to help him.

"But, then other things happened that made me suspicious of Jeremy and his intentions. One of my earlier patients committed suicide, or what we thought was suicide. But this patient was about to be released, so it made no sense.

"That was before you came to us. Then, when you came, he latched onto you right away. Still, I did not want to admit something was suspicious about him. I offered to bring him here when he expressed an interest in witchcraft. Then, only two weeks after he came, another of my patients committed suicide, and, again, it was under suspicious circumstances.

"That is when I began to suspect Jeremy, and I was worried about his intentions toward you. He never latched onto anyone else before he started hanging around you. The only thing I could think of that was different about you was your demon."

I glance down, unable to look into Harper's eyes as the images in the cafeteria run through my head. The figure's build, the sandy blond hair falling from the mask, and the accent and inflections in the figure's tone all pointed to Jeremy.

I started to open my mouth to tell Harper he was right and that Jeremy was an evil person. But he continues with his explanation and I fall silent to listen.

"Anyway, you don't have to worry about that scenario. Lucien's eyes are changing to blue, which means your demon is growing fond of and learning from you. It is a good sign for the future."

"What about Jewel? Where did she get her gorgeous eyes from?" I ask curiously.

"Oh, Jewel is a fully matured demon. The colors for fully matured demons are ultraviolet purple, lilac, navy-blue, and diamond.

"The ultraviolet and lilac eyes are the eyes of demons that have not been appropriately trained or are just as twisted and evil as their owners. The ultraviolet demons are the rarest. They are very powerful, dangerous, evil demons that love violence and destruction and often take over their owners to cause it.

"The navy blue and diamond eyes mean the demon has a partnership with its owner. They work well together and are very obedient. They even care deeply for their owners and, in some cases, have a special attachment to them.

"The diamond ones, like Jewel, are the rarest of all demons."

"Wow," I breathe reverently. "So, Jewel is super rare."

Harper smiles proudly. "Yep, and now she is partly yours too."

"And Lucien is part yours," I say with a happy sigh. "I think I can walk now. Maybe we should go back to the turret and take a shower."

"I hate to ruin the euphoric mood, but we also have to speak to the police about what happened in the cafeteria," Harper says.

He sits up, bringing me up with him, and looks around. He grabs something from the ground and stands, and I realize it is his jeans. I look around for my clothes as well, and we both dress as we talk.

"I will be right beside you, baby girl. You are so much stronger than you know," Harper says as he buttons his shirt, almost mirroring some of my mother's last words to me.

He pulls my chin up to look at him, taking my attention away from my task of pulling on my slip-on shoes. He looks at me as if I am his entire world, and I never want that look to go away.

But we cannot sit in this peaceful little corner of the world forever. We will have to face reality soon, and right now, I have to tell Harper about Jeremy.

I draw in a deep breath and blow it out slowly as I pull away from Harper's touch to finish putting on my shoes. I pull my shirt over my head and am fully dressed.

I let Harper finish dressing as well before saying, "I think I owe you a big apology. I should have listened to you about Jeremy."

Harper frowns as he runs his fingers through his tangled hair. "What do you mean?"

I swallow hard. "I mean, you were right about Jeremy. He is just as evil as his demon."

"Why would you say that, Sophia? I thought you liked him," Harper says.

The shadow mattress melts away, leaving only the bench to sit on. I sit down and pat the seat beside me. Harper sits down, looking at me questioningly.

I clear my throat and say, "It was Jeremy in the cafeteria. He was the one who killed Amelia. That is when I realized that you were right all along and that I should stay away from Jeremy."

Harper sucks in a breath, and I glance at him. The look of utter confusion in his eyes makes me frown. Then a look comes over Harper's face that scares the hell out of me.

He looks at me, and his eyes are…. devastated. That is the only word I can think of to describe the destitute, heartbroken, defeated, doomed look in Harper's gray-blue eyes.

"Harper?" I ask meekly, my voice breathy and laced with worry.

His tone is filled with everything that sits in his eyes as he whispers my name. "Oh, Sophia."

He cups my face in his hand gently as he says in a low tone, "Jeremy did not kill Amelia."

My eyes soften as I cover Harper's hand with my own, pressing my cheek into his hand.

My tone is comforting as I reply, "Harper, I know it may be hard to accept, but I saw him. He was wearing a mask, but I could tell it was him from his body shape. Also, some of his hair was sticking out from under the mask, and his accent was the same as Jeremy's.

"So, you did not see his face?" Harper asks.

I shake my head, rubbing against his hand. "No, but…"

Harper interrupts me. "And there is no way someone could have the same body type, accent, and hair color?"

I frown. "Well, yeah, but…"

Again, Harper interrupts. "Sophia, Jeremy was with me while you were in the cafeteria."

My eyes widen, and I gasp. "What?"

Harper cups my face with both hands, pulling my face up to look at him as he speaks.

"Honey, when I left the cafeteria, Jeremy was coming up the hallway toward me. I forbade him from entering the cafeteria and made him come with me to ask him about Amelia.

"He started to fight me, insisted I let him see you, but I told him about my promise to you. He stopped fighting me. He said I must care if I was willing to make that promise. He wished us luck."

Harper pauses, releasing one side of my face to run a hand through his hair.

He lets out a derisive chuckle before continuing, "He actually wished us luck. He said he would give you the same promise if you asked, and I realized that maybe Jeremy cared for you, too. I was wrong when I said he would never make the same promise.

"I told him that after we found Amelia, I would stop being a dick and let you out of the turret so that you could make your own decision concerning us. I could tell he was ecstatic and couldn't wait to see you.

"He helped me look for Amelia, and when Jewel told me what was happening, he called the police while I ran to get you."

Harper stops speaking and studies my face as I take in everything he had said. His visage still holds the same look as before.

I pull away from Harper's hand, still frowning. My head begins to shake back and forth. "But that would mean…"

"Jeremy really does care for you. If he wanted your demon, he had the opportunity to get him because he knew you were alone. Or, at least, we thought you were alone."

Harper looks stricken as his hand falls back to his side. His tone is laced with misery as he says, "If I had known you chose me because you thought Jeremy was evil, I never would have let it go that far. I never would have let our demons bond."

"No, Harper, don't do this…"

"I should just let you go," Harper says desolately.

"Harper, pay attention," I snap. "I'm trying to tell you…"

"You don't have to tell me, Sophia. I know. I am so sorry about allowing the bond before I fully understood, but we can work something out with Jeremy. This doesn't have to keep you two apart."

I had heard enough. I had already worked out my feelings for Jeremy and Harper, and it had nothing to do with either of them. It had to do with me and how I felt.

Yes, Jeremy felt like home to me. Jeremy was comfort. Jeremy was safety. But Jeremy was like my brother, not my lover. He would never own my heart the way Harper did.

Jeremy does not fill me with an all-consuming passion that threatens to burn me up from the inside out just by looking at me a certain way. Jeremy does not make my heart melt every time he smiles or teases me. Jeremy does not make me want to choke him and fuck him at the same time. Jeremy does not bring out the worst in me, only to kiss it away and bring out the best of me later.

Jeremy is not Harper.

It was Harper who had my heart in his hands. It had always been Harper.

I would explain all of this to Jeremy when I saw him again, but right now, Harper and I had more pressing problems to deal with than a messed-up love triangle, and the fact that Harper did not realize this pisses me off.

We can fight later.

And then have make-up sex.

I let the anger that blooms inside fill me. I let it consume me and make me strong as I firmly slap the side of Harper's face and scream, "Snap out of it, dammit, and listen to me!"

Harper rears back as if the devil himself had smacked him. He places a hand on the side of his face where the smack had connected.

"Did you just hit me?" He asks incredulously.

"Yes, dammit. Shut up for a minute and listen!" I shout.

The devastating look on Harper's face disappears, and the corners of his mouth quirk up in the beginnings of a smile. I swear I see a spark of pride flow through his eyes as he drops his hand from his face.

He clears his throat and says, "Alright. Speak."

"First and foremost, I did not 'choose you'. There was never a choice where my heart was concerned. From the moment I first saw you when I…" I pause for a moment to take a cleansing breath.

"I thought you were the most beautiful thing I had ever seen. I was gone the first time you ever smiled at me. Jeremy is more like a brother to me.

"It was never a matter of who I trusted. If either one of you were after my demon, who's to say you would not lure me into a false sense of trust with that promise you made and then just force me to bond my demon with yours anyway?

"And yes, I realize I messed up by having sex with Jeremy, but I really did believe that I might be in love with him at that time. He had my head all messed up. I admit I let him manipulate me, but not anymore.

"Jeremy will just have to deal with the fact that I am not in love with him if he wants to continue to be my friend."

I was breathless by the time I had finished my rant, and I stomp my foot defiantly as I finish.

Then I see that smile.

We didn't have time for that smile, dammit.

Nevertheless, it's there. It had spread across his face slowly as I had spoken, and now he releases the full power of it on me.

"Why are you smiling at me like that?" I ask, crossing my arms over my chest. "I am furious with you right now."

The smile never leaves his face as he stands from the bench and says, "I know."

Fuck him. He must know what that smile does to me, dammit, and he is giving it to me on purpose. He reaches a hand down to me to help me from the bench.

"Come on," He says. "We need a shower, and you have to give your statement to the police."

I take his hand with a huff. "So, are we done with this annoying conversation?"

Harper's gaze turns serious again as he pulls me to my feet. "We can talk later. There is still more you need to know about Jeremy."

"Harper…" I say, but he interrupts me.

"I know. You have already made up your mind. But you have to know the entire story," Harper says.

I frown. "What about patient confidentiality?"

"That is moot if you suspect the person of a crime," Harper says. "Plus, I'm releasing you from your program and making you a consultant on Jeremy's case."

"Wait, what?" I say dumbfoundedly. "But you said it wasn't Jeremy."

"This time, it wasn't. But, like I said, you don't know the entire story. Come on, I'll explain everything while we clean up." Harper says.

The wall of shadows dissipates from around us, and I gasp when I see it has become dark outside while we had lain in our tiny private circle of the world.

Harper takes my hand, and we leave the garden, heading for the turret and our future.

CHAPTER 30

Jeremy was put into the hospital psych ward because his high-priced lawyer got him a temporary insanity plea, just like me. Only Jeremy was up for murder, not simple assault charges. He was suspected of murdering his mother and father. The fire that had killed his parents was not an accident. It had been the result of arson, and Jeremy was the main suspect.

Furthermore, Jeremy had not even been in the house. So, the story Jeremy had given me about being an only survivor was a lie. Also, Jeremy covering up who he was had not been his doing. The facts had been covered up by the hospital board to prevent a scandal, so that was why very few people knew who Jeremy was. It was not because Jeremy did not want to be treated differently.

That detail had never sat right with me since Jeremy had told me that Harper and Marcel knew who he was. Why cover it up to everyone else when his two primary caretakers already knew?

Furthermore, Jeremy was not due to inherit anything of his parents since he was in custody until he finished his program, so Jeremy had no power as far as the hospital was concerned. Ownership of the hospital was taken by the executor of Jeremy's father's estate until Jeremy was fit to inherit everything.

This is what Harper had told me about Jeremy while we had cleaned up and dressed in preparation for our meeting with the officers investigating the happenings in the cafeteria. Now, we sit in the reception area, waiting for the police to finish their investigation.

"Jeremy always proclaimed his innocence," Harper was saying. "And I was prepared to give him the benefit of the doubt. Especially when I found out that he had an inner demon. I saw the purplish eyes and immediately thought his demon was to blame, so I decided to help Jeremy learn how to control his demon."

Harper pauses, sighing as he runs his hand through his hair. "Then I started suspecting him of killing my patients, and I gave up. Instead of working with Jeremy and his demon, I focused more on the investigations and proving Jeremy was guilty. But now, in light of recent events, I wonder if my suspicions about Jeremy were wrong and if there may still be hope for him after all."

"But, Harper, didn't you say the mature demons had ultraviolet eyes?" I ask nervously. "Because Thorn's eyes are definitely ultraviolet."

Harper frowns. "They are?"

I nod.

Harper slams his fist on his chair arm, causing me to flinch. "Fuck!"

He runs his fingers through his hair and then runs his hands down his face. He looks down at the ground as if in thought and takes a deep breath. I can tell he is trying to calm himself.

"When I first saw Jeremy's demon, his eyes were more red than purple," Harper mumbles to himself, but I hear every word. "They never changed while I was working with him, but then lately….Fuck…No wonder Jeremy refused to bring his demon out during our recent sessions."

He stares at the floor for a moment longer, then looks up at me and asks, "When did they change?"

"I don't know," I say with a shrug. "Thorn's eyes were that color when Jeremy first showed me his demon, the day we…"

I stop myself. Harper is tense enough as is. He does not need me making it worse.

I clear my throat before continuing. "The day I ran away from your office. But that was weeks ago, and if Thorn is mature, wouldn't that mean it is too late for Jeremy?"

Harper sighs. "I hope not, but I have no experience with this situation, so I cannot be sure."

"I have faith you will find a way," I say with a soft smile.

Harper grabs my hand and brings it to his lips. He kisses it softly and then laces his fingers with mine. Our hands swing together between our two seats.

"I love that you have faith in me," Harper says with a smile. "Sophia?"

I shut my eyes with dread at the sound of my name. Harper's hold on my hand tightens.

When I open my eyes, Jeremy stands over me, staring at mine, and Harper's joined hands with confusion. His hazel eyes flick between

Harper and me, and my heart aches when the realization fills Jeremy's eyes.

Fuck…This is not how I wanted Jeremy to find out.

Jeremy's shoulders slump in defeat, and utter devastation fills his visage. He looks at me with such misery that I feel it in my soul.

"Jeremy," I whisper sorrowfully. "Let me explain…"

Jeremy shakes his head back and forth as he backs away from us. "There's no need for explanations, Sophia. I see Harper got to you like I knew he would."

"Wait, Jeremy, that's not fair. Harper…"

But Jeremy does not give me time to say anything before he turns and stalks off toward the living areas.

I stand up from my seat. "Jeremy!" I call after him, but he ignores me and keeps walking.

I start to go after him, but Harper pulls on our still joined hands. I turn to him.

"Sophia, don't tell him about our demons," Harper whispers.

His eyes are filled with a similar look that Jeremy's had held moments ago.

Devastation, fear, worry...

I know he is worried that I will run back to Jeremy, but he releases my hand anyway, dragging his fingers over mine slowly as if letting me go is causing him physical pain.

"Don't tell him," He whispers again, and then adds, "Trust me."

I nod as Harper's hand slips from mine.

"And you can trust me, too," I say softly to him.

Then, I turn and run after Jeremy, following him down the hallway to the living quarters. I see him turn a corner, and it feels familiar. Was this the way to my room? It has been so long since I have been here that I do not remember.

Jeremy stops before one of the doors to the right, and I call to him just before he slips into the room.

"Jeremy, please wait. I just want to talk to you."

Jeremy turns to me as he opens the door. "Well, I don't want to talk to you."

"Please, Jeremy, just let me explain or at least apologize," I say as I catch up to him.

"Apologize?" Jeremy yells as he steps into the room.

I follow him as he turns on me and continues to yell.

"For what? For leading me on and letting me think we had a future together?"

"Jeremy, I…"

"Or for betraying me with the one person I told you to watch out for?"

"But Harper only wants to help…"

"Oh, or maybe it's for pretending to be my best friend."

"Now, hold on a minute!" I yell indignantly. "That's not right. You can yell at me all you want for turning to Harper. I deserve that and more. But you cannot accuse me of pretending to be your friend. I have always been your friend."

"No, Sophia, this is not what friends do to each other," he says, gesturing angrily as he backs further into the room.

I speak up before he can continue, following his movements. "No, it isn't. You're right. This is what lovers do, spouses even, but we are neither of those things, Jeremy. We had sex one time, and I told you before we even did anything that I would always be your friend no matter what."

"It wasn't just one time," Jeremy says, but he is not yelling now. He stops in the middle of the room, his tone turning husky and intimate as he adds, "Don't you remember the second time, and then in the shower…"

I cut him off. "Yes, Jeremy, we had sex multiple times, but it was all one session like I said before…" I stop with a huff and stomp my foot in irritation. "But that's not the point. The point is, I was confused then. I know I was wrong, and I should not have led you on but…"

He interrupts my rant as he moves toward me. "You're right, Sophia. You shouldn't have led me on. But you did anyway."

His movements become predatory as he stalks toward me with lust in his eyes. "So, do it again."

I frown in confusion. "What?"

He draws closer, the carnal hunger in his eyes changing them to a dark gold color. Chills race up my spine as I back away from him.

"Lead me on again, baby. I can take it. Fuck me like you did that day." His voice is low, husky, dangerous.

Fear curls through my blood, but I keep the firm tone in my voice as I say, "Are you listening to me, Jeremy? I am trying to tell you that I am with Harper now. We can't have sex anymore, but we can still be friends."

Jeremy chuckles callously, the sound causing goosebumps to sprinkle across my skin.

"Oh, Sophia, we are definitely going to have sex again, whether you want to or not," Jeremy says, his voice dangerously quiet as he moves closer still.

I back away slowly, fear churning inside my stomach as Jeremy's visage turns wicked.

"I will fuck all thoughts of Harper right out of you until you are screaming MY name, and then I will fuck you some more."

He moves ever closer, rubbing his hands together menacingly.

"Then, when I am done with you, you will be mine and have forgotten all about Harper. Our demons will bond, and we will be together forever."

Terror consumes me, kicking in my fight or flight response, and my body chooses flight. I spin around to run out the door, but I am too late. Jeremy moves fast, moving past me and slamming the door shut before I can get out.

He turns to me with a wicked smile and says, "You aren't going anywhere, Sophia. I will never let you go again."

I open my mouth to scream, but Jeremy grabs me, turning me around and pulling me close to his body. He wraps one arm around my torso, trapping my arms against my body. My back is trapped against his front, and Jeremy clamps his free hand over my mouth, silencing my screams.

It happened so fast that I had no time to react. Now, I am trapped, and my panic kicks in. I struggle, kicking furiously and biting at Jeremy's hand over my mouth, which only makes him press his hand harder over my face. It presses my lips against my teeth, and I taste blood.

Fury replaces the fear coursing through my veins as I change tactics, kicking my legs backward to try to kick past Jeremy's legs and hit the door. Maybe someone will hear the ruckus and come to investigate. Maybe the police officers who should be searching the building right now will hear.

But it is no use. Jeremy lifts me and moves me further into the room so I am kicking nothing but air. He carries me even further into the room and tilts forward, toppling us to the floor. He uses the momentum to fall on top of me while still holding me wrapped up in his arms.

The breath is knocked out of me as Jeremy's weight lands on top of me, and I am momentarily paralyzed. My lungs scream for oxygen I cannot give them as I lay there and struggle to take in a breath. Jeremy wraps my legs up with his to stop my kicking and places his mouth close to my ear.

His voice is breathless from our struggles as he growls into my ear, "You can struggle all you want, but you're not going anywhere until I say you are."

My lungs finally unfreeze, and I take deep, gasping breaths through my nose. I go limp, deciding my struggles are not accomplishing anything other than making me tired. Maybe if I can get Jeremy to drop his guard and think I have given up, he will let me go, and I can escape.

My optimism rises when I see the dark tendrils in the corners of my vision, spreading out and away from my body. This time, I am not afraid. My demon forms, his now blue eyes glowing like a beacon of hope.

"Your demon won't save you," Jeremy hisses in my ear.

"Don't try to save me or Jeremy will call Thorn, and you are not strong enough to fight him yet," I tell Lucien silently. *"Go get Harper and Jewel. Tell them where I am."*

Lucien disappears as fast as he had appeared, and Jeremy growls. More tendrils spread into the room, this time coming from Jeremy. This time I am afraid. The figure forms, and Thorn's ultraviolet eyes stare down at me.

I expect Thorn to disappear and pursue Lucien, but he doesn't. Instead, Thorn wraps me up in his tendrils, replacing Jeremy's arms and hand.

Thorn keeps a tight grip on me when Jeremy's hold is gone, and I struggle against the shadows that hold me prisoner. They hold stronger than Jeremy had. I am not getting out of Thorn's hold. Hopefully, Harper and Jewel will come soon.

"Finally," Jeremy says as he stands up and grabs me under both arms. "I never thought that damn demon would leave. I thought I was going to have to rough you up a bit to get it to come out."

He heaves me to my feet with his fucking demon still wrapped around me, holding me in place. The victorious look on Jeremy's face has chills running up and down my body.

He looks at me wrapped up in his demon and smirks. "Did you really think it was going to be that easy?"

I watch helplessly as Jeremy walks to the opposite side of the room to a seemingly empty wall that holds only a single, small bookshelf filled with some books, a set of skull-shaped bookends, and crystals similar to the ones Harper has in his private office.

Jeremy turns one of the skulls so that it faces the other one, then turns the other one so that they are facing each other. The bookshelf slides, swinging outward to reveal a hidden door behind the shelf.

I gasp behind the shadowy hand that holds my mouth.

Jeremy opens the door and motions for me to follow. I do not follow so much as I am pushed into the hidden room by Thorn, who still holds me tightly wrapped up in shadow.

Jeremy pulls the bookshelf back into place from the inside, then shuts the hidden door and locks it.

Icy tendrils of terror travel up my spine as my heart begins to beat furiously in my chest. I look around the small, simple space with dread. There is only a bed, a single chair, and a large mirror hanging on the otherwise empty wall in this room. There are no windows and no other doors besides the one we came in.

Jeremy motions to the bed, and Thorn begins pushing me that way as I struggle violently. I DO NOT want to be taken to that bed. A feeling of pure dread settles in my stomach when I think of what will happen to me on that bed.

"When Thorn lets you go, just remember, it will do you no good to scream or bang on the walls. This room is completely soundproof and escape-proof. You are stuck here until I decide to let you go," Jeremy says as Thorn deposits me onto the bed.

"What are you going to do to me?" I ask, my voice trembling with fear.

"Just what I said I would do to you," Jeremy answers. "I am going to fuck you until you forget about Harper. But first, I am going to take you somewhere where your fucking demon will not find you."

I scoff. "How are you going to do that when my demon is attached to my soul? He will always be able to find me."

"That's why I wanted him out," Jeremy says derisively. "If he isn't here, he won't see where I hide your body after I take your soul on a little ride. He can chase your soul all over the multiverse of space and time, but he will never be able to take you back if he can't find your body. Now, look into that mirror like a good girl.”

My eyes widen as I look over at the mirror. This is no regular mirror. This mirror does not hold reflections. Instead, the surface of this mirror swirls and coalesces with dark shadows and light, all playing together to create a melding pot of shapes and colors.

It is beautiful and mesmerizing.

I cannot look away.

“Your demon will never find you now,” Jeremy says as I feel icy fingers grasp the top of my head.

No! I know that familiar feeling and what is about to happen.

“Take her soul,” Jeremy says to Thorn. “And don’t forget to come back and get me. I will hide her body in the place we talked about and wait for you there.”

I struggle against the freezing fingers that crawl their way inside my head. I scream and rage against the sensation of being pulled away from my body. I fight against the memories as I am dragged through time and space.

None of it matters.

When I return to myself, I sit in the same room, only the mirror is clear this time. However, it does not show my reflection. The reflection of the room is there, but…

Chills travel down my spine, cold and frozen, freezing the breath in my lungs and stopping my heart. I am there, lying unconscious on the bed. Jeremy stands over me, laughing victoriously as he stretches me out on the bed in a spread-eagle position.

I am inside the fucking mirror, and I can do nothing but watch as Jeremy handles my unconscious body. He turns to the mirror, looking straight at me as if he can see me, and maybe he can. The mirror is strange enough that it could be a window through time.

“I hope you enjoy the view,” he says, and I know he is talking to me. “I’m going to give you quite the show before I take your body away to its hiding spot.”

So, he can see me, and he knows I can see him.

NO…

Oh God, I know what he will do even before he starts, and it makes me nauseous as I stand and helplessly watch. There is nothing I can do.

I have been taken to a place somewhere in space and time through the mirror. My body is back in the world of the living, on the other side of this mirror, and I am at the mercy of Jeremy.

And he is more vile than either Harper or I could have imagined.

CHAPTER 31

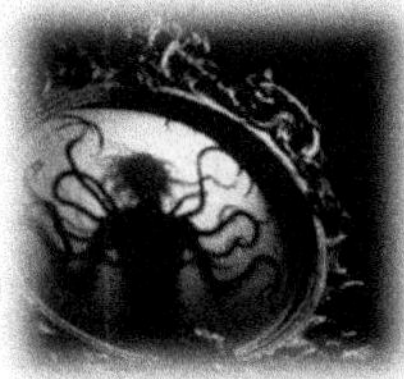

Jeremy smirks evilly at the mirror, at me, for a moment before turning back to my helpless body. I begin to sob, knowing what is coming and helpless to stop it. I know when Thorn moves up behind me because I can feel his icy presence at my back.

He places his cold hands on my shoulders, holding me in place.

"If you look away or close your eyes, I will do worse to you than what Jeremy is about to do," Thorn says in my head.

I gulp and stare at the mirror, wide-eyed and tense, as I wait for Jeremy to do what I already know he is about to do.

And I am forced to watch.

He starts by pulling off my top. I gasp as I feel the sensation of the cloth moving over my skin as Jeremy pulls it up and over my body's head and arms, even though my shirt stays intact here.

It is worse than I could have imagined. I am not only going to watch, but I will also be able to feel every sensation. My sobs grow worse, and I cringe at Thorn's touch as he tightens his hold on my shoulders.

Jeremy moves to my pants next, unfastening them and pulling them down my legs. He pulls my shoes off, then takes my pants all the way off. He tosses all of them to the floor next to my shirt. My body lies on the bed, completely naked.

Jeremy leans down and runs his hand from my shoulders down to my breasts, then pinching and pulling on my nipples. The sensations run through me, and I struggle against Thorn's hold as I scream out in protest. I shudder in revulsion at the feel of Jeremy suckling on my nipples as I watch him kneel down and take each nipple into his mouth.

Aversion and disgust coalesce with the horror running through me as I watch Jeremy take off his clothes. He bends over me, and the sight of his naked body over mine makes me wretch. I choke on a sob and wretch again as Thorn's shadowy fingers dig into my shoulders.

"What's wrong, slut. You begged for Jeremy to fuck you before and even let me fuck you," Thorn says cruelly.

That was before Jeremy had shown his true colors, before I loathed the sight of his naked body lying over me, and before I felt repulsed at the thought of his dick going inside me.

That was when I thought I had loved him, genuinely loved him, and thought he cared for me too.

But I do not say any of that to Thorn. I do not say anything at all to the horrifying, disgusting demon that is forcing me to watch and experience my own rape through a fucking mirror.

I will never be okay with mirrors again.

I gasp when I experience the sensation of Jeremy's weight on top of me as I watch him climb my body. He positions himself between my legs, and I feel every sensation even though I clamp my legs together tightly.

I scream in abhorrence at the feel of Jeremy positioning the head of his cock over my entrance, and nausea rips through me as Jeremy drives himself into me, hard and rough. My body's pussy must have been dry because the friction of his entrance tears through me in a wave of intense agony.

I scream out in pain as Jeremy's cock pumps into me repeatedly. I scream and scream until my throat is raw, and the pain in my head almost matches the pain radiating from between my legs.

My legs shake with anguish, but Thorn's bruising hold keeps me upright. I lean forward slightly and heave, throwing up some sort of weird liquid all over the floor, which quickly disappears with the wave of one of Thorn's hands.

The torture of my rape lasts all of a couple of minutes, but it feels like forever to me. Jeremy finally empties his repulsive load into me with a victorious, satisfied shout of pleasure.

My sobs ring through the room. It was nothing like the rape of my nightmare. This was not a horrified, forced orgasm. This was just fucking unspeakable torturous agony.

I watch wide-eyed in complete loathing and horror as Jeremy picks himself up off me, picks up my shirt, and wipes blood from his still-throbbing dick. He smiles hideously in the mirror the entire time. He throws my shirt onto the floor.

"I will leave the clothing as evidence. I cannot wait to see the look on Harper's face when he finds that," Jeremy sneers into the mirror. "I will leave the hidden door open just so Harper can find it. It will be fun to watch."

I choke on a sob as I watch a tiny stream of blood run down the naked thigh of my body. I can feel it. The horrible agony of my pussy walls ripped and torn from Jeremy's abuse. The pain shoots all the way through my core, tearing through my lower stomach and upper thighs.

If not for Thorn's bruising hands holding me upright, I would have fallen to the floor in a heap of hurt and agony by now. Thorn holds me there while Jeremy picks up my body and slings it over his shoulder.

Turning to the mirror, Jeremy says, "I'll take the trash out, Thorn. Come get me."

Thorn turns, slinging me around with him and shoving me to the other side of the room. I stumble and fall onto the bed as hopelessness and helplessness consume me. I curl up, placing my head into my arms as I cry, great wracking sobs that convulse my body and fill the room with gut-wrenching sounds.

Thorn disappears.

It is useless to hope any longer. Lucien may find my soul, but he will never find my body. Jeremy has taken it God knows where, and without knowing where it is, Lucien won't be able to drag me back to reality.

I am trapped. The only option I have is to wait and hope that Harper finds my body so Lucien or Jewel can rescue me.

I lose all sense of time as I lay there and cry. I do not know how much time has passed before Thorn appears again with Jeremy in tow, and the look on Jeremy's face has me frowning in confusion. He kneels by the bed and brushes my hair from my face, and the gesture is…tender, gentle, almost as if he cares.

His tone matches his worried visage as he says, "Sophia, why are you crying?"

I pick my head up from my arms and frown at him.

"Why do you think I am crying?" I answer sarcastically, my voice ravaged from all the screaming.

Jeremy frowns. "I am trying to be nice to you, Sophia. You do not want to make me angry, do you?"

I do not answer. My head drops back to the bend of my elbow as another round of wracking sobs consumes me. Jeremy sits beside me, rubbing my back in a comforting rhythm, but it is not comforting to me. I shrink from his touch, but that only serves in Jeremy grabbing my arm and pulling me back to him. I decide to endure the touch.

"Oh, now here comes my favorite part," Jeremy says with a sneer. "Come on, Sophia. Sit up and watch with me."

"I d…d…don't w…w…want to," I choke out between sobs.

"Are you trying to make me mad?" Jeremy asks through gritted teeth.

"P…p…please," I beg when Jeremy grabs my wrist and pulls. "Just leave m…m…me alone."

"Sophia," Jeremy says in disappointment. "You know I am not gonna do that. Now, come on and watch this with me. Hurry before you miss it."

Sniffling, I move to sit up when white-hot agony radiates from my core and spreads across my lower stomach. I cry out in pain, but Jeremy only pulls me harder. I scream again as the pain worsens the more I move.

Jeremy pulls me onto his lap, facing forward with my legs draped over his in a backward straddle. He places a hand on each of my thighs and pulls my legs apart further. I scream again as the pain shoots down my legs with the movement.

"Thorn, can you do something about that before we miss the show?" Jeremy says as he holds me in place.

Thorn forms and kneels before me, and I struggle against Jeremy's hold. Jeremy wraps both arms around my torso, and Thorn's tendrils of shadow wrap around my wrists and pull my hands down to my sides. More tendrils wrap around my ankles, holding my legs in place and stopping my struggles.

"Now, now, none of that," Jeremy says in my ear. "Sit still and take your medicine."

Held in place by Jeremy and Thorn, I am helpless as Thorn brings his face in close to my body, blowing a breath of frozen, icy air along the spot where the entrance to my core is hidden under my clothes.

My clothes disappear, and I gasp as I realize I am now naked in Jeremy's arms. I scream.

"Come on, now, love, did you really think I was going to let you keep your pants on?" Jeremy says as he cackles maliciously.

The pain radiating through me lessens as Thorn's icy breath continues to blow across my now-naked skin. The iciness enters my pussy, coiling along my walls and soothing where it touches. I sag in relief in Jeremy's hold as the pain abates, and I am left pain-free.

"There, now isn't that better?" Jeremy whispers softly in my ear. "Now, you are fresh and ready for another round."

I shudder in revulsion at Jeremy's words and the sensation of his lips on the back of my neck. He chuckles evilly and points to the mirror.

"Now, let's watch the show," He says.

I look up at the mirror, and my heart sinks. Harper stands in the room where my body had been, looking around in desperation and worry. Jewel is there with Lucien, and they flank Harper as he screams in rage.

"God dammit, Lucien! You said she was here!" He yells. "Where is she?"

He gets that unfocused look on his face again momentarily before shoving his hand through his hair.

"Mmm, the sound of Harper's suffering makes me horny," Jeremy says in my ear as his hands stroke up and down my thighs, sending waves of nausea through my stomach.

"Well, she isn't here anymore," Harper says in agonizing disappointment, returning my attention to the mirror.

His eyes land on my discarded clothing scattered on the floor, and he freezes. He bends down and picks up the shirt that Jeremy had cleaned his cock on. The blood stands out against the light color of the shirt, stark and bright red, since it had not yet had time to dry to that dull brown color.

Harper stares at it in disbelief momentarily, then slams it to the floor with a string of curses. He throws his head back and screams, the sound filled with pure agony and rage.

"Oh, yes, the screams," Jeremy breaths into my ear as one of his hands travels up my thigh and brushes across the apex. His breathing turns ragged as he strokes above my entrance with two fingers.

"Please, stop," I cry out, writhing against the uncomfortable sensation of Jeremy's touch.

"Watch…the…mirror," Jeremy grounds out, accentuating each word as he swirls his fingers roughly on my clit.

I watch the mirror, writhing and moaning in misery as I endure Jeremy's touch while I watch Harper turn to the two demons standing in the room with him.

"Fucking find her, God dammit," Harper says to Lucien.

Jeremy shoves two fingers inside me and moans in ecstasy. "It makes me so fucking hot to know that he will never find me."

I scream in agony and hatred at Jeremy's violation as I see Harper's eyes turn dark with absolute fury.

"He's doing what to her right now?" Harper screams at Lucien.

Lucien's eyes glow with a sky-blue light so bright that I squint against it.

Jeremy throws his head back and laughs as he snaps his fingers. Suddenly, he is naked under me, and he lifts me up with his hands on my hips.

Thorns fucking tendrils still hold my arms and legs trapped as Jeremy brings me back down on his cock, filling me up as I scream with blinding agony.

"Yes! Scream for me, baby! Hearing Harper's fury at the same time only makes me harder for you," Jeremy cries as he lifts me up and down on his hardened cock.

"Please, stop!" I scream as his dick tears me up inside, the pain radiating through my entire body.

"Go, make him stop!" I hear Harper yell. "Jewel, help him if you can."

"Uh oh, looks like I gotta get this done quick," Jeremy says.

He grasps my hips tightly and stands with me sheathed on him. He turns and pushes my torso down so that I am bent over before him with his dick still embedded in my pussy.

I grab onto the bed and hold on while he rams into me, fast and hard and forceful. His shouts of pleasure as he ravishes me disgust me. The sensation of his dick pounding into me sickens me.

"And if you can, bring that fucking freak to me!" Harper shouts in pure rage.

The vivid fury in Harper's tone runs shivers down my spine even as Jeremy's seed filling me fills me with wrath. It overtakes the hopelessness and misery within me. It sears within my ravaged soul and brings me hope.

Hope that the anger will help me endure until Harper can find my body, hope that he will absolutely destroy Jeremy when he gets his hands on him, and hope that Harper will let me watch.

Hell, I will even participate if Harper will let me.

Jeremy pulls out of me and pushes me to the bed. I turn to look into the mirror, and the look in Harper's eyes makes even me afraid.

Harper takes one last look around the tiny room before turning and leaving it the way he found it. He closes the door, slamming it with ultimate finality.

That last look is seared into my brain. Judging by that look, Harper will find me. And when he does, there will be hell to pay.

CHAPTER 32

My tears are dry. I am done crying. I am done wallowing in hopelessness and grief. I am done with being weak. I glare at the man who I thought was my friend, the man who will be dead when I get my hands on him.

When I am strong enough to destroy him.

I glare up at him as he smirks at me.

"I love this mirror, don't you?" Jeremy says as he strokes the mirror's frame. "This mirror can see through any mirror in the real world."

I say nothing as I continue to glare at him.

"Oh, now come on. Don't look at me like that. This wasn't my fault, you know. I told you to stay away from that fucker. If you would have only listened to me, our demons would already be bonded, and you would be..."

Jeremy stops and chuckles. "At first, I just wanted to kill you and take your demon. But now, I think I will keep you. I just love that pussy. I don't think I will ever get enough."

"When your demon gets here, I will have my way with him and bond him to me," Thorn says. *"Then we four will be an unstoppable force. You will learn to adhere to our ways soon, or I will devour you myself."*

"You will not touch her!" Jeremy snarls. He moves in front of me, shielding me from his own demon.

The mood swings are starting to make me dizzy.

"Fuck you!" I spit at Jeremy. "I'd rather be devoured by your demon than have your dick inside me again!"

Thorn laughs, actually laughs, inside my head. The sound is devious, dark, and dangerous. Jeremy must hear it, too, because the anger in his eyes turns deadly.

"I will deal with you later," He says to Thorn and then turns to me. "As for you, I will teach you to keep your mouth shut."

Fear rips through me as I remember those words coming out of the mouth of whoever it was that killed Amelia….

Come to think of it…

It sounded exactly like that person.

"How'd you do it?" I ask Jeremy as he stalks toward me angrily.

"Do what?" He seethes.

"Kill Amelia while you were with Harper at the same time," I say as I scramble to the other side of the bed, away from Jeremy.

He reaches the side of the bed, and I flinch away from him.

"Oh, that," Jeremy says with a smirk as he grabs my wrist. "Let's just say it was not me walking around with Harper all day."

Jeremy winks at Thorn, who lets out an evil chuckle. I turn to look at Thorn.

"How?"

"Because I can do this," Thorn says, and his body starts to coalesce strangely, twisting and writhing like a mini tornado.

Colors and shapes form in the funnel, and the spinning slows. Finally, an exact replica of Jeremy stands where Thorn used to be.

My eyes widen in surprise. "Impressive," I say sarcastically. "Two psychopaths are better than one, I always say."

"You are going to shut your smart mouth because I am going to shove my dick in it," Jeremy growls as he shoves me forcefully onto my back.

"Why did you kill her?" I spit in his face as I struggle against him.

"Because, like you, she couldn't keep her mouth shut," Jeremy sneers. "She saw something she shouldn't have and then ran to fucking Harper like a bitch…like you…and now I am going to make you pay just like I did her."

"Did she have a demon you wanted too?" I ask sarcastically as Jeremy fights to take me down.

"Actually, yes. Thorn absorbed that bitch of a demon after we fucking killed its whore of an owner. But I am not going to kill you. I am just going to take your fucking demon. You will learn to obey and be a good little bitch after I fuck your mouth."

I scream out in anger and fight, struggling against his hold with everything in me. He slaps me across my face, rocking my head back as I taste blood. I shake it off and lash back, punching and slapping blindly with all my strength. I make contact with flesh and hear Jeremy let out a yelp of pain.

He rolls off the bed and to the floor, holding his injured dick in his hand. I smirk in victory.

"Get the bitch," Jeremy says. "Shove your dick in her ass while I fuck that smart mouth."

I jump from the bed and back away from Jeremy and his deranged shadow. "You won't be fucking anything if you touch me again, I will rip it off next time!"

I back away further, and my back hits something feathery, soft yet cold as the grave. Goosebumps break out along my arms, and I know I have just touched a demon.

But Thorn stands before me, not behind me...

Hope rises in my gut as a shadowy arm wraps around me while a cold hand presses against my head.

I welcome it, waiting impatiently for the feeling of being transported through space and time. I close my eyes against the sensation, taking in a cleansing breath to avoid the usual nausea.

I wait, but nothing happens. I peek open an eye to see Jewel locked in combat with Thorn. I look over my shoulder to see Lucien holding me, watching the combat with worried eyes.

Jeremy stalks toward us, his visage dark and murderous. "Let her go, you bastard. You don't have a body to take her to, anyway."

I hear a demon's scream and look to the fight to see Thorn swipe a clawed hand across Jewel's midsection. Light radiates from the cuts down her chest as she screams. She retaliates with a swift kick to his groin, which he blocks by catching her foot and shoving it away, causing Jewel to lose her balance and stumble backward.

"Get back, you bastard. You have already hurt her enough," Lucien screams at Jeremy.

"Go, help her," I say to Lucien, gesturing toward Jewel, Careful not to say either of their names.

Lucien answers me silently, casting nervous glances toward the fight. *"Harper told me to stay away from Thorn in case he tries to force me to bond. At least, until we find your body and get you out of here."*

Jeremy reaches us and grabs for my arm, but Lucien jerks me away from him.

"I said, leave her alone," He growls.

"She is mine, you stupid demon, and soon you will be mine too."

He turns toward the fighting demons on the other side of the room. "Hurry and finish that one off. We have the one we want right here."

Thorn grabs for Jewel, but she jumps back and swipes at the offending arm. Gashes open up on Thorn's arm and torso, radiating light from them. The light that spills from their wounds is the same color as their eyes, and the colors spin and twine together in a dazzling display of light that belies the brutal fight beneath it.

Finally, Thorn takes one last swipe across Jewel's neck, and light spills from her throat. I hear her scream of pain as her form diminishes.

"NO!" I scream, but Lucien holds me back from running to her.

"Sophia, Jewel will be fine," Lucien whispers comfortingly. *"Demons cannot truly die unless their heads are cut off, and he only slit her throat. She will just go back inside Harper until she gathers enough energy to come back out again."*

Jeremy laughs viciously as he closes in. "Finally. Get over here, and let us finish this so we can finally get out of here."

Thorn brushes himself off, and his wounds close as he stalks over to us. Lucien holds me against him tightly as we both back away together.

"Fuck that God damn demon up his ass and show him who's boss," Jeremy snarls. "While I shove my dick so far up her pussy while she screams. That should do the trick."

I start shaking my head as Thorn backs us away. "Get out of here!" I hiss at him.

"I'm not leaving you," He says as his hold tightens around me.

"How touching," Jeremy sneers sarcastically. "But it won't save you. However, it will serve my purposes if he stays."

Suddenly, the mirror flickers with static, like a television trying to find the broadcast signal. Everyone in the room turns to it questioningly to find Harper standing around the reception area with three police officers.

"I didn't know there was a mirror in the reception area," I say with a frown.

"There isn't," Jeremy says, confused.

"Well, there must be one, or we wouldn't be seeing this now," I say derisively.

"What did I tell you about your smart mouth?" Jeremy sneers, but his eyes are on the mirror.

We all turn our attention to it, straining to hear what they are saying.

"We could not get video footage because your camera was out in the dining room. However, we have found some DNA evidence around one of the small outpost buildings on the property. You were aware this was once a military base, right?" One of the officers was saying to Harper.

Harper nods. "Yes, that is one of the reasons I bought this piece of property. If one of my patients escapes, they cannot get over the wall."

"I see," Says the officer. "There are also not many places to hide a person or a body, which gives us an advantage."

"There may be more places than you think," Harper says. "There are many hidden tunnels under this place with many hidden doors. She could be behind any of those, like the one we scouted earlier where we found her clothes."

"I didn't know Harper knew about the tunnels," Jeremy hisses. "Fucking faggot is getting too close."

I smirk and hear Lucien let out a victorious huff.

"Alpha team, take the outposts," the officer says into a walkie-talkie that has been attached to his hip. "Beta team, you take the tunnels."

He clicks off the walkie-talkie and places it back in its holder as he turns to Harper. "Can you get us a map of those tunnels?"

"Yes, sir," Harper says, offering the officer his hand.

They shake hands, and the officer walks off. Harper turns to the mirror, staring into it like he can see us. He stalks toward it, piercing it with an angry stare.

"Sophia always said she saw the demon in the mirrors," Harper says quietly, glancing around to see if anyone is watching him talk to a mirror.

"Well, if that is true, then I hope you can hear me, Thorn," Harper snarls. "I am coming for you, and when I find you, you and your master are mine."

Harper makes a menacing gesture toward the mirror, punching his fist into the palm of his other hand and then running a finger across his neck.

Then, Harper tosses something over the mirror, and the picture goes blank.

Jeremy turns on Thorn with a look of pure rage and roars, "How the fuck does he know your name?"

He turns back to me. "You told him, didn't you? You found out somehow and told him."

"Yeah, and I am certainly glad I did," I shoot back with a victorious sneer. "He's gonna find me, and when he does…"

I do not get the rest of the sentence out before his fist comes for my face. Lucien tries to jerk me away from the hit, but he is not fast enough. Jeremy's fist clips the side of my face, and I hear a sickening crack.

Pain radiates down the side of my face and along my jawline as stars fill my vision. I hear Lucien let out a terrifying scream of thunderous rage, his black-hole mouth opening wide.

"Let her rot here with her demon!" Jeremy says to Thorn. "We have other pressing matters we need to attend to."

Lucien helps me stagger over to the bed, where he lays me down gently. Pain and nausea overtake me as I curl up into a ball. Jeremy sneers down at me.

"I'll be back, bitch. And, when I return, your demon will bond with mine, or there will be consequences."

Thorn wraps Jeremy in his shadowy arms and disappears. I lie back on the bed and breathe a sigh of relief.

"Do you know how to work that thing?" I ask Lucien, gesturing toward the mirror.

"I think I can figure it out. Do you want to focus on Harper?" He asks.

"I don't know if we should focus on Harper or Jeremy," I say. "If we don't know what Jeremy is up to, how will we know when he is coming back?"

"I need to know if Harper finds your body," Lucien says. *"I am supposed to stay with you until he does."*

"Fine," I say. "Let's focus on Harper."

Lucien walks over to the mirror and touches the frame. The glassy surface glows with an iridescent light as images fly past.

Harper laughing at something I said. He looked so happy and carefree.

Harper staring at me lustfully as I polished a crystal in his private office. That was the day he had asked me to come here.

Harper peeking through the cafeteria door sorrowfully as I sat with Jeremy the first day I came here.

Finally, I see Harper as he is right this minute, sitting on the edge of his bathtub with his head in his hands. Is he crying?

"Harper," I whisper longingly, reaching a hand out toward the mirror. "I love you."

He lifts his head up as if he heard me, and my heart lurches with hope. He glances at his bathroom mirror, and it looks like he is staring right at us.

He runs a hand through his dark auburn hair and whispers, "Lucien, I hope you are keeping her safe."

I glance up at Lucien, and he looks down at me with sorrow radiating from his ice-blue gaze. Has his eyes gotten lighter?

"He is," I say to the mirror, even though I know Harper can't hear me.

CHAPTER 33

My head swims with nausea when I try to rise up from the bed. The side of my face burns where Jeremy had hit me, and it feels puffy and tender when I probe the spot with my fingers. I groan in agony when Lucien tries to sit me up.

"Come on, Sophia, stay with me. It could be dangerous if you pass out here." Lucien says as he pulls me to a sitting position. *"As soon as I get you back to your body, I swear you can rest."*

I blink several times to stay awake. My spirit is tired, and I am sure wherever my body is, it is exhausted. It is also damaged, and I am scared to find out just how severe the damage is.

I shudder as I remember the excruciating pain that radiated from my core after Jeremy had brutally raped my body while ordering his demon to force me to watch.

And experience it.

I hear Harper's voice humming softly and turn my attention to the mirror. He sets up something on his living room floor as he hums a mysterious, dark tune. I watch as Harper brings several items into the tiny room and sets them all up on a table draped with a black cloth.

Four taper candles of different colors, red, green, yellow, and blue, sit in candle holders, one on each of the four sides of the square table. A sizeable purple pillar candle sits in the center, along with several rocks…no wait…crystals surrounding it around its base.

To finish the scene, Harper places his giant skull from his private office on the floor before the table. He pulls a vial from the pocket of the long, black robe he is wearing, uncaps it, and pours the liquid from the vial, covering the top of the skull.

I frown.

"What is he doing?" I ask Lucien.

"It looks like he is casting a spell, though what kind, I have no clue. The altar looks nice, though."

"What's an altar?" I ask in confusion.

Lucien rolls his eyes. *"Jeesh, Harper did not teach you a thing, did he? Did you two do nothing but make out and tease each other when you weren't ignoring each other or fighting?"*

"No," I answer indignantly. "We did other things too."

Though, for the life of me, I cannot think of anything right now.

"The table is called an altar, and the candles represent the four elements. The one in the middle represents spirit. It is all very complicated if you do not know the basics. Jewel and I will teach you some stuff when we get you out of here."

"He is writing something on that big purple candle," I say, pointing to the mirror. "Can you see what it is?"

Lucien moves closer to the mirror, so close that his shadowy nose almost touches the glass. He squints his icy-blue, glowing eyes, then jumps back as if the glass had bit him.

"Fuck!" He curses loudly. *"He's writing Thor's name on the candle."*

"So, what does that mean?" I ask in alarm.

From the sound of Lucien's curses, it is not good.

"He is casting the control spell," Lucien answers.

I frown as the words sink into my mind, and then I gasp. "You mean…"

"Yes," Lucien answers. *"The spell he told you about being able to control another person's demon if you know their name."*

"So, why is that a bad thing?" I ask. "If he can control Thorn, he can force Thorn to tell us where Jeremy hid my body."

"Because, as Harper said before, he has never tried that spell. It takes enormous concentration and massive amounts of energy. If it is done incorrectly, it could be dangerous."

I glance worriedly at the mirror. "I have faith in him. He can do it."

"I hope so," Lucien says and then suddenly blanks out the mirror.

I frown. "Why'd you turn it off?"

"I feel a presence coming. It might be Thorn or Jeremy or both." Lucien answers, gliding over to stand by the bed.

Thorn appears, but Jeremy is not with him. His smile is sly and victorious as he appears.

"They will never find your body now," Thorn growls as he approaches me. *"Jeremy is there now. Enjoy."*

Thorn closes his eyes, and when he opens them, I feel hands all over my body. Only no one is touching me. I scream out in rage, fear, and desperation, reaching a hand out to Lucien.

"No, not again!" I cry. "Make it stop!"

"What is happening to you?" Lucien asks, casting an outraged look at Thorn.

The purple-eyed demon draws closer, looking at Lucien ravenously.

"Jeremy is violating my body, and I can feel everything," I say through gritted teeth as I fall onto the bed. It becomes difficult to stand because of the sensation of a huge weight on top of me.

"And I am going to take you simultaneously," Thorn says to Lucien. *"You will belong to me before this day is out."*

"I don't think so," Lucien growls as Thorn stalks around him, sizing him up for an attack.

I writhe in pain as I feel something enter me, stretching and filling me. I scream at the sensation. It feels like I am being ripped apart on the inside, and the agony radiates through my entire body.

Lucien looks over at me worriedly. *"Sophia,"* He cries out.

I fight through the pain, rolling over and crawling on hands and knees across the bed. I grit my teeth against the urge to scream out again as another wave of agony rips through me from my core.

"Don't worry about me. Fight Thorn," I seeth.

Lucien turns back to Thorn, who launches at him, tackling him to the ground. Lucien screams in anger as Thorn lands on top, pushing Lucien's head onto the ground and holding it there. He straddles Lucien on his thighs and uses his free hand to pull one of Lucien's arms around and lock it in place at a painful angle across his back.

"Stop it!" I cry, enraged and in pain, as another thrusting sensation violates my pussy and sends shockwaves of agony through my walls.

I ignore the pain and get to my feet, staggering toward the fighting demons. Thorn is trying to get Lucien in position to…

Oh, hell no.

Thorn has Lucien's arms pinned, his head held down, and his ass freely exposed. His shadow-man dick is hard and thrusting toward Lucien's ass when I tackle him, bringing him off Lucien and rolling onto the floor beside him.

I scream and writhe, unable to finish my attack as the thrusting becomes faster and the pain more intense. I am thrown onto the floor, back arching from tormenting anguish that I cannot ignore.

The thrusting continues, rendering me helpless as Thorn brushes off my attack and returns to his feet. Lucien has rolled away, nursing his torn arm as he staggers back to his feet.

His eyes glow brightly, the white-blue color radiating through the room. His eyes! They are definitely lighter.

He opens his mouth and screams, the banshee scream that always makes me cover my ears because it hurts my eardrums, but I do not cover my ears this time. This time, my screams rival his as the pain shoots through me, and then suddenly, it is gone.

I look over to Lucien, who has stopped screaming. Thorn backs slowly away from Lucien as a mass of twisting shadows swirls between them. It takes form slowly as the two demons watch, and then pure white light radiates from it as Jewel's eyes come into focus, her form stepping out from the light.

"Hold on to that anger, Sophia," Jewel's sweet, soft voice fills my head. *"It gives us power, and we need all we can get right now."*

That should be no problem, considering I have just been violated yet again, with no way of stopping it. The pain in my lower stomach intensifies with every agonizing step as I struggle to the bed.

Suddenly, Thorn disappears, leaving me alone with the two demons. My two demons. Mine and Harper's two demons. I look toward the mirror, longing to see him again and wondering if he completed the spell somehow.

As if someone heard my wish, the mirror comes alive, and Harper's form comes into view. He is sitting in front of the altar, swaying back and forth as if rocking a baby. He is humming softly, though I cannot hear the words, and holding what looks like a dagger over his head.

He yells Thorn's name and brings the dagger down, sticking it to the hilt into the purple candle. Dark smoke, eerie and silent, permeates from the candle, swirling into the room and surrounding Harper, where he sits frozen in place. The swaying has stopped, and the humming ceased.

Suddenly, Thorn appears with Jeremy in tow. Only Jeremy does not seem too happy.

"What the hell, Thorn? What is this about? Did you bond? I was attending class so I would have an alibi."

Thorn deposits Jeremy before my two demons, backs away, and then turns to Jewel.

"Her body is hidden in tunnel B, room 5, under the old infirmary," Thorn tells Jewel aloud so we all can hear.

"What the fuck, Thorn. Why'd you tell them that?" Jeremy yells in outrage. "What has gotten into you?"

I answer for him, pointing toward the mirror. "Harper. Harper has gotten into him."

Jeremy's eyes widen when he looks at the mirror, and he turns horrified eyes to Thorn.

"Thorn?" He says, and his voice is uncertain, even a little afraid.

Thorn turns to me. *"Fast or slow?"*

Vengeful rage fills me along with the agonizing pain from Jeremy's last assault on my body, and I turn to Thorn with the answer in my eyes.

"Slow"

That one word, filled with all the pain and suffering I have endured over the past weeks because of this man. Filled with all the regret at lost loves and friendships. Filled with all of the anguish of everyone who died because of this vile man.

Thorn nods to the other two demons, and they do their part, wrapping Jeremy up in tendrils of shadow and rendering him helpless. Jeremy screams in outrage, and then his screams turn to fear as he is pushed to the ground in front of his own demon, who stares menacingly down at him with ultraviolet, glowing eyes.

"What are you doing?" Jeremy asks, his voice quivering with nervousness. "Thorn, I order you to stop."

"Thorn is no longer home," Thorn's voice says. *"I will be controlling your demon for now."*

"Harper?" I breathe, staring incredulously at Thorn.

He turns and winks at me with a devious smile. He kneels in front of Jeremy, grabs the pinkie finger of one hand, and pulls hard and fast. Jeremy's pinkie separates from his body, and Jeremy screams in anguish.

His screams fill the room as Thorn continues to tear off his fingers, one by one. The blood that sprays from his hands is unlike any I have ever seen. It is brighter, thinner, and coats everything in the room in a sparkling, red sheen.

Thorn moves to Jeremy's toes next, giving them the same attention as his fingers. The blood coats the marble floor as each toe is ripped away.

Jeremy's screams grow louder, thinner, and higher pitched as Thorn pulls off Jeremy's hands next, tossing them aside as if they were trash.

"Please," Jeremy keens, turning those molten gold eyes toward me.

His voice is quivering with agony and more as he wails, "Please, make him stop. Please, Sophia, make him stop."

I narrow my eyes at him. "You didn't stop when Amelia begged you to. You didn't stop when I begged you to. Why should I make him stop?"

"No, no, please, no!" Jeremy cries as Thorn reaches for him again, pulling each foot off his legs and tossing them aside.

Jeremy's screams are hoarse now, quieter, as Thorn rips off one of Jeremy's arms. The blood sprays everywhere with the loss of that extremity. It coats my body in the thin, warm liquid, running down my face and drenching my hair.

I should feel disgusted, but I do not. I revel in it, throwing my head back in ecstasy and running my fingers through my hair as if I were in a heavenly, hot shower with steaming clean water running over me.

The other arm comes off, and with it, more blood.

"Just kill me," Jeremy breathes, his struggles and screams slowing from the loss of blood.

"It takes longer to die here," Jewel says to me. *"In this dimension, he will not die from blood loss."*

"What will kill him here?" I ask.

"You have to kill his demon," Jewel answers.

"I will kill him when he is done," I say as Jeremy wails weakly.

"Please, Sophia. I can't take anymore," Jeremy cries.

"Too bad," I say cruelly. "You seem to bring out the worst in me for some reason. Keep going, Thorn."

Thorn nods and tears off a leg, then the other. Jeremy is nothing but a head and torso now, his screams quieted to simpering sobs as he bleeds all over the floor.

I look over at Lucien. "Do it," I say.

Thorn holds up a hand and looks over at me. Lucien stops. Thorn comes toward me, reaching for me with purpose. Harper is still in charge, it would seem.

I watch as Thorn comes for me, my heart pounding as if trying to beat out of my chest. Thorn's hand (which is really Harper's hand) cups my face gently as he leans down and softly kisses my lips.

I close my eyes, picturing Harper's face, and my blood pumps furiously through my veins with the rapid thumping of my heart. The demon's lips are cold, but I know it is really Harper kissing me right now.

The kiss is over almost as quick as it began, and I open my eyes to Thorn's eyes, glowing brightly.

"I love you, Sophia," Thorn's voice whispers in my mind, but I know it was Harper who said the words.

"I love you too, Harper. Now, save me so I can kiss you for real."

Thorn gives me a sad smile, looks toward Lucien, and nods. He gestures toward the screen before Lucien takes Thorn's head off and tosses it to the floor with all the other body parts.

"You know how I said I do not drink blood because I am not evil?" Jewel's voice whispers to me.

I nod.

"I think I am going to make an exception this time. Do not watch. This could get messy."

I shudder and turn my attention to the screen while my two demons clean up their mess. I do not even want to know how they do it.

Harper is still in his trance but slowly comes to as I watch. He sways as if disoriented and struggles to get to his feet. He pulls his cell phone from the pocket of his robe and touches the screen several times.

"This is the sheriff," a voice carries from the phone's speaker.

"Sheriff, I just received a tip on Sophia's location. I'm sending you the coordinates now."

"Got it. We will head that way as soon as the text comes through."

"Thank you, Sheriff, for everything."

"That's my job. See you soon, Harper."

Harper's thumbs fly over the phone's screen furiously for a moment, and then the cell phone falls from Harper's hand. He turns toward the mirror. He must have brought the full-length mirror into the living room because I can see Harper's entire, glorious body as he staggers over to the mirror.

He makes it to the mirror and falls to his hands and knees. "Sophia, if you can hear me now, just know that I love you with everything in me. I wanted to tell you while I was inside Thorn, but I wanted you to hear the words from my mouth, not his. I did everything, all of this, to keep you safe. Do not waste that gift."

Harper's breathing becomes ragged, and I can tell he struggles to stay upright.

"What is wrong with him?" I ask Jewel.

"That spell is very intense. Just be prepared," She answers, and

currents of alarm spread through me.

"Be prepared for what?" I ask, not sure if I want to know the answer.

"He is dying," Lucien answers, his tone filled with remorse.

NO. This cannot be happening.

"No, Harper," I say, touching the mirror's surface.

It ripples like water in a pond, and the image becomes clearer somehow. Harper's eyes widen in surprise.

"Sophia?"

"Harper? Can you see me? Can you hear me?"

"Oh, baby, yes, thank Goddess, I see you…I hear you," Harper says, his voice filled with so much emotion.

A lump forms in my throat as Harper's radiant smile lights up his face, although it is a bit weaker than usual. He places a hand on the mirror where my hand is, and I see his throat work as he swallows.

"I am so sorry I could not get to you sooner, baby girl," Harper says.

A sob escapes as I say, "Don't you dare apologize. You saved me."

"I did, didn't I?" He croaks, his voice getting weaker. "Always remember how much I love you, Sophia. Go, make something of your life. Never waste a moment."

"You talk as if you're saying goodbye," I say, my voice breaking.

"I will always be with you through Jewel. She will take care of you for me," Harper says, and then he collapses.

"No, no, no. Harper, please get up! Harper! Harper!"

Multiple hands pull me away from the mirror, and I struggle against them.

"No! Harper, get up," I say as I reach for the mirror. "Harper, please get up!"

He does not get up. I am dragged further and further away from the mirror as Harper lies there and does not move, does not breathe. I open my mouth and scream, the sound filling the room with anguish, despair, heartbreak, and agony.

The mirror shatters into a million pieces, and I am torn from the room with the shattered pieces of my soul.

CHAPTER 34

The room is dark and cold. My head aches. The side of my face hurts. My pussy walls throb with agony. My arms and legs burn from a million cuts all along my skin.

But I am alive.

Harper told me not to waste his gift, and I will not. I will go on, I will fight, I will complete my program, and I will get out of this place with my sanity intact.

I will live for him.

I sit up in the bed and look around the room. I am in a regular hospital room, hooked up to so many monitors that I do not know how I am even going to get out of this bed just to go pee. I spot a chain that hangs down from a light fixture over my head, and I pull the chain.

The room is flooded with light, and I smile as I see multiple flower arrangements sitting around the room. A couple have balloons floating over them, and one even has a teddy bear. The ribbon around its neck says, "Get well soon, kiddo".

Kiddo is my nickname from my Uncle Vinny.

I wonder who all the other ones are from?

"You had many visitors while you were unconscious," The voice of Jewel says in my head.

"Jewel, I am so glad to hear your voice," I say aloud, hoping no one heard me talking to myself.

"I am a bonded demon, which means I do not die unless BOTH of my owners die. You are still alive, so I am still alive."

"Harper is…"

I cannot even finish the sentence. I clear my throat and start again. "How long have I been out?"

"Only two days," The other demon voice whispers through my mind.

My smile widens. "Lucien."

He appears in front of me, standing tall and strong, smiling radiantly with his eyes glowing…

I gasp.

"Lucien, your eyes," I whisper proudly.

"Jewel says it is because I stayed with you and protected you," Lucien says. *"It was a good deed, so…"*

He trails off, and his diamond-colored eyes glow brighter.

I laugh aloud. "It was an outstanding deed, and I am grateful to you. You protected me and made me strong."

"That is what inner demons are supposed to do," Jewel says, appearing beside him.

She takes his hand in hers and starts to fade, but I put my hand up in a stopping gesture and shout, "Wait. Before you go, tell me what happened. According to everyone else, I mean. What happened?"

The images of my demons come back into view, and it is Jewel's soft tones that answer my question.

"You were found, beaten, raped, and bloody, right where Doctor Harper said you would be. You were on the brink of death when they found you. Fortunately, they found you just in time to save you.

"Strangely, the doctor who had made the call and saved you died of a heart attack right after he called the police."

My heart lurches painfully in my chest. The pain and grief of losing Harper threatens to overwhelm me, but I take a deep breath and push it back. I will not be pulled back into the dark depression I had worked so hard to come back from again.

I would live for Harper.

Jewel's voice continues to flow through my mind. *"To wrap up the weirdness and strange occurrences of the day, Jeremy Oakes, the sole survivor of the Oakes family, had a Grand Mal seizure during class and is now in a coma in this very hospital.*

"The very hospital that he would have inherited had he completed his program. It still remains to be seen if he lives. Otherwise, ownership of the hospital will revert to the other owner, who is a silent partner, and no one knows who they are.

"No one knows what prompted Jeremy's seizure, but some suspect it was suicide by drug overdose. According to his labs, his system was full of anti-depressants, the ones the hospital gives out daily. Jeremy's system had an extreme amount of them, more than the daily dosage. "

"It is the medicine Harper used to give you to keep Lucien docile when you first came to us. It keeps a demon in a trans-like state,

making them easier to control.

"They suspect he broke into the nurses' station and stole them. Funny that Jeremy's system would be full of them right after having drinks with Nurse Cora before class, don't you think?"

"Very funny, indeed," I answer with a smirk.

The door to my hospital room opens suddenly, and the demons vanish immediately.

A man in a suit walks into the room. He stands tall and straight as he strolls toward my bed. He fiddles with his red tie and runs a hand over his brown hair, cut short and parted to the side. He pushes his thin-framed spectacles up his nose and clears his throat.

He is carrying a briefcase, which he sets on the table beside my hospital bed, pushing the phone to the side to make room. He pulls out a stack of papers and closes the briefcase.

"Please, come in, make yourself at home," I say sarcastically.

The man ignores my sarcasm as he sits in one of the seats with his stack of papers. He fiddles with his tie and clears his throat again.

That must be his nervous tell.

"Miss Boralis, I am Stan, Harper Andrews's lawyer," The man says.

The pain slices through me at the sound of Harper's name. I grab my chest, where my heart stutters at the physical pain, and breathe around the tightness in my chest. I squeeze my eyes shut for a moment, then open them again, blinking rapidly to keep the tears at bay.

"I am sorry for your loss, Miss Boralis. I understand this may be painful to sit through, but I will be quick," The man says.

I frown in confusion. "I'm sorry, Mr...."

"Oh, pardon my rudeness. I am Silas, and, as I said before, I am Harper Andrews's lawyer."

"Okay, Mr. Silas..."

"Just Silas," The imposing man interrupts, straightening his tie again.

"Okaaay," I drawl. "Silas. What is this about?"

Silas frowns at me as if I should know exactly what this is about. His tone implies the same when he answers simply, "Your inheritance, ma'am."

Bewilderment swirls within me as I look at Harper's lawyer with a blank stare. He stares back, and his condescending frown turns to uncertainty.

"You do know that Harper left his entire estate to you, don't you?" Silas asks, his gray eyes puzzled. "Harper said you were engaged, so I assumed you knew…"

He straightens his tie and clears his throat again. "Anyway, I just need you to sign the papers and it is all yours. I suggest you hire a financial advisor if you had not discussed this with Harper beforehand. There is a lot here to handle, including this very hospital you are sitting in right now."

I am frozen with mystification. The words sink in slowly, swirling with the mayhem and chaos that already lives in my brain. Harper said we were engaged? And this hospital? I knew Harper owned the mental facility, but…

"I thought this hospital was owned by Don Oakes, and now…well, it remains to be seen, I guess. And a silent partner who has not come forward as of yet."

Silas nods and answers, "Yes, Miss Boralis, he was part owner. But Harper owns the other half, and, as you so eloquently put it, the rest remains to be seen. If Jeremy Oakes does not come out of his coma and/or completes his program within three more months, then you will own the hospital in its entirety."

My eyes widen, my heart skyrockets, and my breathing comes in short, rapid gasps.

"But the hospital is called Oakes and Dane, not Oakes and Andrews," I say as the panic threatens to overtake me.

What the hell am I going to do with two hospitals? Hell, what the fuck am I going to do with one hospital? I am a restaurant owner. I do not know the first thing about running a hospital. And not just a hospital, a mental health hospital. I am not mentally stable myself, much less responsible for the mental health of others.

Silas interrupts my turmoil, bringing my attention back to him. "Marcus Dane was Harper's maternal grandfather."

Harper had never told me that. Then again, Harper did not have time to tell me anything. Our entire whirlwind romance went by too fast.

Fuck, I miss him.

I take in a deep, cleansing breath and steady my thoughts. Silas begins to show me places I need to sign as he hands me a pen. I swallow past the lump in my throat.

The first thing I need to do is call Uncle Vinny. I may not get along with his daughter, my cousin Mia, but she is one of the best financial advisors I know. After all, she has her own financial company in Arizona.

That was one of the reasons she came with Vinny to help with the restaurant and chose to take care of the bills instead of running the restaurant.

Hell, maybe it will finally bring us together.

Next, I should find someone who can help me run two hospitals. Nurse Cora and the four hulks may be able to put me in contact with the right people. I will speak with them as soon as I get out of here.

Right away, I decide to give up my rental and live at the hospital, in the turret where I lived with Harper. The memories might haunt me, but I will feel close to him there.

I sign the papers as I think through all of this and more. I will be okay. Harper made sure of that.

The following two weeks go by faster than I thought they would. I am occupied with multiple visits from many people. Some were expected, others were a surprise.

Uncle Vinny and Mia came by to discuss my newly inherited wealth. Mia had some great investment ideas, tips on minimizing my taxes, thoughts on contributing to the community, and more.

She really is good at her job.

After hearing him talk reverently about it, I gave Uncle Vinny the restaurant. He seems to love it so much, and I owe him for taking care of my possessions while I couldn't, especially Mom's grave. He had bought her a beautiful tombstone with a guardian angel statue standing tall over it protectively.

He showed me a picture. I am going there as soon as I take care of one other thing here.

Marcel was my next visitor. She was happy I had improved so much since she last saw me. She even knew a couple of people who could help me with the hospitals and gave me their contact information.

I made her head of the psychiatric ward. Of course, there are channels I will have to go through to make it official, but the people she put me in contact with should be able to help with that.

Nurse Cora came next, carrying something that almost made me leave my bed, running and screaming. Then Cora explained that

Harper had told her how much I loved it. He had told her he was going to give it to me as soon as they found me, so she had decided to go ahead and bring it to me.

The full-length, decorative, fancy mirror that Harper had dragged from his attic now sits in the corner of my hospital room.   It will stay covered and protected until I get out of here and take it back home.

Cora had no idea that the turret was now mine; otherwise, she would have just left it where it was. She promised she would have the turret cleaned and ready for my arrival.

My next visitor surprised me more than any of the others.

When Tamara had walked into my room with a patch over one eye and carrying a bouquet of my favorite roses, I almost lost it.

Tears were shed, apologies were made, forgiveness was given, and hugs were shared. I ordered two cups of the hospital's best coffee and a dozen chocolate doughnuts.

Tamara had forgiven me twice for the doughnuts.

She stayed for hours while I regaled her with my stories about the two hospitals and everything that had happened to me. Of course, I left out some details.

Her hopeless romantic heart went gaga over the story of me falling for my psychiatrist and him reciprocating my love. She cried great hulking sobs, along with me, when I told her of his death. She wants to live with me so I will not be alone.

As long as the pencils are kept under lock and key.

She told me about the others in the group that day and how they had all healed from their not-so-major injuries. No one, other than Tamara, carries any permanent scars or injuries from my psychotic break.

It made me feel less guilty, which was a good thing. It's what Harper had always wanted for me: to let go of the guilt from that day.

Now, I sit here in the chair beside the hospital bed, waiting for the nurse to bring me my discharge papers. My leg bounces nervously as I wait. There is one other thing I must take care of before I leave here, and it scares me.

I do not know if I will be able to go through with it.

"You will. I have faith in you," Lucien's voice flows through my mind.

I close my eyes and smile. I love hearing his voice. It reminds me that I will never be alone.

The nurse brings my paperwork, goes over aftercare with me, and tells me I am free. Besides the mirror, all my things have been packed and moved to the turret.

The mirror stays with me.

Uncle Vinny is bringing his truck to pick me and the mirror up in approximately thirty minutes. It gives me time to complete my final task.

I pad silently, still wearing my hospital slipper/socks, to the open door of my private room. No one roams the halls, and the nurses' station is around the corner. No one will see me when I leave, not even the cameras that are set to play on a loop for the next half hour.

The security guard is a personal friend of Vinny's.

My heart pounds with nervousness and fear as I pad silently down the hallway toward the ICU ward. The doors are locked to everyone except staff, but this is the closest door to the room I need. It takes a keycard to open it. Unconcerned, I dip into the janitor's closet on the right, just before the locked door.

The lab coat with the hanging keycard/ID card hangs in the closet as planned. The janitor I had befriended during my stay here, who knew I was the future owner and wanted a promotion, came through with his promise.

I smile as I slip on the lab coat and into the slip-on nurse shoes the janitor had also left. I open the closet door gently, looking up and down the hall to ensure the coast is still clear.

Satisfied I am still alone, I slip out of the janitor's closet and head for the locked double doors. I scan the keycard and the doors open with a silent swoosh. I cringe at the sound, but no one is on the other side of the doors.

The nurses' station for the ICU ward is around the bend down this hall, but I do not need to go that far. The room I need is the first one on the right.

My pounding heart kicks up its pace as I come closer to the room. I take deep, cleansing breaths and try to stay calm as I approach the door. I open it slowly and peek in.

The room is dark, the monitors trailing a steady 'beep…beep…beep'. I slip in quickly and shut the door silently behind me. I walk up to the bed and stare at the figure hooked to the monitors.

The machine that is keeping his heart beating and his lungs working is daunting. Wires stream from the hospital gown he wears, and the tube that runs down into his lungs protrudes from his mouth, the mask and tape holding it in place hiding most of his handsome features.

The eyes, those eyes that had once looked upon me with such love and devotion and at other times with pure hatred, are closed. There is no movement, not even a flutter, of the eyelids.

The hair, the once beautiful, silky hair, lies flat and dull against the stark white pillows. I reach out a hand and brush a strand of it from his face. I run my hand down the stubble of the strong jawline, being careful of the tubes and wires.

Misery and grief consume me, swirling painfully inside my chest. I put a hand over my mouth to stifle a sob. I pull my hand away and bring it close to my chest.

He looks so peaceful lying there. It is hard to believe that he had been so evil. It is hard to believe that he had never cared for me. My mind races over the memories of our time together, the care and love he had initially shown me. Then, rage fills my chest as I come to the latest memories.

The torture, the violation, and the cruelness of his actions drive the rage that courses through me, overtaking the misery and giving me the courage to complete my task.

I move over to the machines and start turning off the alarms first, as instructed by my janitor friend. I do not want to alert the nurses until he is good and dead.

I shut off the ventilator and defibrillator. Just those two machines should do the trick.

Jeremy is brain-dead. His soul was destroyed. He is never coming back.

I watch in satisfaction as his breathing turns to a gurgling sound and the heart monitor runs a flat line. The breathing stops suddenly. I watch his chest for signs of life, but it lies still as the grave.

Jeremy Oakes is dead.

For good.

"Bye, Jeremy," I whisper softly, then maliciously I add, "See you in hell, fucker."

I turn the alarms back on. The beeping and the noise fill the room. The one drawn-out 'beeeeeeeep' from the heart monitor makes me smile as I slip out of the room, hurry back to the double doors, and leave the ICU.

I slip into the janitor's closet, return the lab coat and shoes, and pad silently back to my hospital room. I check my watch. I had done it with five minutes to spare. The cameras will go back on their live feed, and none will be the wiser that I had ever left this room.

I close the door to my hospital room and walk over to the mirror. I remove the cloth covering it and free the shiny, reflective surface. My two demons appear in the mirror, smiling proudly at me.

I smile back and nod.

"It is done," I say with finality.

Another figure comes up behind my demons. Only this one is not made of shadow and darkness. In fact, it is no demon at all.

The reflection of the mirror changes, fading into a different panorama, and no longer reflects the hospital room. The room that comes into view is a perfect replica of Harper's living room in the turret.

Harper steps out from behind the shadows, sporting that dazzling smile I love. He nods proudly as he drapes his arms over the shoulders of our two demons.

"Good girl," he drawls roguishly, and my heart soars. "Now, let's go home."

FREE DOWNLOAD!

https://mymeshara.wixsite.com/nethersouls**/landing-page**

ABOUT THE AUTHOR

Rebecca Jose lives in a small town in the heart of Kentucky. She has three grown kids, a multitude of "adopted" kids, six grandkids, four dogs, and a parrot. She enjoys her job at a local historical sight in Harrodsburg, Kentucky.

When she is not working at her job, or at home on the computer, she enjoys her time with her husband, grandkids, and the rest of her family. She dreams of creating many stories for many readers and hopes people will enjoy her stories for years.

THANK YOU FOR READING AND FOR BEING A FAN…
REBECCA JOSE XOXO

If you enjoyed this story, please write a review and post it to your favorite reading site. Tell others about Rebecca Jose and her stories so that they may be able to enjoy them as well.

<u>**FOLLOW HER ON SOCIAL MEDIA FOR PR BOX GIVEAWAYS AND OTHER SPECIAL PRIZES FROM REBECCA JOSE…**</u>

TIKTOK…*https://www.tiktok.com/@REBECCAJOSE4080*

FACEBOOK…*https://www.facebook.com/rebecca.maggard.79*

TWITTER…*https://twitter.com/Rebeccajose8*

INSTAGRAM…*https://www.instagram.com/mymeshara/*

GOODREADS…*https://www.goodreads.com/author/show/21408581.Rebecca_Jose*